THE
BLUE MAX...

was the most coveted
decoration in all Germany—
symbol of unbelievable fame,
prestige and power. This is the
story of the men who wantonly
killed and died for it.

BRUNO STACHEL—
Murderer, alcoholic, whose
meteoric rise to glory as one of
Germany's deadliest fighter
pilots forced him away from
companions, conscience,
and ultimately from all human
decency.

KETTERING—The
disillusioned pornography-
collecting philosopher who
became the victim of Stachel's
ruthless ambition.

VON KLUGERMANN—
The haughty aristocrat who
delved too deeply into Stachel's
torment, only to discover a
deadly cobra.

And the woman who knew
them all . . .

KAETI—Stachel's beautiful
mistress, an arrogant noble-
woman, a blackmailing
nymphomaniac.

"HARD-HITTING,
ROUGH-AND-TUMBLE,
SWIFTLY PLACED . . . A
STIRRING NARRATIVE."
VIRGINIA QUARTERLY REVIEW

the Blue Max

Jack D. Hunter

CORGI BOOKS
A DIVISION OF TRANSWORLD PUBLISHERS

THE BLUE MAX

A CORGI BOOK

Originally published in Great Britain
by Frederick Muller Ltd.

PRINTING HISTORY
Muller Edition published 1965
Corgi Edition published 1966
Corgi Edition reprinted 1966
Corgi Edition reprinted 1966
Corgi Edition reprinted 1967

Corgi Books are published by Transworld Publishers Ltd.,
Bashley Road, London, N.W.10
Made and printed in Great Britain by
Love & Malcomson Ltd., Redhill, Surrey

What men or gods are these? What maidens loth?
What mad pursuit? What struggle to escape?

—KEATS

Heroism, says Webster, implies superlative, often transcendent courage—especially in fulfilling a superhumanly high purpose where the odds are against one. This book is dedicated to Shirley Thompson Hunter, who's taught me that heroism can come in dainty guise.

J. D. H.

CHAPTER 1

BRUNO STACHEL stepped down from the truck and surveyed the airfield's forlorn expanse. A cold wind, sodden with the hint of snow, whispered out of the northwest to set up a restless fluttering along the line of tent hangars, and somewhere a loose board swung and thumped. He stood before what appeared to be the station's sole permanent building—a weathered structure that presumably at some dim time had served as a railroad storehouse. Inside someone pecked impetuously at a typewriter. The truck driver, a gloomy fellow with a ludicrous mustache, had unlashed his luggage from the mudguard, and having placed it on the duckboards, now stood in sleepy preoccupation.

"Wait here a moment," Stachel instructed, squinting into the wind.

The airdrome, he noted, was situated at the junction of two highways on the edge of a farm village. The hangars backed up to the north-south road, which itself was paralleled by the railroad spur. Running west on the upper side of the field, the other road crossed a small stone bridge to disappear into the miles of plain beyond. The town had once aspired to greater things apparently, since a two-story factory building—now a vacant-windowed ruin whose chimney etched a tired exclamation point against the sky—brooded on the western horizon. The field's southern boundary was marked by a line of uneasy poplars. It was altogether dismal, and Stachel's loneliness was intense. He struggled to shake it off as he entered the shack.

The office, dominated by a noisily laboring field stove, was heavy with the smell of wet wool and peat smoke. The *Unteroffizier* continued with his typing, his lips pursed around the sopping stub of a cigar, until Stachel rattled the envelope containing his orders. Then, with the comprehensive glance utilized by soldiers since armies had been born, he took in Stachel's rank, the ribbonless spread of *Feldgrau* from waist to shoulder, and face—in precisely that order. He arose, the cigar end vanishing into a cupped hand, to take up a position of attention that was just casual enough to let it be known that here, by God, was an old campaigner.

"Afternoon, *Herr Leutnant*," he said blandly. "You must be the new officer"—his eyes flickered to a paper on his desk—"Stachel. *Leutnant* Stachel."

"Where is everybody?" Stachel was acutely aware of the condescension in the other's tone. He despised being patronized, and to realize that he now was being patronized by one who could base his superiority solely on having been in this melancholy hole first was just short of infuriating.

"On patrol. Sir. They're due back any time now."

Stachel wondered if the Officer's Code said anything about an *Unteroffizier* who made a separate, mocking sentence of "sir."

"The driver outside—where should he put my gear?"

"I'll take care of that. Sir. Simply sign the book there and make yourself comfortable by the stove." Then, as if he sensed Stachel's rising annoyance, the man said disarmingly, "Dirty weather. Cold. Give a man pneumonia."

Stachel considered the peace feeler. He decided to reject it and give the old campaigner something other than a cigar to chew on.

"I'm surprised they're flying," he offered in an equally mild tone.

"They fly in worse than this. Sir. How is anybody's guess. . . ."

"Who are you?"

The other paused, weighing the sharpness of the question and re-evaluating the questioner. An almost indiscernible change came into his eyes, but it was sufficient to show that he'd replaced superciliousness with caution.

"*Unteroffizier* Gerhardt Rupp, sir. I am staff orderly and chief clerk to the *Jastaführer*. . . ."

2

"I didn't ask what you do, I asked who you are. Now see to my bags."

It was the other's turn to be infuriated, but he had soldiered long enough to know that a *Uffz* would always come out second best in a contest with an angered *Leutnant*—even a brand-new one—so he hid his wrath in the business of getting to the door.

When Rupp had left, Stachel signed his name to the duty book, noted the time and date, and was once again struck by the brevity of the interval that had passed since the day he had entered the flying school at Köln. The familiar pang of inadequacy stabbed at him, and his mild satisfaction at having put the *Uffz* in his place was immediately erased by the old anxiety. As tired as he was, and as pleasant as the stove was, he brought up the only defense known to him and strode purposefully to the door and out into the wind. Physical action—a purposeful stride was usually enough—would counter the indefinable sense of impending doom that had been his companion for as long as he could remember. Inadequacy, anxiety, depression, loneliness: would they ever leave him? Did every man resort to purposeful strides, to the exercise of muscle, to stifle a retching of the spirit?

He looked into the large tent adjacent to the head-quarters building and watched a trio of mechanics struggling profanely to hoist the engine from a mud-spattered Albatros. The gloom was fetid with castor oil, lacquer, stale sweat, and damp wool. (God, how he hated the stink of sweat and wet wool; it was rapidly becoming Germany's national odor.) The men ignored him, and he could almost feel the defensive cocoon they had drawn around them by their intimate swearing and calculated avoidance of his eyes. The enormous gulf between the Officers Corps and troops was never more tangible than when enlisted personnel chose to pretend they did not see. He stood tentatively in the shadow, thinking about this and awaiting the biplane's teetering protest as it gave up its engine to the block and tackle.

At first, the new sound was a suggestion—a feeling in the atmosphere. Then, over the men's chattering and the rasp of the chain, Stachel heard a high drumming, and he went outside to peer aloft. A spittle of snow was in the air now, and the dark clouds rolled low. At their base, out to the west where a thin band of lemon sky separated the horizon from the shaping storm, a cluster of dots slanted down the wind. The gentle hum gained in pitch as the dots formed into aircraft. It seemed to Stachel, standing with his hands behind his back and blinking into the flurry, that they were coming in awfully fast. He'd been told that the *Jastas,* as the Imperial Air Service's front-line squadrons had come to be called, were very casual in their flying and frequently made a mockery of operational safety regulations, but these approaching machines were acting as if a landing were the last thing they were about to attempt. There were five of them, and as they slid lower, canting their dual wings to the field, he felt an uneasy puzzlement. Their engines whined strangely. They had round noses and a pronounced dihedral in the lower wing. They weren't Albatroses, of course, since the Albatros had a deep-bellied, barrel-like front elevation and he was quite familiar with the type. No German aircraft he could recall. . . .

A siren croaked down the line, and from behind the railroad embankment came the knocking of a machine gun. Somewhere a man shouted, and there was the clumping sound of running feet. The three mechanics burst from the hangar behind him. One of them, brushing hard against him, swore foully and with no trace of the comfortable tone that had mellowed the wrangling inside. Stachel fought for balance, pacing sideways in indecision and confusion. Dry sticks crackled nastily in the air about him and the rush of engines beat down in a numbing shock wave. Then it dropped in an instant to an angry, dwindling snarl.

"You'd better get down on your belly. Sir. Otherwise our English visitors will punch several extra navels in it."

The *Uffz*'s cold cigar, an inch from Stachel's nose, wagged up and down as the words came around it. His eyes again hinted derision.

"Shouldn't we be doing something?"

"What would you suggest? Sir."

4

"How about shooting back at the Englishmen? Or isn't that fashionable among you old-timers?"

"Suit yourself. Sir. This is one old-timer who's going to get his ass under an umbrella."

Stachel lurched into the cigar's wake and followed Rupp around the hangar, crouching against the returning roar, to the ridge topped by the rail spur. A shallow trench, its sandbags already whitening under snow, cut a sawtooth pattern beside the rise of gravel. They rolled into it, and Stachel was aware of his dry mouth and shortness of breath. The machine guns beyond the embankment were thumping steadily.

"Damned fools. Why don't they wait until the Englishmen get back in range?" the *Uffz* snorted, his face frowning at the sky.

"At least they're doing something."

"The bastards couldn't hit a grounded Zeppelin."

"Why don't you go show them how, Rupp?"

The cigar turned toward him. The eyes above it, old and too wise, were sullen. "I'm on fire detail. If there's a fire in the hangars, I join the pee brigade."

"Meanwhile, you're on the complaining detail, eh?"

"Begging your pardon, *Herr Leutnant,* but you need a sense of humor. Haven't you ever belly-ached about your favorite soccer team?"

"Don't tell me what I need."

"Not a chance. Sir."

"You're a smart aleck, aren't you, *Unteroffizier* Gerhardt Rupp?"

"I get along."

"Sir."

"Sir."

This time the crackling sound seemed inches above their ditch, and the engine sound was a rattling rain of physical blows. Now Stachel caught a glimpse of the buff-colored undersides of the British machines and the large bull's-eye insignia marking their lower wings. Their speed was astonishing, as low as they were, and he could even feel the backlash of their propeller wash. An explosion crashed, as if a great door had slammed, and concussion stung his face. There was another, then a

5

rapid series, but the jarring decreased as the blasts marched away in fretful pursuit of the rushing attackers. Above the sandbags he could see a hangar roof collapse in a shower of dirty snow and spinning turf. He realized with vague satisfaction that he was watching the whole affair with an objective detachment. He had often worried over his possible reaction when he'd come under enemy fire for the first time. For a man as anxiety-ridden as Bruno Stachel could be while lying in his own bed, objective detachment in real danger was droll indeed; for one who perspired gallons over chitchat with a clergyman, a mere dry mouth amidst snapping ricochets was a paradox of almost comic cast.

He sensed the other's eyes on him.

"What are you staring at, Rupp?"

"I was just wondering what you're smiling about. Sir."

"Was I smiling?"

Another truce was in the air.

"Yes."

"I wasn't aware of it."

"Takes a cool one to smile at a time like this."

"Gas pain. I always look like this when I have a gas pain."

Now the *Uffz* was smiling.

"Yes. Cool."

Stachel shot down the white flag.

"Kiss my ass, *Unteroffizier* Gerhardt Rupp," he said.

Rupp's smile faded, and he looked away, Adam's apple bobbing.

The English machines soared in a wide turn over the distant factory. Stachel's gaze followed them; he guessed they were Sopwiths, although he admitted to himself in secret embarrassment that they could just as well be Spads or Nieuports or whatever, for all he could recall of the training manuals. As he watched, another movement caught his eye and he sought it out.

Beyond the line of trees and along the far-off cloud base, a ragged V of specks wheeled with deceptive slowness toward the field. At first they stretched across the sky like a flight of tired geese; but in their approach they edged together and the air throbbed with their bass humming even over the waspish buzz of the circling Englishmen. Stachel nudged the *Unteroffizier*.

"Ours?"

"Ours," Rupp said slowly.

Stachel counted ten machines in the German formation. "Now we'll see something," he thought aloud.

"Not if our people return as usual, out of ammunition and low on fuel. They usually come back as empty as a spinster's belly."

"Not likely today, I'd say. Otherwise they wouldn't barge in like this, but would hang off as long as they could until the Englishmen tired of shooting up an empty lot and went home."

Rupp's pout deepened. "I wouldn't say a company of men, a dozen hangars, and four spare aircraft make up an empty lot."

"You know what I mean." He leveled his eyes at the *Uffz*. "We might as well get this understood right off, *Unteroffizier* Gerhardt Rupp, chief clerk to the squadron leader: don't try your smart-aleck stuff with me. You may be able to use your sly little noncom ways with other new officers—and maybe with some of the old ones, for all I know—but not with me. I'll squeeze you like a flea and poop on the goo."

Rupp studied a thumbnail, his face flushed. "Whatever do you mean? Sir."

"Just this: don't underestimate me."

"You're the officer. I obey the orders. But my thoughts go on." There was defiance there.

"Then think of how sweet I am. It'll be safer that way."

"I've noted that the toughest officers are the most pleasant ones," Rupp suggested angrily.

"A philosopher, eh? It may reassure you to know that I'm really a very pleasant fellow. I am, that is, until some smart aleck presses me. Then I poop on his goo."

Rupp withdrew his crumbling forces. "No offense, *Herr Leutnant*."

Stachel had already feigned absorption in the developing aerial action, but the exchange, as any such

7

acrimony invariably did, had cost him dearly. He wondered if *Unteroffizier* Gerhardt Rupp could sense that truth.

The Englishmen made another sweep, this time down the long axis of the hangar area. Their clattering guns showed tiny flickers of pale yellow, and the truck Stachel had arrived in sagged, its windshield dissolving in a shower of glass dust. Somewhere someone whimpered.

For Rupp's benefit, Stachel shook his head professionally, as he'd seen the instructors do at Köln. "Two-to-one odds. Those Tommies are fools."

But he was thinking: *he's only a frigging noncom, and probably one of those Bolsheviks to boot. What's there to be so upset about?*

At the point of the V, which was now a tight wedge of thunder, Otto Heidemann decided that the raiding Englishmen were fools. Brave, to be sure. But fools. However, such was the history of the English people, and if these five fellows wanted to be conformists, so be it. He glanced over his shoulder at the formation and was pleased to see how well the others had closed in. They were really quite good—even the newer ones were first-class.

The past hour and a half had been uneventful. They had traced a large triangle, flying from the airdrome here west to where the Scarpe crossed the lines, then southeast for nineteen kilometers along the front, and, finally, after several circuits of their area of responsibility, almost due north over Cambrai to close out the patrol. Only once had they sighted enemy aircraft—a low-flying trio of DeHavilland artillery spotters that had disappeared ghostlike in the ground haze. Later, he had considered sending several machines at an observation balloon that formed a swollen obscenity at the end of its tethers south of Croisilles, but Mueller, the *Jasta*'s balloon specialist, was in charge of the *Kette* composed of the newer men, and it would have been too risky to commit them and too time-consuming to organize another section. Besides, Army had been quite specific in its instructions for a high-altitude patrol in squadron strength, so he had dismissed the balloon and had con-

8

centrated on his surveillance of the pale blue vault around and above.

The weather, too, had preoccupied him. The low, rolling snow clouds moving in from the northwest could be very much more dangerous than enemy machines, and he did not want to lose half the *Jasta* simply through inattention to their movements. The sky was a strange and deceptive thing—at one moment bright and cheery, at the next opaque and baleful. In the early days he had more than once found himself entirely lost in a shining sky within a few minutes of leaving a field. And only once had he dared to enter a storm cloud, and he had barely survived the subsequent crash. So Otto Heidemann respected the sky and was wary of its tricks. Someday, he felt, there would be aircraft that could ignore the weather, but not in this generation or the next.

He had been mildly surprised to find the airdrome under attack. Not that anything the English could do would ever really confound him; he had flown against them too long to reckon without their unpredictability. Indeed, it would take an Englishman to fly some sixteen kilometers into alien country during a snowstorm, to launch a strafing attack against a strongly defended station, then, with tanks and ammunition boxes nearly empty, to attempt a return in the teeth of a twenty-knot wind. Like the sky, the English aviator and his eccentricities held Otto Heidemann's unqualified respect.

But his career was to destroy men such as these, so he readied himself for the job at hand. He charged the twin Spandau machine guns nested in the cowling before him, pulled another hitch in the security belt, checked the air pressure gauge (low, but not dangerously so) and tachometer (normal at full), and resettled the glasses over his eyes. His feet were numb with the cold, and he removed them from the rudder bar briefly to stamp them against the boards. Behind and to both sides, their rocking wings somber-hued in the afternoon light, the other machines formed oblique stairsteps upward. Ulrich, in the Albatros nearest his own, stared across the gap at him, his face nearly hidden by a roll of scarf and the blankness of goggles.

9

Heidemann pointed to Mueller on his right, then swept his arm toward the southwest. He could see the answering nod before Mueller stood his Albatros on its side, left wing high, to turn away, trailed by the machines of his *Kette*. With the Englishmen's escape route thus covered, Heidemann teetered the wings of his airplane to signal the free-for-all. His watch said 16:22.

The Sopwiths had finished another run along the hangar line and were climbing in a businesslike effort to meet the onslaught. In the dive, the airdrome formed a black-brown polygon that swelled in size over the yammering rocker arms of Heidemann's engine. He singled out an Englishman at the near edge of the pack, aligned his sights, and, with a tap of rudder, took up the proper angle of deflection. He thumbed the right gun button on his control-column yoke and the starboard Spandau pounded authoritatively. Too high; another correction. Again the jabbing motion, this time on the full fire lever, and both ammunition tracks trembled as the cartridges raced in a dull copper blur. He was close behind the Sopwith now, and the Tommy's khaki wings snapped to the vertical in a full-torque right bank that barely cleared the rushing turf. A quick third burst from both guns tore away the red-white-and-blue rudder directly ahead, then Heidemann pulled up in an arcing climb to watch as the English craft cartwheeled wildly through a farmyard, trailing a welter of junk. Oddly, there was no fire.

Circling at a bare fifty meters, Heidemann took stock. A demolished aircraft was burning briskly beside the railroad, but he was unable to determine its nationality. Another column of smoke traced an enormous, soot-brown question mark in the air above the abandoned factory. The sole Tommy still visible was faltering in the vortex of a twister of Albatroses, and even as he watched, the enemy machine turned on its back to plummet sickeningly into a marsh.

Heidemann throttled back the hammering engine and

sighed deeply, taking his first real breath since the insane plunging and whirling had begun. As usual, his mouth was sticky dry.

It was 16:23, and snowing quite heavily.

CHAPTER 2

OTTO HEIDEMANN'S office was in a corner of the railroad shed that boasted windows on two sides. One wall, an approximately rectangular area of roughly knotted pine boards, served as backing for a map of northern France and a scattering of yellowed general orders and memorandums. His desk and camp chair were placed at an angle, so that when he wearied of shuffling papers he could look out on the field and along the hangar line. Across the room were several packing crates that had been fashioned into rough seats; these were flanked by a table on which he had piled his flying gear. The sheepskin boots, given to him by Elfi on that leave so long ago, stood in careful alignment in the far corner, where he could see them easily in his moments alone. A sputtering oil lamp hung from the ceiling, its fumes mingling with those emanating from a potbellied stove near the door.

Heidemann sipped at a cup of hot chocolate, staring out at the twilight. The fires started by the afternoon's action had long since been extinguished, and the wind had died. The snow came down in large, gentle flakes to rustle softly against the windows. He put down the cup, picked up his combat report form, reread the entries, then scratched his signature across the bottom of the original and copies.

"Rupp!"

The *Uffz* peered around the door.

"Yes, sir?"

11

"Send this to Army with the midnight courier, will you? And ask our new chap—*Leutnant* Stachel—to come up here as soon as convenient."

"He's here now, sir."

"Oh, good. Send him in."

Heidemann was pleased. It was reassuring to find a new officer who observed the proprieties. More and more of the new ones these days were, well, *offhanded* with procedures. For himself, he was convinced that it is the sum of many manners that make for tradition, and it is the aggregate of all traditions that comprise a national stature. The seed of a country lost, he believed, could lie in a seemingly trifling question of propriety. He had often expounded this philosophy over an evening's tankard in the old Mülhausen garrison days, citing the case of Leopold of Hohenzollern. Had Napoleon politely accepted Leopold's gracious declination of the Spanish throne and abandoned his subsequent unmannerly attempt to dictate to Wilhelm of Prussia, the French debacle of '70 might never have occurred. Bonaparte's mortification at Sedan stemmed directly from his own boorishness, and that was that, Q.E.D.

No nation would fall, though, he smiled inwardly, over Stachel's demeanor: his entrance, his half-bow and salute, his manner in presenting his orders were altogether acceptable.

"Sit down, Stachel. Pull up one of those things over there. They aren't much, but they serve. Have you had anything to eat yet?"

"Yes, thank you, *Herr Hauptmann*. After things quieted down, Rupp introduced me to the adjutant and he was kind enough to see that I found the officers' mess." Stachel, seated tentatively on one of the crates, was annoyed with himself for having forgotten the adjutant's name. It would have made a better impression had he been able to use it now. *Hauptmann* Heidemann was reputed to be a stickler for the niceties.

"Good. Good."

Heidemann made a business of filling his pipe. Protocol aside, he was one to place great importance on first impressions. He had discovered early in his career that he'd

12

been blessed (or was it cursed?) with a special ability to read men. Not that a first-rate airman was clearly discernible in a reporting situation such as this, of course; but a man's essential nature as a man frequently showed through during his initial courtesy call, and it was in the probe for this that Heidemann's peculiar sensitivities rarely erred. As for qualities as a flier, only flying established those. In fact, Heidemann often was amused by the marked contradiction between the physical appearance and the aerial capabilities of the twelve men who made up the *Jasta*. Mueller, for instance, the gangling Bavarian who seemed all elbows and teeth, would hardly represent the masterful destroyer of enemy balloons; nor would Von Klugermann, the fat aristocrat with the perpetual pout, strike anyone as a fellow who could cut down four English bombers in as many minutes. Of the entire roster, only Fabian, with his piercing, deep-set eyes, his classically straight nose and high brow, came anywhere close to the popular periodicals' conception of a combat aviator. The others: youngsters to be seen on any weekend ski slope.

And so this new man, Stachel, was another to be assessed. Inexplicably, Heidemann found himself wondering how many days the *Leutnant,* with his wide-set gray eyes, his close-cropped fair hair, had to live. Would he, like Thoma, Linkhof, Krueger—so many others—go early, a whorl of flame, a silently spinning bundle of collapsed linen and spruce? Or would he, like Heidemann himself, hang on, day after breathless day, week after endless week, awaiting, often soliciting, a similar catastrophe? Irritated by this maudlin digression, he picked up Stachel's orders and pretended to study them.

He said, finally, "Tell me about yourself, Stachel. Are you a good flier?"

Stachel paused imperceptibly before answering. The man seated across the desk was much smaller than the press photos had made him appear, a discovery that had already distracted him. But now this question was even more disconcerting. How was a man supposed to answer such a question? Modestly, in the manner of a gentleman? With self-assurance, just short of arrogance, in

13

the manner of the Officers Corps? He decided on the truth.

"I'm comfortable in the air, sir."

Heidemann shifted the pipe to the opposite corner of his mouth to hide the smile that wanted to form. It had been a simple direct answer to a difficult question—an answer that one could expect from a man who knew and accepted his professional strengths and limitations. A competent aviator rarely voiced his competence; his flying spoke for itself. An incompetent aviator would be the last to think of the word "comfortable" in connection with flying. He might claim expertness, or he might turn evasive. But never would he allege comfort.

"How much have you flown?" It was all in the record file under the blotter on his desk, but so much more was revealed when a man talked about himself.

"I've completed the standard military pilot's course at FEA-7, followed by fighter training at *Jastaschule* 1. And there have been assorted cross-countries: Aachen, Trier, and so on."

"Not very much, is it?"

Stachel shrugged. "One assumes the authorities have it all worked out, sir."

"Quite so. Tell me about yourself. Your school. Your home. Your parents—that sort of thing."

Stachel did not relax his attitude of polite alertness, although he sensed that the *Jastaführer* expected him to. The squadron leader seemed the type who would lay the little trap of informality: a commander who would assume a cordial manner simply to see how fast and hard a subordinate would rise to the bait and overstep his bounds.

"My background is quite ordinary, sir. I was born at home in Bad Schwalbe—my father is the proprietor of a resort hotel and several related businesses in the Taunus —and I had the usual schooling. I was working toward a degree in the arts from Heidelberg when I decided to join the infantry regiment in Frankfurt. The infantry soon palled on me, so I requested posting to flight training. And here I am."

Heidemann knew Bad Schwalbe. He and Elfi had spent a week there in the month following their marriage. It had

14

been a dreamlike week in the last June of peace: the tiny village, huddling in its medieval pastels at the base of dark green hills; the concerts in the park by the lakeside *Kurhaus;* the long walks through acres of gardens; their slow, exquisite struggles among the wildflowers on a remote, breeze-haunted sweep of meadow, the benign sun adding a special lasciviousness to the foreplay and ultimate explosion. The ache was suddenly heavy, and to avoid prolonging it, he made no mention of his especial knowledge of this young man's sweet home place.

"What do you want to do after the war?"

Stachel permitted himself a small smile.

"I have to survive the war first, sir. But assuming I do, I rather think I'd like to write. I've frequently been praised for, well, my aptitudes in that area, and I'm the kind, I'm afraid, who needs only a little praise to develop a hunger for more."

"I understand that writing, as such, is a fairly hazardous and unrewarding profession."

Stachel shrugged again. "Perhaps. But I'll take my chances."

"From what little I've done, writing would seem to take more from a man than it gives him."

"So goes the cliché, and I suppose it's true when you talk in terms of cost to the soul or the gizzard or whatever it is a man taps when he writes. Introspection can be a tyrannical creditor. But to have something to say, and then say it precisely as you feel it, is worth the price, I think. Few people pay it unreservedly, so few people reap the rewards that are to be had."

Heidemann chuckled. "Heavy words for one so young. And so you believe that by paying the price you will reap the rewards?"

"I must." Stachel's eyes were thoughtful.

"By rewards, you mean wealth? Fame?"

"Those would be nice, I suppose. But I'm more interested in the peace of mind—the assurances—that come from a man's understanding of himself."

"Assurances of what?"

"That I—that my life has meaning."

Heidemann nodded solemnly, trying to keep his amusement from showing again. He spoke confidentially: "We all want that. But just between you and me, I have long since given up restive self-examination as the key. For true peace of mind, it seems to me, we have much we must forget and much we must resign ourselves to. I've worked up a little philosophy: I can't be at ease by counting and regretting all the things I am not now or ever will be; recognizing this, I count only the things I am, and accept, unnamed and categorically, all the things I am not. This blanket acceptance displaces regret, and, in the absence of regret, I am content." That, Heidemann laughed silently, should jiggle this supercilious youngster's pudding. . . .

"I'm surprised to hear that, sir. No offense, but that seems a rather negative process, and from what I've read of you in the periodicals, it would seem you're quite aggressive and ambitious—a very positive personality, so to speak. It would seem odd that a man of considerable ambition—"

"Nonsense!" Heidemann broke in. "Personal ambition is nothing other than socially acceptable greed, and greed is one of the lowliest of human faults. I aspire, of course, but only to be useful to my God and my Fatherland. The periodicals are full of bean breeze."

Stachel blushed heavily, fearing he'd fallen into the very snare he'd sought to avoid. "Of course, sir. I didn't mean . . ."

Heidemann waved a hand, and his tone was mild. "I know you meant no presumption. As a matter of fact, you merely stated an argument I once used frequently to rationalize my own descents into petty greed. But you'll find as you grow older that you rationalize less and less. And up here, *Herr* Stachel, one grows older very fast. Up here, life takes on a new measure of meaning, and the only assurance you hunger for is that life will continue."

With no apparent pause, he changed the subject. "Why did you choose flying? Between writing and flying, you seem to go out of your way to embrace hazard."

"It's hard to say, sir," Stachel answered, relieved to have escaped the trap. "One day several of us were in Wiesbaden. My father had arranged a party for me and

16

some regimental comrades, and there happened to be a military flying demonstration in connection with a benefit for the wounded. We took it in, and I was, well, intrigued by what I saw. I decided that I wanted to fly."

He could still remember the catch of excitement in his chest as he had watched the sun spank off the wings of the aircraft as they turned and spun in the rich blue void; the long, full thrum of their guy wires as they hurtled down the sky; the A-flat whine as they pulled up and over. He could still see the pilots, climbing in dignified clumsiness from their machines, stripping off their gloves, sliding their goggles jauntily onto their helmeted heads, nodding haughtily to the spatter of applause and shouts of approval from the crowd. There had been no decision to fly. Rather, he had simply known, then and there, that he had to be such a man and would be.

That had been a day, too, he could still associate pleasurably with partying. After the flying demonstration they had gone to the *Zum Schwarzen Bock*. The court had been gayly decorated with lanterns and flowers; the music had been superb, the women lovely, the tables sagging with roasts, fowl, sausages, and cheeses beyond counting, cold salads, hot salads, relishes, cakes and pastries. And the wine. The wine had been cool and keen, and he'd built and retained a fine edge, watching through a wonderful, colorful mist, so that the dancers, the musicians, the diners had moved in the unworldly gauze of a French water color. It was a day he often relived in masochistic nostalgia.

"Well," Heidemann said, staring again at the night, "you'll get plenty of flying here. No doubt you've heard the rumor—God knows everybody else has—that we'll mount a stupendous drive on Paris soon."

"I've heard such rumors, yes. But I've heard similar ones since 1914. It's hard to know what to believe nowadays."

"There's truth in this one. The High Command apparently feels we should finish things up before the Americans arrive in strength. If that's the case, we'll have to be on the move soon; the Yankees have had a year to get ready."

Stachel shifted slightly. He was going to suggest the

17

short work the U-boats were expected to make of the Americans, but he decided it would sound silly. He said simply: "I hope I can contribute something, sir."

Heidemann turned from the window to regard him. His eyes were expressionless. "I hope so, too."

"Is there anything I can do to prepare myself?"

Heidemann sighed soundlessly. How should he answer? Had not this young man seen this very afternoon the ferocity—the fierce, flashing audacity—with which the five Englishmen had paid their visit? What does one do to prepare himself for dalliance with such an enemy? Burn incense? Say a prayer?

"Yes, of course. Tonight, acquaint yourself with your machine. Study it from spinner to rudder post. You'll get a Pfalz. Let's see"—he ran a finger down a page in a worn binder—"forty-two-oh-one-slash-seventeen. Make a note of that: Oh-one. Then ask *Oberleutnant* Kettering for some charts of the area; he'll run over them with you and answer any questions you may have about procedures. Do you have any questions now?"

Only about a hundred thousand, Stachel thought as he arose. The anxiety rapped sharply.

"Not now, sir. Good night, *Herr Hauptmann*." He saluted and turned to go.

"Stachel . . ."

"Sir?"

"Get a good sleep if you can. Tomorrow, if we aren't buried in this stinking snow, I'll take you on a familiarization flight. I'm taking a *Kette* on a balloon run at oh-nine-hundred. Therefore, meet me on the flight line at oh-six-thirty. But sleep—it pays dividends to be bright-eyed around here."

"Very good, sir. And thank you. I enjoyed our chat very much."

"Good night."

Heidemann watched him go, reviewing already the little clues he had gathered. In specifics, the young face had been composed and the voice restrained, and the body, although alert and postured, had hinted an underlying grace and dynamic integration of muscle and nerve. The whole, though, had presented an interesting double image.

18

This lad, he felt, carried with him an unspoken—perhaps even unrecognized—fear. Not so much the restiveness that any of the new ones was likely to show on the eve of his manhood's trial, but something uniquely beyond that. Animal nervousness on the edge of the unknown was one thing; but *Herr* Stachel, he was sure, bent under an even heavier burden.

He stood by the window and noted that the snow was easing off. From down the line he could hear the familiar, busy sounds of the riggers and the engine mechanics at their work. A crew, struggling with a hangar to replace the one damaged by the Englishmen's bombs, argued in good-natured obscenities, their voices drifting on the dying wind.

Yes, Stachel would be a man to watch. Heidemann had seen the type before; such a man at this very moment led *Jasta* 27 a few kilometers up the line. There was ambition, barely concealed behind a practiced façade of impassiveness; a heavily egocentric outlook on the world and the dismaying things it held. A somewhat pompous personality dedicated to itself, with a gyroscopic intelligence to provide the navigational fixes required for the climb up humanity's pile.

All of these were there, he felt. But underlying them was a peculiar diffidence that smelled of a deep, fundamental fear, which the youthful posturizing had failed to hide. Heidemann knew that when a man was alone in the sky, solitary in the trembling box of his cockpit, normal uneasiness could turn into freezing terror in a second's time—a second which, if permitted to lapse into two, could introduce black eternity. He wondered: Was it early in a man's life such a terror was born, to lurk then silently until the ultimate call upon it? Or was it truly something generated of and by the climactic moment of emergency itself?

In Stachel's case, he decided, the terror was already built in and waiting.

"Rupp!"

"Yes, *Herr Hauptmann?*"

"Did they recover all the Englishmen?"

"Four of them are in the tent behind the machine shop,

19

sir, and *Oberleutnant* Kettering has scheduled a burial ceremony tomorrow at noon. The other—the one who fell in the marsh—our party couldn't find. He's under the mud somewhere, I guess."

Heidemann knocked out his pipe. "Poor devil. It's a cold night to be lying out in a swamp."

"Yes, sir."

CHAPTER 3

Oberleutnant KARL-HEINZ KETTERING, the *Jasta* adjutant, was a friar-bald, bell-shaped man whose principal spare-time interest (in fact, Stachel had learned from a garrulous mess orderly, it was asserted to be his civilian occupation) was the collection of erotica. He sat deep in his chair regarding his latest acquisition when Stachel came in. At Stachel's polite greeting he looked up.

"Ah. Our new would-be Von Richthofen. Tell me, *Herr* Stachel, is not this the most extraordinary set of buttocks you've ever seen?"

Stachel considered the photograph for a moment, then shrugged. "There are better."

"Impossible! Look at the elegant curve where they join the hollow of her back, the delightful little smile they make above her thighs. How could there be any better?"

"There are, though."

"Assuming there are, my bucko, and assuming they are within two hundred kilometers of this wretched place, you must take me there at the earliest opportunity. I'll photograph them myself, in person."

Stachel smiled. "I'm afraid you're out of luck—even if this particular set were in the next room. The lady in question is quite discriminating about those she permits to examine them."

Over the exchange of grins, they evaluated one another. Kettering was a man of few pretensions, and if he had

20

any notable characteristic in his make-up it was his willingness to accept the pretensions of others. To him, of course, this was no weakness; congeniality and guilelessness were things to be cherished, he felt, but if others chose to bury them under an armor built of play-acting, so be it. It was not that he was insensitive to the humbuggery life paraded before him; on the contrary, working so hard to be no poseur himself made him peculiarly aware of the sham in others. But he readily conceded that the others must have reasons for their little deceptions, and it was these hidden, tacit things that Kettering honored. Should a man be aggressively hearty, Kettering would suspect (and usually find) the desperate shyness underneath, and, having perceived, would amiably indulge the fellow's bluff. Should another be cynical and hard, he'd give his salute to the plaguing softness that more than likely molded the veneer. Pity, he thought now, that this Stachel youngster felt compelled to smile so tightly, keeping his eyes solemn, so as to restrain the callowness from showing through his pose as the sophisticate. Stachel in his natural state, Kettering was sure, would be a thoroughly likable chap. In his current role, though, he merely came off as a stuffed shirt. Well, no doubt the bitter trials of the year ahead would soon refine away the overlay and leave the real character for Kettering to enjoy. Meanwhile, he would take aboard Stachel's bravado along with the considerable allotment he'd already ingested from so many others.

"Too bad," Kettering said. "Buttocks are God's most magnificent design, combining perfect function with exquisite form. If your lady has such an exceptional pair, she should permit them to be shown, in the Louvre, perhaps, so that the world could come and wonder. She must be a selfish, unfeeling baggage." He slid the photo into an order packet, patting it fondly as he did so. "Ah, well. What can I do for you, *Junge?*"

"I'm supposed to look over some charts of the area. The *Jastaführer* plans to take me on a familiarization flight tomorrow morning."

"The *Jastaführer!* Well, now, you must have made a fine impression on him. Ordinarily the new ones go out first with the *Kettenführer*. What did you do—put him onto a likely brunette?" Kettering's grin turned suggestive.

"*Hauptmann* Heidemann doesn't strike me as the type who'd have to have help in finding his women. He seems quite a fellow." Stachel went carefully, aware that in the Army the wise one never committed himself on the matter of a commander until the subordinate atmosphere had been thoroughly sniffed.

"He's that, all right. Otto Heidemann is one of the toughest and smartest fixtures you'll find in the Imperial Air Service, my boy. I grant you he doesn't look like much, being the skinny little runt he is, but he's got an ironbound belly and a head full of real soldier-type brains. You're a very lucky fellow to be posted to his *Jasta*, I'll tell you. Yes, sir."

Stachel's smile was more relaxed this time, and Kettering caught a meager glimpse of the lurking boyishness.

"You mentioned Von Richthofen. Is the *Jasta* commander that good?"

Kettering snorted.

"Von Richthofen is very, very capable. So is Heidemann. But there the similarity ends. The Baron has that mysterious X-factor—the indefinable ingredient in some people that captures the public imagination. What makes a national hero like Baron von Richthofen? Important friends, that's what. Important friends and the X-factor. The Baron has both. *Herr* Heidemann has neither."

Stachel sat down, weariness dragging at him. "Well," he suggested, "in this line of business, good flying and fine marksmanship have a bit to do with it, I'd say."

Kettering slid a hairy hand into his tunic and scratched reflectively. When he spoke, his tone was confidential. "True enough. But Von Richthofen isn't really good as a flier, you know. Oh, he can get a machine in the air and steer it around, all right. But he doesn't make it dance."

"I find that hard to believe." Stachel's eyes went to Kettering's breast pocket, which was innocent of the pilot's badge. "Have you seen the Baron fly?"

Kettering saw the glance and chuckled. "Of course, I have. He comes over here every once in a while from

JG-1. He marches that saucy little red triplane of his around the field and lands it as if it were a peat barge. No class. You watch Heidemann when he comes in: like a gymnast alighting. Perfect form, balance, execution. And incidentally, my friend, you can't tell a pilot by the badge he wears. I had two sorties in a Rumpler *Taube* back in '14. But I flew like a barge captain, too, and I've a tree limb to prove it." He leaned under the desk and rapped on his lower left leg. There was a wooden sound.

Stachel blushed hotly, angry that he had not remembered earlier seeing Kettering's limp. "Really, I—"

"Forget it, comrade. You'll find my feelings don't bruise easily, and I've managed to turn what at first seemed a liability into a decided asset. You'd be surprised at the number of ladies who are intrigued by the idea of only three feet between the sheets. Somewhat akin to kissing a man with a *Vollbart,* they tell me. That extra something, and so on."

Stachel fell redly silent, and since it made Kettering uncomfortable to see someone else's discomfort, he hastened back to the subject.

"Understand, I don't intend to malign the Baron or to discount him in any way. He's a damned good fighter, and I'll tip my *Krätzchen* to him any time. All I'm saying is that he's lucky to have the X-factor and the High Command working for him. Every move he makes gets into the papers. Meanwhile, Heidemann, a full-fledged *Kanone* with forty victories—not counting the one he nailed right here in our parlor this afternoon—chugs along as obscure as this goddamned itch on my belly."

"I've seen pictures and write-ups on Heidemann in the popular press. Not as many as for the Baron, of course, but good ones," Stachel said dubiously.

"That's precisely my point. He doesn't have the X-factor. Give him three pages in the *Illustrierte Zeitung* and the public turns to the suppository advertisements. Give Richthofen one paragraph in the *Petunia-Raiser's Gazette,* and right off fifty million virgins have an orgasm."

Stachel laughed for the first time that day.

"Drink?" Kettering had produced a bottle.

Stachel hesitated, his amusement dying. When he spoke he tried to keep his phrases from sounding overly casual. "I don't think so. *Hauptmann* Heidemann said he wants me bright-eyed tomorrow."

"Oh, come, now. The charts will look much better to you with something warm goose-stepping around inside." He poured into two tin cups, and the sweet bite of brandy was in the room. "And, as the American cowboys are said to say, 'Never trust a man who doesn't drink with you,' or something similarly ridiculous. You don't want me not trusting you, do you?"

The anxiety, very real now, tugged in a nearly physical way. To stifle it, he capitulated. "Well, no." He took the cup. "All right. *Pros't.*"

The two drank, assessing each other anew over the rim of their cups. Then, after exploding a long sigh of contentment, Kettering leaned over the back of his chair and brought forth a map case. In an easy, practiced motion, he spread several maps across the desk. Stachel took up a position at his elbow, the brandy diffusing within him in a delightful crawl. Kettering assumed a professorial air, which, without the drink, would have been silly, but, with it, was droll.

"Now. You will note, *Herr* Stachel, that our *Jasta* is located here, at Beauvin. On a line running generally north, our other *Jagdstaffeln*—Numbers 2, 26, 27, and 36—are based at Erchin, while *Jastas* 14 and 4 are at Masny, and 20 and 32 are at Guesnain. Your friend Richthofen, as leader of the group of squadrons called *Jagdgeschwader* 1, hangs his trousers at Avesnes-le-Sec with *Jasta* 11, at least for the present, while his other *Jastas*—4, 6, and 10—are at Lieu St. Amand and Iwuy. The battlefront, for your purposes, runs roughly from the Scarpe, where it flows through Arras, south-by-southeast to—let's see—to here. The Somme and the line below the St. Quentin area are covered by eleven *Jastas*. It's this area right along—here—where our particular *Jasta* busies itself. Tomorrow, Heidemann will probably march you up to Arras, then bring you down this way, with the front at a judicious distance off your right wing, to about here.

He'll then more than likely pull you back up this way, over Cambrai. Any questions?"

Stachel reached for the bottle. The apprehension, so strong but moments before, had dissipated, to be replaced by a pleasurable sense of well-being.

"May I?"

Kettering grinned. "I don't want you getting too trustworthy. But go ahead, by all means. . . ."

"Hals und Beinbruch . . ."

"Break your neck and arms," Stachel parroted in proper tradition. Then, opening his collar, he asked, "What are the *Jasta*'s particular problems? I mean operationally, and so on."

Kettering belched delicately. "Well, we've been on a balloon binge recently and have developed a marked distaste for Tommy observation planes. It seems there will be a big push on soon, and the High Command has told the various armies to keep the Englishmen from snooping."

"The *Hauptmann* was saying so earlier. Any success?"

"Mm. But our boys have their hands full, I'll tell you. The only thing about this offensive that's secret is the date, and I'm not so sure the Beefeaters haven't discovered that, too. At any rate, they are very busy little fellows these days, shoving across the lines in those monstrosities they fly, trying to get a peep over our shoulder while we arrange our cards."

Stachel judged that the bottle was less than a quarter full and therefore too low to promote a third drink. He'd been saving the flask of Irish in his bags, but if Kettering made no further overtures with the brandy before he left tonight, he'd nightcap from that. . . .

"Why do the observation planes give our people so much trouble? They're pretty slow and unwieldy, I hear."

"It's not the observation machines that give us trouble. It's those double-damned pursuit bastards they bring along. You pile down on an RE-8 or a DeHavilland, and what do you get? Seven hundred million Sopwiths or SE-5's flying up your backside, that's what you get. Just last month, for instance, the *Jasta* reached into an apple

25

barrel and took out a handful of cow dung. There's this old bedspring of an FE wobbling along at about a thousand meters, see, so Heidemann holds the rest of the *Jasta* upstairs while Huemmel and Fabian go down to polish it off. They just begin to waltz when five Tommies come boiling out of a cloud to lend the FE a hand. Heidemann sends down Mueller and his *Kette*—Mueller didn't have the new boys that day—to even things up. At this, another bunch of Camels comes along to join the wrestling. Heidemann commits the remainder of the *Jasta* just as a squadron of SE-5's happens along at the very same time Von Richthofen and *Jasta* 11 show up. Fabian tells me it was the goddamnedest fight he'd ever seen— at one point there were at least fifty machines having at it. And the old FE that started it all turns around and flies home with nary a hole in his bloomers."

Stachel nodded with interest. "Are we up to strength?"

"Hardly. Oh, our *Jasta* has thirteen pilots against a paper strength of eighteen, which is better than usual, but four of them—Tallmann, Dietrich, Fritzinger, and you— are so new they squeak. *Hauptmann* Heidemann, Fabian, Von Klugermann, Braun, Mueller, and Huemmel are old hands. The other three, Kunkel, Schneider, and Ulrich —Ulrich's only an acting officer, incidentally—are so-so types who've been around since last fall. As for the other *Jastas,* it's about the same. A number of the new lads coming in hail from the Russian front, since they're not needed there now that the Czar's out of business. Operations and aircraft types out that way were a good bit different, so there's some retraining involved. In sum, we are half hotshots, half dilettantes. I hope to God things improve before the offensive begins."

"How about the Englishmen? Are they any better off?" Stachel's sense of well-being was at a fine edge.

"The English, my young friend, are crazy. Pop-eyed mad. You caught a little glimpse of that today. Actual unit strength, they've got numbers, all right, but our Intelligence reports on their quality are somewhat sketchy. But why in pluperfect hell should the English worry about quality when there are so many young Tipperaries who are simply insane in their desire to be heroes? Heidemann says you just can't figure them: you let loose a kick at them and what do they do? They poop on your boot."

Stachel doubted that Heidemann had put it in such terms, but he considered the point. As he did so, the door clattered open, admitting a cold, damp gust and a swarthy man whose black-brown eyes peered over a massive muffler like two raisins atop a bread loaf.

"Tenderhearted Jesus, but that air's cold," he hissed as he stamped his feet.

"Hullo, Ziegel," Kettering grunted. "*Leutnant* Stachel, meet *Leutnant* Ziegel, ground technical officer of this grand organization. Ziegel extorts his 310 *Deutschemark* per month from the Imperial Treasury by pretending to keep our aircraft in operating condition. I might add, however, that I myself would never fly an airplane that had received his attention, since it more than likely would cause me to lose not only what's left of my legs but also what's between."

Ziegel blinked agreeably at Stachel as he unwound the great scarf. "*Herr* Kettering is justified in his concern over what's between his legs, since that's where he carries his meager store of brains. Glad to have you with us—Stachel, is it?"

Stachel nodded and shook the icy, outstretched hand. Ziegel spied the bottle, held it to the light for a moment, then sloshed a liberal amount of brandy into one of the cups. He gulped it down quickly, shuddered, then made as if to pour another.

"Bar's closed, you nuts-and-bolts chaser." Kettering took the bottle, slapped the cork home, and stowed the brandy in a musette bag. So the Irish it would be, Stachel thought.

"Fah. Then I leave." Ziegel turned to Stachel. "Give me the bad news, my boy: are you flying tomorrow?"

"Yes. An orientation flight."

"Oh, that's capital." Ziegel groaned, turning his dark eyes to the ceiling in an attitude of resignation. "Oh-one is the only machine I can't put on the line. Ah, well, I was anxious to work all night anyway. Want to look her over now?"

27

"Very much." Stachel stood. The brandy was leaving him now and the sooner he got to his bags the better.

Kettering yawned, arose, and patted Stachel's shoulder. "You'll probably want to head for your villa after getting your fill of *Herr* Ziegel's abuse. Know where it is?"

"Second house from the edge of town, on the right. Top floor rear. I think that's what the orderly told me."

"Right you are. Well, good night, *meine Herrschaften*. Keep your stickers up."

Outside, as they walked toward the hangars, Stachel asked Ziegel, puzzled: "How did you know which machine the *Jastaführer* had assigned me?"

Ziegel was a Bavarian, and as such he was direct. "The *Jastaführer* assigns our best aircraft only to proven, first-class men. You are still an unknown nobody," he said, not unkindly. "When *Herr* Heidemann decides you're worth it, he'll move you up from the Pfalz to an Albatros—not until then."

"You mean the better the pilot, the better his machine?"

"*Ja*"—Ziegel pronounced it *"Jo"* in the easy Bavarian way—"for our leader, an airplane is a precious jewel. If ever you are authorized an Albatros in this *Jasta, Herr* Stachel, it will be the same as getting the Blue Max somewhere else. In *Herr* Heidemann's eye, there is simply no greater recognition of a man's merit than to entrust a good aircraft to him."

"How, then," Stachel wondered aloud, "do any of the new ones manage to come through? It seems to me a new man in a rattletrap machine would be rather easy pickings in a fight. . . ."

Ziegel nodded solemnly. "It's a cruel world, my boy."

It was the same as always. He had known it would be as soon as he had scented the keenness of brandy. The first one was liberation, an exhilarating release from the tight anxiety, a salving shift of the melancholy and aloneness. The second was nothing special, the clicking sharpness in the chest having fled with the diminishing first. The third and the fourth and the fifth and the others were wooden repetitions, a mechanical process that went on simply because it couldn't be denied or shut off. Now, as it had been from the earliest time, the inevitable dullness was there. Why couldn't he win and retain the soaring reality that came with the first—only the first? That awareness of life, the singing sense of power and cleanliness and rightness in himself, the identity of that self with the etched-crystal world all around? Why did the miracle always die so quickly, to leave nothing but the dullness and the involuntary reflex: eyes to the ceiling, emptily, the liquid sound in the dark?

CHAPTER *4*

THE PFALZ and the Albatros sat wing to wing, slivers of day sparking against their softly ticking propellers. The royal blue of the western sky graduated above through the spectrum to where the cold sun, a featureless hemisphere of metallic white, sat in the cadmium yellow void of morning. The air, quiet, cold, and clear, was an astringent against the taut burn of Stachel's face. The snow crunched, soda-cracker dry, under his flying boots.

Heidemann was between the two machines, standing patiently while a pair of takeoff attendants busied themselves with adjustments to his flight gear. He smiled an answer to Stachel's salute, and when he spoke, little puffs of vapor formed around his helmeted head.

"Good morning, Stachel. We've a good day for your debut."

"Yes, sir. It's a beauty, all right." His lips were stiff, and his tongue moved stickily.

"It's about time. The weather's been appalling for weeks, and Rupp says the French farmer expects a thaw and much rain for several weeks to come. So today is a pleasant surprise."

"French farmer?"

"Yes. Ridiculous, isn't it? All the mechanical marvels of modern science, all the technical resources of the Fatherland presumably at our disposal, and nobody—even the fortunetellers who call themselves meteorologists—can assure us as to the weather for tomorrow. Nobody but a French farmer who, for a jar of jam, will sniff the wind, stare at the sky, and then describe a hunch. But the hunches have, strangely enough, been quite accurate, and I find myself thankful for such little favors." He paused, his gaze direct. "Did you sleep last night?"

Stachel squinted aloft, as if considering the sky, the stab of guilt compelling him to avoid the other's calm inspection. "Oh, yes. It took me a while, but I dropped off eventually. Excited, I guess."

"I wondered. Your eyes are quite red."

The guilt was at once alarm. "I may be catching cold. My eyes always show it first."

"Did you have breakfast?"

"Yes, a tin of fruit I had in my kit. It was all I wanted."

"I didn't see you at mess. Do you feel well enough to fly?"

One of the attendants stooped to check Stachel's coveralls where they bunched into his boots. Stachel started violently and shoved the man away.

"Let me alone, goddamn it!"

The man sprawled, then quickly recovered, shock and resentment in his face. There was a strained, awkward pause in which the others gaped. Heidemann cleared his throat.

"Apologize, *Leutnant* Stachel." His tone was flat. "Apologize at once."

Stachel blushed heavily in astonishment and confusion. "Of course, sir, gladly." He turned quickly to the sullen attendant. "I—I'm sorry. I don't know why I did that. You startled me. And I beg your pardon, *Herr Hauptmann,* for such a rude display."

Heidemann's face was expressionless. He glanced at the *Startwärter.* "Well?"

"That's all right, sir. The new chaps do get tightened up a bit. No offense."

The *Jastaführer* pulled at his helmet strap, a bit of

30

business calculated to mask his own perplexity. He had sensed fleetingly that Stachel's explosion had been directed at him—a volcanic eruption, heavy with fury, that seemed senselessly out of proportion to the situation. But his own outrage at the shoddy tableau was tempered immediately by the unwitting wisdom in the *Startwärter's* words. Excitement, he reminded himself, asserts itself in many ways; for ten people there are ten different reactions to excitement. Sleeplessness and distaste for breakfast were certainly not unreasonable; a startled outburst and an involuntary shove were by no means alien to tension. Go slowly, Heidemann, he told himself: this youngster is growing up today.

"Very well. I'll talk to you about this later, Stachel. Meanwhile, here are my instructions: stay close to me and do what I do as we go along. Fly to my left rear and somewhat above, so you can observe my hand signals. To call your attention to key landmarks, I'll use a simple pointing gesture, like this." He demonstrated. "To indicate other aircraft and their location, I'll first rock my wings slowly then point in their direction. You'll get so that you spot our aerial wildlife quite easily as time goes by, but at first it can be elusive."

Stachel's dismay clung to him like a shroud, and he fought to throw it off. How could he have done anything so foolish? Manhandling of personnel was not uncommon in the Army, to be sure, and he expected no further trouble over that, even from Heidemann, reputed to be the enlisted men's darling. But how in the name of the All-loving could he have lost control of himself that way? *Jesus to Jesus,* he screamed silently, *I've got to stop drinking like that! It's ruining me. . . .*

"We'll confine our course to a simple circuit of the *Jasta's* area of responsibility," Heidemann was saying. "I'll keep an eye on you, but there are times when my attention is demanded elsewhere. So if you have an engine vapor lock or a malfunction of any kind, alert me with a burst from your machine guns. If you must make a forced landing, slap your hand against the fuselage. I'll use that as my cue to lead you to a safe landing place. I'll use the same signal if I get in trouble. In that case, follow me down and note my final position on the ground, so that when you return here, Kettering can set the necessary recovery operations going. Any questions?"

"What if we are attacked, sir?" he managed.

"It's my job to see that we won't be. But if by any chance this occurs, don't attempt to engage but dive for home by the most direct route possible."

"And you, sir?" He felt the Code compelled him to ask, even though he knew the answer.

"What do you mean?"

"Will you engage?"

Once again, despite his determination to sustain the proper amount of suspense over his unfinished lecture on manhandling, Heidemann warmed to this young man. The question had been appropriately solicitous; but more than that, Stachel's air revealed he had not asked it merely as a matter of form. It had been the right question, asked at the right time and in the right manner, and he was pleased.

"I'll protect your withdrawal, if that's what you mean," he said crisply.

"Well—"

"You will not engage the enemy, Stachel. Is that clear?"

"But you might need—"

"I appreciate your concern, but there is one thing you'll learn—rapidly, I hope: never argue with me, even when motivated by altruism. It can cost you dearly." He pulled two slips of paper from the deep cuff of his left glove and handed one to Stachel.

"Here are your compass bearings, in case we're separated. The day's bright, and you can fly by direct observation. But the sky can be confusing, as you no doubt already have learned. Now let's be off, shall we?"

Stachel saluted and turned to his machine. The Pfalz, whose matte-gray color scheme was relieved only by the black and white Iron Cross insignia on fuselage, rudder, and wings, seemed changed in the daylight. When Ziegel had shown it to him in the hangar by the light of a naked lamp, it had been worn and tired-looking. This morning, in the dazzling snow, its lines were racy and dangerous, and it depressed him somehow. He nodded a greeting to

32

the line chief, who stood with one foot in the fuselage stirrup ready to wipe down the windscreen with a wad of porous cloth.

"Everything ready?" He tried to sound casual, but the engine noises were loud and he had to repeat his question in the man's cupped ear. Rather than casual, he'd merely sounded silly, and he hated himself for it.

"Yes, sir, ready and full of spit!" the man shouted. His teeth were wide-spaced, and Stachel thought suddenly of the picket fence around his mother's roses. As the man climbed down to make way for him, Stachel was wracked by a desire to laugh. First guilt; then dismay and confusion, followed by depression; now a compulsion to guffaw. Was this insanity? *Mother of God, was this indeed insanity?*

To fight the turmoil, he made intense physical action of his cockpit procedure. He studied the tachometer, perched directly before him like a single, solemn eye. The engine recorded full normality, bellowing richly as he eased open the throttle and sighing to an even chuckle when he closed to idle. He checked the fuel pressure and quantity gauges, gave the pressure hand pump a series of stabs, ran his thumb over the petrol cocks and magneto switches, and gently tapped the altimeter with his gloved forefinger. Waggling the control column, he examined the aileron and elevator movements, taking them through their full arcs of travel. The rudder bar moved rather stiffly, but that could help him pick up a bit more control through his heavy issue boots. He pulled the security belt's four-way strap to the locking toggle on his chest and settled the webbing firmly against him. Then he glanced at Heidemann.

The *Hauptmann* was shouting something to the line chief, who waved acknowledgment. Then, lowering his goggles and motioning away the wheel chocks, the *Jastaführer* looked across at Stachel, smiled over his scarf, and swept his arm in a forward arc.

Stachel advanced the throttle, and the propeller's flickering dissolved into a mahogany haze. The Pfalz awakened, trembling and vibrant as it waddled through the thin layer of snow. The Mercedes engine surged into a throaty, blattering roar, and with its broad wings rocking in the frenzied flurries kicked up by Heidemann's departure, the machine picked up speed. He watched detachedly as the sheet of white rushed along to disappear beneath the drumming metal of the long, tapered nose. Finally the agonized creaking and slamming of the undergear ceased, and the ground fell away, slowing in its motion as the Pfalz climbed.

At two thousand meters, Heidemann's Albatros eased out of its climb and Stachel brought his machine up close, so that by looking down past the leading edge of the right lower wing, he could see the *Jasta* commander quite clearly. Heidemann glanced back over his shoulder at him, and Stachel saw the sun's glint on his goggles. He returned Heidemann's wave. The Pfalz, he noted, was *schwanzlästig,* and he had to ride the control column to compensate for this tail-heaviness.

Up here the sun was incredibly bright, and the earth formed an enormous platter that moved past in placid laziness, remote and ghostly pale. Impatiently, Stachel awaited the enchantment. Here in the limitless majesty, when immersed in tangy sky scented by exhaust and hot metal, he felt closer to the possibility of a grand concept and a belief that he had a role in it. At times like these, the sensual and spiritual immediacy of the soft blue, the melody of wind in the wires, the reassuring engine throb, the gentle swaying, somehow canceled out the boorishness, deceit, and cruelty that begrimed the earth below.

Stachel was not at all certain there was a God, especially the kind he had visualized during those interminable, droning Sundays when, as a youngster, he had listened in moody discomfort from between formidable parental brackets while Pastor Ehrlich had exhorted the Deity. In those days, God had seemed a gigantic composite of Pastor Ehrlich and Kris Kringel, who sat somewhere beyond the moon and dispensed nice things to good boys and unspeakable punishments to bad boys. He still remembered tempering his attitudes and actions with a sort of polite acknowledgment of this awesome Being's ever-present magnifying glass, smugly awaiting a reward when he felt he had conformed to the pastor's murky code, superstitiously furtive when his conscience told him the code had been violated. As he had grown older and more sophisticated, he rarely thought further on the subject, and in recent times he had been increasingly convinced that Ehrlich-equals-God was a monumental fraud. But if ever there were a kindly, all-seeing Power, Stachel sometimes mused, it would most certainly reside in this magnificent upper place.

Below, Stachel's life was a two-dimensional thing, he knew. Either he was projecting himself into the future, living in advance the undefined torments or unnamed delights to come, or gloomily re-creating the past—its failures and its triumphs, its highs and its lows. In fact, he had become so preoccupied with past and future he was hard-put to be fully aware of the present. Only in two general circumstances did the present ever take on any meaningfulness: with the first gratifying swallow of alcohol, and with the separation of landing wheels from the earth. Only then was there respite from the gnawing melancholy and discontent.

But today the magic failed him. Instead of the exhilarating release, his return to the sky brought only negative uneasiness. For months now he had envisioned this day—the day when he would be mounted in a swift fighting plane, regarding the approaching battlefield over a pair of fatly loaded machine guns. But today was here, the day of days, and it meant only one more dredging of the past, one more struggle with the indefinable guilt. How typical of Bruno Stachel, he reflected bitterly. Two-dimensional Bruno Stachel.

Heidemann banked easily to the right, and Stachel swung too wide on his follow-up. The *Hauptmann*, fortunately, had had his head turned away, and Stachel was satisfied that his laggardliness had gone unobserved. He forced himself to concentrate on business.

The Scarpe was a dark line twisting through the fading white below. Directly ahead, just short of the horizon, a haze hung close to the ground, and there was a faint, fitful flickering within it. At one point a towering column of smoke boiled through the film to a spectacular height, where it flattened into an enormous hammerhead. Heidemann made a 90-degree left turn, and this time Stachel kept with it. Leveling out, the *Hauptmann* pointed off his right wing. Straining, Stachel could make out the porridge-colored smear that marked a town. What was it? Kettering had said. Arras? He studied it for a long moment, since here was the legendary Western Front. It seemed a little too much to accept that over there, under the pall, hundreds of thousands of men were, in the words of the popular press, locked in the greatest struggle of all time. In previous months, in quiet moments, he had fabricated romantically gaudy images of the front, but from here it appeared to be nothing more than a smoky stretch on an otherwise clear horizon. The corner of his mouth twitched. Was this what all the shouting was about?

Heidemann's wings were rocking, and his arm was pointed ahead and down. Stachel sat erect and put his head into the propeller wash. The air stung and flattened his cheeks, but he ignored the blast in his concentration. He peered hard, but could see nothing. He closed his eyes briefly, then tried again; still nothing but the blotched topography. Half-worried, half-annoyed, he began a systematic search of the area Heidemann had indicated, even allowing for the passage of time and space. But it was no use. If there had been another airplane down there, it had escaped him. He wondered momentarily if the *Jastaführer* had been pulling his leg, but he abandoned the thought at once. Heidemann was definitely not the type for foolishness. So he sat back again, aware of the tension that had joined him in the cockpit.

Four more times in the following hour the Albatros' wings tipped, and only once did Stachel spy a general shifting of color that may have been the machine Heidemann's infuriating arm had designated. As they moved finally into the return leg, he was in a truly foul depression. How could he be so blind? How could he hope to amount to anything in this business if he couldn't see even machines that were calmly pointed out to him? To darken his mood further, it wasn't until they had swung around in a full 360-degree turn and had descended to a hundred meters that he first saw the airdrome. He made his landing in hot anger and self-reproach, swearing aloud when the tail-heavy Pfalz bounced awkwardly and yawed at first contact.

Would-be Von Richthofen indeed!

Kettering and Ziegel sat on a bench by the headquarters building, huddled deep in their greatcoats, service caps pulled low against the sun glare. They watched the two machines swagger over the rutted field, engines barking in brief bursts.

Ziegel stirred. "I hope the bastard didn't spring any seams on that landing."

"You say that every time. But it would serve you right if he had. You and your tail-heavy rigging nonsense," Kettering accused good-naturedly.

"It's Heidemann's idea, not mine," Ziegel huffed. "Machines are hard to come by and harder to keep running. It squeezes my scrotum to put a ship out of trim just to indulge the *Jastaführer*'s fancies. He doesn't have to worry with them at night. I do."

Kettering changed the subject with the air of one who'd heard a story a thousand times. "What do you think of this new one?"

"Stachel? Hard to say. Like he can't make up his mind what he is—a man of the world or a wet-nosed kid. One moment he walks and talks like a field marshal; the next, he's wriggling like a puppy. Furthermore, since I get the distinct impression that he's a charlatan, I think I'm not going to like him very much."

"I get the impression that he's never quite with me. I talk to him, but it's as if he's listening to some music that's very far away, sort of. Know what I mean?"

"Mm. Like Klaus in my *Jasta* 27 days. Did you know Klaus, by the way?"

"No. I've heard about him, though. Didn't they call him Forgetful Fritz, or something like that?"

"That son of an ass had no more right flying aircraft than a locomotive does. He had a memory like a mirror, mainly because he never listened, and it finally did him in. We were trying out a Gnome-type rotary in a DR-1 one day and he volunteered to fly it. He came down from altitude on the blip button, forgetting to valve off the fuel. The nacelle filled up to dripping, and when he cut in the ignition to correct his landing approach—Boof!—like Vesuvius, it was."

Kettering grunted. "This Stachel's nervous, too. Did you hear about the Niederhauser incident? Stachel sent him balls over eyeteeth."

"I saw it. As far as I'm concerned, Niederhauser could use a lot more of the same thing. He's a troublemaker, first class. I think he's a Bolshevik. . . ."

"Fabian—he's got the room under Stachel's—Fabian says Stachel walked up and down the whole night. I remember I was all keyed up before my first time out, but I never walked the whole damned night."

"*You* walk, you lard-ass? Ha!"

Stachel had declined the cup of chocolate the orderly offered him but Heidemann, sunk behind his desk, his flying suit flung wide, sipped thoughtfully at the brew.

"Well, Stachel," he asked finally, "what do you think?"

Stachel smiled thinly, his lips dry. He felt his way. "Very interesting, sir."

"Did you note the landmarks I pointed out?"

"Yes, sir."

"And those aircraft?"

The *Hauptmann's* oblique gaze, his carefully casual attitude, suggested a trap. This man, Stachel knew, was the monarch, the autocratic, arbitrary and undisputed high sachem for 130 officers and men and the mud-smeared corner of France they claimed. And beyond him, layer upon fathomless layer, were other monarchs who ultimately looked to the mightiest and most remote of them all—the Kaiser himself—for the word, the nod, the hint that would turn them unquestioningly and ruthlessly to the implementation of the German national whim. A new sense of the manifold laminations of power behind the man who sipped chocolate and of the uselessness of his own impulse to temporize their workings brought Stachel to weary surrender. His inexplicable violence on the flight line, the compounding of his depression with tension

38

and wanderings, his blindness and ineptitude aloft suddenly were more than he could hope to bluff through. *Get it over with now; they'll find out eventually.*

"I didn't see one of them, sir. I can't explain it, but I didn't see one."

There.

Heidemann placed his cup carefully on the desk. He stared out the window to the east. Out there beyond the horizon, somewhere under some sweep of that same sky, Elfi lived. She moved, she talked, she laughed, breathed, thought, felt, ate, slept. The great distance between them did not change those facts, he knew, but he wondered how it could be, really. How could all those intimate, familiar little busynesses really go on when they were beyond the beholding of the one man to whom they had meaning? He recalled the old question: When a tree falls in the wilderness, with no creature there to hear, does the crash really sound? With him gone, did Elfi really live, or did she pause in some sweet suspension until he was there once again to look on and applaud with his heart? Half sick with the pain of his yearning, he closed his eyes. Then he turned to the man across the desk, willing his mind back from his distant wilderness.

"It's important that you do, you know. Not only for your own welfare, either. The Fatherland has gone to a great deal of trouble to put you where you are. It would be an abominable waste to have you wallowing ineffectually around the sky for the few moments it would take an Englishman to find you and stitch up your spine."

"I know," Stachel said in a subdued voice.

"At any rate, you didn't attempt to fool me, and that's very much in your favor. If you'd attempted a bluff, I'd have asked further questions; and once I'd exposed your bluff, I'd have been compelled to post you. Lack of skill can be overcome with patient practice. Lying is hopeless, since lying is symptomatic of weakness beyond correction. I've no place for weak men."

"Stupid and confused, perhaps," Stachel said bitterly, "but I am not a liar."

"Of course. Therefore practice and more practice is

indicated. We'll repeat today's little exercise every morning until next Monday. We'll also take the same run each
evening, and between-times, you'll work in some mock
combat and air-to-ground gunnery."

In the brief pause that followed, Stachel wondered how
best to demonstrate his thanks. Solicitude? Heidemann
seemed to dote on it.

"How about you, *Herr Hauptmann?* Won't that put
undue pressure on you?"

Heidemann hid a smile. This lad would be all right.
Even when crushed he thought in terms beyond himself. It was encouraging, too, that he'd not rationalized a
defense from the tail-heaviness in that Pfalz. Number Oh-
one's sole assignment was to heckle the new ones; it rep-
resented one of his favorite little tests of a man's readi-
ness to find excuses.

"Pressure is my natural element," he said, not without a
hint of satisfaction. He'd planned to lecture Stachel on
the manhandling incident, too, but now he thought less of
it. Niederhauser, an insufferable type at best, wasn't worth
disturbing the pact just concluded. Besides, Niederhauser
would enjoy the notoriety that no doubt now attended him
in the enlisted quarters and so why belabor the thing
further at this end of the field? Moreover, and most importantly, propriety had been served by Stachel's prompt
apology. Case closed.

"How's your cold, Stachel?"

"My head aches a bit, sir."

Heidemann reached into a drawer and withdrew a small
white envelope. He pushed it across the desk. "Take some
of this powder in water. Then lie down. Someday, maybe,
we'll have medical men assigned to each *Jasta,* but in the
meantime we tend the halt, the sick, and the lame from
envelopes. By the way, don't take any alcohol while this
stuff is in you. I understand the two don't mix."

Stachel arose, smiling calmly. Eyes level, he said: "I
only drink socially, sir."

CHAPTER 5

THE FLYING officers' mess was in a large, three-story house with a pocked mansard roof that stood near the center of the village. It had once been the home of the factory manager, and various little abandonments of that long-gone household still gave their mute and melancholy testimony. In the foyer, a blue and white vase, chipped at the rim, still held a cluster of dusty artificial roses. In the drawing room, a stained scarf, patiently and precisely crocheted at a time beyond memory, still covered the scarred piano. Over the mantel, a bewhiskered and fierce-looking old man glared out of the heavily framed oils that had captured him at least a century before. Some wag had used crayon to fit him out in flying helmet and goggles. The bar was in a corner of this room, which now was murky with tobacco smoke and smelled of alcohol, cooking fat, and the inevitable sweaty wool. The noise was thunderous.

Stachel shook the rain from his cap and looked about for a familiar face. For the first time that day he felt hungry.

"Ah!" a voice boomed behind him. "The *Jasta*'s newest Pfalzmauler has arrived. Good evening, my dear Stachel. I haven't seen you all day. Where've you been?"

Kettering had placed an arm on his shoulder. The adjutant's face was flushed, and he held a drink stiffly in his other hand so as not to spill it.

"Oh, hullo, Kettering. As a matter of fact, I've been asleep. I was catching a cold, and the *Hauptmann* gave me some medicine to take. From the way things look outside, I haven't missed much, I guess."

"This rain came up in a hellish hurry, didn't it? The weather in this god-forsaken country is enough to drive a man insane. Snow, seashore sunshine, and rain—all in

41

twelve hours' time. Ah, well, as a Yankee friend of mine was fond of saying: 'Weather is like sex: it's got to be varied to be interesting. . . .' "

"You've got a friend who's a Yankee?" Stachel asked curiously.

"I've got many friends who are Yankees."

"They're enemies. Or haven't you heard?"

"Nonsense! Who's an enemy in a war like this? An individual Yankee or Tommy who, just for the hell of it, dresses up in a soldier suit to search out and shoot an individual German? Nonsense, I say. This war, just like any other, is simply a matter of women. The mistress of some king gets restless and thinks her old man is neglecting her. 'I'd like a country place in Upper Gonorrhea,' she pouts. 'But that belongs to my friend, King Zoop,' he complains. 'I can't simply walk in there and nail up a house.' 'You'd better,' says the dame, 'or no more probing of the bushes at the fork.' The king asks his pal, King Zoop, if he can buy a million-or-so acres. 'For me,' says Zoop, 'it'd be fine. But frankly, old man, my woman simply can't stand that red-headed mattress of yours, and if I gave you the place the two of them would make life miserable for the two of us. Sorry.' The king reports back, and the redhead says, 'Who does that hussy think she is, denying me a country place? Call out the army—I'll show her.' And so eight zillion men, most of them glad to get away from their own women for a spell, march out to settle the matter."

Stachel smiled. "So it would be simpler to let the women do the fighting, eh?"

"Precisely. I say all armies should be made up of women. They cause all the world's unrest; why shouldn't they do the fighting, too? As for me, I'd be perfectly satisfied to stay home and make my sweet, tender body available as spoils for the conquering army—no matter who won. How about a drink?"

Stachel waved a hand. "No thanks. Not tonight."

"What's the matter? Menstruating?"

"I simply don't feel like drinking. I don't drink much anyhow."

For a man who doesn't drink much, Kettering thought,

he was certainly giving the brandy the eye last night. Like Uncle Ludwig. Uncle Ludwig had been a great one to brag about how little he drank and lie about how much he drank. Maybe Stachel was a sneaky drinker like Uncle Ludwig. He laughed.

"What's funny?"

"I was just thinking about something. Uncle Ludwig has thirty years on you. You haven't had time enough."

"What do you mean?"

"Nothing, *Junge*. My mind wanders too much. Come—there are some Daredevils of the Clouds you haven't met yet, and I'd better introduce you while I can still see their faces. Jesus, this brandy is terrible!"

Making a face, Kettering pushed his way to the piano. He slammed the lid three times and the strings hummed. The crowd noises fell off and Kettering held Stachel at arm's length, facing the group. Stachel felt his face redden.

"Gentlemen, I am honored to present *Leutnant* Bruno Stachel, who claims personal acquaintance with a tail assembly superior to that depicted in the photo I've been circulating among you this evening. Because of this especial distinction, he has been gazetted to this *Jasta*."

There was a burst of applause, and Stachel's face grew hotter.

"And now, *Herr* Tail Authority Stachel, these are the chaps who'll help you win the summer place in Upper Gonorrhea. I assure you: there isn't one among them who has the X-factor."

The uproar resumed, and Stachel was pushed into the cluster of grinning, half-drunk young men. He was terribly ill at ease, but he tried very hard to evince warmth in his acknowledgment of the shouted introductions. Eventually someone began to play the piano and the tide surged lemminglike in the music's direction. He was relieved to find he had drifted into a backwater.

"Cigarette?"

A heavy gold case was before him, balanced casually on a long hand with square-tipped fingers. He smiled at the tall blond man.

"No thanks. I don't smoke."

"If you are anything like I am, you haven't the slightest

43

idea of which face goes with which name. This face is Karl Fabian's."

"Yes. I'm terrible at such things, too. But I remember you, all right."

Fabian's teeth were the whitest Stachel had ever seen, and his eyes, deep-set and sun-crinkled at the corners, registered calm good humor.

"Well, what do you think of our jolly group, now that you've been here for all of twenty-four hours?"

"They seem fine. I'm looking forward to knowing them better." He knew he sounded stilted, and he envied Fabian for his easy manner.

Fabian laughed. "Don't waste too much time, my friend. Our cast of characters can change very rapidly in this show."

"Well," he protested, "I meant that I—"

"I know what you meant. And forgive me for sounding melodramatic. It isn't too bad, really; we've been lucky in this *Jasta*. For every one lost, we've nailed four—something like that."

"How long have you been here?"

"With this *Jasta*? Five months, about. A lot's happened."

"I imagine so. Any tips?"

Fabian's smile became remote. "You flatter me. I've learned a good bit, of course. But I'd be presumptuous if I were to advise anybody about what to do and what not to do, really. Every man is different, every aircraft is different, every situation is different. Army writes the music, Heidemann conducts; but each of us interprets the tune in his own way. Have you ever heard American Negro musicians? It's the same sort of thing, this combat flying. Each man works along an agreed-upon theme, but in his particular, individual style."

Stachel shook his head in mock wonder. "There are certainly a lot of experts on the Americans around here. . . ."

Fabian chuckled and made a little motion with his glass. "I don't know anything about them, actually. I was an assistant to the assistant assistant military aide at our embassy in Washington for about six months several years
44

ago. I did get around once in a while to some of their back street cafés, and I became quite enamored of their Negro music. It's very exciting."

"How about Kettering?"

"Who really knows about Kettering? Not I, certainly. You'll hear he's a dealer in pornography and travels all over the world to get it, but it's all rumor, and he just laughs and says nothing. He was in the States for a good while apparently."

"Pornographer or no, he seems like a good fellow."

"There is none better, believe me. He has no serious ambitions, and therefore you can trust him. With him, there's none of this smiling at your face while stabbing your backside, I'll tell you. If Kettering says something, you know he means it; there's no nonsense, no duplicity, no meanness. He jokes and rants around a lot, but if he can't honestly be honest, he says nothing."

Stachel nodded solemnly. He had liked Fabian immediately. He liked him even more now.

"The world could use more people like that."

"Indeed it could."

"This trait—it would seem to be a liability for one dealing in smut, eh?"

Fabian shrugged. "Perhaps. As a matter of fact, I once asked Kettering about that in one of my more sodden moments. (You'll also hear, incidentally, that I drink too much. This is no rumor. It's absolutely true.) But Kettering, true to type, ignored the implication and answered the question. He said: 'Karl, my boy, if you want to determine a man's honesty, ask a dedicated crook. Honesty is a matter of morbid fascination to crooks, and they discuss it in awed, incredulous tones, much as you and I would discuss insanity or perversion. Some of my most intimate acquaintances are crooks,' he said, 'and they do not hesitate to pronounce me incurably honest.'"

Stachel laughed. The fact that he did astonished him mildly. "Remind me to see more of Kettering," he said.

"You could do worse, that's certain." There was a pause while Fabian took a reflective sip from his glass. He said then: "You asked if I have any tips. Well, I do."

"Yes?"

"You feel somewhat low and confused about now, I'll wager. At least you do if you're anything like I was after my first day at the front. My tip's this: take it easy; in a week or so you'll feel right at home."

Stachel tried unsuccessfully to keep the discouragement from his voice. "I wonder. I can't see anything up there. I can't even land as well as I did in flying school. I almost splattered my machine this morning."

"Well, remember this: every day you're alive around here makes you one day ahead. Be satisfied that the enemy you didn't see didn't see you. Be thankful you didn't splatter that crazy damned Pfalz. But there I go— melodrama again."

"No doubt about it, though. I do feel considerably inadequate right now."

"Of course. But it's the system that's at fault, my boy, not you. They send people up here with little more knowledge than how to get a machine in the air and down again. Some of us don't know a camshaft from a bonbon —like Richthofen. Some of us are so sick we shouldn't be walking, let alone flying—like that consumptive wretch Zeumer who was in *Jasta* 11. Some of us can't see, some can't shoot, some are too young, others too old. But someday it will be different. Someday there'll be extensive preparation, tough age and physical requirements, exhaustive academics—not just a spot of engine mechanics, theory of flight, and propeller spinning, but real sciences: aircraft design and related engineering subjects; weather prediction; navigation; perhaps even organized aerial strategy and tactics, coordinated with ground operations. Then, when a man reports to a *Jasta*, he'll be a right smart craftsman, full of pepper and birdseed. Under the circumstances, I think it's astounding that we do as well as we do. And I saw your landing. It wasn't all that bad."

Stachel's smile was wanly grateful. "Do you always go around making people feel better? If so, I'm going to nominate you for Chief of Staff."

"I'm not trying to make you feel better, my friend. I am venting my spleen. I make this speech every evening when I have several liters aboard. Which reminds me: you aren't drinking. What's your pleasure— *schnapps*, cognac? There's even some beer, thanks to the wily Rupp's machinations. Junky stuff, but beer nevertheless."

"No thanks. Busy day tomorrow."

Fabian nodded approval. "Stout fellow. I frequently worry about my drinking. But there isn't anything else to do in this god-forsaken place and so I don't worry too deeply, I assure you. You're smart, though; our work-day is tough enough without carrying along a hangover. I speak from bitter experience."

"Well, I'm no teetotaler or anything like that, but I am careful about how much I take and where and when I take it. Drinking can cause a lot of trouble if a man lets it get out of hand. I know I sound smug, but it's the way I feel. Incidentally, what about Rupp?"

"Rupp?"

"Yes. You mentioned him."

"Rupp is a seventy-five-carat pig."

"So?"

"Yes. A pig. Another tip: stay clear of him. He's one of those noncoms who make a career of getting even with officers for being officers."

"If that's the case, I'm surprised the *Jastaführer*—"

"Tolerates him? Nonsense. The *Jastaführer* has Rupp where he is by design. Rupp's presence in the outer office provides just enough subtle harassment to keep junior officers in a state of imbalance. Consequently they are more pliable and unguarded when they arrive in the sanctum sanctorum. Moreover, Rupp is a·first-class in-former, a useful device for any unit commander in the glorious German Army."

Stachel raised an eyebrow. "You sound bitter."

"I should. I'll tell you about it some time. But right now the subject of Rupp makes me want to vomit. I don't want to lose my carefully stowed cargo, so let's drop him, shall we?"

"Suits me."

In the interval that followed, Stachel made a silent vow to avoid Rupp like the plague. That he'd already made an enemy of the man, he knew; that he'd give the man no opportunity to do anything about it, he swore. A new wave of despondency passed over him

47

when he considered collusion between Heidemann, the stickler for propriety, and Rupp, the seventy-five-carat pig. Was there no escape from hypocrisy?

Kettering returned, beaming, with another large man in tow. "Here, my dear Stachel, is a late arrival to this ghastly party and the *Jasta*'s sole claim to ritziness: The Most Honorable Wilhelm, Count Junior-grade von Klugermann, Commander-in-Chief and Managing Director of the Federation of Imperial Whores. Call him Willi. Willi, your majesty, meet Bruno Stachel."

"That's quite a title Kettering has bestowed upon you," Stachel smiled, taking the fellow's hand.

"Indeed," Von Klugermann drawled in arch Prussian style, *"Herr* Kettering, in better days, would have been strung up by the genitals for his disrespect. But, alas, what with the nobility falling into disrepute in so many quarters of the world, I must discreetly forego arranging such a pleasure."

"Bah," Kettering laughed, "Willi doesn't fool anybody with that snob talk. For an aristocrat, he's real folks, as the Yankees say. Besides, I owe him money."

"Everybody in Germany owes him money," Fabian confided in an exaggerated stage whisper. "He's sickeningly rich. Or his family is."

"Same thing, old bear," Von Klugermann said, feigning a sneer. He turned to Stachel and bowed theatrically. "You'll learn, though, my dear Stachel, that despite my enormous wealth and influence I am really a very adorable fellow. I just naturally generate great admiration and devotion among all who have the good fortune to know me."

"I can see that, all right," Stachel said lightly.

There was a stir at the entrance and someone called attention in a tone that meant business. The piano died and there was a rattling click of heels, and the precise but warm voice of Heidemann urged the group to carry on, please. The *Hauptmann* was in a carefully creased uniform and his boots glowed richly. The delicate cross of the Blue Max at his throat gleamed like expensive jewelry.

"Well, Stachel," he said affably, "I see you're already in the clutches of a fearsome trio."

"Yes, sir. They're ferocious."

The *Jastaführer* smiled at the others. "Would you excuse us, please? I'd like a word with Stachel."

The three bowed, Fabian weaving somewhat. They wandered off toward the reactivated piano.

"Well, Stachel, have you met everybody?"

"Yes, sir. It's quite agreeable, this evening gathering."

"Indeed. A comradely group."

"Yes, sir."

Heidemann regarded him pleasantly for a moment. "How do you feel? Did those powders help?"

"Very much. I got a good rest, too, and I'm as fit as ever."

"Fine. I was worried about you this morning. You looked quite bad. Your eyes—"

Stachel tensed. "They always look that way when I have a cold," he parried.

"So you said."

The tenseness became the old anxiety. Heidemann's pause was strangely long and thoughtful. Stachel wondered whether he could be weighing the subject or actually listening to the singing, as he appeared to be. He struggled to find a new tack for the conversation, but Heidemann selected his own.

"Tell me, Stachel, are you frightened?"

Stachel, confused, asked: "Sir?"

"Are you afraid of what's to come?"

He contemplated the question. The *Jasta* commander was certainly full of little surprises.

Was he afraid of the war? For much of his life he had been playing at war. He remembered those long and sunny times when he and Alois Steiner, game-legged son of the assistant manager at his father's Bad Schwalbe hotel, had marshaled and disposed their small armies of lead soldiers in the bare spot in Alois' rear garden. They would plan and implement great campaigns, and each would take a turn at losing. When the battles had been locked and the heaps of tiny casualties formed, there was

49

always the comfortable awareness that the dragoons or infantrymen, lying there now in sprawling defeat, would soon arise, whole and fit, to win and survive the next engagement. No horror had figured in their pretending, and it had been a good time. Then, when the real war had come and he had been barely beyond the Alois Steiner era, the mass maneuverings and offensives and counteroffensives of the first days—as chronicled in the oddly emotional pedantry of the popular press—had been as idealistic and unreal to him as the battles of the garden plot. Even at Frankfurt he had envisioned his cadet role as simply a sophisticated extension of the game. And then, since that day at Wiesbaden, when the airplanes had sung in the high blue, his single-minded and restless ambition to enter the world aloft had pre-empted everything. Fly he would; excel he must. The war itself was simply a means to that end.

No, he had not as yet felt any physical fear of the war. Such a fear—tangible, understandable, vital—he would welcome any time, anywhere, as a replacement for the fear he couldn't name or fight. From out of the schooldays he heard the old lines: *Death itself is nothing; but we fear to be we know not where, we know not what.*

"No. I don't think so. We all have to take our chances. Why do you ask, sir?"

Heidemann ignored the question to ask another. "Are you really as placid as you make out to be?"

"I'm not certain I understand. . . ."

"I'll put it this way: you remind me very much of a friend of mine in another *Jasta*. In combat, he's a rascal —hard-driving, always in the midst. On the ground he's —well—placid. He and I were classmates at Lichterfelde in 1913 and were gazetted to the regiment at Mülhausen. I learned that behind this façade he's a victim of a special sort of unrest. He's possessed, driven by ambition. He's overly sensitive to criticism. He's torn by two opposing forces—on the one hand, extreme egotism; on the other, inordinate shyness. He is, you'll gather, an unhappy man. He works very hard to disguise that fact."

"And I remind you of him?"

"Uncannily."

Stachel's face was hot. He struggled to mask his annoyance. "They say every man has a twin somewhere in the world. At any rate, your friend seems to be a good airman, even if he is—unhappy—as you say."

Heidemann considered him with steady friendliness. "It's my duty to see that the effectiveness of my men remains at the highest possible level. I get the impression that under that calm exterior of yours you are really an unhappy fellow. This could affect your performance. I don't want it to."

"I'm a German officer, sir. I'll do my duty."

"Good."

Stachel thought: *pompous, self-satisfied son of a bitch. Rupp's been talking to him.*

He wanted a drink badly but he was determined not to have it.

CHAPTER **6**

THE ALBATROS and the Pfalz droned along, their landing wheels skimming through the wispy crowns of cotton-batting clouds. The sun cast their shadows in rainbow-encircled crosses that lifted against the dazzling towers and fell away into the blue chasms between. Stachel glanced across and down at Fabian, whose helmeted head and erect shoulders seemed almost close enough to touch. Fabian was intent on the sky around and above, and his goggles would flicker mirrorlike in the bright morning whenever he turned his gaze upward. His machine, mottled green with white nose and poster-size Iron Crosses, rose and fell easily in the air currents like a large and baleful carrion bird.

It was the first flight of the day on Stachel's seventh day with the *Jasta*. He was taut, a fact he attributed to the hard pace he had set for himself. Throughout the week he had spent virtually every daylight hour in the air or at the hangars, and in the evenings, rather than drifting to the bar like the others, he'd read—heavy-eyed—charts, manuals, aircraft performance data, and anything else that conceivably could prove useful. One of the first things he'd seen to was the rerigging of the Pfalz. He had gone to Ziegel and asked for a manufacturer's specification sheet on the D-3 model and a goneometer and incidence stick. Ziegel had watched over his shoulder in silent amusement as he'd taken a reading that revealed six minutes of negative relationship between the horizontal stabilizer and elevator panel when in presumably neutral attitude. Then, mumbling something as to how too much reading was good for no man, especially amateur engineers, Ziegel had corrected the faulty angle himself. On the next flight, the Pfalz had been free of tail-heaviness, and Stachel had enjoyed his small triumph. He'd flown mostly with Heidemann, as agreed, but also on extras whenever Fabian or one of the other old hands found time to chaperon him. At least twice a day he had connived air-to-ground gunnery runs, and three times he'd ordered the armament section to block up the Pfalz on the machine-gun range—once to bore-sight its guns and twice to adjust their synchronization gear disengagement clutch, which had shown signs of balkiness. With deep night, he would fall on his cot in bone-sore, self-righteous wariness. Once he'd overheard Rupp complaining to Heidemann that that crazy Stachel was burning up a whole month's reserve of fuel and ammunition all by himself, and he'd been smugly gratified to hear the *Jastaführer*'s reply: "You're exaggerating, of course, Rupp—but he is hitting things a bit hard, isn't he?" Two days ago, when Huemmel had come down with pneumonia and had been posted to the field hospital at Courtrai, Heidemann had offered Stachel the use of Huemmel's Albatros. In a dialogue that could have been excerpted from a text on military courtesy, Stachel had countered with a formal request that Pfalz Oh-one-slash-seventeen be assigned to him on a permanent basis. Heidemann had shrugged approval and smiled his distant smile.

Today they would be going right up to the line. Heidemann had made it clear the night before that although the *Jasta* remained on the required two regular patrols a day, any volunteer sorties would have to be fully operational; therefore flights would be ruled out unless they were in an area where they could contribute to the general defense screen established by Army for the *Jasta* as a whole.

So Stachel's rehearsal time had ended.

The *Jasta* had flown in strength this morning, but Stachel had been left behind because Ziegel's crew had found a faulty rudder hinge on the Pfalz. The repairs had been completed by the time the first patrol had returned, and when Fabian had requested permission to fly an extra, Stachel had quickly entered his own name on the sortie roster. Heidemann was of the school that forbade solo flights over the lines, so the pilots had set up a "comrade system," in which the daylight hours between *Jasta* operations were informally blocked out to permit overlapping sorties in numbers of two or more. Since Huemmel had been paired with Fabian, Stachel's request to fly with Fabian had been granted automatically.

They had climbed to three thousand meters in wide circles and then had flown west-by-northwest toward Arras. The plan was to patrol the twenty kilometers from the Scarpe to the bulge in the line before the Awoignt sector. The heavy cumulus would complicate their aim to intercept enemy observation aircraft because these would be operating downstairs where the clouds, although not interfering with their view, would offer a handy overhead hiding place if needed. Since Army had assigned the day's low-level patrols to *Jastas* 2 and 26 and high-levels to Heidemann's organization, Fabian and Stachel knew they'd be hardput to find easy pickings among the *Emils*, as the *Jasta* members liked to call enemy observers.

Stachel still stung from Heidemann's supercilious inventory of his character traits. Even now, when he thought back to that evening, the resentment flared into stomach-tightening anger. Who, he had asked himself over and over in the past week, did that condescending, self-important bastard think he was? Where, he asked himself now, did Heidemann get the right to busy himself with Bruno Stachel's "unhappy" inner soul? A *Jastaführer* was supposed to lead a military unit, not to evaluate the spiritual pluses and minuses of a congregation. . . .

Once he'd even spoken to Fabian about it. Fabian had offered him a drink and he had, of course, refused it. (That was one thing, he thought with satisfaction: he hadn't had a drop the whole week.) But he'd been quite taken with Fabian from the first, and, sensing that this regard was mutual, he'd sat for an hour this night, talking airplanes and trading little philosophies.

"Stachel, my lad," Fabian had said, slowly and thickly, "you'll have to indulge the whim of our esteemed leader. He fancies himself an excellent judge of character. The fact is that he is so infernally preoccupied with detail he is a very poor judge of character. He looks at a man and sees all the trees of attitude, never once catching a glimpse of the forest of total personality. And he's in love. Oh my, how he's in love. And men in love say and do appalling things, they tell me. I don't know; I've never been in love. Have you? How do I know Heidemann's in love? I read a letter, that's how. I was sitting in his office one day, waiting for him. He'd been writing to his wife. It was practically dangling before me as I sat in that chair in front of his desk. I craned a bit, and that, incidentally, is when Rupp came in. He saw me, I know. I also know he will mention it to our glorious chief at some auspicious time. So I'm still waiting for the other shoe to fall. *Herr* Heidemann is analyzing my soul, too; *Herr* Heidemann is analyzing everybody's soul. Piss on Heidemann. I'm going to bed."

And so he'd gone to bed. And Stachel had filed away another piece of *Jasta* intelligence.

He glanced again at Fabian, sitting now a few meters beyond a touch but a whole universe beyond a word, and wondered about him.

They had just begun their southward turn when out of the fluffy floor below and to the left three brown shapes, dark and malevolent, hurtled into the sunlight. They came at an astonishing speed on that peculiar side-sliding rush of aircraft working a diagonal course. The large bull's-eyes on their upper wings showed with startling clarity, and Stachel could see the flashing of their big four-bladed propellers. There was no maneuvering, no wheeling for position—simply a near collision of forces, with the shock of surprise momentarily freezing both sides.

Stachel snapped upright in his seat, fighting a rush of panic. As reflex, he twisted the auxiliary throttle grip on the control column yoke and the Mercedes bellowed. He booted full left rudder and hiked his right wings to the vertical and was conscious of the leaden feeling that came with the enormous centrifugal effect of the flipper turn. A spatter of dirt and gravel whipped up from the floor and stung his face, and he cursed the wind's crazy vacuum action. The Pfalz went into a bad skid and he fought to correct, at the same time throwing in his gun clutch and clawing at the security belt, which was cruelly cramping his right thigh. He became aware of the muted but insistent thumping of machine guns that worked an angry counterpoint to the monstrous engine-racketing and wire-shrieking engulfing him. Continuing his wild, wide swing, he threw a glance out over the top wing and saw Fabian's Albatros roll out at the top of a loop and hammer away at a turning SE-5. Another Britisher was below, far down and climbing. The third was in a long flat glide to the west, its propeller windmilling without power.

Now curiously calm and detached, Stachel weighed the situation. Fabian had winged one and was doing all right with the other, and the third, lower SE-5 would be out of things for long seconds while scrambling for a return to altitude. The disabled Englishman, apparently assuming he was in the clear and trying to stretch his westward glide, floated toward the clouds. Stachel put the Pfalz into a wingover, followed by an open-throttled, humming dive.

The crippled machine's propeller was barely turning now, and its broad wings expanded in Stachel's sights. He could see the Englishman's head, turning and twisting, bobbing from side to side as he searched for an

55

opening in the cloud floor ahead. Stachel's thumb caressed the triggers, and the machine guns crashed and sent a trembling through the cockpit. The powder sting was in his nostrils, and out ahead the tracers made deceptively slow, arcing streaks.

The English machine collapsed. From a gracefully soaring thing it reduced instantly to an ugly tangle that fell in an anguished, slanting tumble into the shifting mists below. A piece of it lingered behind, turning and spinning and casting flashes of sun as it drifted.

As he came around, Stachel saw that he had been wrong about that lower SE-5. It had already joined the other in a sweep on the green Albatros. Fabian was in a split-S, belly to the sky, but the Tommies were close behind, their guns flickering pale yellow. Stachel could see that Fabian was in deep trouble; if the enemy fire didn't get him the split-S would, because even Stachel knew that an Albatros wouldn't take such a maneuver under full power. Maybe Fabian had already been hit; he was certainly familiar enough with the Albatros to avoid a fool thing like that. But Stachel saw immediately that it made no difference.

A stream of whitish vapor spun out in the wake of Fabian's machine. Its edges rapidly became stained with brown, and there was a flag of flame flapping along the fuselage. Stachel blinked, and when his eyes had refocused, the Albatros was in an inverted flat spin, hell-fire boiling in its center-section. A small, fork-shaped booted thing detached itself from the mass, trailed by its fitful, private burning; it tumbled beside the wreck for a moment, then arced away for its long and solitary return to earth.

Stachel dived for the safety of the clouds, a strange exhilaration surging in him. As the blue mists closed around, he became aware of the most incongruous, insane paradox of his life. He was sexually aroused. The incredible discovery set him to wild, soundless laughter. He had participated in high tragedy and he was sexually aroused. He wondered in his near hysteria what Heidemann the Alienist would make of that.

Kettering listened intently, the phone tight against his ear, his eyes staring vacantly at Stachel.

"Yes," he was saying, "that's right. An SE-5. It fell at about eleven hundred hours some three to four kilometers south of the Scarpe. What? No. No." His eyes became direct. "Did it burn, Stachel?"

Stachel shook his head. "Not while I was looking."

"No, it didn't burn, as far as we know. Just fell apart. Yes, that's right. About three kilometers." He listened for a long time, nodding his head. "Very well. The flamer must have been ours. All right. Well, thanks anyway." He rang off, then sank back in his chair.

"I'm afraid you're out of luck on this one, Stachel. The *Flugmeldedienst* has no information on an SE-5. The observers at the balloon station at K-15 have reported a machine falling in flames about five hundred meters beyond our trenches but they weren't able to determine whose it was. Burning too heavily. They said they could hear the action, but it all took place above the clouds. The flamer just dropped out of the ceiling, and they couldn't tell much for all the smoke and so on. But the FMD hasn't a scratch on any SE-5. . . ."

"Seems strange," Stachel said irritably. "My SE-5 must have fallen right onto their frigging balloon. How could they have missed it?"

Kettering's face was blank. "The sky's a funny place, Stachel."

"Yes, but this Englishman fell like a burst paper sack. He must have come down in a very elaborate sprinkle. Christ, how could they miss it?"

"There'll be others."

"I want this one. I want credit for my victory, do you understand? I risked my ass to get him, and he's mine."

"Look, the *Flugmeldedienst* has to nail down a victory before you can confirm it for yourself. You can claim your SE-5, but unless we get more information it'll have to remain as an unconfirmed on the *Jasta* listing, that's all there is to it. If Fabian had come back he could have verified your claim. But he isn't coming back."

"Somebody must have seen that plane crash."

C

"Sure. Maybe seven hundred thousand people saw it crash. But how in the name of pluperfect hell are they going to know who got it? If the FMD lists it, you do, too; it doesn't, you don't."

"I don't like it at all."

Kettering arose, his face red, his eyes watering. "Then sue me, you son of a bitch!"

Ziegel's head was deep in the dusk of the empty engine compartment of an Albatros when Kettering tapped him on the behind. He turned around, straightened his oil-stained *Krätzchen*, and sat down on the top of the step-ladder.

"Well, what's on your mind, Fatso? I'm fresh out of dirty pictures."

"I simply want to talk, that's all." Kettering's face was good-natured even in its solemnity.

"Oh, fine. That's capital, really it is. Wait a moment while I put all these dirty old airplanes back in the pantry and I'll make hot tea and we'll have a nice long chat, just the two of us. Christ, man, I'm busy; can't you see that?"

"I know you are. But——"

Ziegel was immediately sorry for his sarcasm. Kettering, he saw, was just beginning to feel Fabian's loss. The two had been great friends.

"All right. So you want to talk. I'm a brilliant conversationalist, as a matter of fact."

Kettering was silent for a long moment. His eyes, remarkably blue in the hangar shadow, traced the progress of a brace of aircraft that skittered across the field and churned away to the southwest. Finally he spoke.

"This war is a filthy thing."

"I'll make a note of that."

"It really is, you know."

"I get the point."

"I mean, you run into so many nutty types."

"You have to take some bad with the good. Everybody can't be as gracious, courageous, and true as I am."

"Ambitious people make me want to vomit."

"There are a lot of them."

58

"Fabian will be missed around here."

"He was a fine fellow."

"Why couldn't it have been that ambitious son of a bitch if it had to be somebody?"

"Stachel?"

"Stachel."

"The breaks, Fatso. Never argue with Kismet. It was the breaks."

"People are pigs, mostly."

"Right you are."

Kettering fell silent again. Ziegel sat there, looking at nothing in particular. It occurred to him that he had never before heard Kettering call anybody a son of a bitch and sound as if he meant it.

The Pfalz had scarcely cooled from the pre-noon sortie when Stachel was aloft again—this time with Von Klugermann, the pouting Prussian. He had stalked out of Kettering's office and signed his name to the extra list. Then he'd gone to the latrine and afterward stopped in his room, where he'd taken four deep pulls at a brandy flask. Von Klugermann, who had just come from lunch, stopped by and said he was all set so what were they waiting for?

The cumulus had rolled on, leaving a low broken cloud pattern over most of the front, while a sheet of cirro-stratus had formed overhead to diffuse the cold sun glare and give an eerie light to the sky. They were flying at three thousand meters, due west to the lines, when Stachel—still nursing his indignation over his loss of the SE-5—saw the RE-8 observation plane cruising in wide circles over the road junction at Nauroy. He glanced over at Von Klugermann, huddling in the cockpit of his mud-colored Albatros, and realized the Prussian had not seen the Englishman. He eased open the throttle and brought the Pfalz wing-to-wing with the other machine. Von Klugermann saw the motion and gazed quizzically across the gap. Stachel jabbed his thumb downward, then tapped it against his helmet. Von Klugermann watched the RE-8 below for a long time, it seemed; then, after peering all around the sky, he gave an exaggerated nod.

The Pfalz lifted over in a long descending curve, and as the horizon tilted away, Stachel rode back on the throttle. The engine's drone hushed, and the humming of the guy wires increased in pitch. As the earth came up, magnifying deliberately over the engine, he engaged his gun gear with an angry motion, took another quick look at Von Klugermann's Albatros protectively circling above, then concentrated on the Englishman. The big khaki machine continued its unconcerned turning course, and Stachel decided its crew hadn't seen him yet. He dropped below and behind, slowing his speed to a point slightly exceeding that of the British craft, so that the RE-8's broad tail screened him from its two occupants. At fifty meters he opened fire, and the racing needles of his tracers disappeared into the silhouetted mass ahead. He swore, realizing suddenly that his speed was too great, and he dropped away in a shallow dive. The RE-8 was an enormous shadow above him for a fleeting moment, then was gone.

Correcting, Stachel brought the Pfalz up and around. The English machine was descending in a flat, uncertain power glide. In the front cockpit, the pilot was hunched over, and Stachel could see that he was frantically operating a wobble-pump. Behind him, a gloved hand clutched the spade grip of the rear cockpit's Lewis gun, whose muzzle was pointed crazily at the sky. The hand was all he could see of the *Emil,* who presumably had collapsed on the floor.

Stachel prepared to deliver the *coup de grâce,* but as he dropped behind the wallowing Englishman, his thumb hesitated on the trigger. A tight smile formed on his wind-numb lips. He peered at the ground, and, fortunately, was able to orient himself at once.

He rode the throttle briefly and brought the Pfalz alongside the RE-8. The pilot, his face pale below the lozenge-shaped goggles, regarded him as if hypnotized. Stachel pointed at him commandingly, then jabbed his finger to the east. He repeated the gesture, but this time, after indicating the direction he wanted the Englishman to fly, he emphasized his meaning by patting the butts of his machine guns.

60

The Tommy nodded mechanically, then turned his head stiffly to the front. The big biplane, with the awkward funnel-type scoop on its nose and its queer, bent-in-the-middle profile, lifted slightly under increased power and turned slowly toward the darkening afternoon. Stachel took up a position behind and slightly above.

They flew that way for long minutes, and once, when the RE-8 drifted somewhat off course, Stachel fired a brief burst to one side. The Tommy corrected and maintained the proper direction, although he seemed to have trouble holding his altitude. The airdrome appeared off the port quarter, a large flat scar on the drab countryside. The RE-8 pilot glanced back, pointed to the field, then to himself, questioningly. Stachel nodded and pointed. The British machine began to sink, not bothering to circle the field first.

From behind, Stachel saw the *Emil*'s other hand appear on the circular gun mounting enclosing the rear cockpit. It was followed by the arm, then the head and shoulders. The man wavered and pressed his gloves against his face. He slumped again; stiffened again.

Stachel judged that the RE-8's momentum would cause it to fall well within the field's boundaries. He eased the control column forward and thumbed the trips. As his guns hammered, the English observer spun around twice, and a piece of cowling tore away in the wind. He fired another burst. One of his tracers seemed to fly directly into the RE-8 pilot's open mouth.

The ponderous machine turned on its side, slanting, its rudder flapping. Idling his engine, Stachel thought he could hear the moan of the now-derelict craft's wires as it fell away. He watched without expression as the RE-8 mushed through the line of poplars, whipping wildly as a wing tore away. It continued on, slewing sideways into the ground, skidding across the rutted turf, rolling into a shambles that shuddered into a steaming heap directly before the entrance to Heidemann's railroad shed.

Stachel noted that the erotic phenomenon had repeated itself.

Stachel shouldered his way through the crowd. The

excited babble fell off to a murmur as he strode up to the wreck. His service knife glinted as, with four sweeping motions, he cut away the RE-8's serial number. Rolling up the piece of fabric and returning the knife to a pocket of his flying coat, he turned to regard the crowd. Kettering was there. Wordlessly, Stachel went to him. He shoved the roll of khaki linen against Kettering's chest, then stalked away to get something to drink.

The bottle was half empty when Von Klugermann came into the room.

"Hullo, Your Serene Highness. Have a drink."

"No thanks."

"It's right fine stuff. Hennessey. Put hair on your plumbing."

"I don't want a drink, thank you."

"Well, what in hell do you want?"

Von Klugermann lit a cigarette, then leaned against the wall, his little eyes regarding Stachel thoughtfully.

"You're a real cobra, aren't you, Stachel?"

"What do you mean?"

"I mean you're a real, sly cobra."

"I'm not reading your semaphore."

"That RE-8. Special delivery on the front doorstep."

Stachel laughed, reaching for his glass. "Pretty neat, eh?"

"Very neat. But why did you shoot him?"

Stachel paused, the glass still at his lips. He shrugged, then downed the drink. "The *Emil* came around and was getting ready to argue again. There's a war on, they say."

Von Klugermann dragged deeply on the cigarette and blew a stream of smoke toward the ceiling. "I was up there, you know."

Stachel poured again, the gurgling sound loud in the room. "You were a considerable distance away."

"I was directly above and behind you. You would have seen that if you had bothered to look around."

"So?"

"That *Emil* was in no mood to fight. I don't think he could even see."

"C'est la guerre."

"That RE-8 crew could have proved to be quite informative for Intelligence."

"Too bad."

"Yes. You're a real cobra."

"That's me."

"You fascinate me."

"Naturally."

Draining the glass, Stachel vowed that never again would he forget to look behind.

CHAPTER 7

HEIDEMANN STOOD by the piano. The scarf had been pushed aside to accommodate a sheaf of charts and a small stack of notebooks. Seated in a semicircle around the room, the *Jasta* pilots concluded their shuffling and coughing and settled into polite silence.

"Gentlemen," Heidemann said in his pedantic way, "I've called this assembly this evening to brief you on impending developments. As I go along, you'll no doubt have questions. Please hold them until I've completed my few remarks. That way we should have this over in jig-time. Rupp, if you please . . ."

The *Unteroffizier* came around the piano, took a rolled chart from the *Jasta* commander, then tacked it to the bulletin board on the wall. He shifted his cigar and made a face when the map slipped free at the bottom and began to furl. There was a soft snickering among the pilots. Heidemann tapped his walking stick against the piano, and there was an awkward pause while Rupp struggled to subdue the sheet.

"I'll wager you're better with corsets, eh, Rupp?"

Heidemann rapped the renewed tittering to silence, his eyes narrowing. "That will do, Stachel."

Rupp sat down finally, throwing an angry look at Stachel, who sat, one leg over an arm of his chair, regarding the ceiling.

After sweeping the room with a searching look (which, Stachel felt, was ridiculously dramatic) Heidemann began.

"The day after tomorrow—March twenty-first—our artillery will open a bombardment at oh-forty-five hours. It will signal the greatest offensive in the history of warfare. Four hours after the barrage has begun, fifty-six divisions will advance on the territory held by the British Fifth and Third Armies—here and here." His stick traced swishing arcs across the chart, and there was a burst of comment and a few claps of hands. Again he held up his stick, and a smile pulled at his mouth.

"I'll not go further into the disposition of the ground units, but pertinent extracts of the general field orders will be available in *Oberleutnant* Kettering's office. Right now, I want simply to discuss the part our aerial forces will play in this most significant operation. The ultimate objective of the push is, of course, to reach Paris before the Yankees can reinforce the French and English in sufficient numbers to influence German operational effectiveness. Intelligence informs me that several American ground units took up positions at Toul—down—here" —he pointed—"on or about February first. So, as you see, time is pressing. In our favor, of course, is the fact that the Russians have surrendered, releasing many thousands of our people for duty here on the Western Front. We must make this advantage pay dividends."

Stachel stifled a yawn, relishing the warmth of the cognac he'd had. The Americans, he reflected, had arrived in the war even before he had. He went back to studying the elegant cross of the Blue Max at Heidemann's throat. Now there was something worth having, all right. . . .

"The German Second Army front has been divided into two general sectors for aerial operations. The northern sector will be covered by a regrouping of *Jagdgeschwader* 1, augmented by *Jastas* 5 and 46, under the command of *Rittmeister* von Richthofen. In the south, *Oberleutnant* Kohze will be responsible for the operation of two *Jagdgruppe*, designated Numbers 9 and 10, which are comprised of *Jastas* 3, 37, 54, 56, 16, 34, and our own. Advance airfields for the use of these units are in preparation. As the offensive progresses, our *Jastas* will move forward to occupy them."

Stachel thought: Kohze, eh? How come Heidemann hadn't been given the *Jagdgruppe* command? Perhaps he wasn't the big executive he liked to pretend he was. He recalled Kettering's little speech on the X-factor.

"This *Jasta*," Heidemann droned, "will fly low-level cover for the troops in the southern sector. There will be three daily sorties in *Jasta* strength during the hours between oh-eight-hundred and dusk. Specific times will depend on the weather and Army's requirements. Meanwhile, I expect every man to fly as many volunteer sorties as he feels capable of. Knowing your capabilities, gentlemen, I'm sure the sorties will be many."

Several of the group leaped to their feet, applauding. The others joined in. Stachel swung down his leg, arose, pulled his tunic straight, and clapped several times, embarrassed by this cadet-school demonstration. For German officers, everybody was certainly acting like kids. Heidemann's eyes met his as he signaled for order.

"There must be some questions, gentlemen. You seem to be in eloquent form tonight, Stachel. How about you?"

Stachel sustained the gaze, eyes level. "Yes, sir. How about new equipment? Any chance of our replacing these apple barges we fly?"

Heidemann slid the stick under his arm and leaned on the piano. "You've probably heard reports of the new Fokker being built under contracts awarded after the trials at Johannisthal last January. The reports are correct. The new machine—designated the D-7 type—is said to have remarkable characteristics. It was selected by a panel of leading combat airmen, and therefore we can expect that it will be an outstanding aircraft indeed."

Stachel coughed gently against his fist. "When will it be delivered, sir?"

"As soon as possible. I have not been given a date."

"How will they be apportioned? To the *Jastas*, I mean."

65

Heidemann felt he knew very well what Stachel meant: when would *Herr* Stachel receive a Fokker D-7? Stachel was a very strange young man, no two ways about it. The past month had brought noticeable change in him. A month ago, Stachel had been a likable, somewhat faltering, and overly serious fellow, struggling to resolve the issues of shyness over ego, outer calm over inner turbulence; today he was still serious, to be sure, but elements of arrogance and mockery had entered the picture somehow, and the likableness was rather more difficult to discern. At the outset, Heidemann had sensed ambition in this youth; today the ambition was obvious to anyone—from the lowliest rigger helper to the commanding general of the Second Army and only God knew who else. It had been extraordinary, really, how the RE-8 incident had electrified and amused so many. Heidemann, in his three full years of combat flying, had witnessed many spectacular feats (had even participated in some, he admitted mildly to himself). Few of them had won so much as a note of commendation from *Kofl*. How was it, then, that by shepherding an old English observation tub to his own airfield and polishing it off when it showed signs of resistance, Stachel's name had traveled so far so fast? Any run-of-the-mill line pilot could have duplicated the job with his eyes shut. Perhaps it was the colorful arrogance (there was that word again!) with which he had torn away a trophy to vouch for his win that had done it. Or, perhaps, the idiotic fortune that had dropped the Tommy on the *Jasta* doorstep, so to speak, as if it had been a postal delivery. Whatever the reason, the *Jasta* was being talked about favorably in several important areas, and this, Heidemann knew, was not to be scoffed at, justified or no. So whether he liked it or not, whether good or bad, he'd begun to feel a vague obligation where Stachel was concerned. And, in some indefinable way, he knew Stachel would figure importantly in the future of *Hauptmann* Otto Heidemann, and he was uncertain as to the desirability of this. He liked Stachel, but still. . . .

He was aware suddenly that his mind had wandered, and he answered the question more quickly than became the man in charge of things. It vexed him, but he kept his voice calm.

"They'll be assigned according to the greater need." He saw the puzzled looks and elaborated. "The D-7's should arrive at the front in sufficient numbers to enable their distribution to all *Jastas* in considerable strength. I understand the *Albatros Werke* are under contract to build them, since the D-7 is to become the standard fighting machine for the Western Front. Of course, as is customary in this *Jasta,* the new models, as they arrive, will be assigned to the more experienced pilots first, with subsequent deliveries assigned in the same manner."

Stachel flushed slightly. "By experienced pilots, sir, just what do you mean? Length of service? General performance?"

Heidemann felt a new flash of irritation. The question had been presumptuous. Nevertheless he succeeded in retaining his impassive expression. "I will be the judge of that, Stachel. Any other questions, gentlemen?"

As several voices broke in, Stachel sat down, his anger rising over the haughty dismissal. Von Klugermann leaned over the back of his chair, his little mouth smiling wryly.

"Well, my cobra, know any more than you did?" he stage-whispered.

"Go to hell."

"Tut-tut. Tony Fokker can only do so much at a time, you know."

"I'll get one of those D-7's."

"Perhaps. We'll see. Actually, though, I believe you've annoyed our esteemed *Jastaführer.* And when he's annoyed, he can be obtuse and vindictive."

"So can I. So watch out."

"The secret is to be nice to our beloved leader. He dotes on those who fawn."

"I'll get one of those D-7's."

"We'll see."

"I'll get one somehow."

Heidemann signed his name under the final endearment,

then fondly scrawled Elfi's address on an envelope. God, how he missed her! He would simply have to do something about a leave, or something. They'd been married nearly five years now, and in all that time they had spent no more than several months together, all told. In the past year her letters had fallen off considerably, and when they had come, they were oddly disconnected, out of sequence and syntax, not at all reflective of her orderly mind. They would range from almost aloof formality to fervent passion, from idle chitchat to melancholy philosophizing. It wasn't good for a couple to remain apart for so long a time. Just another reason, he mused, to question the wisdom of his choice of soldiering as a career. True, the war would have caused the separation regardless, but after the war, if he'd be lucky enough to survive, there no doubt would be many another separation. The thought depressed him.

Rupp knocked.

"Yes?"

"*Leutnant* von Klugermann to see you, sir."

"Have him come in."

The petulant blueblood was pressed and polished to the teeth. Von Klugermann, Heidemann guessed, would manage the *Wilhelmstrasse* gloss even in a coal mine.

"Hullo, Willi. Something up?" He gave a friendly wave in answer to the precise salute.

"There's something I'd like to ask you about, sir."

"Ask away."

"Well, I realize that every man will have to give his utmost to help our push succeed, and I will certainly try to do my part. But I've just received some news. My uncle, the *Graf* von Klugermann, will visit Army for several days next month, and I was wondering if you could spare me for a day. I'd like very much to see him."

Heidemann began to scrape the bowl of his pipe. "The *Graf* von Klugermann. He's the eminent physician, isn't he?"

"Yes, sir. As I understand it, he's on tour of various Army units to consult on field medical problems. We've been quite close, and since he'll be relatively nearby, I'd like to take advantage of it." He paused politely.

"Do you have any leave coming to you?"

"Yes, sir."

"Well, by all means then, plan your visit. Unless something very drastic occurs, I don't see why you shouldn't." How wonderful it would be, he thought in a momentary flash of irrationality, if officers could take their wives to the front with them. Wasn't there some place in history where such had been the practice? "And never mind the leave—keep it intact. We'll just say that the time you take is my present to you and the *Graf*."

"That's very kind of you, sir." Even when he smiled, Heidemann noted, Von Klugermann appeared to sulk.

"Anything else?"

"No, sir. Good night."

Heidemann motioned with his hand. "Before you go, let me ask you something."

"Of course, sir."

"What really happened up there with Stachel and the RE-8?"

Von Klugermann's smile faded and his eyes grew cautious. His answer was quick, as if he had rehearsed it.

"Well, sir, nothing more than what I put in my combat report form. *Leutnant* Stachel disabled the machine and forced it to fly back to the field. When its observer appeared to be returning to the fight, Stachel shot it down."

Heidemann tamped a fresh load into the pipe bowl. His gaze was averted and thoughtful. "Appeared to be? Perhaps. Did you know that the observer had been blinded? That his eyes had been shot away?"

Von Klugermann shifted uneasily. "Not up there, sir. As you know, it's difficult to see detail at a time like that."

"Of course. But there are times—" He paused. Rupp's voice, bawling for a better telephone connection, came through the wall. Down the line, an engine barked, coughed, surged into a steady drone, then dropped to idle.

"How is Stachel getting along? I mean, how do you and the others feel about him now that he's been here a month or so?"

69

"He's quite a fellow, sir."

Which could mean just about anything, Heidemann meditated. He should have known better than to ask. If only Rupp were more communicative . . . No. He'd not lower himself to collect gossip from an *Unteroffizier*. Information, perhaps. Gossip, no.

"Yes, he seems to be. Well, good night, Willi."

"Good night, sir."

When he'd left, Heidemann went to the window. It had begun to rain again, and the drops made liquid pinging sounds against the tin roof. Dampness had put a chill in the room, a clinging coldness that made his cheerlessness even more acute.

"I've got to see her," he told the night outside. "There *must* be a way."

CHAPTER 8

OUT TO the west the artillery still grumbled, and Stachel imagined briefly the great swarms of men cowering in the mud and struggling in their various ways to cling to life for another hour so they could cower some more. It had been three days now, and for all that time a heavy ground mist had made low-level operations out of the question. The gigantic offensive had gone on nonetheless, and *Jasta* personnel, at the outset excited by the prospect of climactic events, had by nightfall of the second day subsided into a moody taciturnity. They had sat around the bar mostly, playing *skat* or reading old newspapers and listening to the far-off thunder while pretending not to. Heidemann had attempted to keep them keyed up with little lectures and reviews of the progress being made out there, but even he had seemed let down by the "operations suspended" orders that kept coming down from *Kofl*, and he had eventually withdrawn to his office to tinker with those mysterious occupations that commanders always find behind closed doors.

This morning Stachel had awakened before dawn after a fitful, sweaty half-sleep. His head ached dully, and there was a foul tackiness in his mouth. He hadn't meant to drink again, but he'd been as nervous as a cat as the long evening had worn on and so he'd come to his room and begun to work on the cognac. He noted now that beads of moisture still clung to the dark panes and he welcomed the prospect of another wet morning in which to doze away the aftereffects of his solitary bacchanal.

He poured some water into the tin on the crate in the corner and held his face in it until his breath strained. After moving the wan candle closer to the field mirror, he soaked his face again, then worked a full five minutes to shave as well as the hard water, dull blade, and poor light would permit. He did not look directly into his own eyes at any time. He knew they'd be red and puffy but he avoided the confirmation the mirror would give.

When he went to the table in the center of the room he saw the paper, and he remembered the writing he'd done. Somewhere in the night he'd been moved to write, and he had sat silently and let the pencil stub trace the thoughts as they'd come. The stool was overturned now, and he righted it, holding the paper to the light. As he read, he felt a dying somewhere within him.

Notes of a man at the front: Loneliness is, of course, everything. Loneliness is my eternal comrade, and I take a measure of solace from the quiet companionship it offers. . . . I hear the mechanics hammering, and I recall awakening in the cool summer bed and hearing the merry knocking of carpenters across the valley and the smell of breakfast, and my mother calling, it's late! It's late! . . . The rain falls and makes lonely sounds against the window, cold in the outer dark and wanting to be in. . . . That pigtailed girl in the cellar of the big old hotel, chortling over the mewling kittens and then surprising me with the clutching and the groping and

71

the lascivious laughter springing from some primeval corner that had been tapped by her stroking of the furry warmth. . . . Even the Almighty Orgasm is nothing but an enormous seizure of loneliness; why does the world seek it so? God grant me a D-7. God? Grant me? God is a yearning. How can a yearning make grants? A D-7 is real. I must win it as I win other realities. D-7. D-7. D-7. I must. I must win. Piss on Heidemann. Piss on his D-7's. God: be real. I am not. . . .

There were three full pages of such madness. He burned them, wanting to retch.

He heard footsteps coming up the stairs and he fought an instantaneous and unreasoning panic. When he opened the door to the knock, he noted his hand was slick with sweat. It was Rupp, his sly eyes blinking against the candle.

"What do you want?"

"Pardon, *Herr Leutnant*," he said in that oily voice, "but the *Jastaführer* wants all pilots on the line in fifteen minutes."

"Why?"

"The weather's breaking, and Army has ordered low-levels. Right away."

Stachel wondered why this man got under his skin so. Ever since that first afternoon they'd avoided one another as much as routine would permit, the mutual dislike tacit in the carefully formal correctness between them. But now, simply to look at the man brought a surge of annoyance and resentment that was impossible to mute.

"I'll be there."

"Very good. Sir."

Rupp turned to go, but then he paused, staring around the room, his nostrils flaring almost imperceptibly.

"These quarters ought to be aired and scrubbed. Sir. The smell's awful."

"That's none of your goddamned business. Get out."

The *Uffz*'s small eyes glinted, and he smirked. "I'll send up a crew while you're out. Sir."

"Just don't bother me, that's all."

"Heavy night, *Herr Leutnant?*"

"Get out, I said."

"Take a tip? Draw on the nipple that fed your head. Clears up things in short order."

Stachel opened his mouth to shout, but then the door was closed and Rupp's boots were clomping down the stairs, and so he simply stood there, foolishly. Someday, he vowed through his fury, he'd kill that smart-aleck son of a bitch. . . . He went to the corner where his flight gear lay piled and dressed with stolid, deliberate motions. His head swam sickeningly when he stooped to pull on his boots, so he fell back on the cot to do the job. The bottle under the blanket gurgled softly. He drew it out and held it to the light and saw it still held several drams. Drawing the cork from the neck, he sniffed tentatively and was mildly surprised that the sharp grape spoor did not cause him to gag.

He took Rupp's tip. Then he sat, motionless, watching the candle flame.

As finally he stood and headed for the stairs, the panic was gone, the anger had subsided, and his brain—no longer surging—was aware and at ease.

Thank you, God, for this wonderful discovery. And thank you, Rupp. I hate your guts, Rupp, but thank you anyway.

Heidemann stood in the center of the group, his back to the line of racketing, trembling aircraft, looking dumpy and swollen in his padded flight gear. The men were in high spirits again, and they pounded each other on the back and laughed when he reported that the offensive was going famously. The German armies were plunging deep into the territories once held by the now bewildered and shaken enemy, he said, and today the *Jasta* would be right down on the ground, hitting targets of opportunity. When he gave the order to mount machines, the pilots whooped and scurried like schoolboys. As Stachel moved off toward the Pfalz at the far end of the line, Heidemann motioned to him, smiling easily.

"This low-level business is new to you, Stachel, so I want you to stay as close to me as possible. I suggest you take the inside left of the lead *Kette* so you'll be easier for me to watch." His voice strained to top the engine noise.

"I'll be all right, sir."

Heidemann considered him, his smile fading. "Do you have another cold?"

"All this dampness. It makes my eyes water."

"They're certainly red this morning."

"I'll be all right."

"Well, let's get going. Remember, keep close. We'll break up a bit as targets present themselves, but I don't want you to wander off. Understand?"

"Yes, sir."

Stachel thought: *Heidemann's not a bad sort, really. A schoolteacher, an amateur alienist; but not a bad fellow after all was said. . . .*

Kette by *Kette,* the squadron rumbled into the westerly wind, picking up speed, skittering across the soggy turf, rising in seesawing clusters. At two hundred meters, Heidemann circled widely to the left, while the others, climbing in sky-filling thunder, closed in to form on him. After two circuits of the field, the *Jasta* headed west, still climbing.

Stachel was completely at ease for the first time in weeks. The drumming and sighing and creaking of the machine around him were pleasant, hinting of power and speed; even the oil and exhaust smells that rolled up from the Pfalz's dusky interior had an excitement to them. The other machines of the *Jasta,* hanging around and above and behind in the pewter sky, gave him a sense of the might of a nation and its will, and for the first time since his arrival at the front, his identity as a German officer swelled in him.

How, he wondered, could his mood have changed so quickly, so completely? How could he have gone so long without encountering the glorious secret?

"Gezeigt was er vertragen kann, schon früh am Morgen fängt er an . . ."

In all the times he'd sung those lines from the old drinking song, not once had he perceived the clue. *"The first thing on the morrow he begins again . . ."*

He was still smiling at his own stupidity when Heidemann signaled the descent.

They went down to thirty meters, where the ground rushed by in a blur of crazy patterns and chaotic color. In icy detachment, Stachel stared over his machine guns at the hurtling panorama, managing a few hurried glances at Heidemann's Albatros to keep himself oriented. What in one instant would be an indistinct smudge ahead would balloon in the next into a fleeting but precisely detailed image—like a ghostly face forming from a smear of ectoplasm to hover in hideous clarity for a jot of time before vanishing. A shattered farmhouse, swaying over the engine for a moment, then sweeping sickeningly under the straining wings; a sagging church tower, cross askew; a patch of tortured woods; an ugly snarl of trenches; the fast-whipping snake of a road—they came, then were gone.

A stream, crisscrossed with pontoons and wagons and horses and men, swam into sight beyond the crest of a rise. Somewhere there was the muffled staccato, and Stachel took up the fire. The bridges dissolved behind curtains of spray, and dark shapes sprawled, leaped, writhed, and made private little splashes in the foam. Then, across a plain, on a road slanting away to the left, a column of troops scattered before the insane chattering like tiny beads from a broken string, while beyond them, in a wash, a bubble of flame rolled up from a hive of vehicles.

Stachel's mouth was leather-dry.

From nowhere, a khaki machine, one wing high, slid past in a swift diagonal. Another. Two more. A cloud of them, rushing. He yanked on the controls and the open sky surged ahead, tilting. A Camel arced across it. He thumbed the trigger release and the guns vibrated for an instant. The tracers went wide, but, unaccountably, the brown machine rolled on its back, trailing a sheet of flame. As he corrected, there was another, below and to the right. Instinctively he slid into positon and hammered out another short burst. Again he missed, but even so this one, too, flew on, sinking fast, to slam full on into a building. A Pfalz (was it Dietrich's?) whined past, rolling

75

over and over, its tail a fluttering shambles. A second one, Tallmann's, obviously, its black crosses vivid in the final moment, careened into an orchard, slewing wildly and tossing as it shredded the trees.

In the air beside him was the dry-stick crackling, echoed by a knocking to the rear. Beyond his rudder post, a white-nosed Camel danced, the head of its pilot an indistinct blob behind the propeller blur. In unthinking reflex he kicked and pulled, and the horizon rolled over, twice. When he looked again, the Camel was even closer, and he could see the guns bucking, the oil spray from its rotary lathering the air. Again he rolled away, and this time his face was stung by gravel from the floor. He cursed in rage and fear.

When he dared another glance behind, the Camel was a torch, and banking along abeam of the hurtling wreck was Heidemann's Albatros. The *Jastaführer* pulled alongside, his goggles staring blankly. Fighting nausea, Stachel managed a wave. Heidemann did not acknowledge it.

The Pfalz trundled to a halt, and after a final burst of power with elevators full up, Stachel cut the magnetos and, remembering, put the guns on safe. He sat there, breathing deeply of the sweet air and soaking up the blessed silence. He turned his head with an effort, finally. Heidemann had dismounted and was striding toward the office shack.

A stumpy man from the ground crew trotted up and pulled himself onto the stirrup.

"You all right, sir?"

"I'm all right."

"Can I help you out?"

"Get away, goddamn you. I'll get out myself."

The man dropped off the step and backed away, face red.

Stachel eased himself out of the seat, steadied himself against the turtleback, and, holding a center-section strut for support, slid to the ground. The impact sent a tingling through his board-cold calves. He leaned against the fuselage, his breath still catching. The desire to throw up was strong.

Von Klugermann sauntered over, his flying boots making sucking sounds in the mud.

"The cobra at rest."

"Go away."

"Now you know what it can really be like, eh?"

"Go away, I said."

"Got quite busy out there for a few minutes, didn't it?"

Stachel made no answer.

"Did you get any Tommies? An RE-8, perhaps?"

Von Klugermann laughed briefly, then walked away, whistling tunelessly.

Ziegel was at the corner of a hangar, hands on hips, supervising a ground crew that struggled to roll an Albatros out of the gumbo onto the lath floor. Stachel took one of his elbows and spun him around.

"Easy, Stachel, easy. I've already promised this dance."

"You'll dance across the field on your head if you don't clean up those filthy goddamned machines of ours."

"My. We are in a temper, aren't we? Simmer down, for Christ's sake."

"I'll simmer you, you bastard, if you don't clean up my airplane."

Ziegel's dark eyes grew hot. "If you'd just stop raving long enough to tell me what in hell ails you, maybe we can make some sense. Meanwhile, this is one bastard who doesn't like to be called a bastard."

"You wouldn't like to be sprayed in the face with gravel, either, if you had to risk that slab-sided ass of yours in a dogfight. If ever again I roll that Pfalz over and get a face full of gravel, I'll kill you. Understand? Just once more and I'll kill you."

He gulped down half the flask's contents before taking a breath. He stood quietly for a moment, staring absently out the window at the slate roof across the court, then drank some more, slowly this time. Finally, after a deep sigh, he returned the flask to his kit and dropped onto the cot to count the cracks in the ancient ceiling. Three times he had flown during the day, and each experience had punished him heavily; four times he'd had

77

enemy machines under his guns, and four times he'd missed his aim. *D-7? The Blue Max? Indeed!* His fist hit the wall, hard.

He had lain there for some time, concentrating on the plaster overhead until the brandy could counterbalance the weight of insistent frustration, when someone came up the steps and knocked.

"Come in." There was that panic again, fleeting but powerful.

It was Heidemann, and Stachel was suddenly glad that Rupp's crew had cleaned up the room. As Stachel moved to swing his boots to the floor, the *Jastaführer* waved a hand in short little arcs.

"Rest, Stachel, rest."

"Thank you, sir."

Heidemann tossed a pad of forms onto the table. There was an odd expression on his face. "You haven't filled out a combat report form for this afternoon's action."

Stachel arose, blushing. "Oh, I'm sorry, sir. I'll do it right away. I'm afraid you've caught me trying to steal a few minutes on my back."

"No matter. We've all had a rather full day. I could sleep for a week, myself. But there's still much to do tonight, I regret to say."

"Anything I can help with, sir?" He knew he was groveling, and the knowledge galled him.

Heidemann shrugged. Stachel noticed his lips were pale.

"Unfortunately no. These are the mountains of maddening routine that are the privilege of a unit commander. I've often thought that if I fired as many bullets at the enemy as the numbers of papers I launch toward headquarters, the British Empire would have been destroyed by the Christmas of '14."

"Well, that's the Army, as they say."

"Yes."

Heidemann went to the window and watched the evening gather. After a while he said: "You did not follow my orders."

"Sir?"

"On that low-level. You did not follow my orders."

Stachel's defense apparatus went on the alert. "I don't understand, *Herr Hauptmann.*"

Heidemann turned. His face was gray in the late light. "I told you to stay close to me."

"I tried, sir—"

"To try is not enough. My orders must be followed, precisely and with no shade of default."

"Those Camels. The Camels were all around, and it was a *Freie Jagd*—a free-for-all—"

Heidemann stiffened, and his eyes were opaque. When he spoke the words were sharp and measured. "I want no excuses. Camels, earthquakes, or the Four Horsemen of the Apocalypse. If I tell you to stay with me, you stay with me. You almost got yourself killed. I will not permit you to be killed. I cannot afford to have you killed. There is too much at stake. I forbid you to be killed. Do you understand? I forbid you!"

His words echoed even after the door had slammed shut behind him. Stachel listened as his footsteps died away below, and then he sat on the cot, his eyes thoughtful. Absently he reached for the flask. He studied it for a long time before drinking.

Once he laughed and shook his head.

Ziegel and Kettering leaned against the bar, staring at themselves in the clear spots in the fogged mirror. It was quite late. Except for Mueller and Braun, who bracketed the chess board like bookends, the mess was empty. The phonograph rasped *Der gute Kamerad,* and the takeoff attendant who doubled as bartender was deep in a worn volume of pornography.

"I ought to write a letter to Gretchen." Kettering yawned. "But I get so double-damned tired of scribbling all day I just can't seem to bring myself to it."

Ziegel, for whom a yawn was always contagious, squinted his eyes and took a huge bite of air. "Why write? She'd only have to read it over her boy friend's shoulder."

"Not Gretchen. She wouldn't do anything like that."

"Like what? Read? Or read while fornicating?"

"I think she's being true to me. I really do."

"No doubt. I also think that Jesus will take command of the *Jasta* tomorrow morning at eight o'clock."

Kettering sipped his drink thoughtfully. "Gretchen's an upright person. You'd like her. Upright."

"Mm. I could tell that from that picture you have of her."

"She posed for that in the interest of art, pure and simple," Kettering said, elaborately defensive.

"Well, she and the fellow in the beret were upright, I'll admit that."

"You know any girls around here?"

Ziegel reflected a moment. "Well, yes. Three young nuns at the school. And there's the mayor's secretary. She must be a girl. She wears dresses."

Kettering, enjoying the idle foolishness, began to tell a story about a secretary for a police inspector he once knew, but he broke off when the door banged open and Stachel came in. Stachel wore no tunic, and his face was puffy.

"Our favorite air hero," Ziegel said from the corner of his mouth.

"Mm. And I do believe he's had a pick-me-up."

"Yes. One or two, I'd say. Enough, perhaps, to put a fine gloss on his natural charm. If the son of a bitch starts in on me again, I'll slit his throat."

Stachel came over to them, walking carefully as if the floor were tilted and bejeweled. To their surprise, he smiled.

"Good evening, gentlemen. Having a late one?" His eyes were glassy, and they roamed about the room, empty and without focus.

Ziegel and Kettering exchanged brief glances. Kettering, relieved at Stachel's reasonable tone but going tentatively, smiled faintly.

"Just entertaining each other with jolly patter."

"Mind if I join you for a nightcap?"

"As the Yankees say, it's a free country."

Stachel laughed outright. Again Kettering caught that glimpse of the boy, and as usual, he was softened at once by the poignancy of a reality suppressed.

"Freedom?" Stachel nodded. "Freedom is a sweet word, eh? 'Freedom has a thousand charms to show, that slaves, howe'er contented, never know.' "

"You've been reading." Kettering chuckled, forgiving Stachel with the easy forgiveness he had for all boys.

"Not for some time, I'm afraid. It's one of the freedoms this contented slave no longer knows. Barman—a double cognac, please." The man put down his book and consulted a ledger.

Stachel turned to Ziegel, who was staring into his half-filled glass. "How are you this evening, Ziegel?"

The black eyes came around, a hint of belligerence in them. Then they went back to their study. "Fair enough."

"I apologize."

Ziegel looked at him again, warily this time. "What for?"

"For my angry words this morning. I was pretty tense. Things magnify under tension, they tell me."

Ziegel shrugged. "You were right. I should see that the cockpits are clean."

"You and your crews do remarkably well, all in all. I'd rather swallow a bit of gravel than have an engine that falters. Your engines don't falter." He spoke the words slowly and with the precise diction of a drunken man fighting for control. Kettering watched him in open interest.

"No need to apologize. Let's forget the whole thing, shall we?" Ziegel said unconvincingly.

"Good enough. I like you, Ziegel. And I like you, too, Kettering. Let me buy you both a drink," he said expansively. "Barman?"

The man made a nervous swipe at the bar with his cloth. "Sorry, sir," he said uncomfortably, "but the chit book shows your ration has been used up for the period—"

Stachel looked at him blankly. "Used up? How could that be?"

"I don't know, sir. That's what the ledger says."

Stachel's face darkened. "You mean I can't buy my friends a drink?"

Kettering put up a hand. "That's all right, Stachel. I've had enough anyway."

"Me, too, thanks," Ziegel put in quickly. "Me for bed."

Stachel leaned across the bar, glaring full into the barman's eyes. "Let me see that frigging ledger."

"Of course, sir." The man had it on the bar and open in one fast motion. Stachel considered it for a time, weaving slightly. Kettering, sensing a storm, reached out and closed the book.

"Never mind, Stachel. The next ration periods begins the day after tomorrow. Meanwhile, if you need something to drink you can borrow on mine. I don't use the stuff very much anyway. Makes me fat."

Stachel brought his eyes around, rolling, to peer at Kettering. He smiled crookedly. "Well. That's a neighborly thing to do."

"I'm a very neighborly fellow." Kettering instructed the barman: "Fix it, will you? *Leutnant* Stachel is to draw from my account until the day after tomorrow."

"Yes, sir," the man said, relieved.

Stachel pulled himself erect and ran a hand through his hair. "I wonder if I may have a bottle now. To take to my room for visitors. . . ."

Kettering nodded at the barman.

Placing the brandy under his arm, Stachel gave an exaggerated salute and bow, then took an angular course to the door. There he turned, repeated the gesture, and intoned solemnly: "You may be interested to know that the *Jastaführer* has forbidden me to be killed."

After he'd gone, the phonograph's grinding was the only sound. Sighing, Kettering said finally, "A very strange fellow."

"You're very kind," Ziegel grunted, lighting a cigarette.

"He's—mercurial. You never can figure how he'll act or what he'll say."

"True. But I like him more when he's drunk."

"He's certainly carrying a bundle tonight, eh?"

"The last time I saw somebody that drunk was in Bad Tölz. My girl friend's old man was something of a sipper. This time she was in the mood for a little game of Hide the Wiener, and to keep him out of the way I slipped him a bottle of American corn whisky. It had cost me the equivalent of a trip to Australia, but it was worth it. Like anesthesia, it was."

"Did you get away with the game?"

Ziegel nodded. "I was just sneaking out at daybreak when the old man wobbled out of the potato cellar."

"What did he say?"

" 'Good morning, Pastor. It was an excellent sermon.' "

Kettering yawned again. Ziegel yawned again.

"What the devil do you suppose he meant by that remark?"

"Who? What remark?"

"Stachel. About Heidemann forbidding him to get killed, or whatever."

Ziegel rubbed his eyes. "Who knows what madness wanders in the mind of a drunk?"

"Odd, though."

"Our friend Stachel is a very odd fellow. Like this evening, earlier. I went into Hangar D to clean out his cockpit—personally, mind you—and he was just leaving. He looked very pleased with himself."

"So?"

"So I don't know what to make of him, that's all. Guess what I found in his machine."

"A pipe organ?"

"No, but something just as nutty. When I lifted the seat cushion I saw a slit in it. I pried it open and found a rubber hose coiled up and stuck in the gap."

"A rubber hose? What kind of rubber hose?"

"You know—one of those long, thin ones, about the diameter of a Luger barrel. In my time I've run across all sorts of things in cockpits—good luck charms, and so on—from douche syringes to brass knuckles. But what kind of a good luck charm is a rubber hose?"

"He's a quaint one, all right. Well, I'm turning in. Make sure I'm up at five, will you?"

CHAPTER 9

AT FOUR thousand meters, the sky was a brilliant blue, and the patches of clouds drifting below were like flocks of grazing sheep. The Pfalz's guttural rumble was even and strong, and the wind sighed dreamily in the rigging. Up here, Stachel found with gratification, his senses had become alert and finely tuned. He was alone in the void, and his machine seemed to purr with the pleasure of the lazy circling he permitted it. For April it was a beautiful day, and momentarily he experienced the once-familiar exhilaration. He knew better than to be disappointed when it faded. Instead, he began to think about things, grateful for the opportunity to turn them over calmly and objectively. At times like this he could hold up and examine many things without the discontent that such probing invariably brought when attempted below. It was almost as if the higher he climbed away from the irrationalities and inconsistencies of life aground, the more rational he himself could become.

The primary inconsistency these days was Heidemann, of course.

There had been a subtle change in Heidemann. Just how or when it had come Stachel was unable to say, nor was he able even to define the change. It was simply there. He was aware now of the *Jastaführer*'s especial surveillance, a watchfulness and an attitude of waiting. It was as if Heidemann were evaluating Bruno Stachel in the manner of a biologist observing an alien cell, a botanist scrutinizing an exotic bulb. Several times Stachel had caught Heidemann at this; in each instance the *Jasta* commander had withdrawn quickly behind his wall of correctness. At first Stachel had been irked, but lately he had been able to dismiss the thing as just one more of the other's peculiarities. What he'd not been able to shrug off was the inconsistency. Since that afternoon in his room, when Heidemann had issued his extraordinary mandate, he had been the model flying officer; he had behaved himself meticulously in all departments. In every *Jasta* engagement he had stuck to Heidemann like a surgical plaster, even passing up two easy kills in the process. The inconsistency was underscored upon landing after this sortie: Heidemann, far from noting Stachel's resolute adherence to orders, had instead spoken irritably and at length about how important it was for Stachel to seize such opportunities.

"You must," he'd lectured, "kill them whenever you can, wherever you can. A great deal depends on this— more than you know. If you have the chance, kill them. Understand? Kill them."

What, Stachel asked himself now for the thousandth time, had he meant by that? It had not been a commander merely exhorting a subordinate to destroy the enemy; it had held an even deeper urgency. In any event, it was a clear and classic case of damned if you do, damned if you don't.

He was still weighing this when far below something readjusted itself against the blue-green earth, something he had sensed rather than seen. He dropped a wing and circled slowly, his eyes studying the magnificent relief map shifting beyond the interplane struts. There—now he saw it. A Britisher. One of the new Bristol Fighters. A nasty, fast-moving machine that performed like a pursuit but carried a crew of two armed to the teeth. The Englishman was an incredible distance behind the German lines, and flying still deeper as he climbed. Since Stachel had been trying out a new engine—the original Mercedes had begun to throw oil and overheat alarmingly—he had hung well back in German territory. The last thing he had expected to see in this remote area was a lone Englishman. Stachel congratulated himself for his decision to try the engine under full war load, because he had better than half a tank of fuel still remaining and ammunition boxes that were packed to the brim.

He began to stalk.

The sun was at its zenith, so it would be difficult to use its glare as cover unless he came down on the Bristol in a near vertical dive. He dismissed that prospect immediately, since he questioned the ability of the Pfalz to sustain the forces such a drop would involve, considering present attitudes and angles of convergence. He would probably do better if he were to spiral widely, dropping behind the Englishman in a *Kurvensturz*, the classic curving dive, then use his momentum to pull up and under. If his first burst missed he would have a job on his hands, for the new Bristol was reputed to be willing and able to take on all customers, even odds or no. But if it didn't he'd have confirmed Victory Number Two, since half the German armed forces were arrayed below under the bright, sunlit sky.

He had just charged his guns and had tightened his belt when he saw the second machine. It hung below and behind the Bristol, climbing fast. Studying it, he recognized it as a Fokker triplane—a brilliant red triplane with black crosses neatly outlined in white. The sighting was a disappointment. With the triplane on hand he could no more than share the victory at best. However, this was as good a way as any to test the mettle of his new engine, so he eased the yoke forward and tapped light left rudder, throttling back to slow the downward rush. While in the descent, a sparkle of sunlight on a polished surface caught his eye. It had come from a point to the north beyond the uptilted tip of his right lower wing. Trimming the Pfalz to the horizontal and pulling up a bit, he studied the area. He shut his eyes briefly to rest them, then resumed his scanning. Almost immediately he found them. A trio of Bristols slanted down the wind to the rear of the climbing Fokker.

Stachel considered the situation. The lone Bristol, presumably having lost its mates, was being stalked by the triplane several kilometers to the rear. The Fokker pilot, absorbed in his work, could not have seen the other Englishmen; four Bristols were simply too much for a single triplane to handle, and a pilot with a shred of experience would have discreetly made haste to escape the forming trap. As for his own position, Stachel knew that the sun screened him from all parties, so that made him the trump.

Flying instinctively now, he eased the Pfalz around, keeping the sun behind him as well as he could, then began a rushing power glide. He glanced rearward again, twice for good measure.

A trail of white smoke dots fell behind the uprushing triplane and a second later he heard the far-off stutter of its guns. The lead Bristol dropped off on one wing, hurriedly. The Fokker closed in behind and below it in craftsmanlike precision, and its guns rattled again.

Stachel's airspeed was climbing rapidly, the keening of guy wires shrill and penetrating. He closed fast with the trailing triangle of Bristols, and, adjusting slightly for proper lead, he caught the left rear machine in his sights. A slight pressure of his thumb, and the machine guns crashed a brief but furious burst. Another. The Bristol, huge and dark-hued, seemed to fill his center section. Another burst.

Then, in one of those insane compoundings of coincidence experienced only in the sky, his target mushed, one wing low, into a skid to the right just as its flanking machine began a vertical turn to the left. Stachel watched, almost as if it had been a series of photographs like those you could flick with your thumb and see the pictures come to apparent life. The stricken Bristol's propeller marched up its companion's top wing, methodically chewing away great sections. In a blinding instant the two aircraft had locked together in a hideous slamming and tearing. Then he was beyond, under full throttle, and glancing hurriedly over his shoulder past his rudder post, he saw the two Englishmen dropping away in their horrid embrace.

The Fokker's victim was at the top of a hammerhead stall, flames gushing from under its engine housing. As he watched, the observer crawled free of the smoking rear cockpit, skidded along the turtleback, and rolled off into empty sky. The Bristol seemed to bulge slowly at all its seams, then it disintegrated in a thudding explosion. Its pieces drifted in the wind, spinning.

The remaining Britisher cut for home, but the red triplane was again coming up fast from below. A short thumping—it couldn't have been more than fifteen rounds all told—and the large brown biplane fell into a sickening spin. Stachel's gaze followed it for a long time, breaking off only when he had seen the splash of earth below.

The red triplane had pulled up close alongside, and he could see the fabric drumming along its fuselage. The figure in the Fokker's cockpit was swathed high in black leather and fur, but under the goggles he saw an easy grin. He returned the friendly wave.

As usual, he was physically stimulated, and, as the red machine arced away, he decided he had earned a reward. Steadying the control column with one hand, he reached between his legs and pulled the hose from its cache in the cushion. Hanging it over his arm, he felt for the flask in his inner jacket pocket. Flipping its top open with an expert twist, he inserted the hose in its neck. Then, holding the flask upright between his thighs, he sucked out a long and satisfying draught.

If he was to have a bottle along for emergencies such as this, it wouldn't do to have somebody—somebody like Heidemann, for example—seeing him raising an arm and bending an elbow. You never could tell who might be watching.

As usual, he noticed, no one from the ground crew climbed up on the stirrup. Two of them caught each tip of his lower wing and guided the Pfalz through its taxi and final turn-around, but once he had cut the switch they walked off silently. To hell with them.

He walked to the *Jasta* office and had just completed his combat report when the rasp of a rotary engine beat down through the roof. He heard the motor blipping as the machine slowed for a landing. Kettering, peering up from the door, said, "Well, I see the big boy is making a call."

Signing his name, Stachel muttered, "Who's that?"

"The Red Baron. The great Von Richthofen himself. Wonder what he wants?"

Stachel looked up at the adjutant. "Does he come here often? I mean I've never—"

"It's been some time now."

Curious, Stachel went outside. He recognized the triplane at once. It came around behind the trees, its red wings flashing in the sun as it made the final approach. Leveling out, its engine snorting in little blasts, it lifted over the trees, touched down gingerly, bounced once, then settled. As it taxied up to the line, its stairstep wings waggling, the *Startwärter* gang fell to with precision and élan. There was a commotion around the fuselage, and, when the propeller had gasped to a halt, much heel-clicking and saluting. He joined the crowd of pilots and other ranks that had magically gathered.

The man who climbed from the triplane's cockpit was smiling gently. When he removed his helmet, the sun shone in his short blond hair, giving him an incredibly youthful appearance. The glistening cross of the Blue Max showed at his throat. Stachel was bemused. So this was the fabulous ace of aces. Despite himself, he was caught in a rush of hero-worship and he joined the applauders. Heidemann stepped forward and saluted smartly.

"Delighted to see you, *Herr Rittmeister*. It's been some time, hasn't it?"

Von Richthofen shook Heidemann's hand warmly, nodding affably at the group as he did so. "Yes, Otto. I'm afraid I never get around as much as I like."

"Won't you step into the office? There's some excellent chocolate—"

The Baron held up his hand, smiling. "Thank you. But first I want to meet your gentleman who so gallantly saved my neck awhile ago. Where is he?"

Heidemann looked puzzled. "I'm not sure I understand. Our *Jasta* is refueling and rearming for the afternoon patrol—"

"A gray Pfalz it was. I saw it headed here."

Heidemann's eyes lighted in sudden comprehension. "Why, Stachel, of course. He was trying out a new engine."

"I'm glad he was. He pulled me out of a trap and nailed two Englishmen to boot. Is he around?"

Stachel saluted and bowed, blushing violently with the

89

knowledge that everyone was looking at him. "Here, sir."

The slight blond man strode over to him, hand outstretched. Stachel took it, and the clasp was firm.

"Stachel, is it?"

"Yes, sir. Bruno Stachel."

"I'm Manfred von Richthofen. You were a handy fellow to have around up there."

Their eyes meeting in mutual appraisal, Stachel said: "My pleasure, sir. But you ought to look around a little more when you're stalking."

Heidemann's smile faded. There was a moment of strained silence. Then Von Richthofen threw back his head and laughed.

"You're absolutely right, *Herr* Stachel! Absolutely. It was a dunderheaded thing I did. A rank novice could have done better, and that's all the more reason I appreciate your helping hand."

Stachel smiled slightly. "No offense, sir. But I'd hate to have somebody as valuable as you lost for the want of a mere glance over the shoulder."

Heidemann coughed. *"Herr Rittmeister,* won't you come to the office?"

"Of course, Otto. But one thing more. Would you let this very observing and—I might say—blunt fellow join me in JG-1? I can use men like him. He flies like he talks—straightforward and businesslike. Would you release him?"

Heidemann glanced at Stachel, his eyes noncommittal. "Would you like that, Stachel? It's a very great honor the *Rittmeister* proposes."

Stachel paused. Then he said: "I'm quite aware of that, sir. But as grateful and flattered as I am, *Herr Rittmeister,* I'd like to remain where I am. *Hauptmann* Heidemann and his unit are a great inspiration to me, and, in view of the current situation, I'd feel as if I would be letting him down if I were to leave just now. I hope you understand, sir."

The Baron's hand rested on Stachel's shoulder. His expression was kindly.

"Of course I do. Your answer makes me think even

more highly of you, and"—he turned to Heidemann—
"it reflects great credit on you, Otto. You must be every
bit the fine leader I think you are if you can hold the
loyalty of men such as this."

Heidemann reddened in his pleasure. He studied Stachel's face. When he spoke, it was softly.

"Stachel does *me* honor."

The *Jasta* commander poured chocolate into two cups,
handed one to Stachel, then sat down in his creaking
camp chair. His face was a dark profile against the sun-
set glowing through the office window. He sipped his
drink in preoccupied silence. Turning then, he said: "Con-
gratulations on your two new victories. That makes three
confirmed now, doesn't it?"

"Yes, sir."

"It was a good thing you did."

"I was lucky."

Heidemann put down his cup and took up his pipe.
"Do you smoke, Stachel?"

"No, sir."

"Pity. Pity that you can't enjoy the peace that comes
with a slow pipe. This one was given to me by *Frau*
Heidemann many months ago. It is very precious to me."

"I'm sure it is."

"Do you have a girl, Stachel?"

"Well, I can't say that I do, actually. Oh, I keep company with a few back home, but nothing serious. There
has never been time to be serious, I guess."

"You must make time. It's very important, you know.
Life goes so quickly, and a man needs to share it; otherwise, loneliness saps and warps his personality." He lit
the pipe, and the smoke clouds made twisting patterns
against the twilight.

Stachel rested back on his chair. What, he sighed inwardly, did Heidemann know about loneliness? Bruno
Stachel had invented loneliness.

"I suppose so, sir. But first you have to find someone
to share it with."

"The search isn't as difficult as you may think. It's a
91

matter of being receptive, of knowing when the search has been ended. Do you know how I met *Frau* Heidemann?"

God, Stachel thought, *here's another new one: a Heidemann who confides family secrets.*

"I had been commissioned from Lichterfelde and was in Munich for a short leave. I was strolling along the Isar one afternoon—waiting for another girl, as a matter of fact—when some flat-faced little urchin smashed me a good one with a snowball. Before I carried through my natural desire to box his ears, I thought, 'Well, if there'd been snow, and I'd been his age, and if I'd seen a pompous Army type just asking to be smashed with a snowball, I'd have done the same.' So I merely laughed. It was the luckiest thing I ever did, because Elfi—it was her younger brother—hurried up, apologizing. She said later she never would have given me a second glance if I hadn't laughed. Confidentially, though, her brother's an insufferable boor, and I've boxed his ears soundly several times since."

Stachel smiled politely. "Strange, how people meet."

"Yes."

Stachel wondered why Heidemann had called him in.

"I guess you're wondering why I called you in."

"No, sir."

Heidemann shook his head, chuckling softly. "That's one of the things about you that intrigue me, Stachel. Your unconformity. Almost anyone else would be wondering, 'Now why did the *Jastaführer* call me in?' and sit defensively and ill at ease. Not you. You simply wait, assuming I'll let you know when I'm ready."

"That's the way I am, sir."

"Only two others I know are like that."

"Your friend in *Jasta* 27?"

"He's one. The other is Elfi."

Oh, Christ. Now I remind him of his wife! Why couldn't I have had a plain, everyday thickheaded, unimaginative pain in the ass for a commander? Some squareheaded farmer who thought personality analysis to be a veterinary term for cow plop?

"You are certainly good at figuring people, sir."

92

"It's a trait I've cultivated."

"It makes for good leadership, I'd say."

Heidemann made a minimizing sound. He turned to look out the window at the coming darkness.

"That was a fine thing you did today."

"As I say, I was lucky."

"No. Not the victories. I mean what you said, when you turned down Von Richthofen's offer."

"I meant every word," Stachel said deliberately.

"Well, it helps more than you know. Unhappily, politics plays a role in the German Army—too big a role, really—and it helps to have a man in his position hear such things. It was good for all my men to hear it, too. It will be discussed widely, and it can't help but reflect well upon me."

"You deserve it, sir."

"You're very kind. But now there's something you deserve. Von Klugermann will soon visit Army for a day or so. His uncle, the *Graf*, will be there, and I've given Willi permission. How'd you like to accompany him? For a change of scenery, so to speak. You both can fly up in the C-3—I like the brass to see my men with their machines, even with an old flatiron like the C-3."

"That would be fine, sir. But perhaps Willi wouldn't like my butting in on a personal matter—"

"Oh, you won't have to stay with him all the time. Just accompany him to headquarters and be seen around. I can give you a little business to attend to while you're there, just to make it all look official and so on. You can pop in, be seen, then pop out again. Who knows" —he chuckled again—"you may even meet some girls. They say the place is crawling with nurses and Red Cross women from the field hospital."

Stachel registered appreciation. "Well, that sounds first-rate, sir. But certainly others in the *Jasta* deserve such a treat more than I do."

"Nonsense." There was a hint of swift annoyance in Heidemann's eyes.

"I hope you don't think—"

"That I need to reward you for your kind words this afternoon? Nonsense. You've earned a day off. Now don't belabor the issue. Get there. And let the brass see you. Let them see you. Understand? See you."

Stachel took the stairs two at a time. As he passed Von Klugermann's room, he paused, wondering whether to prepare Willi or to keep his peace and let Heidemann break the news. He decided on the latter and went up to the next flight. He heard the Prussian's door open and he glanced down through the banister rail. Rupp came out with a thick envelope under his arm.

"Remember, Rupp," Von Klugermann said from within the room, "not a word."

"Naturally, sir."

"And there'll be more. I'll let you know when."

"Any time's all right."

Stachel shrugged, then went on to his quarters. He lit the candle and brought out the good stuff, ignoring the cheap Spanish that sat on the table. After holding up the bottle and toasting himself in the mirror, he drank deeply. He sat on the cot, waiting for the magic to work and speculating once again as to the origin of that Spanish slop.

After a while he pulled off his boots and sprawled out, placing the cognac on the floor within easy reach.

Once, when the purple beyond the window had turned to black, he sneered audibly.

What, he wondered then, would Heidemann think if he were to discover why Bruno Stachel had really turned down Von Richthofen?

Raising a hand oratorically, he told the cracked ceiling, "*Anybody* worth his salt would shine in Otto Heidemann's mediocre and colorless presence. . . ."

CHAPTER *10*

THEY HAD completed their business with the office of the *Kommandeur der Flieger* in fairly short order and had spent a pleasant quarter hour with the captain who served Army as its staff aviation officer. Von Klugermann, by virtue of his uncle's presence nearby, had been fussed over a bit, of course, and the aide to the *Kommandeur* had brought him special greetings from the *Kofl* himself, who regretted he was tied up in an all-day meeting. Stachel had stood about somewhat uncomfortably, answering questions as politely as possible and agreeing frequently and with rapidly diminishing patience that the spirit up at the front was excellent, excellent indeed.

As they came down the stone steps of the large old school building that housed *Kofl*, Von Klugermann laughed aloud.

"What's the matter?"

"You're very amusing, Stachel."

"How so?"

"The way you were while we bummed around in there. Like a schoolboy at a headmaster's tea. A real cobra in the air, but a shiny-faced schoolboy when back in civilization."

Stachel admitted lamely, "I won't deny it. Sessions like that bore me stiff. I wasn't aware it showed through so much, though."

"Well, try not to let it show through while we're at dinner with the *Graf* and my aunt. They're good sports, and you don't have to pucker your lips for them. Be yourself. The *Graf* is very quick to recognize a poseur. And Auntie is, I believe, secretly fond of loutish types like you."

"Your aunt? She's here, too? I didn't realize they permitted ladies to come up this far," he said, mystified.

Von Klugermann stopped briefly to light a cigarette. His face glowed orange in the dusk.

"This isn't really up very far, you know. Furthermore, the old boy has bundles of pull and does pretty much as he pleases. Berlin has long since given up trying to make him conform."

"He must be a very important fellow."

"He's that, all right."

Stachel was depressed with the prospect of an evening with an old but very important fellow and his aunt-type spouse. He'd much rather have looked up a side-street bistro for a bit of contemplative drinking. He wondered if there was some way he could beg off. After all, they'd be returning to the *Jasta* the following afternoon, so he'd have to get in his licks tonight, if at all.

As Von Klugermann led the way across a square toward a large and very ornate hotel with wide terraces and reasonably well-tended shrubbery, he laughed again.

"Now don't try to connive a way out of this, my cobra. The *Graf* and *Gräfin* are expecting us, and I don't imagine even you could be crude enough to disappoint them out of hand."

Stachel's face reddened. "Why do you bother with me if you think I'm so—beneath you?" His tone was testy.

"Now don't get your hair up. I told you: you fascinate me. You're a cobra, and I like to watch cobras."

"I don't imagine your dear old aunt will be very at ease in the company of a cobra."

Von Klugermann smiled distantly. "Wait until you see my dear old aunt."

The foyer of the hotel was dim and cool, and somewhere a string ensemble brooded over some Strauss. The scent of fresh flowers sweetened the air. Two Red Cross nurses passed them as Von Klugermann gave his card to a stooped old man in hotel livery. One of them regarded Stachel with an open but noncommittal gaze. She was quite pretty.

The cadaverous attendant led them through the stained glass doors at the rear of the foyer to a large piazza that stretched along the length of the hotel and looked over a pleasant garden. Candles had been placed on the small round tables dotting the terrace, and white linen and sparkling glass made each a warm little island of elegance in the hushed twilight. The people at headquarters, Stachel noted, lived very well indeed.

The *Graf* was seated at a table in a corner formed by an angle of box hedge. Stachel saw that he was old and quite heavy, and candlelight reflecting on his polished monocle created a peculiar Cyclops-like effect. His close-

96

cropped, bullet-shaped head gave him an air of great dignity.

"Good evening, my dear uncle," Von Klugermann purred. "I do hope you haven't been waiting too long. We were held up at headquarters, I'm afraid. May I present *Leutnant* Bruno Stachel, one of the more promising members of my *Jasta?* My uncle, the *Graf* von Klugermann, Stachel."

Stachel clicked his heels and bowed stiffly. "I'm honored, sir."

The *Graf's* nod was affable. He smiled thinly. "Come, come, my lads—sit down and do stop the Palace Guard business. I'm looking forward to an evening agreeably free of all this slap-and-crash-and-click military posturing. Lord knows I've seen enough of it in the past few days. Well, Nephew, you're looking fairly fit, despite your tendency to emulate your father's obesity."

"I feel in the best of form, really. We Von Klugermanns simply appear to be fat. Something about the way we're built."

"We're simply built fat, you rationalizer."

"Mm. Where's Auntie?"

"She's due here any moment now. Something involving a letter to be mailed, I believe. Mail service has been atrocious lately." The monocle turned to Stachel. "Tell me, young man, are you a famous flier? My nephew's name has been conspicuously absent from the communiqués, and I should like to advise certain of my friends that I've dined with at least one of our air heroes."

Stachel blushed heavily. Despite his determination to be himself, he was painfully aware of the enormous social gap between him and these drawling aristocrats, and he felt that whatever his answer, it would sound foolish and banal.

"No sir. I'm not famous. In fact, I'm quite new to the game. Your nephew is an accomplished pilot, and I only hope I can eventually equal his skill."

The *Graf* smiled his wan smile. "Acceptably put. But altogether unconvincing, I'm afraid. My nephew is an ass, and I have the distinct impression you are aware of

97

that fact. So, if you think he's an ass, say he's an ass. I consider candidness to be mankind's sweetest and most worthy aspiration. I admire only those who have the temerity to use it."

Von Klugermann laughed. "My uncle admires candidness because he's old enough and rich enough to afford it."

Stachel's blush persisted. He told the *Graf:* "I was speaking of his skill, not his personality traits. He doesn't think too much of me, for that matter."

The uncovered eye twinkled. "So? Why?"

"He thinks I'm a cobra," Stachel chafed.

"A droll thought. What do you mean by that, Nephew?"

"Stachel, under that clean-scrubbed, blushing-boy manner, is coiled and tense and watchful, and, well, deadly."

The *Graf* peered at Stachel with an odd expression. "Interesting. But isn't deadliness implicit in the very uniforms you're both wearing? What makes *Herr* Stachel more so than any of you young fools?"

Von Klugermann's smile was a caricature of his uncle's. "We kill for duty's sake. Stachel kills for enjoyment."

Stachel felt anger rising in him. "I don't think this is the occasion to talk of such things."

The *Graf* lit a long, thin cigar. "Tut-tut, *Junge*. If my nephew's analysis is correct you have nothing to be ashamed of, actually, because you have a lot of company. Many men kill for enjoyment. As a matter of fact, I once collaborated on a paper on homicide as a sexual manifestation. There are case histories in that work that leave little doubt that the act of slaying can actually trigger sexual release under certain conditions. Blood lust is, I am personally convinced, in the immediate family of sexual lust. For this reason I've always suspected that history's great warriors have had more than patriotism on their minds."

"You're correct on two matters, sir. I don't feel I have anything to be ashamed of. And your nephew is an ass," Stachel said evenly. "Now do you mind if I have a drink?"

They were interrupted by the arrival of the *Gräfin*.

She was a medium-sized woman, somewhat on the plump side, but she had the striking blue eyes and the creamlike skin of a *Nordländer*. Her lips were full and wide, and her teeth were quite attractive. Stachel guessed she was not even half the *Graf*'s age.

"I'm sorry, gentlemen, but I simply had to attend to something. I do hope I haven't been awkward." Her voice was a fine contralto. Stachel and the others arose. "Dear Nephew, how nice it is to see you again. You look stunning!"

"Dear Auntie," Von Klugermann murmured, brushing her hand with his lips, "how I've awaited this day. You are a darling to come all this way to see me. May I present *Leutnant* Stachel, one of my favorite cobras?"

She gazed steadily at Stachel for a moment. He took her hand.

"Delighted, *Leutnant* Stachel."

"My pleasure, madame."

"Well, for God's sake, sit down, Kaeti," the *Graf* rumbled. "We were just preparing to launch some serious drinking. Or at least such seemed to be the intention of *Herr* Stachel. Will you join us?"

"An apéritif, please," she said as Willi guided her to her chair. The *Graf* nodded to a waiter, who had been standing discreetly at the hedge.

"Now, *Leutnant* Stachel, what is all this about cobras?" the *Gräfin* asked, amused.

"Just a joke between us two fellows, Countess. Your nephew likens me to one." He smiled to himself when he considered his squadron mate as the nephew of this woman. She was probably all of five years older than Willi.

"You don't look very reptilian to me. I'd say you're rather well set up, actually."

When the waiter had served them, Von Klugermann lifted his glass and said quietly: "To the Kaiser."

They drank, and Stachel caught the *Gräfin* studying him. She blinked, then turned to her husband.

"Hugo, my dear, what's become of the packages we've brought for Willi?" she asked in the manner of a woman who already knew the answer. To Von Klugermann she chortled: "I have no way of knowing what you need most up at the front, since you're such an abominable correspondent sometimes—at least when it involves writing about yourself. So before we left Frankfurt I simply sat down and thought of all the things I'd want if I were a man living at the edge of nowhere. I hope my empathy proves adequate."

"Your very presence here in these primitive surroundings is all I could ever wish for, dear Aunt Kaeti. You have brightened not only my day but also that of every man in this miserable town," he answered her smoothly.

The Graf snorted. "Good God, Willi, but you're sickening when you try to be gallant. You know very well that the woman's presence at a headquarters location so near the front has proved to be a prime source of annoyance and distraction to half the German Army. But she demanded to come, and you know how she is when she demands."

The cognac was resting well with Stachel and he laughed briefly. The *Gräfin* smiled, her fine teeth brilliant in the candlelight.

"My, that's better. *Leutnant* Stachel can laugh. I'd begun to think that that preoccupied, grim expression was the only one he had."

Von Klugermann chuckled sardonically. "You should see him out at the factory. When compared with Stachel, Mephistopheles becomes a study in benevolence."

Her expression grew solicitous. "How is it out there? Really, I mean. Is it very horrible?"

The *Graf* made an impatient sound. "Kaeti, how many times have I told you? Never ask a soldier what it's like. It's the same as asking him about his bowel movements."

"Hugo! You don't have to be so crude."

"I've earned the right to be as crude as I want. Any man who has spent all of his life in the turgid, smug, and deceitful wallows of Germany's so-called upper society should be permitted the blessed purgative of bluntness now and then."

"What will *Leutnant* Stachel think?" she asked, brows knitted.

100

"I don't particularly care what *Leutnant* Stachel thinks. I suspect, however, that he has had his own belly full of the arrogance and inequities our benign despotism has engendered."

"However," Stachel observed dryly, "I haven't had the advantage of seeing it from within. After all, I'm only a hick from the Taunus, and therefore on the receiving end."

The *Graf* nodded. "Quite so. The ancient story of the ins and the outs. It amuses me these days, for instance, to hear of the Bolsheviks' agonized cries for a rise of the common man. All they want, in the final analysis, is to throw out one tyranny so they can establish another. Whenever you have two men, one will always seek to be dominant. Whenever you have a society, there will always be the upper and lower classes, the rulers and the ruled."

Von Klugermann shook a finger. "Easy, my dear uncle. The Kaiser would be very displeased to hear you referring to his rule as a tyranny."

"Nonsense. The Kaiser is a mustachioed brat, and, as one of his few friends, I've told him so to his face. What makes any society's ins so insufferable is that they always cloak their rottenness in trappings of self-righteous altruism, always put up a self-defensive protest that what they do is in the best interest of all. And the Kaiser and the class he personifies are master protesters of this sort."

"We are of his class," Von Klugermann pointed out wryly.

"Indeed we are. I wouldn't have it any other way. So long as there are ins and outs, I must prefer to be an in. But that doesn't alter my distaste for the system. More cognac, please."

Stachel noted that the nurses had taken the table near the door. The pretty one met his glance, the hint of a smile at the corner of her lips. The other one appeared to be quite drunk. She sat stiffly upright, and her gestures were the slow and deliberate movements of one who fought for control.

The *Gräfin* said impulsively, "I do wish someone would help that poor woman. I've been watching her, and I'm afraid she'll fall over any minute now."

The *Graf* shifted his glance to the nurses. He grunted. "Why should anyone try to help her? She's enjoying the opiate of the outs and would resent any intrusion. I dare say if you were as plain as she is and were forced to accept the company of someone as attractive as the other is, you'd feel very much the out. Alcohol is her particular escape from the intolerable knowledge of her outness, that's all."

His wife shrugged a shoulder. "I'm quite plain myself, but I don't seek escape in alcohol."

"You say that so smugly, my dear, because you don't understand addiction. Addiction is a physical manifestation of a psychological hunger for escape. Alcohol is only one form of addiction. Drugs are another; overeating is another; fanatical religious evangelism is another. I could go on, naming gossip, butterfly chasing, reading, dancing, scores of human preoccupations which, when overindulged, are signposts of addiction. But the most widespread form of addiction—second to alcohol, of course—is sex. Sexual preoccupations, from flirting to perversion, comprise perhaps the most common escape of all for the psychologically and socially trapped. The people down in Vienna are arriving at some startling things in this regard."

Stachel was aware that the *Gräfin* had reddened slightly. Von Klugermann put in whimsically: "My, aren't we profound tonight?"

The *Graf* considered him, somewhat disdainfully. "If you think I have time for banalities you are more of an ass than I believed. Life is closing out for me, and if I'm going to bother with conversation at all I'm not going to devote it to frivolity.

"Consider that girl over there. I'll wager I can give you an accurate précis of her unhappiness despite the fact I've never spoken to her in my life. First of all, and mortally so, she's an alcoholic—at least an incipient one. Secondly, her plainness has assumed the stature of both cause and effect of her vast loneliness and discontent.

The first feeds the second, the second feeds the first. She is in a hideous squirrel cage of push and pull, and she has found that alcohol, once a salubrious medicine, is now a despotic poison."

Stachel interrupted: "Let's define our terms. What is an alcoholic?"

The *Graf* smiled faintly. "Who's to say? I've made an exhaustive study of the subject, and for every treatise there is a definition. I'm personally convinced, however, that an alcoholic—whether old, young, man, woman, fat, skinny, blond, brunette, tall, short—is one who is afflicted with a peculiar allergy, a flaw, if you will, that took form within the womb. When alcohol is administered to such a body, the allergy asserts itself in a physical compulsion and a mental obsession for more. The ultimate result is the spiritual disaster—the collapse of personality—that engulfs our nurse over there."

"You mean you believe a sot is born, not made?" Stachel put in mildly.

"Precisely. In my studies I've come across cases of advanced alcoholism in children who had barely begun to grow pubic hair. Their first exposure to alcohol came as tots in families in which table wine was a staple."

"Hugo!"

"Proprieties, Kaeti?" He did not look at her and went on doggedly: "Everyone has seen and can easily recognize the advanced alcoholic, such as the pasty-faced man who sleeps in doorways. But, believe me, he's in the considerable minority. For every one of him there are scores of men, women—yes, and children—who live in constant misery, who go through life in lonely torture, because they consume alcohol in one form or another, either as medicine or as a social amenity, innocent of the knowledge that their especial susceptibility is domineering them by inches. Then, by the time the malady becomes well established, they've entered a half-world—outwardly respectable and well adjusted; inwardly miserable, terrorized by the fears, doubts, and anxieties that unaccountably belabor them. These unfortunate individuals may live out entire life spans, never comprehending what has caused their appalling unhappiness.

"I've often wondered how much of history has been influenced by these half-world people. It seems that those who are the most vulnerable to this malady, this allergy, are more often than not those of great ability and high intelligence. Therefore, just think of how many of them may have held vital positions in government, education, business, industry, the military—even the clergy—in ages past. Think for a moment of how even the fate of nations may have rested with some whose alcohol-induced frenzies and discontent, lurking behind their externally calm and cogent demeanors, motivated their decisions and actions. It makes my flesh crawl."

Stachel's fingers drummed the tablecloth. "Very interesting, but hardly convincing. It's all a matter of will power—or lack of it, that is. For instance, if I ever had trouble with my drinking, I'd simply stop drinking."

The monocle glinted. "Perhaps. But I doubt it, because I find it's the nature of the ailment that the more the victim deteriorates under its influence, the more he resents and rejects any suggestion that it exists at all, the more he lies to himself about his secret awareness that something is wrong with his drinking. Furthermore, you accept the popular conception of dipsomania: the belief that it is caused by a weak will combined with moral degeneracy, that the victim drinks because he's a brute. I believe the contrary: the victim is a brute *because* he drinks, because he must drink. The victim can no more will himself from drinking than a hay-fever sufferer can will an end to his sneezing. And, by way of additional example, consider the tubercular. As advanced as society is in this year 1918, it still condemns a tubercular as the victim of his own degradation. This is patently ridiculous. The tubercular has a physical disease. He should be helped rather than pilloried. But society is organized stupidity, so the tubercular—like the alcoholic—is condemned for a sin he never committed in the first place."

Stachel's tenseness was acute. He noticed that the *Gräfin* was regarding him curiously, and he was relieved when Willi changed the subject.

104

"Well, I'm addicted to food, for one thing. May we order?"

The *Graf* signaled the waiter. "You all must forgive me. It's one of my favorite subjects, and I'm a windy old fool."

The breeze coming off the balcony was sensuously cool and full of night smells. In the half-light, Stachel's heaving chest slowed to normal cadence. For a long while he studied the dim rain clouds rushing over the trees outside.

The *Gräfin* stirred, her body an area of smoothness against the deeper dark.

"Tell me something?"

"What?"

"Why didn't you go after that nurse? She's much prettier than I."

Stachel smiled at the dusky ceiling. "Perhaps. But you were much hungrier."

Her laugh was moist against his throat. "Could you tell, really?"

"Of course. I can always tell. Women get an odd look around the eyes when they're hungry. The nurse was merely bored with her drunken company and wanted a way out. You had the look."

"You're an amazing man. For one so young, I mean."

"That's what the midwife said as she tied off my umbilical."

Her fingers traced a delicate oval on his stomach. Her hair was rich with the scent of cleanliness, and its tingling against his face was a pleasant thing.

"My husband was right in one way, you know."

"I know. As the *Graf* would say, you're addicted to this. This is your escape from a social entrapment symbolized by a husband twice your age. By frequent practice you have become a virtuoso at your chosen method of escape. Or something like that."

She laughed again, softly. "You make me sound so whorish."

"Nonsense. You're simply expert. You're a virtuoso.

You played me as if you were a concert performer and I was your clarinet."

Her laugh accelerated. "What a ridiculous picture!"

They lay silent then for long minutes, luxuriating in the rain sounds, the soft stir of the air. Finally she whispered: "There must be more to it than that."

"What do you mean?"

"There must be a reason other than my odd look, as you call it. That nurse would probably be an exciting experience for a man. And I honestly believe she was hungry, too."

He thought a moment. "Yes, there's another reason."

"Tell me."

"I get more out of this kind of thing when I steal it."

"Steal it?"

"Yes. To know that the *Graf* is right at this moment snoring away in a room across this suite makes you all the more exciting to me. I love to steal, that's all. I love to take."

She considered that for a moment, then chuckled. "If that's the case, you must be the world's champion rapist."

"Not at all. Rape would not meet my test for stealing. For me, there has to be a sense of participation—a sense of sharing a common, and perhaps desperate, risk. Would you believe it if I told you I'm"—he gestured—"like this at the height of combat? I'm attempting to steal a man's life. But he participates by agreeing to the conditions under which the theft is aspired to. When he loses, that's his loss. He has shared the common risk. The *Graf* has accepted the risk of such clandestine sport as this by taking a young wife; he participates in the game by snoozing while someone consummates the theft."

She arose to her knees, and her torso was silhouetted against the window as she studied him.

"You are a very beautiful young man, even if you are crazy."

"Think so?"

"Now just lie there like that," she instructed. "It's my turn to do a little stealing."

106

CHAPTER 11

VON RICHTHOFEN was missing.

Stachel learned this when he and Von Klugermann returned to the airdrome on Sunday evening. The whole *Jasta* was talking about it, and there were rumors that the Baron's *Jasta* 11 people were volunteering all sorts of crazy stunts to rescue him, or, if the worst had happened, to recover his body and bring it back for appropriate rites. As Stachel understood it, Von Richthofen and five others had left the advanced field at Cappy that morning to patrol between Marceux and Puchevillers. The Army had launched a probe in force to determine enemy potential near Bretonneux, and British observation planes were to be kept away. Apparently a large-scale wrestling match had developed near Corbie when the Baron and his *Kette,* augmented by *Jasta* 5 in strength, had begun to maul a pair of RE-8's. A group of Camels had come out of the southwest, and, after a lengthy and involved fight, the Baron's triplane had been seen crash-landing behind the British lines north of Vaux-sur-Somme. The *Flugmeldedienst* was unable to report further details.

At the bar, Von Klugermann was pensive.

"You know," he said, "it seems hard to believe in a way that someone so experienced could let himself be dragged that far into Tommyland. Something odd must have happened out there today."

Stachel rolled the drink on his tongue before he swallowed. He motioned for a refill.

"Experience," he said, "is good up to the point it becomes overconfidence. Nobody dragged the Baron—he went there."

Willi was silent for a time, thinking that over. He knew that if he were completely honest with himself he would admit that the sense of regret he'd felt at the news of the Baron's fall was more a depression that stemmed from the heightened awareness of his own vulnerability. If Von Richthofen could be shot down while permitting himself such a lapse, certainly Von Klugermann——

"Still, it seems odd."

"Why? I know from personal experience that Von Richthofen tended to get all wrapped up in his work. What's so frigging odd about somebody getting his pants full of lead when he neglects to look over his shoulder in a sky full of machines?"

Von Klugermann gave Stachel his pouting smile. "The cobra speaks."

"I wish you'd get off that cobra stuff. You bore me."

"Where did you go last night?"

Stachel's defenses came up. "What do you mean?"

"Well, I'd left my bar of soap here at the field so I went by your room to borrow yours. You weren't there. The desk man said you'd left the hotel a little after midnight."

Stachel was annoyed, but glad he'd tipped the desk man against such an eventuality.

"Checking up on me?"

"Certainly not. I merely wondered, that's all."

"I wanted some fresh air, if you need an explanation."

Willi took a thoughtful sip of brandy. "I hope the *Graf* didn't wear you down with all that slush he was handing us."

"On the contrary. I think he's a very fascinating old potato. Germany could use a lot more like him."

"Maybe. I'm rather fond of the old boy, myself. He does talk a lot though."

"He has some strong ideas. I don't mind anybody talking when he's got something to say."

"Yes. But some of his ideas are silly."

"I didn't say I agree with him. I said I don't mind him talking."

"Kaeti sort of puts up with him. She's not a very intellectual type, I'm afraid."

"She does all right," Stachel parried.

"I guess her life is somewhat empty, in a way. She's not too old, actually, and not exactly a raving beauty. And the *Graf* becomes engrossed in all his machinations and leaves her alone in that huge house day after day with nothing to do but supervise a platoon of servants."

"He brought her along on this trip, didn't he?"

"Yes. But only because it pleased him to demonstrate his great influence. She may have asked to accompany him, but she certainly didn't demand it, as he said. She wouldn't dare. Any way you look at it, it must be an empty life for her."

Stachel thought about her: the practiced fondling, the lewd instructions, the smoothness and damp heat, the scented hair, the furious maneuvering, the heaving and silent explosions.

"Perhaps. But she has her own little interests, I'm sure."

Kettering stumped in, his leg squeaking. "Anybody seen Ziegel?"

"Down at Hangar G, I think," Stachel said. "He was rigging the replacement D-5."

Kettering considered him for a moment. 'I checked there." Turning to Von Klugermann, he asked, "Have a good time?"

"So-so."

"Any women?"

"There were some around."

"Shoot any down?"

"Sightings only. No combat."

"Pity."

"Yes."

Stachel said, not knowing exactly why, "Let me buy you a drink."

Kettering showed mild surprise. "Don't mind if I do. I never was one to deny little visitors a tour of my insides. I think there are some *schnapps* on hand. . . ."

The three of them drank together. Ziegel came through the door, his dark eyes brooding.

"Oh, there you are, Ziegel. I was looking for you."

The Bavarian muttered a dirty word. "You and everybody else. Tenderhearted Jesus, but I wish people would

109

let me alone long enough to get something done. How about a drink? Or are you out of gas again? I've noticed you're quite ready to give away your bottles these days."

Kettering laughed nervously. "Not very often, I don't."

"Kettering, giving away bottles?" Von Klugermann snorted. "He wouldn't give a bottle to the Kaiser. You must be dreaming, Ziegel."

"Not hardly. Ask Stachel."

Stachel became vaguely perplexed. "What do you mean?"

"Christ, don't tell me you don't remember that night last month? That night you wandered in here with your eyes looking like red billiard balls? You were ready to geld the barman until Kettering cut you in on his ration."

Stachel struggled to conceal his confusion. All of them were staring at him with amusement.

"Oh, yes. Of course I remember. I've been meaning to repay you, Kettering," he said jerkily.

"Your credit's still good."

"Have another drink now."

"Well—all right. I've got work to do, though. But, as the Yankees say, 'Here's mud in your eye.'"

Von Klugermann blew a column of smoke at the mirror. "Ziegel tells me you were in the States at one time, Kettering. Do you speak much English?"

"Enough to get around."

"What's it like over there?"

"Like any place else. Only more so."

"What are the people like?"

"Oh, they're all right, I guess. They get livelier the farther west you go. On the East Coast they tend to be more like their stuffed-shirt English cousins. Out beyond Chicago they're more like us, I'd say. But from me to you—don't ever let anybody try to sell you the idea that the Yankees are all sweetness and love and full of openhearted democracy. That's horse manure. They're just as class-conscious and full of little snobberies as any I've ever seen. They talk out of both sides of their mouths all the time. They'll say: 'Brotherly love and sharing are the way to peace in the world.' And even while

110

they're saying it they'll be kicking some poor bastard's ass and snatching his wallet as he grunts."

Ziegel humphed, his eyes showing surprise. "Well. This is the first time I've ever heard you say anything nasty about anybody—especially the Yankees." After a while, he added: "That's certainly the way they've treated us. Wilson yammers about how alarmed he is over the war and all, protesting neutrality, and all the time supplying the beefeaters and Montmartre pimps with all sorts of hardware. My God, look at the so-called Lafayette Escadrille they've set up in the Frenchman's air service. If that's a volunteer outfit I'll swallow my *Krätzchen*. I haven't seen any volunteer *'Von Steuben Jasta'* in *our* flying corps. . . ."

Stachel broke out of his reflective silence. "Well, the Americans should make for some fine shooting, at any rate."

Ziegel nodded vigorously in a burst of unfamiliar patriotism. "We'll give them a warm welcome to the little war they've come into so unwillingly, by God."

Kettering stirred. "Speaking of warm welcomes, that's what I wanted to see you about, Ziegel. Heidemann tells me that a new D-7 will be delivered here for familiarization. He wants you to pop over to the Army Aviation Technical Center next week. A representative of the Fokker Company and a man from the Aircraft Production Directorate will give you an orientation. How to put one together and take it apart and that sort of thing."

Ziegel grumped, "What a pile of nonsense. I don't have enough to do without making trips, eh? All I need is a screwdriver to put any machine in the air; you know that and so does Heidemann."

"I know that. But I also know that when Heidemann says poop we drop our suspenders."

Stachel's eyes narrowed with interest. "When is the D-7 due, Kettering?"

"Not sure yet. But soon."

"How soon will we get enough for the whole *Jasta?*" he demanded.

"How should I know? I'm not the frigging commanding general."

"Will we all get a chance to try out this one that's coming?"

"Why not? That's why they're sending it, I suppose."

Von Klugermann laughed. *"Herr* Stachel is very anxious to fly the D-7, I take it."

"You're damned right. The Pfalz is a barge."

"There's an Albatros available. Heidemann will let you use that and you know it. Why don't you use that?"

"There's a matter of principle involved, that's why. If it's not a Fokker, it's the Pfalz."

Heidemann was not happy with the duty he faced. Ordinarily such matters were routine—fundamental to the complex and imperturbable process by which the needs of an operational fighting unit and its hundred-some souls were defined, weighed, and acted upon. And with Otto Heidemann, routine was a way of life; routine was the spine and neural system upon which the Army's diverse parts assembled to become a vast and homogeneous whole. There was little room for emotion in such a scheme, and it occurred to the *Jasta* leader that he should be confronting Kunkel's case with no particular feeling either way. Nevertheless, he was distinctly aware that if Mueller hadn't complained he would have been able to confine his actions to a reprimand, and be content. Then, perhaps, he could have avoided the uneasiness he now felt.

He buried the thought as he returned Kunkel's salute. Kunkel, he noticed, was nervous, and sweat brought a fine sheen to his hairline. Heidemann deliberately allowed several minutes to pass, shuffling and signing a few papers before resting back and regarding the young man.

"I suppose you know why you're here, Kunkel."

"I—not exactly, *Herr Hauptmann.* I—"

Heidemann picked up his pen and toyed with it in preoccupation. Finally he said, "That's precisely it, Kunkel. You're inexact."

"Begging the *Jastaführer's* pardon, I don't follow—"

Heidemann decided to get it over with. "Propriety and

absolute obedience, Kunkel: those are the two most important ingredients in a successful military organization. Determination of the proper thing is the genesis of accomplishment; adherence to the proper thing, at all costs and under all pressures, brings the seeds of accomplishment to maturity. The proper thing must be established, defined, and pursued with unquestioning dedication in all facets of military life—whether it be the courtesies observed at a garrison ball or the planning of high strategy."

Kunkel licked his lips. His look was anxious. "Yes, sir."

"You are a high type of young man. You are intelligent, decent, fairly skilled at your specialty, and, above all, loyal to the Fatherland and our cause."

"Thank you, sir."

"But you are not good enough to remain in this *Jasta*."

Kunkel's face paled, and his fingers plucked at the center button of his tunic. "I don't understand, sir. Have I been improper somehow?"

"Not in the usual sense, of course. As I say, you're a thoroughly decent type."

"Well, then—"

"But you disobeyed me. And I will not tolerate disobedience."

"Disobeyed? How, sir? Please—"

"During the patrol this morning your assignment was to keep close to Mueller. You did not do so."

Kunkel's eyes blinked as he struggled to reconstruct the morning's events. "I can't recall having failed to do so, sir. I—"

"No doubt you will recall our return approach to the field here?"

Again Kunkel's tongue ran along his restless lower lip. "Yes, sir. It was altogether routine. The patrol was ended, and we made normal landings, so far as I can remember."

"Yes. Except that as we began to break up for the landing in pairs you dropped away from Mueller."

"But for God's sake, sir, that was no more than two

113

kilometers from the field. I clung to Mueller like a leech from takeoff all the way through the scramble with the DeHavillands and—"

"I'm aware of that. But you dropped your guard, and therefore disobeyed."

"But the flight was ended! There was no danger—"

Heidemann pounded the desk with his fist, his eyes hard. "There's always danger, Kunkel! Always! Don't you remember that afternoon when the Camels shot our base to pieces? Don't you know that the English can be expected to repeat the performance at any hour of any day in the week? From takeoff to touchdown we're game for stalking Englishmen. What more hazardous time is there than when a man prepares to make a landing? Can you think of any other time when a man is more totally absorbed in flying for flying's sake? What better time for a prowling Tommy to move in on a German pilot? Eh? Tell me: what better time?"

Kunkel flinched visibly. He opened his mouth to speak but the words were long in coming. "I'm sorry, sir," he managed finally. He seemed to sag.

"Mueller would have been sorrier if he'd been picked off by a marauder while you buzzed your merry way."

"Yes, sir."

"Pack your gear. Kettering is preparing the papers posting you to FEA-1. There, perhaps, you may ultimately receive reassignment to another *Jasta*. If so, I hope you'll remember the lesson you learned here. That's all. You may go."

"Sir—"

"That's all."

When he was alone again, Heidemann sat down and gazed out the window. His annoyance with the Kunkel incident was done, an irretrievable part of the past. He sensed, though, that his annoyance with himself would continue.

After a while he turned to the desk and began a letter to Elfi.

Stachel opened his kit bag and removed the bottle of

114

whisky he had promoted from the *Gräfin*. He stared at it for some time, thinking—not about the whisky but about the borrowing from Kettering.

So that's where the bottle of Spanish brandy had come from. He remembered the dull surprise he'd felt when he'd awakened that morning and had seen it there on the table. The acid taste of the stuff had never appealed to him, so he always traded his ration of it for Kettering's second-grade cognac, since Kettering wasn't much of a drinker and therefore didn't care. Consequently, until today it had remained an open question as to how that bottle had arrived back home.

He wondered: *Jesus, how can I wander around borrowing bottles and not even remember it?*

CHAPTER **12**

STACHEL'S FIRST impression of the new machine was that the Fokker Company had designed a long casket, placed an engine at the front, a tail at the rear, square-ended wings to the sides and above, and landing wheels below. The D-7, in sum, had none of the gently curved lines and tapered sleekness that he had come unwittingly to admire in the Pfalz. The Fokker was big, angular, and thick-winged, and had a squarish nose. Its engine was partly exposed, and an exhaust stack jutted out to one side as if it had been an afterthought. Sitting there in the brilliant sun, the sweet spring breeze nudging its comma-shaped rudder into a dreamy, side-to-side swing, it struck him as being somewhat dowdy, and he felt a disappointment.

Ziegel's Bavarian sibilants sounded a monotone as he walked slowly up and down before the pilots seated on the grass. Stachel was reminded of a Spanish instructor he'd had at the *Gymnasium*, a smallish Latin type who

115

had always been torn between his efforts to conform to the stolid impassiveness of the German teaching form and his natural instincts to enthuse.

"You'll note, gentlemen," Ziegel was saying, "that the engine is the Mercedes D3-a, with a rated horsepower of one-sixty. This power plant is standard for the aircraft type. The machine itself, as you can see from the stencil on the fuselage, weighs some seven hundred kilos empty, and, with a payload of one-eighty kilos, a total of eight-eighty kilos. With twenty gallons of fuel and four of oil, she'll stay up for an hour and forty-five minutes."

As he droned along, lecturing on cantilever spars, balanced ailerons, and unequal chords, Stachel studied the machine in more subjective terms. In time, and at Heidemann's pleasure, in a cockpit like that one there, he would travel many high and lonely paths. Seated in the coffin, he would feel the fabric and metal and lacquer and petroleum and wire and wood become, slowly but inevitably, amalgamated extensions of his own flesh and nerve. Those twin guns, mounted atop the fuselage in a precise and malignant parallel, would constitute his power of debate wherever the god of war might lead. This machine, in its dull battle dress of muted greens and browns and pinks and violets, would serve as his testing place, a tiny laboratory in which the extremes of his courage and cowardice would daily be defined.

Late that afternoon he had his turn. The waiting had been interminable. Heidemann was the first to take the machine aloft, and upon his return he was smiling that faint smile that more and more served as a source of irritation for Stachel. The *Jasta* leader had designated the order in which the pilots were to fly, and it was with a sense of mixed despair and chagrin that Stachel had learned he was to be second from last. It was inconceivable that Heidemann could rate him so low on the list. Below even Schneider, the worry wart; below even Fritzinger, the timid; below even Von Klugermann, the one whose sole distinction was the freakish kill of four bombers that had been wandering, lost and out of fuel.

Only Ulrich, the sissy, was rated lower. He had expected, of course, that he would not be among the first, either to try the machine or to be awarded one—he had long since made up his mind to that. But this was ignominy.

He was still burning as he eased into the D-7's cockpit. After Schneider's return another refueling had been necessary, and precious minutes of daylight had been consumed during the additional wait.

Ziegel climbed onto the stirrup. His voice was pitched high to make himself heard over the engine.

"All right, Stachel, note the instrumentation. You have an auxiliary throttle lever here on the control column, along with the firing buttons—here. Main throttle control on the port side—here—magneto switches, fuel tank switches, hand pump"—he pointed in little jabbing motions—"altimeter, compass, fuel gauges, and tachometer. Machine-gun charge handles are within easy reach of—"

Stachel broke in. "For God's sake, Ziegel, I'm no idiot. I can see the charge handles."

Ziegel paused, his eyes narrowing. "What's eating you, sweetie?"

"None of your goddamned business. Just haul your ass off this aircraft and let me get going."

"You certainly are a pleasant fellow, aren't you, Stachel? Been eating more gravel?" he suggested with a smirk.

"Climb off."

"If I didn't have to return this barge I'd shove it up—"

Stachel cracked the throttle and the machine began to roll. Ziegel yelled something unintelligible, then swung off the step. The oncoming port elevator barely missed him as he fought for balance.

The Fokker's tail came up almost at once, and Stachel stirred with surprise. Collecting himself, he settled back to feel the machine. It was more immediately alive than any mechanical device he'd ever known. Once, when Oskar Frisenius had allowed him to drive his new Renault phaeton, he'd felt a similarly startling bewilderment; again, when first experiencing the recoil of his father's fowling piece he had had a fleeting impression that the gun held a separate life of its own. But this airplane offered no such momentary illusions; it strained to

117

be up and away with an urgency that continually communicated itself.

Absorbed now, Stachel gave the craft its head. The turf rushed by in a dun-colored blur; the undergear sprang easily with the accelerating jolts; the wheels spun in well-lubricated sighs as they topped the grass. Then, as the ground fell away and the nose lifted into the evening, he experienced the sensation of riding a darting fish in a clear and endless pool.

He laughed into the wind.

"Christ!"

He took the Fokker to three thousand meters, nearly breathless with the speed of the climb. The long flat rays of the sun were deep gold, and the earth was a mosaic of sharply contrasted yellows and purples. The rich, sweet exhaust mixture coming back from the engine was, in the high coolness, an ambrosia, and even up here he could identify the lacquer and oil and clean metal smells that spoke of the machine's virginal newness.

Circling back toward the field, he moved the control column forward, and the long nose, topped by its saucy little radiator fill cap, sank away. The deep earth colors came toward him, and the tingling of his downward rush was an unrelenting excitement. He pulled back, and the daubs of shadow and mounds of last light fell below and behind, the nose climbing steadily up the evening clouds to the royal blue beyond, to the zenith, to the golden sky, to the far-off but enormous wedge of sun, then back again to the twilight horizon. Again he looped, cutting back the engine as he hung against the seat belt, his head giddy with the blood rush, gently opening the throttle as he resumed the earthward plunge. As the D-7 flattened, he pulled back on the control yoke and shoved hard against the left rudder bar stirrup, and the machine snap-rolled to the left. He repeated the maneuver, this time to the right. Wingovers, stalls, chandelles, Immelmann turns, spirals, slow-rolls, and lazy-eights—he tried them all.

Never had he experienced such exhilaration, such intense pleasure. The airplane was magnificent. He began a long, fast climb, and, when he had gone high enough, he lifted the nose and reduced power until the entire machine shuddered. Kicking full rudder as it fell off, he waited, smiling, for the spin to begin. The soaring, weightless feeling came, then the horizon whirled, and the ground colors, separate and distinct at first, began to merge as the twisting began. For five full revolutions he let the craft fall, and the whipping and sighing were an exquisite insanity. Almost reluctantly, he recovered.

As he made his approach to the field, the engine burbling and the wind softly singing, he knew that nothing could match this incredible beast he commanded; he knew that there had been a courting and a mating.

Heidemann had stood apart from the others, squinting into the evening sky, his face a golden brown in the late light. Overhead, turning and lifting and rolling, its engine alternating between whispers and moans, the Fokker had been a tiny dark cross whose surfaces would send out sparkling beacons when occasionally they caught the low-lying sun.

Ordinarily the sight would have been a source of pleasure for him, but the depression he'd felt since receiving Elfi's letter was still too deep to set aside. Of all the strange letters she had sent him in recent months this had been the strangest. It had been full of rambling, disconnected, and nebulous philosophies; it had been, he felt, heavy with overtones of self-pity and bitterness; it had contained a caustic passage on the war and the hardships it was causing at home, immediately contradicted by a sentimental discourse on how any discomfort, any sacrifice, was worthwhile if it assured Germany's fighting men even the smallest advantage over the barbaric oppressors. But what disturbed him the most was the minute detail, the bizarre relish, with which she reported a suicide that had occurred in the apartment block. It wasn't good, he decided, for a woman to dwell on such things.

I must see her, he told himself, still watching the sky. *I must.*

With the way things were going, the American pressure building up and all, it would never do to request a leave right now. This he knew, and so knowing, dismissed the thought at once. A *Jasta* commander who took leave—even though well earned—when the issue in the field was so doubtful was no *Jasta* commander. He thought about that for a moment, but was distracted by a loud obscenity from the group nearby.

"Isn't that bastard *ever* coming down?" It was Ulrich, whose turn with the Fokker was last. "I'll be damned if I'll fly a strange machine in the *moonlight*."

Ziegel grunted. "I wish the son of a bitch would never come down."

"Pretty *inconsiderate,* I'd say," Ulrich complained in his effeminate, whining way.

Kettering laughed. "You don't think Stachel really has a considerate bone in his head, do you? Compared to him, a Hamburg pimp is an altruist."

Ziegel wondered, "Where do people like him come from? I mean, does he really enjoy being a pain in the ass?"

Kettering sat down on the sod, the harness of his false leg creaking loudly. "You know, I'm not so sure he does. You have to look hard, but there are some good points about him."

Ziegel snorted. "You name one and I'll do a clog dance on the Kaiser's belly button."

Kettering held up a finger. "I'll tell you one thing, gentlemen: *Herr* Stachel has the X-factor. He's got that, all right. Did you ever notice how he has the knack of getting people to talk about him? He can simply sit on his ass in a mud pile, and people will talk about him. There's something about Bruno Stachel that gets people going. He makes them mad, or he makes them snicker, or he makes them whatever; but never do they ignore him. It's the fattest case of the X-factor I've ever seen."

"Balls," Ziegel fretted.

"It's true. Look at us: I'd much rather be talking about the twenty-five positions in intercourse, myself. But no, we're gabbling along about Stachel. It's remarkable, I think."

"I think it's a sore on my sweet rounded buttocks. And so is he."

"By the way, which position do you favor, Ziegel?"

"An echelon—featuring a fast takeoff up the valley, followed by a series of low-level rolls."

"Any stalls?"

"Possibly. Somewhere along in the third day."

Ulrich sniggered. "You fellows are *crazy!*"

Heidemann watched the Fokker descend from the mackerel sky. After a time he said: "Ulrich?"

"Yes, sir?"

"Take your turn in the morning before the nine o'clock patrol. Ziegel, see that the D-7 is serviced, will you? I'm going to prepare for dinner."

As Heidemann walked toward his billet, he was mystified. It was ironic, really, how Kettering's idle conversation had congealed and organized so many abstruse elements, so many vague and nagging things over which he'd been puzzling for weeks now. The forest and the trees, he grumped silently. Kettering was right, of course. Stachel did have the X-factor. In great quantities, he had it. How could that key have been so evasive and difficult to perceive over these past weeks?

The restless watching, the uneasy guilt and discontent, the contradictions—they all tumbled into place and the plan took magical form.

For the first time since reading the letter, his spirits rose.

CHAPTER *13*

VON KLUGERMANN sat on the cot in his underwear, a field desk pulled close so he could write in relative comfort. Outside, the rain was a steady roar against the gables, and flickers of lightning made the night clouds an eerie, shifting backdrop for the restlessly dancing trees. He liked nights like these because he liked to write, and the sound of rain against a window seemed to gen-

121

erate a delicious dreaminess in which the words would come, fast and clear. It was, therefore, with a sense of irritation that he listened to someone come up the stairs, pause, then knock on his door. He hoped that whoever it was would not stay.

"Come in," he called resignedly.

It was Stachel. He stood in the doorway, his poncho streaming water, holding two bottles side by side and looking down the necks as if they were field glasses.

"Ahoy! Two bells for'rd of the starboard poopdeck! Periscope sighted through open fly!"

Von Klugermann, prepared to be quite cool, laughed despite himself at the ridiculous pose. He could see that Stachel's face was highly flushed.

"Oh, it's you. Well, come in, if you're going to. But I warn you: it's too late already, and I have some writing to do. So don't expect to stay long."

Stachel bowed deeply. "Of course, Your Royal Arrogance. However, I have fallen heir to this pair of slim-necked beauties whose maidenheads remain—as of this moment—challengingly intact. I thought you might like to help me rectify the situation. One for you, one for me."

Von Klugermann shook his head. "I'm not in the mood, Stachel. I don't know if you realize it, but you have just diverted a stream of consciousness in which priceless prose was being born."

"Well then, let's unleash a stream of unconsciousness." He dropped his steaming rain gear on the floor and placed the bottles on the desk. His smile was crooked.

"All right. I'll have one with you. But not that cheap stuff." Willi reached into his kit and withdrew a silver flask, then placed a pair of cups on the desk beside Stachel's bottles. Each poured his own. They touched cups, then drank.

"Ah, that's better. Much better." Stachel sank into a camp chair. "What are you writing?"

"I'm making some entries in my diary."

"Diary? Don't you know that's against regulations?"

"Yes, so I hear. But I also note that the late Baron von Richthofen's battle diary is already selling at fantastic rate at every bookstall in Germany. I feel, therefore, no

122

particular guilt in keeping track of my own modest affairs."

"You're going to have to go some if you expect your diary to outsell his."

"I don't plan to sell it. Von Richthofen had to. His family—although among the ins, as Uncle Hugo puts it —are as poor as church mice, you know."

"That's not the way I've heard it," Stachel said knowingly.

"I'm talking about real money."

"Like yours, you mean?"

"As you will."

"Must be nice to be stinking rich," Stachel suggested darkly.

"It has its points."

Stachel poured another drink. He stared into it, his eyes bright and restless. "What are you going to do after the war, Willi? Besides spend your money, I mean."

"I don't know. Write, I guess."

"Write what?"

"I've always wanted to take a turn at journalism. Not the junky pap you see in the penny sheets but more chewy kinds of things for opinion publications. And, I must confess, I have an idea that I may have a novel or two bubbling around inside. What about you?"

"I haven't thought about it much," Stachel lied. "But whatever it is, there'll be airplanes in the picture."

"You like airplanes, eh?"

"I like them."

"What do you think of the new Fokker?"

"It's all right, I suppose." He tossed off the drink and reached again for the bottle.

"You certainly seemed to enjoy it this afternoon. Ulrich was getting ready to pull you down with a rope."

"Ulrich is a silly pattycake. He can't even pull down a pair of bloomers."

Von Klugermann tried to visualize Ulrich pulling down a pair of bloomers. He couldn't.

"Why is the D-7 so important to you, Stachel?"

"It's part of a scheme."

"Oh? You have a scheme?"

123

"Doesn't everybody in this frigging world?"

Von Klugermann shrugged. "I suppose so. What's yours?"

"Money."

"I see. How do you propose to get it? With a D-7, that is."

"The D-7 is only the starting place."

"How so?"

"As I see it, to make money—make it, I say, not come into it the way a fat bastard like you comes into it just because he happens to be a particular fat bastard—to make money you've got to get attention first. I simply know that with a D-7 I can get some attention."

"How do you know that?"

"I just do."

"What comes after the D-7?"

"The Blue Max."

Von Klugermann smiled faintly. "Oh. You want the *Pour le Mérite,* eh? You want to be a hero."

"That's right."

The Prussian shook his head in sad amusement. "Stachel, my boy," he drawled, "the Blue Max is becoming common coin in our glorious flying corps, don't you realize that?"

"You don't have one."

"Of course not. And I won't. I'm a coward, actually. Medals are for suicidal idiots."

"You can say that. You and your frigging money."

"Money doesn't buy all the things you think it might."

Stachel sneered. "Oh, Christ's holy robe, don't give me that junk. You rich bastards give me a pain in the water pipe. You sit up to your navels in gold and make little preachments about how it's the real things in life that count. You keep telling the poor how really unrewarding and unhappy it is to have a lot of money so that the filthy beggars will feel sanctified and noble because of their filth and therefore be disinclined to reach out for part of your pile. You rich bastards make me want to puke."

"Then why do you want to become one of us rich bastards?"

"Because you have the power, that's why."

"Power? So it's really power you want?"

"Of course. Anybody who says he doesn't want power is a goddamned liar."

"Power to do what? What do you want power for?"

"To do as I want, when I want. To tell everybody to kiss my ass."

"Everybody? Who's everybody?"

"The whole frigging, lying, covetous, dirty, stinking world, that's who."

"Why are you so angry with the world?"

"Because it has the ins and the outs, that's why."

"You sound lik a Bolshevik. Why don't you join the Bolsheviks? If they succeed, you'll be riding high."

"I don't want anything to do with those crybabies. They stink like Russians, and I hate the goddamned Russians."

Von Klugermann lit a long, flat cigarette and exhaled twin streams of smoke from his nostrils. "You're a real hater, aren't you? But don't you find it somewhat unsatisfying to hate so indiscriminately? I, for instance, have very few hatreds, but I cherish those I do have because I've thought them through and have decided I can intellectually and morally afford them."

Stachel's eyes were red and puffy. One of the bottles was nearly empty, and he shook it before he poured another drink. "Anybody can afford to hate anybody."

"Not so. And I'm not speaking in the purely moral sense. To be effective, any emotion must be selective. What is the opposite of hate? Love, of course. Would you derive real satisfaction from loving everybody, so to speak? I doubt it. Your love, like your hate, would become onerous because of its very copiousness. The world is currently going through what is called an orgy of hate, but if you'll listen to people—not merely to the words but what's behind the words—you'll see that the hatred, once so piquant and exciting, has long since palled."

Stachel grinned lopsidedly. "Like sex, eh? The first couple of times are fine. Then the rest of the night you wonder how you can break off with the least amount of embarrassment all around."

"Precisely."

"Here's to sex."

"Pros't."

Von Klugermann drew deeply on the cigarette and studied the stream he blew at the ceiling. "After the war, Stachel, there will be an international parallel to your night of sex. The thought's not new, of course, but nobody wins a war any more than one partner wins the struggle of the copulative couch. The man may experience considerable physical gratification, the woman none. You might say, then, that the man comes out the winner. But does he? I don't think so. He's had a momentary triumph of the nervous complex, which later leaves him embarrassed and more than likely disgusted. The woman, though, has made a moral conquest; she knows that although the combat has left her physically beaten she has made the man responsible. She knows he may spend the rest of his life attempting to fulfill his sense of obligation to her. No matter who wins the physical battles of this war, the other side is going to react in woman fashion."

"Do you think we'll win?"

Von Klugermann smiled. "I don't think we have a chance, *Junge.*"

"That's traitor talk."

"So have me arrested. It's true."

"It had better not end too soon."

"So you can become a hero?"

"Something like that."

"Well, I hope you make it."

"I will. Let's have another drink."

"Let's see you get out of here. I've some writing to do." Von Klugermann was aware that Stachel had become very drunk, and he was anxious to be rid of him. Drunken people always made him nervous. "Good night, Stachel," he said firmly.

"Good night, you rich bastard. I hope you choke on your money."

"Stachel?" His voice was soft.

"Well?"

"You don't hate the world. You hate yourself because you don't understand where you fit in this world."

"Piss on you."

Stachel walked stiffly into the office, a singing in his ears, a heat baking behind his face. Only one lamp burned, and Rupp slouched below it with a newspaper on his knee. His lips moved as he read.

"I thought I'd find you here, Rupp."

"Want something? Sir." The man peered up, squinting against the raw light.

"Get off your ass when you talk to me, you pig."

Rupp folded the newspaper carefully, removed the cigar from his mouth with his little finger extended delicately, placed them both on the desk, then stood. His face was blank.

"Want something? Sir."

"Von Klugermann and I will fly an extra tomorrow at ten-forty-five. Put it down."

"As ordered. Sir."

"And for the same time the day after tomorrow."

"Can't do it. Sir. The new Fokkers are coming in the day after tomorrow, and the *Jastaführer* has suspended operations for that morning."

Stachel wavered slightly. "How many new Fokkers?"

"Five."

"Any assignments made yet?"

Rupp's lip registered a faint sneer. "You'll have to ask the *Jastaführer* about that. Sir."

"How did you get to be such a pig, Rupp? A slovenly, smirking pig?"

"Lucky, I guess."

Stachel slurred, "You get around to the village a good bit, don't you?"

Rupp hesitated, straining to follow the new course the conversation was taking. "A bit, now and then. Sir."

"Want to make some extra money?"

"How's that?"

"I'll pay you ten per cent for every bottle of acceptable liquor you can dig up. I know those French pigs you wallow with have it. You bring me a bottle, I'll give you a ten-per-cent markup."

Rupp's sneer became more obvious. "Don't you officers get a ration?"

127

"Don't ask questions, you smart-aleck son of a bitch. Do you want the money or don't you?"

"I want the money."

"Well, then. Start tomorrow."

"There's only one thing. It's against the rules for me to sell officers anything."

"Who'll know?"

"I might be seen making the—ah—deliveries."

"Well, we'll meet some place. How about that stone bridge over the creek?"

"That'll do, I guess."

"Each day at dusk. Be there. And, Rupp—"

"Yes? Sir."

"Stop acting so goddamned superior. You're a pig. A bootlegging pig who sells himself for ten per cent."

He wandered out into the rain, laughing.

CHAPTER *14*

THE SPADS had come out of nowhere, fat, stub-winged, and fast. It was the first time Stachel had directly encountered the Spad, a French machine that the British seemed to favor on occasion. He had been horribly sick that morning, and had barely been able to pull himself from his cot, even after a heavy dose of brandy. He had thrown up twice, a rare event for him, and he had avoided the mess hall, heading directly to his machine at the end of the line so as to escape the *Jastaführer's* questioning eyes. Throughout the uneventful low-level *Jasta* run he had remained queasy and shaky, cursing himself for failing to bring along a bottle. Behind the physical upset, the anxiety and remorse had been the most severe he had ever experienced. Upon landing he had virtually run to his billet and had gulped a great quantity of white wine, pausing only to fill his flat flask with the good cognac. It had helped considerably, and, after completing his combat report and checking on the refueling of the Pfalz, he had felt somewhat human again. He and Von Klugermann had climbed away from the field on their extra at five minutes to eleven—ten minutes late.

The five Spads had jumped them above the clouds when they had completed the southeasterly leg of their swing and were preparing to turn northeast toward Cambrai. One minute the sky had been empty; the next, the Englishmen were all around them, snapping like terriers.

It did not take Stachel long to sense that the Tommies weren't of the most experienced breed. They scattered their attacks, they wheeled widely on recoveries, they tended to get in the way of one another. He selected one Spad and gave it his full attention.

The Englishman was a great one for acrobatics. As Stachel rolled the Pfalz into a *Kurvensturz,* eying the Spad over his top wing, the Tommy did a slow roll for no apparent reason. This enabled Stachel to close the gap with gratifying speed, and his first burst for range startled the other pilot into a ridiculous snap-roll. His second burst for effect needled through the Spad's lower wing just abeam of the cockpit. He could see the Englishman's white face looking backward at him. The Spad, incredibly, attempted a loop, and as it hung high on its back, Stachel fired again. This time the tracers danced around the center section and he could see pieces flying. The enemy machine never recovered from its inverted attitude, but mushed down the sky, upside down and spinning wildly, a fire flaring brightly from its engine louvers.

Stachel took inventory.

Von Klugermann was just putting the finishing touches to one of the Englishmen, whose machine collapsed and tumbled end-over-end toward the cloud floor. A third Spad had preceded it, a huge blob of flame whose only resemblance to an airplane came from the stubs of wings that jutted from its core. So the fat Prussian had scored twice, Stachel once. A good bit of shooting all around.

Stachel reached into the seat cushion, assembled his siphoning gear, and drank deeply of the cognac. The remaining Spads were scurrying west, tails high.

As they headed home, Stachel was sullenly pensive.

129

The new Fokkers would arrive tomorrow. Once again he reviewed the list. Heidemann, of course, would keep one for himself, leaving four others to be distributed. Mueller would get one because, next to Heidemann, he was the *Jasta*'s high scorer. Braun, Mueller's eternal chess partner, no doubt would get one because of his exceptional skill at *Kette* tactics—he was even contributing to a manual on the subject; a fourth would go to Huemmel, now well recovered from his illness, who was simply a good, all-round pilot with a comfortable score. The fifth— that was the puzzle. Ulrich, Fritzinger, and Schneider could be considered out of the race, as could the two new replacements, Hochschild and Nagel. That left Von Klugermann and himself. Willi's score as of this morning stood exactly even with his own. Counting the two Spads he'd just nailed, the Prussian was now ahead by one.

Stachel thought about this for long minutes. Then, nodding once to himself, he eased back on the throttle.

He pulled on the machine gun charge handles, threw in the clutch, then fired a brief, stuttering burst.

Von Klugermann turned in his seat and let the Albatros fall back alongside. Stachel reached out and thumped the side of his fuselage, then pointed ahead to his engine. He repeated the gestures, but this time motioned to Von Klugermann to go on without him. The Prussian stared across at him questioningly, the wind distorting his cheeks. Stachel repeated the signals for a third time, then dropped away. He noted with satisfaction that Von Klugermann made no attempt to follow.

When the Pfalz had sunk into the cloud blanket, Stachel pulled up and restored power. He retained his altitude just below the surface of the mist and headed toward the airdrome at full throttle. Once or twice he permitted the Pfalz to rise to the cloud surface, stalking, he smiled to himself, like a U-boat. In these fleeting intervals he could see Von Klugermann's Albatros continuing its lonely course.

As the Prussian's dirty brown machine began a wide spiral, Stachel went into a fast power-glide, the sunlight surrendering to the solid gray vapor that formed beads of water on his face and rivulets on the surfaces of the Pfalz. The blind descent seemed interminable.

He broke free eventually, but noted in sodden satisfaction that the ground mists had all but obscured the field, just as he'd hoped they would. He took another long pull from the hose, waiting, his cheeks tight with brandied numbness.

The Albatros appeared finally, and as Stachel hung at the fringe of the overcast, he watched Von Klugermann make a tentative, exploratory circle above the lower haze. The Prussian arced around again and began a long power-glide. He had obviously elected to avoid the poplars and make his approach from the opposite end of the field. Stachel, feverishly alert, made rapid revisions to his calculations. Satisfied then, he gave the Mercedes full throttle and slanted down the sky toward the pocket of mist. When he saw Von Klugermann's propeller slow from a hardly visible blur into a windmilling of blades, he also cut power. The Pfalz's wires moaned with the speed of its otherwise silent plunge.

The Albatros sank out of sight into the fog, and the Pfalz was close behind.

Straining, Stachel could make out the shadowy outline of Von Klugermann's machine ahead. As the haze grew thinner and ground detail appeared to float by in enlarged and wispy procession, the Albatros began to correct and ease away from the long finger of the factory chimney that reached upward through the mist to the right front. It was then, hovering directly above and to the left rear, that Stachel fed full power to the Mercedes.

To Von Klugermann, whose open-mouthed, wild stare was clear even from the Pfalz, the sound must have been like that of an express train.

The Albatros went into a frantic turn with full power on, its nose high. As Stachel's machine screamed for altitude, he saw the Albatros' wings slam into the chimney, dissolving in a ghastly tangle and sending a shower of bricks cascading through the air. Then there was a muffled explosion below, and the mist brightened with an unearthly glow.

"Now go over this again for me, Stachel. Just what happened?" Heidemann leaned across the desk, his face stony.

"We were jumped by five Spads above Bernes. In the fight, the enemy lost three. We—"

"Who knocked down the Spads?"

"I got all three of them."

"What was Von Klugermann doing all this time?"

"Well, we were up to our hips in Spads. He gave a good account of himself, of course, but I was luckier in the shooting department."

"Then what happened?" Heidemann demanded.

"We returned here, but on the way my machine acted up. A vapor lock, I think. I signaled Willi to go on, since there was nothing he could do and I didn't want to risk him in the nearby air while I made a forced landing through that deep overcast."

"Yes?"

"Well, I straightened out the trouble, then came on back here. I decided to avoid the usual approach over the trees because of the mist. As I made my final glide, Willi's machine suddenly appeared right in front of me. I turned on full power and he did likewise. However, I guess he didn't see the chimney and flew right into it. . . ."

Kettering came into the office.

"Well?"

"Sir, the *Flugmeldedienst* confirms three Spads. They fell in a triangle near an antiaircraft battery at L-Twenty. But because of the overcast they couldn't trace the action." He looked at Stachel. "I suppose you'll have to console yourself with another moral victory."

Heidemann said in a warning tone: "Do you doubt Stachel's claim, Kettering?"

The big man's face reddened. "Why, no, sir. But the rules—"

"The wreckage of three Spads has been found. *Leutnant* Stachel claims the victories. Do you doubt his word?" His voice was flat.

"Well, of course not, sir, but—"

"Credit Stachel with the three Spads and send the claim forms, with my endorsement, to *Kofl*. At once."

Kettering wallowed hard. "Yes, sir."

"And arrange a full military burial ceremony for *Leutnant* von Klugermann."

After Kettering had left, Stachel sat in tense silence while Heidemann studied some papers on his desk. The *Jasta* leader signed his name twice, then looked up, a smile in his eyes.

"No doubt you've heard that the first five Fokkers arrive tonight."

"I admit I've heard the rumor."

"It's no rumor. And one of them will be yours, of course."

Stachel barely restrained a smile. "That's fine, sir. I wasn't certain you'd consider me eligible. . . ."

"Why?"

"Well, on those tryouts I was next to last, and knowing your habit of assigning all such things in descending order of merit—"

Heidemann laughed easily, shaking his head. "Stachel, you amuse and baffle me. You are so infernally sensitive, so wont to evaluate events in terms of your own egoism. If you had just used a little sense instead of emotion you'd have seen that I established the Fokker tryout sequence on a purely alphabetical basis."

Stachel was conscious of a roaring in his head.

"And, Stachel, let me point out that, next to me, you are the best pilot in this *Jasta*. It would have been asinine not to assign a Fokker to you after that spectacular exhibition you gave with it. Now—you've had a busy day. Take a rest. But first, I suggest you go by Von Klugermann's quarters and pull together his personal gear. I want you to compose a note to go with it when it's sent to the family. After all, you were Willi's friend."

"Yvette," Rupp said, "roll a bit this way. There. That's better."

He made the exposure, satisfied for the moment. He stood for a long time, his eyes distant, as if he listened to something far beyond the farmhouse walls. He nodded once to himself, ignoring the idle chatter of the two women. Then, returning to the business at hand, he readjusted the camera and walked to the threadbare couch.

"Now, Yvette, let Dominique take the couch again for this last one."

The little brunette pouted. "But, monsieur," she complained, "you have already made so many of her. I thought I was the one who appealed."

"Yes, you appeal a great deal. But my client has not yet seen Dominique, and so we all stand to gain by favoring her in these new ones. So shut up and give her the couch."

The tall one arranged herself and smiled. "Like this, m'sieur?"

Rupp considered the scene, shaking his head. "It's too much like the others." He stepped backward, fingers to his chin, lips pursed, as if he were an artist evaluating a half-finished canvas. "No, for this one we'll have the two of you. Yvette, move in and make love."

"Zut! I am a man-girl, not a girl-girl!"

"All right, so you are. But the camera and the client make no such distinction. Just pose. If you make it good we should get a premium price for your several moments of make-believe."

The tall one laughed. "Come on, Yvette. It can be fun, really. Come. Relax, and I'll show you."

"But if someone should see—my reputation—"

Rupp chuckled absently. "No one will see but the client. He is a fat, one-legged pig who gathers these things like a squirrel and shares them with none. Would you begrudge a fat man his illustrated daydreams? Especially when he pays us so well?"

Yvette tossed her head. "You said he was a painter. For art, I pose. But for a filthy, peeping—"

"I'll double your share of the fee."

"Well—"

"And I'll bring you a jar of jam."

She shrugged and got on with it. Once, while Rupp tinkered with the big army camera, she spoke, her voice muffled by the embrace.

"It doesn't seem very much."

"What?"

"The fee. For something like this, I mean."

Dominique giggled. "It's the easiest money there is."

134

"Shut up, you two, and hold the pose. I'm about ready."

"Money is everything, isn't it?"

"Shut up, I said. And raise your right leg a bit. Yes. Like that, but keep the knee bent. He'll want to see."

He concentrated, whistling softly between his teeth.

"You're right, my pigeon. Money is everything. Enough of it could make even me happy, and that's a tall order."

He continued to work silently for a time, then, seemingly unable to control an inner exultation, he laughed outright.

"And today," he said thickly, raising a hand and whispering theatrically, "today in the mist, I found my way to happiness."

He made the picture then, still laughing. After a protracted pause he said, again as if to himself: "I honestly believe I've found the way. No more underground mail duty. No more filthy pictures. No more conniving of cheap swill for drunken officers. No more. And if it works, ladies, I'll treat you each to the grandest roast pork dinner you ever had."

"You, m'sieur," Yvette said, sitting up, "are crazy."

"No," he grunted. "Not crazy. Heartened. The tall order is to be filled at last."

"Crazy."

CHAPTER *15*

VON KLUGERMANN's personal effects were Spartan, considering his great wealth. In addition to the extra uniforms, the dress boots and bathrobe, there were a razor with stag horn handle, brush and comb with his initials inset in the mother-of-pearl, a piece of soap (which Stachel slipped into his pocket), a small mirror, a nail file, three volumes that appeared to be in English, a Bible, a silver flask half full of whisky (which Stachel drained), and the diary.

Lying on the cot, Stachel opened this. The Prussian's script was small and neat, his language easy but precise. In moments, Stachel had become absorbed, and he read for a long time. Once he laughed at length. When, finally, he closed the fat book, he sat up and laughed again.

Aloud, he said thickly: "Well, Willi, you've given me my first leg on some real cash."

It was the first patrol with the new Fokkers. Heidemann was at the apex of the *Kette,* his D-7 lifting and falling on the thermals. Stachel and Mueller held the outside left and right. The day was faultless, with a stunning indigo sky and warm sun, and the earth below was a gigantic table of pleasant greens and browns and purples. The engines made a deep bass rumble, and the early summer wind sang sweetly.

For Stachel, nothing was wrong on this delightful afternoon. After his acquisition of Von Klugermann's astonishing diary the evening before, he had bathed, shaved, and dressed to the hilt. He had enjoyed a full dinner at mess—the first in many days—and the chattering and joshing the others had used to mask the afternoon's tragic accident had been amusing. He had even joined in, and the others, convinced that he, too, was attempting to absorb the shock of his unfortunate role in Willi's demise, had cooperated by laughing overly loud and long at his jokes. He had ended dinner with only one cordial, and, drinking nothing more, had turned in for the best night's sleep since February. He had awakened this morning, refreshed and eager for the feel of the Fokker—his own Fokker. The D-7's had arrived on the railroad siding the previous evening, and Ziegel and his *Abteilung* had worked throughout the night to uncrate and assemble them. By three o'clock, the five glistening craft had been poised in a muttering, businesslike line before Heidemann's office shack, and the entire personnel roster had turned out to wave them off.

The thick wings of Heidemann's Fokker were rocking. Stachel eyed the *Justaführer* closely.

Heidemann, sitting high in his cockpit, pointed at him, then at Mueller. Next his hand traced a little circle in the air above his head, then thrust downward and to the right. Stachel followed the line of the pointing arm and saw the three observation balloons. They were in a line, about four kilometers apart, swaying like fat grubs. Even as he watched they began to bob as the winches below sought to wind them in. He glanced at Mueller at the far side of the V. Mueller's buck teeth showed in a grin as his Fokker tilted over in a rocketing peel-off.

Laughing, Stachel followed.

Between the machine guns and beyond the flickering rocker arms, the earth came up. Mueller's machine was well out in front, diving in a clean, breathless arc. The air ahead became stained with an antiaircraft barrage —pale yellow flashes first, then puffs of white smoke followed by claps of concussion. A delicate netting of tracer trails formed amidst the blooming air-bursts.

They pulled out just above the trees and raced for the first balloon. As Mueller's Fokker leveled off, it staggered, one wing high. Flame raged along its fuselage, and Stachel sensed rather than saw the sluggish roll, the skidding impact, the cartwheeling, the bouncing, the shattering and final explosion. Then the first balloon was ahead, filling his center section. His initial burst was low, and he raised the nose. His second stream of incendiaries stitched up and across the swollen gray bag. There was a soft whoomp, and, as his head was pressed down between his shoulders in the centrifugal force of his vertical turn, he felt a wash of heat from below.

He was in the clear and roaring flat out for the second balloon. The zigzags of a trench system flashed below his wheels, a road junction, a forest of barbed wire, a line of poplars, a cluster of farm buildings, a creek, a railroad, and then he was firing again. The big gas bag, close to the ground now, seemed to fold in on itself as a mountainous roll of flame and smoke shot skyward. He saw the observer topple away, the thin parachute trip line trailing behind him from the tossing wicker basket. The Fokker darted through the smoke column, bouncing badly in the uprush of heat, and he nearly lost control. But he corrected quickly in the bright sun, and, nosing down slightly, he picked up a few knots of speed for the final rush.

The third balloon exploded almost atop its winch, and Stachel could see the figures of men running from under the descending shower of fire.

He could have turned right on his climb away, but on whim he went to the left. As he did so, a Spad, rushing along in a steep slant, sat directly ahead, the angle of deflection as perfect as if it had been a lantern slide at gunnery school. He fired a burst of ten rounds through pure reflex, and was incredulous when the Spad disintegrated, sprinkling its parts toward every point of the compass.

A second Spad came in off his beam, its guns chattering. Stachel kicked the D-7 into a wrenching chandelle and came around off the Britisher's right rear. He fired once, but the shots were wide, ticking along the Spad's left wing. The Englishman attempted a vertical bank to the right, but he had sunk too low and instead flew at full throttle into a tree.

Stachel headed east, still at full speed, not climbing until he was well behind the German lines. For the first time he took count. Three balloons and two Spads.

It was a fine day, indeed.

To celebrate, he treated himself to a huge drink.

Kettering and Ziegel were dug in at their usual positions at the bar. The phonograph was mercifully silent, and Braun sat alone at the chess board, stolidly playing Mueller's men against his own. He was icily drunk. Ulrich and the new man, Nagel, were tossing darts.

"I've got a belly-ache," Kettering announced vaguely. "World's biggest ache."

"I think it was those queer preserves Gretchen sent me."

"Oh? Speaking of queer things, how is she doing with that fellow in the beret?"

"Very funny."

"I'm the funniest."

"How could he be a queer? You saw what he was doing in the picture."

"Yes, but who else would wear a beret at a time like that?"

They fell silent for a while.

Ziegel stirred and said: "Stachel's a bullet-catcher, all right."

"How so?"

"You should have seen that D-7 when he brought it back today. It looked like a piccolo. We'll be patching all night. They say he did quite a job out there today. Three balloons and two Spads, singlehanded."

"Mm. Confirmed by the *Jastaführer,* no less. Which is nothing new, of course," Kettering added blandly.

"What do you mean?"

"The *Jastaführer* tends to be lavish when it comes to *Herr* Stachel. He confirmed those three Spads on Willi von Klugermann's last run on Stachel's word alone."

"Strange. Old Proper-ass usually requires an affidavit from the Holy See."

"Yes. But stop me if you've heard this before: the X-factor is at work for *Herr* Stachel."

"I've heard it before."

"Then why didn't you stop me?"

They drank slowly, analyzing the mirror. Kettering grunted, then chuckled.

"What's the matter with you? Piles?"

"No. I just happened to think of a story I heard in the States. I guess the balloons reminded me of it."

"How does it go?"

"Well, it loses something in the translation, but there's this big circus being held in New Orleans—that's a city down in the South. The big event is a balloon ascension. A fellow in white tights, gold spangles, and a fancy gold helmet with thingamajigs all over it climbs into the basket and the balloon goes up amidst much cheering. However, the bag gets caught in a stiff wind and drifts for miles. Finally it comes down in a cotton patch where a bunch of black Americans are working. Being a superstitious lot, they take one look at the balloon and disappear in a cloud of dust. All except one very old fellow who sim-

139

ply hasn't got the steam to run. He stands there, transfixed, as the chap in the white tights climbs out of the basket. Finally the little old man lifts his hat and says, his knees shaking: 'Good morning, Master Jesus. How's your papa?' "

Kettering guffawed.

Ziegel, stony-faced, said, "As you say, it loses something."

"Well, in Yankee English, it goes like this: 'Mo'nin', Massah Jesus, how's you' paw?' And to Yankees, that's very funny."

"No wonder we're at war with them."

They realized suddenly that Stachel was at the bar. Neither had heard him come in. They traded nods with him, but the air was tense. They could tell he was very drunk.

"You speak English pretty well, eh, Kettering?"

"So-so."

"Do me a favor?"

"What is it?"

Stachel took out a stub of pencil and a combat report form. Steadying himself against the bar, he scrawled a brief phrase. He handed the paper to Kettering, weaving slightly.

"How do you say this in English? In the fewest possible words, that is."

Kettering read, then looked up at Stachel. "My, my. That's a dirty word. A dirty two words, I should say."

"Write them down. In block letters."

Kettering shrugged, then, tongue between his lips, traced out one four-letter word and a second one with three.

"There you are. They're not very complimentary, I might mention. Say those two words in polite society and the English will seal your ass in paraffin."

"Good." He turned to Ziegel, his eyes hot. "Ziegel, I want you to paint my Fokker. Jet black all over, except for the national markings, which you can outline in white."

"Jet black? All over? It's against the rules."

"Von Richthofen had an all-red machine, didn't he?

And all the people in his *Jasta* are still using the color, aren't they?"

"Yes, but that's *Jasta* 11. Heidemann wouldn't stand for it. He demands we stay with standard factory colors."

"I already have Heidemann's permission. He said to tell you it would be all right."

"Well, all black it is, then," Ziegel murmured, frowning.

"And one other thing: in large white block letters, running the full chord of the top wing, I want you to paint on these letters, just the way Kettering wrote them."

Kettering snickered. "You'll have every Tommy in France running after you."

"That's the idea."

Ziegel shook his head doubtfully. "This is going to take awhile. . . ."

Stachel shrugged. "Certainly. Just so it's all done by tomorrow morning."

"Are you insane? It'll take until dawn simply to patch the holes in that Schweizer cheese of yours. And my men haven't even had their meal yet, let alone a rest."

"I want a black airplane carrying these two words on the top wing by tomorrow morning at ten o'clock. If it isn't ready I'll put another crack in your backside."

"All right, sweetie. Black is your color, to be sure."

It was early evening when he met Rupp by the stone bridge. The *Uffz* wheeled up on his bicycle, the one with the big basket on the steering bar. His gaze was oblique.

"How long will it take you, Rupp?" he demanded.

"I don't know. The stuff is getting pretty scarce around town. The Frenchies are starting to jack up their prices, too."

"Pay them. Here, you'd better take this, in case you need it."

"I've got enough money. Enough for their junky grape juice," Rupp said glumly.

"Well, hurry then. And listen, if it's all the same to you, we'll stop these meetings. You just get the stuff directly to my quarters and I'll pay you the following morning. Nobody will ask any questions. I promise you."

Rupp took the cigar from his mouth, regarded it speculatively for a moment, then spat. "You really put the stuff away, don't you? Sir."

"That's my business."

"That's your problem, I'd say."

"Don't get smart with me, goddamn it. You're getting your cut."

"You'd be in bad shape if you had to go bumming around the village for your own sauce, wouldn't you? German officer—rapping on back doors like a vagrant? Heidemann would love that, wouldn't he?"

"I said don't get smart. Where else could you get such an easy ten per cent?"

"Twenty-five per cent. As of now, it's twenty-five per cent."

"You're a goddamned pirate."

"You're a goddamned sot."

Stachel was shaking, his eyes glassy with fury. "Get going, you bastard, before I kill you."

"Ta-ta. Sir."

For a long time he waited, and he kept off the gnawing despair with the Spanish he had brought in the pocket flask. The sky had turned a soft rose, and the sun was a great yellow disc caught in the snarl of trees on the rise across the road. The small river gurgled the quiet sounds of deep, swift currents. He wasn't drunk, nor was he sober. Rather, his nipping had suspended the deadness in him and his mind registered plodding, disconnected thoughts. He despised himself for bringing Rupp into his privacy like this, but the *Jasta* supply was limited and always rationed and therefore never enough. So their pact had been sealed, and still another facet had been carved on the nugget of guilt under Stachel's ribs. Standing there now, the brandy sullen within him, he was aware of the abysmal guilt for the first time and for the thousandth time.

A gaggle of schoolchildren came down the road, pushing and shoving and shouting that insane language of the region. Stachel turned his back on them to lean over the bridge and stare at the black water below. Each note of their voices, each scuff of their shoes, each suck of their panting laughter was a corruption, a violation of his nerves. As he fixed his eyes on the current, there was a whoop, a sudden hush, then a splash. He had sensed the rolling of a checkered skirt and the slithering of a book down the river bank. The book floated. The skirt went out of sight in a sodden whirling.

Unthinking, he tore off his coat and vaulted the stone railing. The water was ether-cold and he fought to retain his breath in the rushing darkness. His uniform pulled heavily and his boots were leaden. He blinked his eyes in the murkiness, straining for another glimpse of the skirt. Gasping, he surfaced, oriented himself, then returned below. His boots touched bottom, lifted, touched and scraped again as the stream grew shallower. In his numbness, it was suddenly a matter of great importance that he find the skirt. He struggled in feverish outrage against the vision of a child bumping along the cold dark rocks of a miserable back-country creek, coughing out a life that hadn't really begun.

You! You pastor's God! You can't get away with this!

He found the skirt and the icy-slick legs it enclosed. It tore, and he lost it for a hideous moment, then he had it again, and he was splashing through the rocks to the marshy grass beyond. He dropped beside the girl, retching. Eventually someone threw a great warm coat over him, a coat that smelled of cigars.

Rupp was astride the sprawling youngster, his hands pounding her back. Stachel shivered and gagged as he watched.

Rupp's cigar waggled. "Stachel, you're absolutely the nuttiest cookie that ever came out of the oven."

"Go to hell, you bastard."

"Absolutely the nuttiest."

The girl coughed and began to cry.

Stachel said: "Where's my cognac?"

CHAPTER 16

HEIDEMANN HAD to admit that the Fokker looked impressively ominous in its coat of black paint. As he sat in the cockpit of his own idling D-7, waiting for Stachel to get settled, he smiled to himself over the vanity of men, particularly very young men. It had always seemed a bit absurd to him that a serious, responsible, and altogether businesslike fellow such as Manfred von Richthofen could have permitted himself an all-red aircraft. Heidemann was familiar with Von Richthofen's officially professed reason: red was easy to spot in a dogfight, thereby facilitating recognition and so on. But he suspected the real truth was that the Baron had been vain, vain enough to believe that his red machine would become sufficiently well known to strike fear into the hearts of the British. Aside from the fact that the English took a lot of scaring (and certainly would not be abashed by mere color), the idea was silly for a more practical reason. Things happened so fast in combat it was difficult enough to recognize friend and foe by outline, let alone by a single characteristic such as a splash of color. (What would the Baron have done if everybody had started using red?) For these reasons he had been amused by Stachel's request to have his Fokker painted black. Expecting a Richthofen-like rationalization when he'd asked Stachel why, he had laughed outright at the answer: "Because, goddamn it, sir, a black airplane gets attention." Most importantly, though, a black airplane for Stachel would be another link in the chain of his own, private little plan, so he had been happy to approve the request.

He noted that Stachel's Fokker was not all black. There seemed to be white stripes painted on the upper wing between the national markings. They appeared to be letters, but he couldn't make them out from this angle.

Stachel waved, so Heidemann opened the throttle and gave the D-7 its head.

Once aloft and headed west, Heidemann waited for the black machine to close in on him, then settled himself for some thinking. Twice he smiled, and once he actually grinned. He decided that with luck it should work quite well, all things considered. His main struggle would be to remain patient.

He was still deep in thought when he noticed Stachel directly alongside. He sat up, alert now to Stachel's waving and pointing. Below, sliding along at medium altitude, were three DeHavilland 9's—big, broad-winged day bombers. They flew arrogantly low for DeHavillands, and Heidemann once again shrugged at the unpredictable English. Amazing fellows, really. He pointed to Stachel, watching impassively across the gap. Then he pointed to the left. He tapped himself on his leather helmet, then pointed to the right. He could see Stachel's acknowledging nod. With no further sign, they split apart in gigantic, singing arcs, each slanting down the sky at the Tommy wedge from opposite quarters. The engine noise was strident and overwhelming.

Heidemann hurtled in from the English flight's left front, keeping below the enemy's course. He singled out the leading machine, and the aiming point of his sights wavered along the DeHavilland's left lower wing to the wing root, to the center section. He thumbed the trips. His guns stuttered once, then were silent. He cursed bitterly, and in stupefied surprise. Furiously, he clawed at the charging handles, but neither would budge, so he rolled over on his back and fell out of the tangle. Safely aside and below, he struggled with the Spandaus, but they were hopelessly jammed. He threw an anxious glance at Stachel.

The black machine was climbing at a dazzling speed, coming up below the Englishmen with its guns chattering. The DeHavillands, following customary two-seater tactics, held their V formation, seeking to cover one another with their free-swinging Lewis guns. But Stachel was having none of that. He was coming in from the rear

145

lower quarter, where he was hard to see and harder to hit. Despite his anger at having to stand by helplessly, Heidemann felt grim approval. He observed that the English planes moved sluggishly, presumably due to their full load of bombs.

Stachel's guns hammered again, a trail of powder smoke spinning out behind the up-rushing Fokker. They drummed a third time.

The leading DeHavilland exploded. It was there, then it wasn't. A huge ball of red-tinted, oily smoke hung in the air, sprinkling small dark things. The right outside machine teetered off to one side, badly damaged from the blast; it went into a tight spin as the left half of its wings folded up alongside the fuselage. The remaining two-seater dumped its bombs, then fell away in an erratic spiral. It recovered sufficiently to begin a series of confused turns.

Stachel, Heidemann smiled, was a great one for getting two stags with one arrow. How he and Von Richthofen had laughed that day over Stachel's carom shot with the Bristols. . . .

But apparently Stachel wasn't finished. The black D-7 rolled out of its climb, went into a fast vertical bank and sliced menacingly at the surviving English machine. Instead of trimming out into a gunnery run, however, it swept into a wide turn around the drifting enemy. The sun glinted dully on the slanted wing surfaces, and Heidemann could barely make out a legend blocked out on the upper one. It was meaningless to him.

He sat up when he saw the English observer secure his guns, then hold his arms high above his head. The big biplane was smeared with oil all along its starboard side.

"I'll be double-damned. Stachel's got himself a prisoner!" His words were lost in the wind.

Laughing, he closed in to take up a position on the left flank of the now eastward-bound DeHavilland. Stachel's black machine soared easily along on the opposite quarter.

Stachel's head was hunched down, and he didn't answer Heidemann's wave.

The English fliers sat on two of the converted packing crates across from Heidemann's desk. One, the taller of the two, had a lean, aesthetic face topped by a tuft of silken hair whose color matched exactly the burnished leather of his knee-length flying coat. The other was an Irish type—fair-skinned, with green eyes, blue-black hair, and a neatly trimmed mustache. They sat stolidly, thin-lipped and determined.

So this, Heidemann reflected, was the enemy. Change their khaki for *Feldgrau* and you'd have a pair of *Jasta* members. He was swept by a renewed sense of the idiocy of men like himself devoting every waking hour to schemes calculated to slay men like these. But such thoughts were dangerous, and so he motioned to Kettering, who stood by the window, trying to look grim and military.

"Tell them we are honored to have them as our guests."

Kettering's voice rattled some English. The two exchanged glances, then the black-haired one—obviously the aircraft commander—stared levelly at him and spoke.

"What did he say?"

Kettering cleared his throat and said, "It's difficult to translate precisely, sir."

"Well, what's the sense of his comment?"

Kettering thought for a moment. "It comes out something like 'go copulate with yourself.'"

Heidemann remained expressionless. "Ask them the name or number of their unit and where it's based."

Kettering did. At the answer, he shrugged.

"Well?"

"He said he can't remember."

"Tell them it will do them no good to be flippant, that we know their unit is located either at Poulainville or Cachy. Tell them that our Intelligence has pinpointed virtually every British squadron between Dunkirk and the Vosges."

Kettering's voice sounded strange as it formed the English words. The Irisher commented finally.

"His answer, Kettering?"

"He says if you know so frigging much why do you ask?"

"Ask Captain—O'Brien—if he realizes that the war is over for him and his friend Watkins. Ask him why they continue to be so evasive and belligerent when a cooperative attitude could make things so much easier for them both."

Kettering translated, then listened blank-faced to the Irisher's answer. To Heidemann, eyes averted, he said: "The captain says you have their names, ranks, and serial numbers, sir, and if you think you're going to get anything else from them you have a diamond-shaped, felt-lined anus."

Heidemann sat straight-faced for a moment. Then his shoulders began to shake. Finally he burst into open laughter. Kettering blinked, confused. The Englishmen continued to sit impassively, their eyes narrowed.

"Tell them," Heidemann said chokingly, "I'd be delighted to have them as my guests for dinner tonight. And that there'll be no more questions."

When Kettering had finished, the black-haired O'Brien stood up and lisped some of his crazy language.

"Well, Kettering?"

"He said they want no favors."

"Of course not. I expect they'll be interrogated at length by Army later on, but now that I've sung my little tune they can relax. I'd be very disappointed in Captain O'Brien and Lieutenant Watkins if they had reacted in any other fashion," he added amiably.

Kettering chattered and Heidemann called: "Rupp!"

The *Unteroffizier* entered. Strange, Heidemann noted digressively, how Rupp looked positively radiant these days.

"Where's *Leutnant* Stachel? I want him to meet these gentlemen."

"He completed his combat report form, sir, then, I believe, he went to his quarters."

Heidemann started to say something, thought better of it. Still smiling, he told Rupp, "Very well, I'll see him later." To Kettering he said, "Ask the English officers if they'd like to freshen up a bit. They can use my own quarters. Under guard, of course."

The man called O'Brien nodded as Kettering spoke and answered briefly.

"The captain says they'd be happy to accept your invitation, both for dinner and for the use of your rooms. Meanwhile, however, they can make no promises not to try to escape."

"Tell them I understand. You might add that if they try such a thing they will, of course, be shot."

Kettering translated. There was an exchange of salutes, and the three departed, gabbling easily in English. Heidemann watched them go. He laughed again, shaking his head.

He went to the window and contemplated the De-Havilland, which had been parked in front of Hangar A. A sizable crowd of ground officers and enlisted men had gathered to inspect Stachel's trophy, and someone was standing in the rear cockpit, experimentally swinging the twin Lewis guns. This was the first enemy machine the *Jasta* had taken intact, and it was apparently a source of great pleasure to Ziegel, who paced importantly up and down, hands on hips, bawling instructions at a pair of mechanics struggling to remove the engine cowl. Heidemann had just decided to stroll out and examine the big machine when Rupp knocked.

"Yes?"

"Sir, this is most unusual. The security guard says there's a bunch of French civilians at the main sentry box. They want to see you."

"What about?"

"I'm not sure. There's a language difficulty there. The guard—Schwarz, it is—can't speak much French and none of the Frenchies understands German. Do you want me to run over there and see what's going on?"

"Yes, of course."

As Rupp turned to go, Heidemann gave the matter second thought. "Rupp—wait. Better yet, bring the Frenchmen in."

"Isn't that a little risky, sir? The Frenchies have been acting a little queer the past few days. I know. I think they have something going on," he added confidentially.

149

"Nonsense. What can they do? Are Germans to grow nervous over the silly machinations of some senile snail-eaters? Bring them in."

"Yes, sir. As ordered." Rupp, oddly, seemed suddenly crestfallen.

Heidemann filled his pipe. He went to the desk and from a drawer withdrew a letter to Elfi he'd begun the previous night. His eyes scanned the words. No, that wouldn't do. He'd have to begin again. He mustn't let his loneliness show through so much. (Don't, under any circumstances, be maudlin; don't include those saccharine terms, those juvenile endearments. Show her you're in command.) As grim as things must be for her, a little cheerfulness would be more in order. Perhaps if he told of the British prisoners—cleaning up the dialogue a bit, of course—yes, that was it. Be amusing. Lighthearted. He sat down and scribbled a few tentative sentences across the top of a clean paper. He crossed them out, then sat back in the chair, the tip of the penholder between his compressed lips. Several minutes went by, the only sound the busy ticking of the dashboard clock he'd had mounted for desk use. His pen began to scratch again, and this time he continued with no further pause.

There was a shuffling in the anteroom, and he caught a few phrases of softly spoken French. His own command of the tongue left much to be desired, and, although he could read French fairly well and speak it laboriously, it seemed to take on entirely different characteristics when he heard it spoken by natives. Therefore, he had chosen the easy way and had appointed Rupp to serve as his interpreter on the rare occasions he had any dealings with the populace. Heidemann smiled. Today seemed to be his day for language lessons.

Rupp's face appeared. "They're here, sir."

"How many?"

"Three old men, two women, and a girl."

"Well, have them come in then."

Heidemann pulled down his tunic and rubbed a hand quickly over his hair. The six civilians entered, slowly and with deference. At their fore was a hunched oldster with a snowy Van Dyke whisker arrangement. His skin

150

was leathery from the wind and suns of at least seventy summers and his eyes were watery dots of faded brown. The other two men were dressed like their leader, affecting worn but neatly pressed dark suit coats of long-forgotten fashion. They were somewhat younger, but not enough to make any real difference. The women, blank but well scrubbed under their shawls, hung to the rear of the tiny formation. At the elbow of one was a child who held a bouquet of wild roses. She shifted uneasily from one foot to the other, her cordlike legs nicked and soiled-looking where they showed between her skirt and stockings.

"Well, what is it, Rupp?"

"They say they want to see you about something important, sir. But they'd give me no more than that. They want to speak to the head man, as they put it."

Heidemann regarded the old man. He smiled in a friendly way and asked: "What can I do for you, old one?"

Rupp's French sang. He waited while the man answered, his words musical and reedy.

"His people, he says, want to show their gratitude."

"Gratitude? For what?" Heidemann inspected the old man with puzzled interest.

Again there was the sibilant, nasal exchange. Rupp's face began to take on a muddy color.

"Well?"

"The old man says the mayor has authorized him to make this visit and to tell you that it was a magnificent thing one of our officers did."

"What does he mean by that?"

"Well, sir, it seems the little girl there fell into the creek over by the bridge and one of our people rescued her at the risk of his own life, the way they tell it. The town thinks it was a fine thing for him to do. These people here are members of the girl's family. She has some flowers to give her rescuer."

Heidemann stood silently for a time, seeming to listen to the clock. Then he said, "Who was it, Rupp?"

Rupp swallowed, his eyes averted.

"Come, come, Rupp. Do we know who it was?" His voice had taken on an edge. The girl came forward and

151

said something. Rupp reddened, and he looked slightly sick. He appeared finally to make a decision.

"It was *Leutnant* Stachel, sir."

"How do you know? What did the girl say?"

Rupp explained lamely: "I—I happened to be approaching the bridge when I saw *Leutnant* Stachel standing there. There were a number of children running and playing. The girl fell down the bank into the creek. *Leutnant* Stachel jumped in and pulled her out. I helped bring the girl around. She says she remembers me, that's all."

"When was this?"

"Last evening, sir."

"Why haven't I heard of it before now?" Heidemann's tone had become sharp. Rupp was pale.

"I—*Leutnant* Stachel ordered me not to say anything about it."

Heidemann's eyes narrowed, hot anger showing. "Don't you recall, Rupp, that I have a standing order that any incident—no matter how minor—involving the local citizens and the members of this *Jasta* are to be reported to me at once?"

Rupp looked miserable. "Yes, sir. But—"

"There are no buts to any order I give, Rupp. However, I'll get around to that later. Right now I want you to get *Leutnant* Stachel up here at once. Quickly."

"I'm not sure where he is, sir. He—"

"Find him!"

When Rupp had gone, Heidemann once again turned to the silently waiting delegation. They had not moved, except for the girl, who by now had returned to her former station beside the woman. He was suddenly conscious of the great chasm between these people and himself.

"Would you ladies like to sit down?" he ventured in his halting school French.

The women traded glances, then looked at the man with the beard. The old one nodded, his thin blue lips showing a slight smile. They sat uneasily on the packing crates.

Heidemann considered the girl. She had the pinched expression and large eyes that made all French children

152

appear somehow the same. He held out his hand, and as he spoke, the alien words came slowly.

"Come here, little girl."

She hesitated, throwing a nervous glance at the women. One of them nodded briskly.

"What is your name, my dear?"

The youngster made no answer, but approached him slowly.

"My name is Otto. Do you know anybody else with a funny name like that?"

She shook her head, looking up at him from behind the bouquet.

"I'm happy you weren't hurt in the accident."

The child lisped a few words, but he couldn't follow them.

"Would you like a piece of chocolate?"

Her expression remained unchanged, except for a barely perceptible widening of the eyes. She nodded. He went over to the desk and shuffled through the large center drawer. He brought out a square of issue chocolate and, bending down, held it out.

"Here you are. I hope you like it."

One of the women said something and the girl curtsied. She murmured a thank you, and Heidemann smiled inwardly; that was at least one phrase he'd understood in the afternoon's seemingly endless mish-mash of foreign languages. He watched as the youngster returned to the women, and felt depressed when one of them took the chocolate and slipped it into her coat pocket. Where were Rupp and Stachel, for heaven's sake?

The old one, smiling again, spoke at length, and the others nodded approval.

"I'm sorry, old man," Heidemann slipped back into German, "but I simply can't get what you're saying." In French again he recited slowly: "I don't speak French very well."

The man made a minimizing gesture and spoke again. Heidemann thought he caught something about "very well indeed," but he couldn't be sure.

Stachel came in, trailed by Rupp. His face was flushed

153

and his eyes were strangely vacant. "You called for me, sir?"

Heidemann was alarmed at Stachel's appearance. "Yes. Are you all right?"

"A bit tired. What's up?"

The *Jastaführer* motioned toward the visitors, and sensed that Stachel had not noticed the small group until that moment.

"These people are here to thank you."

"Thank me?"

"Yes. For saving this little girl's life yesterday."

Stachel studied the youngster. She smiled openly now and came forward, the bouquet held out stiffly before her. Her small voice sounded a few phrases.

"What's she say?"

Rupp coughed. "She says she's very grateful for what you did. She wants you to have the flowers."

Stachel's redness deepened. He took the tired roses. "Tell her it was nothing. Nothing at all."

The old man spoke before Rupp could comply. The *Uffz* listened. To Stachel he said: "The entire village is grateful, according to this one. He wants to know if there is anything you need or want they can take care of."

Stachel stared at the aged Frenchman. "Yes. Tell him to tell his women to keep their goddamned brats at home where they won't get in trouble."

Heidemann stiffened. "Don't tell him that, Rupp. What's the matter with you, Stachel? Are you sick or something?"

"No. I just want the silly old son of a bitch to tell his slatterns to keep their brats out of my hair, that's all."

To Rupp, Heidemann snapped: "Say something. Something diplomatic." Turning again, he said, his voice toneless, "Meanwhile, Stachel, I suggest you go to your quarters for a rest."

CHAPTER 17

KETTERING LOVED parties. He stood beside the piano, viewing the orgy in high good humor, nodding his head in cadence with the mad crashing Schneider's playing produced as stiffening for the vocal meringue. Tobacco smoke formed a motionless nimbus just below the ceiling, and the reek of alcohol was almost palpable. The fierce old man in his crayon flying helmet hung upside down, and the rudder piece from Stachel's RE-8, suspended from a beam, would turn lazily like a tricolored windmill paddle whenever a weaving head nudged it. It was a noisy, smelly, altogether riotous shambles and Kettering was relishing every moment. He was even amused when the man called O'Brien, who sat on the piano swinging his legs and la-laing to Schneider's bawdy lyrics, spilled his drink.

"Watch it, O'Brien. This is my only fresh uniform."

"Fresh? God, I'd hate to smell your dirty ones."

The man called Watkins, his eyes out of plumb, leaned over confidentially. "I say, Kettering, wherever did you pick up your English? In an American whorehouse?"

"Can you think of a better place?"

"Certainly: in an English whorehouse."

They all laughed loudly, agreeing between gasps that this was rich, very rich indeed.

Kettering said, "That reminds me of the business trip I once made to East St. Louis. I was walking down a street just off the red-light district when I came upon a vacant lot between two buildings. Some kids had fixed it up like a fair ground, with booths made of packing crates and signs scrawled in crayon, and there was this kid loafing by what looked like the main entrance. 'Want to look around, mister?' he says, and since I had some time to kill, I said, 'Why not?'

"Well, it was quite a place, I'll tell you. For instance,

there was a booth with a picture of a bearded fellow with a halo holding a big bumblebee, and this picture was inside a bigger picture of an old crone—a real battle-ax she was. On the counter was a neat pile of stones and a sign that read: 'Mad at the Old Lady? Knock the bee-Jesus out of her—one cent.' That gives you the idea.

"But I was intrigued most by a little booth with nothing but a fancied-up matchbox on the counter. The sign there read: 'Are you destined for great things?'—or something like that, and—'Ask the Egyptian pharaoh for five cents.' I asked the kid about it. He said, 'Wait, I'll get my brother; this is his business.' A few minutes later he came back with this other kid who stood about as high as my boot here. The bigger one told me that the box had been passed down to him through many ancestors, and it contained the innards of a mummy. There was a legend, he said, that if somebody opened the box and heard the pharaoh's message, he was a very special fellow who'd have a glorious future. 'Open the box,' he said, 'and maybe you'll hear the message.' I did, and—Phoot!—the little one let an enormous, blattering fart. I was so charmed by the ingenuity of it all I tipped them each a dime."

The O'Brien asked, incredulous, "You mean the little blighter could do that at will?"

"Apparently. With a talent like that, he should go far. . . ."

Heidemann despised affairs like this. It was incredible to him that grown men could let themselves go so. Not that he was against relaxation in principle; the good Lord knew that there was little enough to ease the pressures under which these fellows lived. But it had always depressed him to see clear eyes go to marble, friendly faces turn arrogant, true wit fall into filth, propriety deteriorate into slovenly indecorum. He was not of the school that could easily condone such degeneracy by a mere indulgent nod toward the bottle. It had never seemed an adequate excuse for one to explain a lapse into oafishness with a knowing wink, an apologetic smile, and an "I was drunk, you see." Momentary release from pressure was

156

one thing; compounding pressure with the next morning's guilt was quite another.

He registered amusement, however, when young Braun undertook to explain his theory of balloon attack. Braun stood on the piano, lecturing in thick tones that were meant to be an overt parody of the *Jastaführer* himself. To illustrate a final point, Braun hurled himself into the air and swept three of his applauding audience to the floor.

A few moments more, to demonstrate that he was not offended, then he'd leave, Heidemann decided. There was a great deal to do yet tonight. The events of the day had been just about perfect, and he was anxious to get things under way.

He signed the bar bill, which Zimmermann, the mess officer, had placed at his elbow, and turned to go. Stachel was beside him, his face pale but composed.

"Well, Stachel. I don't remember releasing you from quarters."

"Was I in confinement?"

Heidemann studied him. "You behaved wretchedly in the presence of those civilians. You know that, don't you?"

Stachel shrugged. "You confined me to quarters because I can't stand Frenchmen?"

"I sent you to quarters because of Rupp. He was there, you know."

"Oh. So then you were showing Rupp you're still boss, eh?"

"Don't make me angry, Stachel."

"Of course not. Sir. I simply can't stand Frenchmen. I'm sorry it showed through."

"You certainly got wet feet in behalf of someone you can't stand."

"Kids don't count. French kids aren't Frenchmen."

"They grow up to be."

"I'll hate them then."

Kettering came over in a cloud of brandy fumes, his face beaming and sweaty. The Englishmen weaved along under his bearlike arms.

"Ho, Stachel! There you are! These beefeaters have

been asking all evening to meet the man who snapped their suspenders."

Stachel turned, his back to the bar, and regarded the foolishly grinning trio. His face was blank. "So?"

"Here on my right is Captain James O'Brien; on my left, Lieutenant David Watkins." Kettering switched to English then, and the Tommies examined Stachel in drunken solemnity. They began to nod in understanding, their eyes amused. The O'Brien one held out his right hand and said, *"Wie geht's?"* sounding the "W" as if it were a combined "U" and "I." Stachel was slow to take the hand. Without dropping his stare, he told Kettering: "Tell them it was a good fight they put up. It wasn't, but tell them anyhow."

Kettering did. The O'Brien began to laugh, and the Watkins made a comment from the corner of his mouth.

"What did he say, Kettering?"

The adjutant's expression was a mixture of amusement and concern. "Well, this one says he'd have put up a better fight if he hadn't been laughing too hard to aim."

"What does he mean by that?" Stachel's voice was flat.

"Oh, nothing, really."

"I said what does he mean by that?"

Kettering looked confused now. The O'Brien said something to the Watkins and they both howled, punching each other in the ribs.

"What did he say, goddamn it!"

Kettering shrugged, attempting to minimize it all. "Well, he said you'd soon be known far and wide as the 'Men's Room Ace.'"

Stachel's expression was mean. "What's that supposed to signify, if I may be so bold?"

"Take it easy, Stachel. They're drunk. We're all drunk. This is all in fun."

"Tell me."

"That legend you have on your machine's top wing. It's the kind of thing you see scrawled on walls in public comfort stations, that's all. It amuses our guests. They say you must have a wonderful sense of humor. . . ."

Everybody began to laugh then. Braun, Huemmel, Ulrich, Zimmermann, Schneider, Ziegel—they'd formed

158

a circle and were roaring and stamping their feet and slapping their thighs.

Braun choked, "Stupendous! *Herr* Stachel will kill the enemy with laughter!"

Stachel, his face white, turned on his heel and stalked from the room.

Heidemann, Kettering noted, had already gone.

Heidemann wrote two letters. One was to Army, outlining in precise detail the events of the day. He struggled long and hard to obtain the proper emphasis in the part that involved Stachel's visit from the grateful French. He also rewrote his praise of Stachel's proficiency as an airman: once, when he'd decided it had been a shade overdone; a second time, when he realized he had omitted reference to the demoralizing effect Stachel's black airplane seemed to have had on the English. In fact, he wrote, a DeHavilland crew had surrendered rather than fight this fearsome machine. . . .

The other letter was to an old friend of Elfi, Ludwig Niebergall, an elderly newspaper publisher who had doted on *Frau* Heidemann since she'd been a tot. Heidemann had met the old gentleman at parties several times, and twice he had exchanged cordial notes with him. This was a third such note, simply to send best wishes and, as a conversational aside, to mention how fine it was to be associated with men such as those to be found in his *Jasta*. One of them, Bruno Stachel, had even risked his own life to rescue a child of a Frenchman—a child whose father even now was no doubt fighting and killing brave Germans. . . .

When his writing was done, he sealed the letters—the one to Army in a top-priority *Feldpost* packet, the other in a plain envelope carrying nothing but Niebergall's address. Army would get the report in the morning; Rupp's little extra-censor postal service would take several days to get the note to the publisher. After a second thought, though, he took the Niebergall letter from the drawer reserved for Rupp's pickup, scratched his *Feldpostnummer* across the top, and placed it in the out-box with the other. He'd said nothing he wouldn't say to anyone. Besides, the more people who read the letter the better. Censors, especially.

He turned out the light and sat in the darkness, thinking, for a long time.

Stachel was lying on broken glass and crumbled rock. A mountain had fallen across his belly, and a bayonet had been shoved through one ear to emerge from the other. His arms and legs had been sawed off. His mouth and throat had been crammed with sand. A bass drum had been inserted in his chest and was sounding dull, agonized thuds.

He tried to open his eyes, but they had been puttied over and lacquered. He stopped trying and lay there, rolling in a void.

Many centuries later he tried again, and this time light seared his eyes. He shut them to wait some more.

There was a sound. It defied recognition. Later, something in the darkness pulled a string of intellect and a tiny gate opened to admit understanding. The sound was that of rain, a heavy drenching rain that whipped against a window.

The drum beat a cadence now, and through the rain, over and over in a mad irrelevance, came the soundless words of the ancient soldier's song:

> *Eine Kugel kam geflogen.*
> *Gilt's mir oder gilt es dir?*
> *Ihn hat es weggerissen,*
> *Er liegt mir vor den Füssen,*
> *Als wär's ein Stück von mir,*
> *Als wär's ein Stück von mir.*

Kettering and Ziegel sat in the adjutant's office, sipping chicory coffee and listening to the storm. A wild burst of wind moaned around the hut and the rain crashed.

"What a delightful morning!"

"Perfect."

They sipped some more.

"It couldn't have come at a luckier time, this rain."

160

"Any time's lucky."

"Yes. But can you imagine what it would be like to have to start an airplane engine this morning?"

"Like sticking your head in a tuba. I'm glad we don't capture Englishmen every day."

"If our people had gone up this morning we'd have had one hundred per cent losses."

"Lovely day."

"Gorgeous."

"Lovely."

"Indeed."

The door burst open, and in the brief sweep of rain and wind, Stachel entered, a poncho thrown over his head. Ziegel turned to stare out the window. Kettering, irked by the disruption in his luxurious mood, asked: "Help you?"

"Morning, gentlemen. What's new?"

Kettering looked at him with new interest. Ziegel shot him a glance, one eyebrow raised.

"Well," Kettering said, "you seem in a good mood. I thought you'd still be eating nails."

Stachel, his eyes puffed and sore looking, managed a smile. "What do you mean?"

"What do I *mean*? Sweet Jesus, man. I thought you were going to shoot down the Englishmen all over again right there in the bar last night."

"Englishmen?"

Stachel's redness was something to see, Kettering thought. Ziegel coughed and said: "You seemed to be a bit put out with the men's room thing. Funny though, eh? Ha-ha."

Stachel asked, "What's the date?"

Kettering pointed to the wall calendar. "Right there. Help yourself."

"Let me see yesterday's combat report forms. The copies."

Kettering pulled a clipboard from a drawer and handed it across the desk. Stachel read for several minutes. Then he returned the board and left without a word.

Ziegel poured another cup of coffee from the pot on

161

the desk. He said, "I've seen people dead five months who look better than he does on this beautiful day in June."

Stachel drank another cognac, but the terror refused to leave. Shaking, he sat on the cot, his poncho staining the mattress with running rivulets.

Once he said, aloud, "Ah, God. God."

The last thing he could remember before his agonized awakening this morning was returning to this room to remove the uniform he had soaked in the creek.

Somewhere in the two intervening days he had destroyed two English bombers and captured a third. His signature and Heidemann's confirmation and endorsement said so.

He stood up and began to pace.

Englishmen? He *talked* with *Englishmen?*

CHAPTER *13*

THE PHOTOGRAPHER, a fat little man with a ratty Kaiser's mustache, came out from under his black cloth. He elbowed aside the cadaverous major from *Kogenluft* and announced imperiously: "Now, *Herr* Stachel, after this pose we want a picture of you standing beside your flying machine. Is that it there?" He pointed to the broadwinged C-3 two-seater the *Jasta* used for general utility.

"No, that's not mine."

The major giggled. "Gracious, *Herr* Hugelmaier. All of Germany is talking about the 'Black Angel.' Haven't you read that *Leutnant* Stachel flies a black airplane? That's his over there."

"To read the journals is for editors and onanists. I am an artist."

"Well, after all . . ."

All of Germany. Stachel, poised nervously, hands be-

162

hind his back, felt the real irony. This kind of attention had been his compelling goal for many months, and now that he had won it, he was as nervous as a cat in a new house. It was still an awesome, numbing thing to look back over the incredibly few weeks in which it had all taken place, and he was convinced that he would never become used to the discovery that reputations could be made of such filmy stuff. Nor was he at all sure, even now, how it was that whatever he'd done could make so many seemingly rational types suddenly begin to act like fatuous, fawning idiots.

It had all begun with the mail one evening. There were, for *Leutnant* Bruno Stachel, no less than eighty-nine letters in that one delivery—eighty-nine letters for a man who, until then, had had a good week if two notes from his mother had arrived. The mail was from people he'd never heard of: farmers, professors, policemen, schoolteachers, schoolboys, mechanics, promoters, and women —many women. Each letter, in its way, had gushed over the ridiculous and embarrassing affair involving the French girl at the creek. It hadn't been until several days later, when the mail had risen to enormous piles and a tent had been set aside for the gift packages alone, that he'd seen the newspapers themselves. His mother had sent them, of course, and each gave prominent space to a story of the incident. At first he'd been nearly delirious with pleasure, but once the initial impact had been absorbed, he'd fallen into nervous, somewhat sullen confusion. It had been no better when Heidemann had called him in one noon to advise him of today's parade, and as he'd dressed this morning he had been in a deep depression that even yet burned under the nervousness. Heidemann was approaching now, trailed by the pair of official news-agency people he'd been showing around the field. The *Jastaführer* was smiling and chatting animatedly.

"How are the pictures coming, *Herr* Hugelmaier?" Heidemann asked expansively.

"This light is atrocious."

"Looks like a decent day to me," the *Jasta* leader suggested.

"Shadows are too hard."

"Well, I hope the pictures turn out. They should— you have a fine camera."

"Someday," the fat man grumped, "people will understand that good photographs derive from the photographer's skill—not from the camera."

The journalist with the slouch hat and trench coat looked Stachel up and down. "You don't seem very deadly to me. The first reports described you as deadly."

Stachel reddened. "I'm not deadly. I'm really very sweet and lovable."

The one with the black bowler and the porcine eyes asked: "What's it like to kill somebody?"

"Hilarious."

Heidemann coughed. "Our visitors are anxious to get some background information on you, Stachel—data to augment the earlier articles that have appeared."

"So I see." He was determined to cooperate with these people, but to be picked at was maddening.

The slouch hat said: "About this little Frenchie. When you went off the bridge, what were your thoughts?"

" 'I'm going to have to get these trousers pressed.' "

The man's sallow face remained expressionless. "No need to be sarcastic. Our readers want to know these things."

"Why?"

The bowler asked, "Are you in love with somebody? A girl, I mean?"

"If I were to be in love with somebody it would be a girl."

"Well, are you?"

"No."

"Why?"

"We don't have any girls in the *Jasta.*"

"How about at home?"

"I'm never at home."

The slouch hat was scribbling. He looked up from under his brows.

"*Herr Leutnant,* the youngster you pulled from the creek says you are a very brave man. Isn't that odd coming from the daughter of a French infantryman?"

164

"Ask the infantryman."

"Did you know the girl before the creek incident?"

"No."

"Will you keep in touch with her?"

"I doubt it."

"Why?"

"I like my girl friends to be a little older."

"Oh, then you do have girl friends?"

"I didn't say that."

"You inferred it."

"I thought you people wanted information on my activities as a flier. My love life's my own business." His voice was low and tense.

"You're a hero now, Stachel. People want to know everything about you."

The bowler broke in: "All right, so you're a flier. Do you like to fly?"

"It's fine."

"What kind of airplane do you fly?"

"Fokker D-7."

"The black machine over there?"

"That's right."

"I understand you once had a bawdy legend painted on it. I don't see any now."

"I took it off."

"Why?"

"I heard you were coming," he lied, writhing inwardly at the recollection of the days of joshing he'd taken over the men's room business.

"What difference does that make? We couldn't tell our readers what it said anyhow."

"Your camera might. My intention was to anger Englishmen, not to offend Germans who may read English."

"What do you think of *Hauptmann* Heidemann?"

Heidemann's face remained blank. The major from *Kogenluft* blushed, and stammered: "That's hardly a proper question. Can't you confine yourselves to less personal matters?"

The slouch hat and bowler ignored him. The latter asked, "Well?"

"You heard the major."

"I understand you were a flying mate and close personal friend of Willi von Klugermann, nephew of the *Graf* von Klugermann and heir to one of Germany's greatest fortunes. Did you see him die?"

"Yes."

"How did it happen?"

"He was returning from a sortie. He ran into a chimney while landing."

"Isn't that an ironic way for an air hero to die?"

"The sky is full of irony."

"Have you ever been frightened while in an air fight?"

"Have you ever been frightened by a snake?"

"What I mean—what do you think when you prepare to dive your machine on an enemy?"

" 'I hope this frigging airplane holds together.' "

Heidemann smiled faintly. The slouch hat said, with an air of one of special privilege: "In Mainz, before we came out here, we were permitted to talk with the Englishmen you captured. They said you are a first-rate fighter, but as a person, a pain in the ass. Any comment?"

"Do you want me to be modest, or do you want me to agree?"

"It's up to you. I don't particularly care."

"The Englishmen are correct. On both counts."

The bowler scratched his buttocks and asked, "What are you going to do after the war?"

"I've got to get through the war, first."

"What should Germany do after she beats the English and French into submission?"

"Worry about the Yankees."

"Don't you think the Americans will be glad enough to pull out once a decision's been made here?"

"What do you think, Mr. Journalist? You get around."

"I'm no politician. I merely write what they say."

"I merely fly where they say."

"Well, we need some words of encouragement from a war hero to the people at home. Can't you give us some? I mean, above all, what should the German people hope and work for?"

"To come out even."

"How does it look to you, here in the war's fourth summer? Is victory in sight?"

Stachel glanced at Heidemann, who was studying a machine that droned in lazy circles far overhead.

"It depends on what you mean by 'victory.' We've got to turn on plenty of steam if we expect to beat the people across the way. At the rate we're going, we'll be lucky to hold our own."

The *Kogenluft* officer stirred uneasily. "What *Herr* Stachel means—"

The bowler cut him off. "We know what he means. Stachel, what do you say to a picture of you and the girl by the bridge?"

Stachel looked at Heidemann again. "What do you say, sir? Is that acceptable?"

Heidemann turned his gaze from the sky.

"Of course. I think it's a fine idea."

The photographer snapped, "Well, hurry then. The light's changing."

Stachel stood stiffly at attention, the late afternoon sun hot against his face. A trickle of sweat coursed down his spine under the heavy tunic. Behind him, flying personnel to the right, ground officers and troops to the left, the *Jasta* was a solid block of gray-green and polished black. The unit's aircraft were aligned wingtip to wingtip before the hangars, and on a ladder to one side of the black Fokker, *Herr* Hugelmaier struggled under his cloth to record the scene.

Heidemann and the *Kogenluft* major stood before him, and Kettering was reading from an official-looking document, his voice strained and high-pitched.

"—for bravery of the highest order: On twenty-five June, 1918, above-mentioned *Leutnant* Stachel, in company with the leader of his *Jagdstaffel,* sighted and attacked three heavily armed enemy day bombers. Despite the fact that his *Jasta* leader was forced out of combat due to mechanical failure, *Leutnant* Stachel continued to press the attack singlehandedly. During his vigorous harassment of the enemy formation, *Leutnant* Stachel destroyed two of the bombers and forced the third to surrender. By virtue of this and other meritorious actions, *Leutnant* Stachel is awarded the *Ordre Pour le Mérite*. By Imperial Decree. Wilhelm, Emperor."

Stachel had gone directly to his quarters once the parade had been dismissed. To Heidemann's invitation that he have a drink in the mess, he had pleaded a headache from the sun.

He stood in his room now, staring at himself in the small shaving mirror. A single beam of last sun cut diagonally from the window to the opposite wall, casting the rest of the room in somber eclipse. The blue-and-gold cross at his throat glowed richly in the half-light.

The Blue Max: Germany's highest award for an individual act of gallantry. In a nation that had—from the beginning of history—idolized its military and lavished baubles of all descriptions on its warriors, only the select and illustrious few could hold this delicate cross, a cross created by Frederick the Great himself. But as always, of course, what Stachel had envisioned as a moment of triumph and giddy elation was a time of despondency. Instead of presiding at the bar below and receiving the toasts of his admiring colleagues, he was standing in his room, solitary, and consumed by the especial aloneness that defied description or understanding.

The Blue Max: for an action he couldn't even remember.

He considered the bottles on the table, but only for a moment.

He had not had a drink since his awful discovery on that rainy morning last June.

He would not have a drink again, never again in his life. This he had promised himself. This promise he would keep.

Hanging up his cap, he sprawled on the cot fully dressed and watched the day fade. The first thing he'd have to do, he decided, would be to settle a few debts. . . . And the first of these would be the delivery of Willi's strange diary to the safekeeping of the *Gräfin* von Klugermann. That was the least he could do for Willi.

Heidemann held the receiver tight against his ear, the phone close to his lips. He heard the *Kogenluft* operator make the final connection.

"Wurfl here."

"This is *Hauptmann* Heidemann, *Herr General*—"

"Oh, yes, Otto. How are you? I understand you had a gala at your place today."

"Yes. That's what I've called about—"

"The press people: did Major Klingel get them there in time for the award ceremony?"

"Yes, but—"

"Amazing fellow, that Stachel. No one ever heard of him a month or so ago. Now he's the subject of discussion in every home in Germany. Amazing. 'Death to the French soldier; long live his child.' And so on."

"Yes, indeed, but—"

"How about a leave for him? Are you arranging one? You really ought to let him circulate a bit. People are hungry for heroes, signs of military successes, and that sort of thing."

"I haven't thought about that. If you—"

"Well, don't think about it; give him a leave. As soon as possible. And have him bring that damned-dong black flying machine with him. Give the people a boost."

"Very well, sir. But I've called you to—"

"How's your father?"

"Quite well, I believe. In his last letter—"

"Good man. Good man indeed."

"General, I wanted to talk to you about this afternoon. This Major Klingel—"

"Saw Elfi the other day at a reception."

Heidemann's heart leaped. "Oh, really? How is she?"

"Handsome woman. Handsome. Can't understand how she ever settled for a funny-looking scalawag like you. Ha-ha."

Heidemann made appropriate chuckling sounds. "She's looking well then?"

"A bit peaked. Wan. Not getting outdoors enough, I'd say. Handsome, though."

"I keep writing her, telling her she must—"

"Well, Otto, I can't chat all evening, you know. When are you going to get down to business?"

Stupid, pompous old bastard, Heidemann thought. "Sorry, sir. I have something I want to report about this afternoon—"

"Can't you write it out and forward it through channels?"

"I would, sir, but I don't want to make a formal issue of it, and, frankly, I wanted to have the pleasure of talking with you again. As Papa says, he's always refreshed and stimulated after talking with you, and—"

"And you need a little of that, eh? Well, delighted, delighted."

"Thank you, sir."

"Now, what about this afternoon?"

"The press, sir. I'm afraid Major Klingel didn't do a very good job of handling them."

"How so?"

"Well, he just doesn't understand fighting men. Fighting airmen, in particular. The press people were a bit boorish, and he made no attempt to control them. As a matter of fact, they were quite presumptuous in their interviews with *Leutnant* Stachel. He—Stachel, that is —was considerably annoyed and upset, and Klingel made no move to ease the situation. Actually, I don't think he even recognized Stachel's distress."

"Klingel is a fathead. If he were worth anything, he'd have more responsibility in assignment. We can't really trust him on anything else, so we have him play escort to the more important war correspondents."

"Well, General, that's just my point. Klingel's position could be extremely important to *Kogenluft*. A calculated publicity program, properly handled, could do much toward creating strong public—even military—support for Germany's air service. Look what's happened in the case of Richthofen, Boelcke, Immelmann, Stachel—all of them—despite the amateurish effort on Army's part to bolster their images. If such men can electrify so many

170

in spite of an impersonal and ponderous and unimaginative communiqué system, think of what could be done with a shrewdly devised scheme, unprecedented in its dexterity. You need a very clever man in Klingel's spot. A very clever combat airman, an air-minded planner with a strong sense of publicity values. When I saw how badly Klingel handled the situation today, I was convinced of this, and I feel you are probably the only officer in all of Europe who would immediately grasp the significance of what I'm saying."

The general was silent for a moment. Then he rasped: "He let the press walk on Stachel?"

"I'm afraid so, sir."

"Publicity, eh? Calculated publicity. A formal program . . ."

"Yes, sir."

"Whom would you suggest for such a job?"

"I wouldn't presume to say, sir. But I can suggest something to you."

"What's that?"

"You can check with *Herr* Niebergall. *Herr* Ludwig Niebergall. He's the well-known newspaper publisher. He can advise you on what kind of officer to look for."

"I've met Niebergall. Elfi introduced us, I believe."

"Good. He can give you some fine suggestions."

"Well, all right. Like the idea, Otto."

"I knew you would, sir. Papa always said you were very quick to grasp a situation."

"Good man, your father. Too bad he can't be on my staff. Terrible waste. Talented officer, sitting on the sidelines in a wheel chair."

"Yes. He feels badly about it, too. He's a great admirer of yours—"

"One thing, Otto."

"Sir?"

"Let's just keep this publicity thing between us for a while, shall we?"

"I've forgotten the conversation already, General. As a matter of fact, the whole thing's your idea."

"Well, then. Nice to talk to you, my boy."

CHAPTER 19

THE DRIVE from Munich to the Ammersee had been pleasant. It was high summer now, and the meadows were soft in their pastels and the white birch trunks provided interesting, geometrical accents to the green-black fir forests that quilted the rolling hills. Stachel rested easily in the rear seat of the phaeton the *Graf* had sent to the airfield for him, breathing deeply of the scented air. For the first time since his return to Germany he realized how sweet was home. His two days at Bad Schwalbe had been almost farcical if considered as a rest period. His parents, bemused by their son's new fame, had struggled ineffectually to balance their desire to monopolize him against their compulsion to exhibit him. Consequently his time there had been fitful periods of family small talk between lengthy parades of sight-seers. At first there had been well-wishers from the town and a clutch of relatives he'd hardly known, but soon there had been pomaded commercial promoters from Frankfurt (how had they escaped conscription?), a platoon of journalists, and even a theatrical producer who envisioned a postwar aerial circus with Stachel as a sort of flying ringmaster. Gifts, from flowers to wolfhounds, had crammed the hotel's storage facilities, and the mails had produced sacks of obsequious, frequently ridiculous letters. He'd sat up until dawn the second day reading these; most of them he'd thrown away, but some he'd speculated over and saved.

But here on this country road, he reminded himself, was the Germany he loved: the large *Hof* there, where several generations of a single family worked, slept, ate, argued, laughed, and loved under the deep-slanting eaves; the roadside crucifix, with its pot of cut flowers; the hamlet, its wood and plaster buildings leaning against one another for mutual support; the stain of centuries-old manure mingling with the aroma of freshly baked bread; the onion-shaped steeple across the valley, golden against the velvet blue; the geese, scattering and hissing before the murmuring car. Here a man could take account of things, by God.

Once more he felt the kit bag and the diary's bulk. He smiled. The *Gräfin* would spend the rest of her days wondering if he'd peeked at its contents. He knew she'd grasp at his assurances otherwise; he also knew the assurances would serve only to increase the wonder. Well, he laughed silently, it would probably do the little lady some good to wonder a bit. She certainly had everything else going her way. . . .

"A beautiful day," he told the back of the driver's head.

"Indeed, *mein Herr*. A gift to men from their God."

Finally the car turned through a large and ornate gate, where a small group of *Landsmänner* in their *Lederhosen* and knee socks waved and their women, starched and scrub-faced, threw bouquets onto the tonneau and called friendly calls. He returned their hails, delighted.

Ahead, up the broad avenue and beyond the high and arching elms, he could see a rambling villa backed against the sparkling Ammersee. This was *Sonnenstrahl,* the patriarchal summer retreat of Von Klugermanns since the days of Charlemagne. As the car curved to a halt, Stachel reset his cap, straightened his tunic, and reached for his kit. Already a man in knickers and brass buttons had brushed past the car attendant to lift it away.

"I'll take that."

"My pleasure, sir."

"I said I'll take it. Give it to me."

The man bowed, his expression unchanged despite this appalling breach of historic procedure.

"*Leutnant* Stachel. Good of you to come." The *Graf*'s voice rolled from the entrance. "Come in, and welcome to *Sonnenstrahl.*"

"*Grüss Gott,*" the *Gräfin* said in the amiable custom of Oberbayern. "It means a great deal to the *Graf* and

173

me that you've been willing to spend some of your precious leave with us."

Stachel, once he'd reached the piazza, clicked his heels, bowed, then took the *Gräfin*'s hand and touched it to his lips. He avoided her eyes, and spoke in carefully formal tones.

"I'm honored to have been invited. I confess I'm relieved to escape the annoyances that seem to attend—" He hesitated.

"Notoriety?" the *Graf* boomed joshingly.

"Well, I—"

"Not notoriety, Hugo; rather the attentions of a whole grateful nation." The *Gräfin*'s contralto was full of amusement.

Stachel smiled at her. Her ice-blue eyes were excited and her fine, even teeth caught the sun. The scent of sweet soap came to him. She was appealing and girl-like in the full-skirted peasant *dirndl* with its puff sleeves and apron, its black vest and velvet neckband and ivory cameo.

"I'm afraid the *Graf* is right, Countess. Notoriety is the word for it."

The three of them laughed together, and the *Graf* and *Gräfin* each took one of Stachel's arms. The kit swung heavily against the *Graf*'s leg, and he pointed to it, still chuckling.

"The rationing and food shortages are ghastly, *Junge,* but you needn't bring your own sausage and cheese when you come to *Sonnenstrahl*. We still have plenty here."

"No sausage in there. Just a little something for the *Gräfin*." He was glad now he'd brought the brooch. It had come among all the other booty in the mail at home, and at the last minute he'd placed it in the kit, along with the diary.

"That's sweet of you, *Herr Leutnant*."

"Wait until you see it, Countess, before you decide that."

"Whatever it is, I'll love it."

"We've set up a table on the lakeside patio," the *Graf* confided, "and we've managed to scrape together some first-rate refreshments. Do you like American bourbon? I've featured it in my little display."

"Bourbon? It's a whisky, I believe. I like whisky very much. It's a man's drink." He felt a sinking.

"I like it, too"—the *Gräfin* laughed—"so I hope I'm not disqualified."

He fought to throw off the seizure. He heard himself saying, involuntarily: "Not by me, Countess. Today all restrictions are off. All restrictions."

The large hallway led directly from the front entrance through to a panel of ceiling-high French-type doors at the rear. These were open, and framed in the villa's deep, cool shadow was an expanse of the blue-green Ammersee and the far-off hills beyond. The house was heavy with the smells of rich wood and ages of polish and care. The man with the brass buttons was adjusting a large floral display on the baronial table at the foot of the massive, carved stairway, and another strode silently across the thick pile of the carpet ahead of them.

The patio that edged the lake-facing side of the villa was broad, part of it in shade, most of it yellow under the sun. A table, protected by a mushroom-shaped umbrella and surrounded by cushioned wicker chairs, was adorned with glistening crystal, bottles with exotic contours, a roasted duck with one flank expertly carved away, a spread of fruits, nuts, and cheeses. A soft breeze whispered in the trees, and the lawn stretched invitingly down to the rim of the lake. Butterflies fluttered in the grass, and somewhere a honeybee droned.

"What a delightful place," Stachel observed in admiration. The food intrigued him. His father had made a long speech on how rations were now at little more than starvation levels. Not here, certainly. . . .

"It seems we're forever destined to meet on piazzas or patios, doesn't it, *Herr* Stachel?" the *Graf* rumbled as he poured three drinks.

"I can think of few more pleasant places to meet."

The *Graf* raised his glass, and Stachel and the *Gräfin* answered.

"To the Kaiser."

"The Kaiser."

Stachel held a chair until the *Gräfin* had settled in it, then pulled up one for himself. The whisky's sting was already sharp and exciting in him. How foolish he'd been to worry about his drinking!

"How was your trip, *Herr* Stachel?" she asked.

"So-so. I flew, you know. The *Jasta* commander gave me permission to take my own machine to Frankfurt. Once there, it wasn't difficult to obtain *Kogenluft* permission to fly on to Munich via Mannheim and Augsburg. Fuel is very short, and I imagine I've been selfish in flying, but I'm afraid I wouldn't have been able to include this splendid side trip any other way. And, frankly, I need a rest badly."

The monocle caught the sun as the *Graf* raised his head. "Well, no one will interrupt your rest here, you can be sure of that, my boy. You have a thousand-some acres to roam, a gorgeous lake to soak in, a private stock to hunt—regardless of season and controls—and, if you're so inclined, a village full of *Mädeln* who are simply panting to hold your hand or whatever."

"Hugo!" the *Gräfin* protested. "Must you be so—?"

"Crude, Kaeti? Is reality necessarily crude?"

"Well, after all. What will *Herr* Stachel think?"

"Of me? Or of you?"

"Well—"

Stachel laughed easily.

"I admire directness, Countess. And I assure you that the *Graf*'s directness does nothing to lessen my respect for you."

She made a little face. "He's an old boor."

"If I were a young boor I'd be pottering around down in the village myself."

They laughed together again, and then slipped into a long and wandering discussion of the history of *Sonnenstrahl* and the Ammersee region. Finally Stachel arose, went to the table, and poured his third whisky. With his back still to them he said: "I'm deeply sorry about Willi. He was a grand fellow."

There was a silence. The bee swung across the patio,

its hum loud and determined. The *Graf* coughed. "It was the game."

"Yes."

The *Gräfin* stirred. Her voice was bitter. "Game, indeed. You men and your horrible, deadly games. It makes me ill."

Von Klugermann ignored her. "We appreciate your note, *Junge*. It was very thoughtful of you."

"Willi was my friend."

"Yes. He wrote about you several times."

"I think I appealed to him more as a laboratory specimen than anything else."

"Willi was like that. I believe he would have made a great writer. He studied people, always trying to find what went on behind their eyes. But he did like you very much. He said so. He would not say so if he didn't."

"I'm glad. I was very fond of him."

The *Gräfin* stood, her lips pressed together. She said: "If you gentlemen will excuse me, I believe I'll go and take a nap before dinner. I'm suddenly quite weary. I've been up since dawn, *Herr* Stachel"—she managed a smile—"supervising the preparations for your arrival and keeping the backroom servants and tradesmen at arm's length in their little plots to get a glimpse of Germany's newest hero. I confess I'm not used to such activity here at *Sonnenstrahl*. In Berlin, of course, one gets accustomed to bustle, but Oberbayern is more conducive to dreaming."

Stachel murmured, all solicitude: "I'm sorry to cause you trouble. I was hoping I wouldn't."

"Bah," the *Graf* snorted, "she's simply using you as an excuse to go and primp for several hours before dinner. Kaeti needs a nap like I need a third buttock."

She regarded her husband levelly. "I don't need an excuse to primp."

"You don't need to primp at all. You're too lovely for that," Stachel put in.

"Why, *Herr* Stachel. How gallant."

The *Graf* grunted. "Don't delude the poor woman, Stachel. Besides, that courtly stuff sickens me. But how about you? You must be tired yourself after bashing all

177

over the sky between here and Frankfurt. Would you like to freshen up?"

"I'd like to very much. Traveling puts a suit of armor on a man. . . ."

"Heinz!" the *Graf* bellowed. The set of brass buttons appeared. "Show our visitor to his rooms, will you?"

The *Gräfin* smiled diffidently. "Well, good then. Dinner will be at eight, gentlemen. Excuse me now."

Stachel bowed and the *Graf* waved his hand casually. She disappeared into the house, her skirt swinging.

"I hope my mentioning Willi didn't upset her," Stachel said, looking after her.

"I don't know, *Junge*. She's taken it all very hard. She was very fond of Willi."

"She seemed to be." Stachel found it difficult to hold back the laugh that wanted to form. "She's a charming lady, and I'd hate to think anything I said—"

"Nonsense. It had to be said. It's been said. Now we can get on with our visit with no further discussion of the matter."

"Well," Stachel said, "I'll be off then. See you at eight?"

"Right you are. I plan to stay right here for a time and catch up with some reading. I've begun a piece by the American, Mark Twain. Do you know Twain?"

"Can't say that I do. I've little time for such things lately."

"Too bad. Twain's quite good. In the original English, that is. Although I confess some of the dialects he uses are a bit thick for me now and then. But his situations are amusing."

Stachel nodded to the brass buttons.

"Well, at dinner. Excuse me."

He soaked for a luxurious half-hour in the huge, sunken brass tub that dominated the bath adjoining his bedroom. Then, rubbing himself to glowing with a thick towel, he padded across the suite to survey the view from the casement, whose diamond-paned windows had been flung wide. He sank onto the cushioned window

178

seat in the bay, and abandoned himself to the sensual pleasure of the warm breeze's playing on his still-damp nudity. The lake had turned to a deep blue in response to the oncoming dusk, and the far hills had become a lustrous gold. On the patio directly below, legs jutting out from the swollen mound of his belly and making twin bridges to the footstool, the *Graf* sat nodding over his book. Somewhere a brook splashed, and Stachel recalled the childhood poem his mother once loved to chant:

> *Du Bächlein, silberhell und klar,*
> *Du eilst vorüber immerdar,*
> *Am Ufer steh' ich, sinn und sinn,*
> *Wo kommst du her? Wo gehst du hin?*

He yawned sleepily, and, dropping his feet to the floor, prepared to arise. A soft hand slid over his mouth.

He turned, startled.

She held the forefinger of her other hand to her lips, signaling silence. She was in a dressing gown, her hair loosened and falling to her shoulders. Again he caught the scent of soap.

"Hello, my dearest," she whispered.

"How did you get in here?" He wrapped the towel about his midriff, clumsily and in haste.

"This is a very old house. It has an interesting passage between the walls. The passage links so many rooms."

Stachel jerked his head toward the patio below. "Won't he hear us?"

"He's as deaf as a nail. Besides, he's asleep. He's always asleep. . . ."

She slid onto his lap, and he found that under the gown she, too, was nude. Her lips, full and hot, pressed against his, softly at first, then crushingly and moist. Raising slightly, she pulled away the towel. Against his mouth, after a while, she breathed a salacious command. As he positioned himself to comply, her swollen but tautly upright breasts were silhouetted against the wash

179

of yellow light on the patio. Still visible, at the moment her breath hissed an ecstatic obscenity, was the figure of the dozing *Graf*.

Stachel made a languid business of his theft.

They rested across the canopied bed. She sighed deeply, then chuckled.

"I thought you'd never get here. I was awake all last night, thinking about this."

"All I can say is thank God for the foresight of those old architects. They must have been a bawdy lot."

"Gormann says the passage was originally an escape device for use during the ancient wars."

"Who's Gormann?"

"The head man here."

"You mean Brass Buttons? Did he show you the passage?"

She laughed. "Not for the reason you think. He's an old *Sauerpreuss,* and I don't particularly like him. But he showed me the passage in one of his more communicative moments. He's an amateur historian."

"Did he show the *Graf?*"

"No. I don't think so. He doesn't like Hugo."

"Friendly bunch around here. Nobody seems to like anybody."

"I like you. You have the most stunning, boylike body I've ever seen."

"That's nice."

"Now, my darling, I want you to do something. Something especially exciting."

"What's that?"

"Take me over to the window again. I want to look over your shoulder at the *Graf* von Klugermann. I want to watch him snore while you demonstrate the difference in your ages."

He poured a heavy dose of whisky into the tumbler on the table and downed it in three gulps. She rolled over and said through the pillow: "You're drinking a lot. Almost a whole bottle in two hours—in the two hours since you arrived. That's a lot. . . ."

He turned, holding the glass and bottle poised for another pour. "Not so much. I simply like whisky, and it's been a long time since I've had it."

"There's a lot of whisky, and a lot of time ahead. Ten days. Ten wonderful, stolen days."

He served himself another drink and studied her. She was full-figured, but firm and smooth. Her waist was slender and her belly flat, and her breasts, although large, were in pleasing proportion to her shoulders. Her hips swung in rounded, easy curves to slightly thick thighs. But her calves were trim and gently tapered to slim ankles.

"Like it?"

"Like what?"

"This." She made an indolent gesture.

"Why shouldn't I? It's the playground of the elite."

Her eyes narrowed slightly. "What do you mean by that?"

He smirked, his stare bright and glassy. "I found Willi's diary."

She raised up on an elbow. Her look was anxious. "Willi's diary?"

"Yes. It makes for very interesting reading."

"Give me an example," she demanded softly.

"Well, there's one entry—dated October seventh, 1917, I believe—that begins something like this: 'To-night I found Kaeti. It's unbelievable; wildly, madly unbelievable. She's my aunt by name. But in reality, she's my toy. She's my instructor. She's my soul.' Or something equally ridiculous."

She was pale. Swinging her legs around and putting her tiny feet on the glistening oak floor, she took the glass from him and gulped half its contents. Eyes watering, she asked, huskily, "Willi wrote that?"

"Willi wrote that."

"What else?" she persisted.

"Let's see. There was one passage that told, sigh by sigh, gyration by gyration, giggle by giggle, of an afternoon in front of a large mirror somewhere here at *Sonnenstrahl*. Then there was another that described in similarly glowing detail the night you spent hilarious hours attempting to massage some of the weight from him. And so on and on, *ad nauseam.* . . ."

She smiled, but her pallor remained. "I never did like heavy men. I like them slim and hard."

"How come Willi, then?"

"He was young. And so comfortably available when Hugo was safely away on those silly trips of his."

"You're what they call a nymphomaniac, by God."

"Yes. I suppose so. But the diary. What do you propose to do about that?"

"Make some money."

"How?"

"How much is it worth?"

She pulled the robe over her shoulders. Her blue eyes were thoughtful. "You are attempting to sell it to me?"

"Not attempting; selling."

"That's blackmail, isn't it?"

"I believe so."

"Why should I want to buy it?"

"You're pretty comfortable as a countess, I dare say. You would not be able to pose as a countess very long if certain sections of Willi's diary were to be slipped in among the Mark Twain pieces."

She stared at him, her face solemn. "Where would I get the money—the amount you no doubt want? I—"

"You forget that Willi was a scribbling fool. I know of your immense personal fortune—the one inherited from your dear old papa and cached away in the Swiss bank."

She shrugged. "If I am so wealthy, why would I pay blackmail to remain the wife of that pompous old windbag out there on the patio?"

He smiled, his mouth slack, his eyes vacant. "Because you like being a *Gräfin.* You cherish your storybook elevation to this from your former status as the daughter of a mere shipping clerk who tumbled onto Arabian oil. I know. Willi said so. You would not want to be known as that incestuous whore the *Graf* von Klugermann tossed out on her well-worn ass."

"Willi was not incestuous. He was a nephew by marriage."

"Do you think the German upper crust would make

182

such a distinction? As I get it, they don't think very much of you as it is."

She tossed back her head and smoothed her silver-blonde hair with a hand. The robe fell away, but she made no attempt to recover it.

"Well," she said tonelessly, "now I know why you wrote and asked to come here. And I thought it was me you wanted. So, then. What's your price?"

"Two thousand marks a month. At the end of each month. Upon receipt of that sum, I'll send you one carefully selected page by special confidential messenger."

She was incredulous. "Two thousand marks per month per page! You *are* drunk, aren't you? Why, that could go on for years. . . ."

"True. There's a bonus, though. My physical favors, whenever your—hunger—grows unbearable."

She arose, her motions deliberate and unhurried. "I have no choice but to pay."

"Exactly. Now, I suppose you'll want me to leave. I'll make some excuse to the *Graf* and go."

She smiled remotely. After a while she said: "No. I'll send word to him I have a headache and can't join you for dinner. As a matter of fact, I do have a headache, and you've given me some things to think over."

"You mean you want me to stay? Even after our, ah, business deal?"

"Of course. If I'm going to support a blackmailing male whore, I'll want my money's worth."

CHAPTER **20**

HIS AWAKENING was an appalling series of sluggish recollections. With each came a stab of remorse approaching physical pain. He lay across the huge bed, listening to his heart, his eyes shut tight against the awful succession of shocks, his tacky mouth locked against a shriek that

183

pressed against his teeth. It wasn't solely what he had done that tore at him and stirred the nausea; it was more the knowledge that what he had done had been unpremeditated, involuntary and unwanted.

The *Gräfin,* he told himself in despairing mockery, was getting no bargain. Who wanted a male whore who was insane? Not even she could want that. . . . God! *God!* How *could* he have?

Groaning, he crawled erect, ignoring the beaming, scented morning, and dressed. As he shaved, once again he found it impossible to look into his own eyes. He actually dropped the razor when he realized with a burst of memory that he had not made dinner, that he had summoned Brass Buttons and, in a grand speech, had told him to inform the *Graf* that Germany's newest hero was indisposed. He hoped in mute anguish that Kaeti had left the room by then, but he was unable to remember. He did recall at some time ringing for more whisky. The bottle lay now on the window seat, unopened.

By the time he had reached the breakfast table, however, most of his control had returned, leaving him only a vague, indecisive queasiness. When he greeted the *Graf,* who hulked behind a plate of fruit and studied the distant hills, he noted his voice was husky and retained a hint of the thickness.

"Good morning, sir."

"Good morning, *Junge,*" the old man grunted non-committally, looking around at him.

"I'm sorry I wasn't able to join you for dinner last evening," he ventured.

"Perfectly all right. As a matter of fact, I dined only lightly and turned in early myself, and I feel better for it."

"Good."

There was a pause. The *Graf* selected a piece of apple and munched thoughtfully.

"Didn't the *Gräfin* come down, either?" (*God, oh God—please! Please!*)

"Yes. She seemed a bit put out she didn't see more of you on your first day with us."

(*Thank you, God.*)

184

"Well," he managed, "I was more exhausted than I realized. Caught cold, too, I'm afraid."

"I have some powders that will fix you up."

"Oh, I'll be all right, thank you."

Suddenly he wanted to run, to get away from this place at any cost, under any pretext. Real panic surged, and his stomach turned with its impact.

"Actually, sir," he invented, "I want to confess one of the main purposes of my visit. I wanted very much to see you and the *Gräfin*, of course, and to express my condolences. But there's something else, too. I want your advice. For a friend. I wasn't going to bring it up until later, but I think I ought to go immediately, leave for the front. My friend needs help, the *Jasta* needs me, and I—well—I simply won't feel right loafing here when so much is required of me."

"So? What can I do, *Junge?*" The *Graf* turned to regard him, and it was with relief that Stachel saw concern and interest in the old man's face. He sat down then, and an impassive Brass Buttons appeared with fruit and coffee for him. He took a few experimental sips and found the brew established a base from which he could go on. Prompted by a separate, inner voice, Stachel heard himself saying: "I remember that evening at Army, when you and the *Gräfin* and Willi and I had dinner. I remember you had some things to say about drinking. . . ."

"Mm. I spout off on that sordid subject altogether too much. It is the most irrational, mysterious, and vexing malady known to me; therefore it preoccupies me to the point of fanaticism."

"Well, I'm worried. There's an officer in my *Jasta*— Schmidt, a first-rate flier—he, his drinking is becoming . . ." He paused.

"Unmanageable?"

"Yes. I guess that's it. I thought perhaps you could advise me on how to help him."

"Tell me about it," the *Graf* said, studying the end of his cigar.

Again in that alien voice, Stachel explained: "This fellow isn't a bad sort, really. At least he seems like the right type when he isn't drinking."

185

"Go on."

"Well, I've noticed that when he drinks—with the rest of us, that is—he changes. Something seems to come over him and he gets, ah, unpredictable. . . ."

The *Graf* continued to contemplate the cigar, remaining silent.

"Now, I understand that anybody gets a little crazy and does silly things when he drinks too much, and there's a lot of drinking that goes on in a front-line *Jasta*, I'll tell you. But this particular fellow is rather peculiar the way he goes about it."

"Have you," the *Graf* broke in, "talked to him about this? I mean, has he told you anything about how *he* feels about his drinking?"

"Yes. Quite a bit. I'm his closest friend, his confidant. That's why I'm concerned about him, you see."

"Of course. But I can't comment sensibly unless I have some idea of what he himself thinks. You, for instance, can tell me in great detail what you observe about him, but that's not too useful unless it can be coupled to his own impressions." He smiled, as if recalling a secret joke. "Secondhand symptoms rarely lead to first-rate diagnosis."

Stachel gathered himself, realizing the die had been cast and somehow feeling grateful for the fact. "Well, my friend complains of such things as an appalling loneliness, a feeling of inadequacy, anxiety, a teetering of spirits—elated one moment, depressed the next. He says the see-sawing evens out and he experiences a sense of relief and calm when he drinks. At first, that is. Then he grows melancholy and remorseful—nutty, as if another personality had taken over. When this becomes alarming to him, he tries to stop drinking, but he continues on until he's unconscious." Strange, Stachel noted, how one began to talk like a textbook whenever discussing something with a physician. Why in hell couldn't he have said, "The son of a bitch is unhappy when he drinks and unhappy when he doesn't"?

The *Graf* put in, "How often does he do this—drink himself unconscious?"

"Not too often. He can stop for considerable periods, as a matter of fact."

"This change of personality: is it obvious to others?"

"It is to me."

"How so?"

"It's as if this fellow is really two people and he can't decide which is the real one. When he drinks, it's never guaranteed which will show up. And sometimes, both intermingle."

"What kind of person do you think he is? Really, I mean. Basically."

"He's quite decent, actually. Rather shy, reasonably intelligent, well mannered, dedicated to the Fatherland and our cause."

"And when he drinks, he's none of these?"

"Frankly, when he drinks he can be a dirty bastard, and usually is."

"I see. Anything else?"

Stachel compressed his lips and toyed with his water tumbler. "He says he sometimes can't remember things. People will tell him about things he's done and he won't have the slightest recollection of them."

The *Graf* nodded. "Does he experience physical illness? Nausea? Tremors?"

"Sometimes."

"Does he drink alone? Does he hide a supply? Drink in the morning? Drink the most when he wants to the least?"

"I believe so."

"Does he lie a lot? Rationalize truth?"

"I've found that he does." He put in anxiously: "But understand—he's really a very nice fellow. . . ."

"To be sure."

Stachel fell silent, and the *Graf* appeared to be in deep thought. The elegant clock on the sideboard ticked politely.

"There's nothing," the *Graf* said finally, "that anyone can do to help your friend—Schmidt, I believe you said his name is."

"What do you mean?" Stachel asked tightly, the sinking sensation strong in him.

"Your friend Schmidt is an alcoholic. And probably an aspiring schizophrenic to boot. But it's the alcohol that will do him in, I'm afraid."

"So?"

"So unless he stops drinking he'll go insane or die a rather nasty early death."

To Stachel, the clock was thunder. "That's easy to say, isn't it? Stop drinking? Don't you think he would if he could?"

"Of course," the *Graf* agreed softly. "But nobody else can stop for him."

"Isn't there some way—?"

"There is no other, simple way. If I could name some alternative, my name would go down in history. There is no known cure for what ails your friend. Only preventive action."

"And that's for him to stop on will alone?"

"Correct. To put the cork in the bottle and pray it isn't too late."

Stachel shook his head in disbelief. "He's pretty young for such a thing. . . ."

The *Graf*'s cigar waved. "Age does not enter into it at all. Does diabetes, cancer, consumption, hay fever—even the common cold—respect or await age? I've been ridiculed from here to Chicago and back for saying this, but alcoholism is a disease, the same as these others. It differs only in that it is self-inflicted and in that the sole chance for recovery rests with the victim himself. And the odds of even this succeeding are infinitely small, no matter if the sufferer is ten or a hundred and ten. Your friend has my deepest sympathy. Only a miracle can save him."

Stachel said in a halting whisper, "Some of them recover. There's a man in my town—"

"Some of them experience miracles."

"You mean the Bible kind of miracle?"

"Miracles are all around us. I am not a specialist in such things. But I do know from my years of practice that strange, inexplicable things happen in hospitals and on deathbeds. I personally have seen men live when every clinical indicator demands that they die. Since I can find no explanation, I assume a miracle. Any modern physician will tell you the same."

In his numbness, Stachel heard his voice say: "Is there anything I can do to help my friend?"

"You can pray for him. If you're so inclined."

After a time, Stachel arose.

"It's been difficult, all this. If you don't mind, sir, I'll get my things ready. And may I use the car to return to the airfield?"

"Of course."

He went to the door. With his hand on the massive handle, he turned. The *Graf* was regarding him thoughtfully.

"Thank you, sir."

"You're welcome, *Herr* Schmidt."

She whispered, "What's the matter, darling? You're not responding."

"I've got to get out of here quickly. To make things look right downstairs. . . ."

She giggled. "You may be expensive, but you're sweet for all that."

He was silent, and stood rigidly against her fondling.

"Darling?"

"What?"

"Just once."

"I've got to leave. Now. And you annoy me."

"Don't talk sharply to me, darling. I'm paying for smiles."

"Will you stop that frigging stuff?"

"Sensitive, darling?"

"Shut up. Now get out of my way. I'm leaving."

"Want a drink?" Her tone was conciliatory now.

"No."

"It isn't too early for a drink. . . ."

"No. But it may be too late."

CHAPTER 21

PASTOR EHRLICH was a wispy man with sunken cheeks and an aquiline nose which, for as long as he could remember, had struck Stachel as being a monstrous incongruity in the clergyman's otherwise gentle configuration. Standing beside the desk in his dim and musty study, clad in his somber uniform of black, he appeared to be a tiny figurine calculated to symbolize the Moral Law. He held out his nearly translucent hand, and as he spoke, Stachel was reminded of sifting sand.

"Bruno. I'm delighted to see you again. And surprised."

"I've been recalled to the front and I was anxious to see my parents again, at least for a day. I thought I'd take a few minutes and pay my respects to you while I was here."

The pastor nodded, the light from the casement glowing in the white arc of his hair. "It's good that you did. Much time has passed."

"Yes."

"Have you been well?"

Stachel hunched a shoulder and gazed out into the garden. "I suppose so. I've escaped the enemy up to now. Which is more than many have done."

"Too many. It has been an appalling waste. But sit down, my son; tell me if there is anything I can do for you." Pastor Ehrlich sank into the large leather-backed chair behind his desk and contemplated his caller.

"I'm not sure, Pastor. I've been——" He paused, thinking.

"Searching?"

"What do you mean?"

The pastor's face readjusted itself to accommodate a small smile. "As I say, much time has passed since you and I had frequent association. You have entered the world and found it wanting. I sense you have been searching, and, having been disturbed by the nature of the answers that have suggested themselves, you have returned to port for reorientation."

"That's part of it, I guess."

"I think, really, that's the all of it."

Stachel regarded him. "How so?"

"Although I'm a simple clergyman in an obscure mountain village, I've seen a great deal of life, my boy. If there is one thing that is common to all men it is their constant rummaging for the key to their own identities. Whoever they are—rich, poor, honest, false—they roam their

190

worlds, searching for answers as to who they are and what they are, and why they hope their vague hopes. It would all be so easy if they'd merely recognize that what they seek, what they yearn for, is God."

Stachel rested back in his chair. "And would they find what they look for?"

"It's all around them. It's they, themselves."

"Then you think I'm just another searcher? A spiritual shopper, so to speak?"

"Why else would a young man, heaped in the glory of arms and the rewards of self-righteous conquest, take the time to visit one of God's interpreters, unless it were an acknowledgment that the fruits of triumph are wormy?"

Stachel made a steeple with his hands and touched it to his lips. He said, stiffly: "I must admit that there are many times I feel restless, dissatisfied; all in all, I'm not a very worthy fellow, and this makes me somewhat—uncomfortable."

The pastor stared out the window. "And your discomfort has brought you here?"

"Perhaps."

"Why do you think you're unworthy, as you put it?"

Stachel was silent for a time. Then he shifted in the chair and said, "I seem to be two people sometimes. There's one of me that compels me toward—good, I guess you'd call it; there's another of me that acts otherwise."

"All men feel this through divine design. How can one appreciate the sweetness of righteousness unless he recognizes and experiences evil? God has given us the power to make a choice. He has made goodness difficult to attain and hold, so that in the attainment we demonstrate our worthiness in God's own eyes. You are no different from any of us."

"I feel I am."

"Why should you be so smug as to feel that?"

"I sometimes believe I'm going insane."

"Tell me about it."

Stachel studied the polished planks of the floor. "I accept your theory that we have a choice for good or evil. But somehow I no longer seem to have a choice. I no longer seem capable of deciding what I'll do is to be right or wrong. I do good in the midst of evil; I do evil when my only intention is to do good. I'm never certain which it will be at any given time."

"Are you merely making excuses? Be honest, now. Are you merely covering a secret knowledge that you are weak and enjoy your weaknesses?"

"I don't think so. Honestly, the things I do make me sick."

"I've read of your rescue of the French child. Is that an example of what you believe to be the good you do in the midst of evil?"

"I suppose."

The pastor looked at him. "A solitary act of goodness to another doesn't constitute goodness *per se*. I, for example, can actually do any number of good things—good, in that they may be selfless and righteous in themselves—but unless I do them in the *spirit* of goodness, in an honest *aspiration* to total and continuing goodness, they will never make me a really good man. God will perhaps credit me with them, as a sort of partial payment on ultimate righteousness, if you will; but what He really wants is my complete surrender to the good. Not until I see and hunger for the whole and not the parts, my greatest good deed—the hugest partial payment—cannot make me truly good. In other words, your rescue of the child was laudable; whether it was a partial payment on or total acquisition of goodness depends on the spirit in which the deed was done and the spirit in which you consider it now and forever."

Stachel nodded. "I follow your reasoning. But does it hold true for evil? If I do one evil deed, and it's done without an honest aspiration to total evil, am I really evil?"

"Good and evil are not an equation. Any evil is the absence of God."

"I want to be good."

"Is this true? Or do you merely want to want to be good? There is considerable difference, you know."

Stachel considered that. Pastor Ehrlich studied him through half-closed eyes. "There's something else, isn't there?"

192

"Something else?"

"Yes. You didn't come here simply to philosophize, I'm sure."

"I'm not exactly certain why I came here."

"What has happened, my son? What has hurt you?"

"I've hurt myself, I guess."

"How?"

"I don't know. I—"

"I can't help you if you are evasive."

Stachel sighed. He leaned forward in his chair. "What does God say about drunkenness?"

The clergyman picked up a letter opener and balanced it between bony fingers. "This is your 'something else'?"

"I—I think so. The only time I do the worst things is when I've been drinking. Do I drink because I'm evil, or am I evil because I drink? My God, Pastor, it's driving me out of my mind. . . ."

There was a catch in his voice. He recovered quickly, blushing.

"Are you compelled to drink?"

"I must be. I drink the most when I want it the least."

"God pity you, Bruno."

"Yes."

The small man in black shook his head slowly. "I know very little of drunkenness and its causes. But like all human maladies, it's something that certainly, if submitted to God by a repentant victim, can be borne with the dignity that comes with the knowledge of God's help."

"You mean if I ask God He'll forgive my drunkenness, the sins it's caused me—"

"God does not forgive sin, any sin, because to do so would be to tolerate and thereby compound the sin. God forgives not the sins, but the sinner. . . ."

"But if I can't control my compulsion to drink, am I to spend my life sinning, then asking forgiveness, then sinning again, then asking again? Over and over?"

"Much of mankind does this without drink. Who is the greater sinner—the man who commits a foul act while sodden with drink, while wallowing in alcoholic confusion and despair, or the man who does an equally reprehensible act while in control of all his faculties? I don't know—I

193

merely pose the question. However, it would seem to me that the latter has an edge on true evil."

"You mean you don't know the answer either?"

The clergyman shook his head again. "As I say, I'm not God; I merely seek, through as honest a dedication as I can muster, to serve as an interpreter of His word. But in my opinion, a drunken soul is a soul nonetheless. Should that soul ask God's help, why would God ignore the call? I dare say God would hear with greater compassion a drunkard's miserable but sincere plea than He would the beautifully articulated petition of a teetotaling, self-righteous pharisee. Furthermore, God loves his children, whether they're sick or healthy. If that love is returned from the depths of despair, is it any less worthy than that stemming from a serene heart? I doubt it very much. But in any event, God's love must be returned—totally."

"So you don't know, either?" Stachel arose and straightened his tunic. He said: "Well, thanks for giving me this time. I'll have to be getting along now."

A thin hand came up. "Wait—I don't believe I've really helped you yet. We've just begun to talk."

"Nobody can help me. Good-by."

"Bruno?"

"Yes?"

"When—and only when—you've become sick enough of yourself do you have a chance. I know nothing of your—malady—but I do know that only when one surrenders completely, when he forgets himself and turns the direction of his life over to the All-Loving, only then can he be helped. Surely this is as true of the man bedeviled by drink as it is of anyone."

"Lovely words, Pastor. But as you say, you know nothing."

"You must surrender yourself, my son."

"I can't surrender a self I can't even find to a God I can't even imagine."

"Then stop looking. Just admit defeat and wait. God will step in and show Himself."

"I haven't got the time."

"One minute—one second—is enough."

"Not for the fire I have going."

194

"For any fire."

"A friend of mine said all I have to do is put the cork in the bottle. He's right."

"If that were all that's required, there'd be no drunkenness in the world. When you put the cork in the bottle there will have to be something to fill the void—"

"Your pious semantics won't do it, I'm afraid."

The little man's eyes dimmed. "Someday, when you've become sufficiently revolted with yourself, my pious semantics may have a bit more meaning."

"Perhaps. But don't hold your breath until then."

"You can't do it alone, you know."

"I can do it alone. I'm used to being alone."

Pastor Ehrlich sank back against the leather. "Why did you come here, Bruno?"

"Damned if I know."

"May God have mercy on your poor soul."

"Thanks, Pastor. Say hello to God the next time you see Him. I know He means well."

CHAPTER 22

SOMEHOW HE and Heidemann had become separated. Their two-machine echelon had held closely all the way from the new field near Coucy to well beyond the line's southward curve at Autreches, but there they had found turbulent cloud conditions, and after skirting a colossal pile of cumulus, Heidemann had vanished. Stachel flew two large circles, hoping to catch a glimpse of the *Jastaführer*'s D-7. His own Fokker was singing like a sewing machine, a fact that reassured him, since in the past week, two of the *Jasta*'s D-7's had crashed due to mechanical failures. He had witnessed one of these incidents. The *Jasta* had been flying in strength (what strength remained, he mused dryly) and had just risen to altitude. Ulrich's machine had begun to smoke, and Ulrich sought to turn the Fokker back to the field. He had no more than tipped his wings when fire broke out openly from the fuselage below the gun mounts. Ulrich was wearing one of the new parachute rigs that nobody trusted, but apparently he had decided to risk a jump rather than continue riding in that furnace. He'd gone over the side, but no one had seen any sign of a parachute. A day later the *Flugmeldedienst* reported that an infantry work party had found Ulrich's body impaled on a fence post. Ziegel, of course, was quite rattled by the whole thing and was working night and day to duplicate the conditions that may have caused the accident. He had some wild theory that the incendiary ammunition the *Jasta* was using these days had somehow ignited a pocket of fuel vapor in the cockpit well, but the pilots secretly believed that he or his crews had simply overlooked something while servicing Ulrich's machine. The other D-7, Schneider's, had been destroyed when its engine failed on takeoff. The piano-playing Schneider had lost an arm in the crash. All in all, Ziegel was none too popular at the moment.

Things were going badly in just about every department, Stachel reflected. The Americans had poured into the war in fantastic strength, both on the ground and in the air. The enormous pocket the German forces had laboriously hammered into the line between Soissons and Rheims all the way to Château-Thierry had been rolled up in jig time by the Yankees. It had been due to this turning of the tide that the *Jasta* had been moved south to Coucy. That had been a mess, all right. The pilots had flown their planes to the new field at the time specified, having allowed the trucks a full day to relocate ground equipment and supplies. They had landed to find no trace of the ground parties, and it hadn't been until the following morning that the first elements arrived. Luckily, the August night had been warm and the pilots had been able to get a fairly decent sleep under the wings of their aircraft. But the whole fiasco had been typical of the deterioration afflicting German operations these days.

The first he realized he was under attack was when a section of the padding on the cockpit rim next to the machine-gun butts exploded and stung his face with leather fragments. Instinctively he threw the D-7 on its back and hauled back on the control yoke to roll down and away.

The Spad clung directly behind his rudder post, and in his glance rearward, he could see its machine guns winking. The crackling was close, but wide. He began a dive, knowing, of course, that the Spad could outdive his D-7 on any day of the week. But after the engine had wound up and the Spad had begun to close in, he hauled back on the yoke and the Fokker went up like a monkey on a string. There was no Spad built that could recover from a dive or climb faster than a D-7.

He had won a break in the business, and as he circled above the frantically climbing Spad he saw that it was still another American. The machine had bull's-cye insignia on its wings, but the red was on the outside and the white in the center. A large white numeral One had been painted on the top wing, and on the fuselage he could make out a splash of color that appeared to be an Uncle Sam hat with a ring around it. He made sure his guns were charged by firing a brief clearing burst, then he kicked rudder and gave full aileron to a tight wingover.

The Yankee was good, all right. Stachel knew he should have nailed him on his first pass, but the Spad stood on beam's end and whipped around in a turn that should have wrenched its wings off. His tracers had needled through empty air. He saw the green and brown camouflage daubing on the other machine's wings run tantalizingly through his sights, but his second burst for effect had proved again to be anything but effective.

He followed the American into a tight vertical turn and realized they had fallen into a *Kurvenkampf*—a ring-around-a-rosy that would break only when someone's nerve or machine gave out. Staring straight up, he could look directly into the Yankee's cockpit. The other pilot was looking straight up at him as each machine flew top-surface to top-surface in madly opposite directions. He could see the other's blankly staring goggles and how his head hunched against the centrifugal force.

During the fourth revolution, the drumming of the

Mercedes altered. It was an almost indiscernible change in pitch, but Stachel had felt it at once. His eyes, alarmed, swept the instruments. Everything appeared normal. But when he looked up again, the Spad's position had altered slightly, meaning it had gained a hair in the revolving pursuit. Again there was a change in the yammering ahead, and now he felt a slight vibration in the floor where his heels rested in the rudder-bar swing races. A *Kurvenkampf* with a faulty engine was suicide. His only chance lay in a quick break-off and a race for the cloud bank two kilometers or so to the north.

He waited until the cloud came around to a point just above his upper wing, then skidded out of the vertical turn with the slight additional speed the lobbing effect provided. Tight-lipped, his breath suspended, he began his dash. The Spad pilot was a real professional. He barely missed a wink as he closed behind.

Stachel was numbly aware that he'd never make it. He was afraid.

There simply wasn't enough time, and the Mercedes was balking badly now.

His mouth was choked with cotton. The terror was like a pain. God. God.

The Spad was alongside.

Stachel stared stupidly.

The Spad pilot was grinning and pointing to his guns. Stachel could see his jutting jaw and easy, wide grin. The American shrugged, pointing to his guns again, and made a gesture Stachel finally understood.

The Yankee's guns were jammed.

Just as the Fokker plunged into the mists, he was aware of the Spad making a vertical turn to the west, the big white One on its wing bright in the sun.

Kettering tapped Ziegel on the rump. The Bavarian, his face streaked, looked back over his shoulder to peer between the engine supports of the dismantled D-7.

"Morning, Master Jesus; where's your balloon?"

"I brought you some hot soup, Ziegel."

The black eyes, puffed with fatigue, regarded the steaming mess tin. "Thanks. Just set it down some place."

"You'd better take it while it's hot."

"I'll get to it."

"How long since you've caught your breath?"

"I don't know."

"Don't you think you're pushing things a bit?"

"No more than anybody else."

"You've got to rest sometime."

"Sometime."

Kettering shook his head wryly. "You're not going to be able to win the war all by yourself, believe me."

"I can try."

"Come on, *Junge*. Sit down a minute and have some soup."

Ziegel slipped the wrench into his hip pocket, straightened his *Krätzchen*, and turned to descend the ladder.

"Well, I can see I won't get anything done while you hang around."

They squatted in the airplane's shadow. Ziegel picked up the mess tin, rested his back against the D-7's landing wheel, and sighed. "Jesus."

"How are you coming?"

"Losing battle, Fatso. No tools, no parts, no nothing. I don't understand how these barges can keep going much longer. I fix, I fit, I scrape, I sand, I daub, I tighten, I loosen, I screw and I unscrew. But it isn't going to be enough pretty soon."

Kettering nodded, his eyes thoughtful. "I don't know how you do what you do. . . ."

"I'm not doing well enough, that's certain."

"I think so."

"Just ask Ulrich. Ask Schneider."

"You can't blame yourself for what happened to them."

"I'm responsible for the condition of the *Jasta*'s aircraft."

"You're not responsible for the whim of God."

"God didn't wreck those planes."

"Neither did you."

They both sat for a while, watching the breeze ripple through the grass. Ziegel sipped at his soup, then put it aside.

"Too tired to eat, I guess."

"Like I said: you can't do it all by yourself."

"I've got lots of help. But if we only had some parts."

"Heidemann says we've got to start rationing fuel."

"I know. Rupp told me."

"Rupp's got a big mouth."

Ziegel sighed again. He rubbed a greasy thumb over a crack in the toe of one of his jackboots.

"Kettering?"

"Mm?"

"Do you think there's any chance?"

"Of what?"

"That we'll win this war?"

"How should I know?"

"It doesn't look good."

"Depends on how things are on the other side of the street. If they're just as bad off as we are, then we have a chance."

"Huemmel says the Yankee machines are getting as thick as flies around a cow's ass."

"I can't argue with that."

They turned to look west when they heard a drumming. "Heidemann."

Kettering nodded. "Wasn't Stachel with him?"

"Yes."

"Wonder where he is."

They watched the *Jasta* leader's Fokker make a circuit of the field, sigh into a wag-tail slip, then drop daintily onto the turf with a muffled thump. It rolled for a long time, then turned in an awkward wing-rocking arc at the end of the strip to come jouncing back, its engine snarling in intermittent blasts and its propeller-wash beating the grass. They could see Heidemann's head looking over the cockpit coaming, first one side then the other.

They helped Heidemann climb from the machine, and he stood for a moment, absently unbuckling his helmet.

"Kettering?"

"Sir?"

"Put in a call to the FMD and see if they have anything on *Leutnant* Stachel."

"Right away, sir. Where did you last see him?"

"I lost him somewhere near Autreches. In the clouds.

There had been no engagement. He was there with me, then he wasn't."

Kettering lumbered off toward the office, his fake leg creaking.

"How many machines will be in shape for the afternoon patrol, Ziegel?"

"Six, sir. Seven, if Stachel's is counted."

"That's all we have, isn't it?"

"Yes, sir. With three others down for repairs. I doubt if two of those will do any more flying. That is, if we don't get some parts, they won't."

Heidemann stared west, one hand shading his eyes. A pallor showed through his windburn, and it struck Ziegel that he had never seen the *Jastaführer* look so openly worried, so, well—really worried, sort of.

"Well, we don't have the pilots to fly them, anyhow."

"I know."

"How's the fuel?"

"We've enough for three more ninety-minute patrols in *Jasta* strength, sir."

"Any word when more will come?"

"No messages have come in since you left. Kettering would have said something."

Heidemann nodded. "I'll draw up a rationing plan. We'll simply have to cover assigned patrols with *Ketten* of three machines. That will give us six more patrols. There will be no more voluntary missions until further orders."

"Very well, sir."

"I'll send you a copy of the plan. Check it when it comes to see if I've thought of everything, will you?"

"Certainly, sir."

"And, Ziegel—"

"Sir?"

"Get some rest. You look awful."

"I'm all right."

"That's an order."

"As ordered, sir."

Heidemann walked off toward the office, his pace heavy, his anxiety over Stachel's disappearance a coldness in his chest.

Ziegel went back to the ladder and took out his wrench. As he worked, he was pensive, his dark eyes brooding. He was thinking of the girl in Bad Tölz, for some strange reason. She wasn't such a bad type, really, and he *had* acted rather shabbily. He wondered what it would be like to have her as a wife. Not so good, he decided finally. He *must* be tired if he'd begun thinking that way.

His sensitive ear caught the sound long before it was any more than a hint in the air. He peered toward the west, his eyes squinting against the hot glare that sent little waves up from the field. It was a Mercedes, and it was running very raggedly. He climbed down from the ladder and took several steps out into the noon sun.

The black Fokker came in directly, a scud of dirty smoke trailing. As he watched, the coughing engine sounds died.

"Damn. He's too low."

Ziegel began to run, hard, his arms pumping.

The D-7 teetered slightly as it struggled to reach the field.

Already Ziegel's lungs were straining, and his legs were leaden.

"Damn. Damn. Stay up!"

The Fokker was drifting in a flat, singing glide, its nose just short of the stall point.

The pounding of his feet made individual agonies. Sweat stung his eyes.

"Stay up, goddamn you, stay up!"

He fell, the wind bursting from him in a great sob. He arose to his knees, crawled crabwise, then staggered to his feet again. His run had become a jerky, mechanical weaving.

The black machine's landing gear whispered through a hedgerow. There was a cracking sound, and one wheel went bounding crazily off across the field.

"Damn. Damn. Damn."

The broad upper wing of the D-7 showed for a fleeting moment, and Ziegel realized numbly that this was the only time he had ever seen a *Jasta* machine flying up-

202

side-down and backwards. Then the dirt surged up, and the aircraft spun around laterally, belly to the sky, a tearing and shattering and banging clapping through the air. An aileron flipped out of the dust cloud, spinning. Metal squealed. Then the only sound was that of his feet pounding.

The Fokker lay on its side, a piece of wing flapping in the drifting dust. The reek of fuel stained the air.

Barely able to speak, Ziegel rasped: "You all right?"

Stachel's face was partially hidden. "I think so. But I'm caught on something."

"I'll get you out."

"This is going to go any second now. You'd better run."

"I'll get you out." His hands tore at the fuselage side. He sobbed for air.

"You'd better get the hell out of here, Ziegel. The fuel—"

"Shut your goddamned mouth and try to help."

"I can't move my arms."

"Try, you bastard. Try."

Somewhere there was a crackling.

"It's started."

"Shut up and kick. Push!"

Ziegel remembered his screwdriver. He groped frantically.

"It's gone. Damn. Goddamn. It's gone."

His eye caught a glint of metal. It was lying in the grass. He clutched it up and made a wild, slashing swing. Fabric tore.

"Hurry."

Ziegel's fingers seized the fabric at the tear, and he pulled, wheezing. Smoke drifted, and the crackling was louder.

"We aren't going to make it."

"Shut up, I said. Push! Push!"

"Don't let me burn, Ziegel. Shoot me."

"I haven't got a gun, you crazy bastard."

"Use the screwdriver. Just don't let me burn, that's all."

"Shut up and push!"

Ziegel fell back, grunting, when the fabric gave way in a sizzling whine. He came back up, yelling. The fire sounds were insistent now, and the smoke was thick. A flare of flame shot across his face and he shook his head, eyes tight.

"Oh, God. It hurts. It hurts."

"Run, Ziegel!"

Ziegel ducked through the hole in the darkness, his hands groping. He felt the seat belt toggle and tore it open. Seizing Stachel's collar, he pulled.

"It's no use. My feet are caught."

"Kick! Kick!"

He could feel Stachel's heaving. In the gloom, he saw two tubular longeron sections collapsed over the ankles of Stachel's boots. He crawled in, got a shoulder under one of the pieces, and, cocking his legs, gave a huge shove. The section groaned, and one foot was free. Then the other.

"Get out! Get out!"

The two of them scrambled onto the oil-soaked grass, rolling. There was a dull whoomp, and a searing surge of fire. Hands seized them and tugged, and there were shouts.

Ziegel was crying like a baby. His seared face was all screwed up and his mouth was open and he cried, tears running. His eyebrows and lashes were gone.

"Lie down, Ziegel. Lie down!" Heidemann's voice commanded.

"Son of a bitch. Son of a bitch. Son of a *bitch!*"

Stachel coughed, his chest heaving. He rolled over and squinted at Ziegel. "You all right, Ziegel?"

"Damn. Damn."

"You lie down, too, Stachel. Are you all right?"

"I'm all right. How about him?"

"He's fine. Merely lost some of his decorations and got a sunburn in exchange. He'll be fine. Fine."

"What's he crying about?"

Ziegel opened his watering eyes. His sobs were loud and dry. "I've done it again."

"Done what?"

"I've lost another of my machines."

Stachel looked at Heidemann, then back at Ziegel, blushing.

"God's name, Ziegel. Stop bawling."

CHAPTER **23**

WHEN HEIDEMANN came in, he was lying on his cot in the tent, listening to the frogs grumping in the nearby pond. The *Jastaführer* demonstrated that this was an informal call by carrying his pipe, which exuded a rancid odor that could be caught even before the tent flaps had parted.

Stachel swung his boots to the boards, but Heidemann waved his pipe in that condescending motion men of command use when they want subordinates to be at ease, but not too at ease.

"Rest, rest. How do you feel?"

"All right, sir. Considerably sore in the muscles here and there."

"That was a nasty one you had today."

"I don't want one any nastier."

"Did you get something to eat?"

"I didn't want anything."

"Still shaky, eh?"

"I suppose."

"We should have a doctor on a full-time basis."

"That's not all we should have. How's Ziegel?"

"Oh, he's fine. Nerves are shot mostly, I guess."

"I never saw a man cry like that."

"I did once. It was shortly after I came to the front on my first assignment. There was a fellow who was sitting at mess one night. Right in the middle of soup, tears began to run down his face. He stood up, and while we tried not to look at him, he started to cry—just like Ziegel did. The only difference was that he also wet his

205

pants in the bargain. He simply stood there, crying and wetting his pants. It was revolting."

Stachel shrugged. "I can understand a pilot getting all wound up like that. But a ground technical officer—"

"Pressures work strangely on men. What eats at one man may not bother you or me at all. On the other hand, what would make us wake up in a wet bed would make the other fellow yawn."

"Perhaps. I don't know much about such things. But Ziegel has been going pretty hard lately. I'm not surprised he sprang a leak."

Heidemann tamped the pipe bowl with his index finger. "You've been going pretty hard yourself."

"Who? Me? Not any more than you or anybody else around here."

"Ever since you returned early from that leave you've spun like a windmill."

"Nothing else to do. I can't find anybody to play cards with, so I fly. Is that wrong?"

"No."

"Well, then."

The *Jasta* leader struck a match, and his eyes shone like agates as he held it to his pipe, sucking. Through a mat of smoke he said, "You've been tensed up, I've noticed."

"So? I haven't been aware of it."

"Is something bothering you?"

"Yes. Approaching senility."

"I mean really. I know you better than you think. And something is bothering you."

"Oh, in Christ's good name—are you going to begin analyzing me again?"

"Why does it bother you when I ask you how you are?"

"It doesn't bother me when you ask me how I am. It bothers me when you tell me how I am. Everybody just loves to tell me what I am, how I am, why I am. I'm just naturally appealing to alienists, I guess. It makes me want to vomit."

"Did something happen on your leave? Something that's disturbing you?"

"You'll never believe this, but I spent the first part of my leave giving stud service to a female aristocrat in heat. I got very drunk in the bargain."

"Why did you come back so early?"

"The well went dry. In both departments."

Heidemann sat down on a camp chair. His boots sparkled in the yellow lamplight as he crossed his legs. He stared into the glowing pipe bowl.

"Those sound like natural releases. Certainly nothing to bring an early end to a well-deserved leave."

"Please. No more interrogations. I came back early because I thought I'd be useful around here. Pardon me if that's not the case."

"Are you beginning to take yourself seriously? As a hero, I mean?"

Stachel sat forward, his eyes murky. "I hope you're not trying to amuse me. Because you're not. You're making me very angry."

"Relax, Stachel. You're a valuable property now. I'm interested in my valuable properties."

"Valuable? How? As a stud? Or a hero?"

"I have only two interests in you. First, as a pilot—a very good pilot—in my *Jasta*. Second, as a friend."

"Your stinging little questions don't sound very goddamned friendly to me."

"Watch your tongue. I may be fond of you, but don't take liberties with me. . . ."

"Oh, so now you're putting on your official hat."

"Not yet. Only if I have to. Meanwhile, I sincerely want to know if there's anything I can do to help you."

"Yes. Stop prying."

Heidemann looked around the tent. "Do you have anything to drink? Some sherry, perhaps? I'm in the mood."

"No."

"Nothing?"

"No. Nothing."

"You used to be fairly well stocked. Is your ration out? I have plenty—"

Stachel arose and walked to the flap. He stood there, looking up at the stars.

"I don't want any. Thank you, but I don't want any."

Heidemann knocked out his pipe. "Well, I guess I don't either, really."

They both fell silent. The frogs' grumbling was loud.

"Herr Hauptmann?"

"Yes?"

"I'm sorry."

"So am I."

"I mean it. I act like a pig, sometimes."

"We all do. The war—"

"No. Not the war. I mean me. Bruno Stachel. The way I'd be even if there hadn't been a war."

Heidemann shifted, and his chair creaked. "Men get taut when they're lonely. And afraid. They can be both— even without a war."

"Are you lonely?"

"Yes. Very." Heidemann nodded.

Stachel said: "I'm always lonely."

"I was sure of that."

"How so?"

"Elfi. You remind me of her. Remember?"

"Tell me about her. Is she a good woman?"

"The finest."

"What's she like?"

"I have a photograph of her here in my—"

"No. Just tell me. I don't want to see her."

"Well, she's not very tall. Not very short, for that matter. Medium. She has blue eyes, a—"

"I mean, what's she like? Not what does she look like."

Heidemann leaned back, his eyes half shut. "She's a very dear girl. But puzzling. Simultaneously she can be as soft as an eider pillow and as hard as a brass button. She's mercurial, unpredictable. Therefore, she's exciting and interesting. To me, at any rate."

"Because she doesn't fit into the little categories you like to assign to people?"

"I admit that's part of it. I can usually figure people in a wink. But she keeps me on the alert, has me guessing. It appeals to me. I remember one time. She had a cat. I dislike cats very much, but I permitted her to keep it because it gave her company while I was away. The animal, which she called Big Karl, turned out to be anything but a Karl and had kittens on our back stairs just after I'd arrived home from the front the first time. She asked me to take care of the little darlings, or some such. I drowned them in a rain barrel. When I returned, I found she had decided to take the kittens to an orphanage instead. Instead of what, I asked. Instead of my giving them away just to anyone, she said. When I told her that everything was already taken care of, she seemed to dismiss the subject. Later that evening, while I was reading, she came in from the kitchen. I looked up, and what do you know? She had a pitcher of water and she emptied it on my head, saying that it was too bad she couldn't accommodate me with a rain barrel. . . ."

Stachel smiled. "Spirit, eh?"

"Yes."

"What did you do?"

"Boxed her ears. Hard. What else could a husband do in such circumstances?"

"Nothing, I suppose. A man has to keep discipline in his house."

"Mm. But she's stimulating."

"It goes to show you, though. One never knows where he'll find spirit. Look at Ziegel, for instance. Who'd ever think he'd hang around a burning airplane, working like an ox to pull out someone he doesn't particularly like?"

Heidemann smiled. "Ordinarily I don't give much to Jews. But I'll have to admit Ziegel showed some stuff today."

"Ziegel's a Jew?" Stachel peered at him.

"Certainly. Didn't you know?"

He shrugged. "I simply hadn't thought about it."

Boots sounded outside and Kettering came through the flap, blinking against the light.

"Oh. There you are, sir. Excuse the intrusion, but I have a flimsy here from *Koft*. It's classified *dringend,* so I expected you'd want to see it right away."

"You did well to look me up, Kettering." Heidemann took the message and, holding it close to the lantern, read

209

slowly. He read it a second time, then folded the paper and placed it in the cuff of his tunic sleeve. He smiled, broadly for him.

"You may go, Kettering."

The adjutant, piqued by the offhanded dismissal, saluted sullenly and creaked out of the tent into the night. When he'd gone, Heidemann leaned forward, his eyes bright.

"Good news, Stachel."

"So?"

"Yes. You and I are going to visit Berlin."

"Berlin!"

"Yes."

"What for?"

"This message"—Heidemann tapped his sleeve—"advises me that there will be tryouts of new aircraft types at Johannisthal. I'm ordered to report there in company of another *Jasta* member of my choice. My choice is you."

"Well, as much as I'd like to see the big city, wouldn't you do better to take a technical type like Ziegel?"

"No. Flying personnel are involved only. This, I suspect, is the same general arrangement used last January. Leading pilots from leading *Jastas* try the various new models, then select the machine they believe comes closest to combat needs. The D-7 was so selected."

"I know. Well, I must say I'm flattered."

"Why? You are now a darling of the German public. You have nearly thirty victories to your credit. What would be more natural than for you to go?"

"Piss on the German public. I'm more interested in what you, a professional, think of me. I saw how the press works."

"As a professional, I think you are a professional."

"When do we leave?"

"Tomorrow morning. We'll take the C-3."

"This will leave the *Jasta* in pretty bad shape. We're at rock bottom as it is."

"Orders."

"Yes, but—"

"But Berlin awaits."

"And—Elfi?"

"And Elfi."

"Good orders, eh?"

"Excellent orders."

Stachel was preparing for bed when he heard someone outside.

"Who's there?"

"I."

"Oh. Rupp. What do you want?"

"Can I come in?"

"I suppose so. This seems to be my night for callers."

The *Uffz* sauntered in. The cigar looked to be the same one he'd had three weeks ago. A bottle was tucked under each arm.

"Well?" Stachel felt the old irritation. Rupp looked around the tent, his small eyes insolent.

"Comfy in your new little nest?"

"It'll do."

"Where's the bar?"

"There isn't any bar."

"How come? A sauce-lapper like you ought to have a very big one."

Stachel's neck muscles tightened, and his face paled. "I'll kill you yet, Rupp."

"No you won't. You need me. You're a sauce-lapper."

"Get out."

"Not yet. Business."

"You'll get no more business from me. The agreement's off."

Rupp sat down in the chair Heidemann had occupied. He placed the bottles on the board floor.

"Get up and get out."

"Business, I said."

"I don't want any more of your cheap swill. Do you understand? Not now or ever."

Rupp shrugged. "Not until you want it again. But meanwhile, there's the little matter of the sum you owe me for your last—delivery, shall we say? The big one I made before you went on leave?"

Stachel's pallor deepened. His lips were compressed.

"How much?"

211

"Two hundred marks."

"Two hundred! Are you insane?"

"Two hundred."

"I'll give you half that. And you'll still be ahead."

Rupp's eyes hardened. He dropped the cigar butt to the floor and ground it with a heel.

"Do you want Heidemann to find out that you're a sot? That you've been misusing a noncommissioned rank? He'll squash you like a flea and poop on the goo, as you once put it, I believe."

Stachel turned, reached into a pocket of the trousers he'd hung on a nail driven into a tent post. He counted out one hundred marks. Silently he faced Rupp, who lounged arrogantly in the pool of light. Then, in a single, animal-like bound, he crossed the tent, seized the man's tunic, and heaved him erect. The camp chair skittered against the canvas wall and rebounded with a clatter.

"Open your swinish mouth!"

Rupp's eyes were frightened. His face reddened under the pressure, but his mouth remained tight. Stachel jerked a knee into his groin and shoved him to the floor. Sitting astride the struggling form, he pressed a thumb and forefinger against the other's jaw hinges. Rupp's mouth sagged open and sucked air, the whistling sound loud.

"Now, you stinking pig, take your money."

He crammed the crumpled bills into the gaping, salivating mouth. Then he scooped up the shredded cigar and added it to the wad. He said, his voice toneless: "Get out of my sight."

He sent the man stumbling into the night.

"You'll see, you dirty bastard," Rupp's voice choked from the darkness. "I'll fix you! I'll take this to Heidemann —to the frigging Kaiser, if I have to! I'll fix you good!"

He stared at the bottles. They lay on the floor where they had rolled. His hands trembled, and there was sweat on his forehead.

What had the *Graf* said? What?

Pray that it isn't too late?

An agonized moan burst from him, and, half running, half crawling, he clawed up the bottles. He weaved out

212

into the coolness and threw them, hard, against the stars.

Then he re-entered the tent and fell on the cot. He lay there for a long time, his chest heaving and his eyes staring.

Heidemann's shock was deep but relatively short-lived. When he had retraced his steps to Stachel's tent, his sole purpose had been to remind Stachel that the Fokker Company would have a suite at the Hotel Bristol, where they could make their off-duty headquarters while at the capital. And now, as he groped his way quietly through the darkness toward his office, he was aware, for the latest of uncounted times, of the idiotic capriciousness of events— once again impressed by the irrational process by which a prosaic errand could in an instant become a dramatic revelation. Life, Heidemann reflected bitterly, was mainly a protracted series of fantastic haphazards. What he had seen at Stachel's tent had, consistent with all these inconsistencies, brought together many answers; but it had also posed an immediate, pressing problem that demanded immediate corrective measures. For a moment there, he had been overwhelmed by the insane uselessness of attempting to prearrange fate, and the temptation to surrender to the tyranny of futility had been great. But being as he was, once a problem had been recognized he had no choice but to devise a solution. Surprisingly, the solution had suggested itself quickly. Deep in thought, he paused before his office door as if listening to the night. He nodded once to himself, then turned and strode the few meters to Kettering's office.

The big adjutant was treating himself to a drink. When the *Jastaführer* entered, he swung his bulk erect, returning the flask to his desk drawer in hurried confusion.

"Carry on, Kettering. Have your drink, if you wish."

"Thank you, sir. Care for one?"

"No."

Kettering waited, his eyes cautious, while Heidemann paced back and forth over the duckboards. The adjutant was impressed again by the difference that had come to the *Jasta* leader in recent weeks. Heidemann had always served to reassure Kettering that even in the enormous confusions and vagaries of war, certain constants would remain. Heidemann had personified these; Heidemann had demonstrated that solid men could survive and retain their solidity even in the face of the most seductive invitations to dissolution, temporization, and degeneracy. Heidemann had been Kettering's kind of man, because Kettering knew that what the *Jastaführer* was, he could not be. But in recent weeks, things had changed. There was nothing Kettering could point to and say, "There—that's what did it"; rather, it had been an intuitive thing he'd felt. Heidemann simply no longer came across as Heidemann.

If there were any single causative factor, Kettering felt it was Stachel. Somehow, in some way, Stachel had worked a subtle influence on the *Jasta* leader. It had, for example, been a distinct shock that day when Heidemann had confirmed those three Spads out of hand, the Spads that had been downed on Willi's last sortie. It had also been a disturbing thing to see Heidemann's preoccupations elsewhere those many times when Stachel's boorishness had asserted itself. For a commander with an overriding sense of propriety, Heidemann had developed a curious blind spot for some of the most peculiar and arrogant improprieties. If ever, Kettering told himself, he'd been asked to point out any one member of the *Jasta* whom Heidemann might be expected to dote on, Stachel would have been his last choice.

Well, he shrugged inwardly, *c'est la* frigging *guerre*.

Heidemann fished out his pipe and dug its bowl into the tobacco pouch he had unrolled. "Kettering, please make certain that the C-3's radiator leak has been repaired. I don't want to land for water every five kilometers tomorrow."

"Ziegel says he's already taken care of it."

"Good."

Heidemann sucked the pipe to life under a match. He spoke through the cloud. "Kettering?"

"Sir?"

"I want you to take a letter for me."

"Yes, sir." He scooped up a pad and held a pencil stub ready.

"Make it to whom it may concern. And attach it to the

214

necessary papers posting Rupp to the Army replacement center. I want him out of here by oh-seven-hundred to-morrow."

Kettering's eyebrows lifted. "Rupp, sir?"

"Rupp. I want him out of here and beyond my sight by oh-seven-hundred."

Kettering swallowed noisily. "Has he done something wrong?"

"Take this letter for my signature: 'Subject Rupp'— first name, rank, Army number, and so on and so on— 'served under the command of the undersigned officer from'—dates, whatever they are—'and although he has demonstrated technical proficiency during this period, he has revealed character traits that make it inadvisable to entrust him further with confidential information.' "

Kettering looked up, his face puzzled. "Begging your pardon, sir, but this will ruin Rupp. He won't be able to—"

Heidemann ignored him, continuing his dictation around the pipe stem. " 'Subject *Unteroffizier* has not committed overt acts of irresponsibility, and therefore has received no punishments, summary or otherwise. However, it is the undersigned's considered judgment that subject *Unterof-fizier*'s word is open to serious question in all matters.' "

"Sir, goddamn it, this makes out Rupp officially to be a liar."

Heidemann's eyes narrowed. "Are you disputing me?"

"Well, no, sir. Of course not. But—"

"Then shut your mouth."

"Very good, sir."

"Mark the letter *Vertrauliche Personalsache* and append it to the copies forwarded by courier."

"Pardon, *Herr Hauptmann,* but as a Confidential Per-sonnel Matter Rupp will never see the charge. He'll have no idea—"

"Precisely. Write the letter."

"As ordered, sir."

CHAPTER 24

THE BIG Albatros C-3 sat in the twilight that precedes dawn, the night's moisture streaming slowly down its flanks. Kettering leaned against a wing, watching Ziegel and one of his mechanics screw the engine cowl in place. A swarm of birds swept by, their chattering oddly muffled in the morning air.

"Finished?"

"I suppose. Seems idiotic to be testing new machines in Berlin when we can't keep even the old ones in shape."

"I thought Heidemann told you to get a rest."

Ziegel yawned. "I get more rest walking around, doing something. I lie down, I start thinking."

"That never hurt anybody."

"You don't know what I think about."

"The Melancholy Dane, eh?"

"Dane?"

"Never mind."

Ziegel waved the mechanic away, then sat on one of the airplane's tires. He yawned again, noisily. "You look like a cow plop in a mud puddle. What's the matter?"

Kettering shook his head woefully. "I just packed off Rupp. It was pretty awful. He never knew what hit him."

"Just what was all that about, anyhow? Freihofer told me something was up when he brought the coffee at oh-three-hundred."

"Rupp flew out on his ass, that's what."

"I'm not surprised. He's a surly one. What did he do?"

"Damned if I know. Heidemann simply walked in last night and told me to draw up the papers. Then he dictated a letter to the effect that Rupp is a frigging liar—said letter to precede said Rupp wherever in said hell he goes."

"A firing squad couldn't be more effective. No explanation?"

"None. Just the *coup de grâce*. Rupp will be digging latrines for the rest of his life and never know why."

"Heidemann must have caught him in a beauty, all right."

"I don't know. I simply don't know. My intuition tells me Stachel had something to do with it."

"The *Hauptmann* doesn't do things without a reason."

"That's what binds me. He usually states his reasons. This isn't like him."

Ziegel snorted. "A lot of things aren't like they used to be. So why shouldn't Heidemann change?"

"It's beyond me. Heidemann changing is like the Iron Cross turning to pink and green. Take him and Stachel, for instance: there's something for you."

"They've been great chums these days, that's certain."

"Chums! I admire Heidemann. He's a damned good soldier. But he's a nitwit when it comes to Stachel. Have you ever seen Heidemann drop in and visit in anybody else's tent? No sir. But he wigwags into Stachel's digs like a leaky little puppy. Can you imagine? I can forgive Stachel a lot of things, but when he messes up a good officer, I draw the line. Think he has something on Heidemann?"

"Not likely. The *Hauptmann*'s too correct to be compromised. I dare say he even clicks his heels and bows before he climbs into bed with his wife."

"How do you click bare heels?" Kettering said, rising to the bait.

"Who says they're bare? Haven't you heard that our leader always is in dress uniform when he copulates?"

Kettering smiled reminiscently. "Did I ever tell you about the American wench? The one in Albuquerque who always wore cowboy boots?"

"Not more than seven thousand times."

"Those spurs nearly tore me to ribbons."

"What do you hear from Gretchen, Fatso?" Ziegel asked, cheered to see his old friend returning to type.

"She's sent me a batch of periodicals. They're full of Stachel, of course."

"So?"

"Yes. It's almost funny, actually, how they've roman-

217

ticized him. It's like reading about an entirely different fellow—a character in a play, or something. I make him out as insolent, they say he's determined; I think he's sarcastic, they find him to be a wit; I say he's an egotist, they do him up as self-assured; I think—"

"I get the idea. Well, the readers love that kind of manure."

"And the pictures. You remember the one that little fat bastard took of Stachel and the kid holding hands? They've printed it as big as my backside and label it, 'His Only Sweetheart.' Jesus. Stachel's only sweetheart is himself."

"As I say—they love it."

"It makes me want to throw up."

Ziegel touched his face with his fingers, gingerly, testing the singed skin. "Stachel isn't a bad sort, really. You used to be pretty high on him yourself."

"He's an arrogant, tampering son-of-a-bitch politician, that's what he is. I simply don't trust him."

"Suit yourself. But I saw him yesterday."

"What do you mean by that?"

"Out there. On the field."

"So?"

"He has guts."

"I never said he didn't," Kettering huffed.

"I know. But there was more than that. He kept ordering me to run."

"From the wreck?"

"From the wreck."

Kettering considered that awhile. "Wasn't that a bit out of character for him? Maybe he's starting to believe his own publicity."

"I'm not so sure. All I know is, he was sitting in a bonfire and he was telling me to run. Nobody loves his publicity that much. I honestly think he didn't want me to get hurt."

"I'll bet you my adorable ass that he never thanked you for all your trouble."

Ziegel was silent.

"Well? Did he?"

"I don't remember. I was blubbering too much." He

218

seemed wrenched by the memory. "Tenderhearted Jesus —what made me blubber like that?"

"We're all jumpy. At any rate, you did just fine. And Stachel was lucky you were there. By the way—why were you all the way out there, anyway?"

"I don't know."

"You don't know?"

"No."

Kettering rolled his eyes skyward. "Everybody's going crazy."

They turned when they heard someone coming. It was Stachel. He was in his lightweight flying suit, and his face glowed from a recently completed shave. It struck Kettering that there were times when Stachel appeared to be quite a fellow. The chameleon.

Stachel himself was mildly surprised that he felt as serviceable as he did this morning. He had lain awake for a long time, and the struggle against himself had been total. It was puzzling, really, to recall how in the first days after that murky and degrading leave, it had been relatively easy to deny the impulse. Perhaps it had been the newness of the realization of how heavily the *Graf* had scored. But as the days had passed, the fear, the certain knowledge that he was fighting for survival, had paled under the absence of tangible reward. As the immediacy of the threat had diminished and the body and mind had begun to recoup the losses they'd suffered in the leave's debauch, the lack of compensation for all the sacrifice and effort had become more wearing. And now, not to drink called for an especial output of mental energy; not to be rewarded somehow for the huge expenditure had become disheartening and frustrating. It was difficult to see how he could hope to survive Berlin, the City of Baal and Bacchus.

But he had come to one decision during the night, at least, and now he moved to implement it.

"Kettering?"

"Yes?"

"I've left a package at your shack. Will you see that it goes out with the Rupp Postal Service?"

"Rupp doesn't live here any more."

"What do you mean?"

"Heidemann fired him, that's what I mean. He's gone, for now and evermore, life without end."

"I'll be damned. I didn't know. . . ." He smiled faintly, and there was relief in his face. Kettering regarded the face, calm and direct, the eyes quietly level. He had not seen Stachel look so well set up in a long time, and he was vaguely impressed.

"I've inherited the postal service. I'll take care of your package."

Stachel nodded his thanks. To Ziegel he said: "The machine—is it ready?"

"Yes. It's ready."

"Gravel off the floor?" There was an amused sound in the question.

"Yes. But I hope you don't have to roll that old bedspring. It'll never make it."

"I hope so, too."

"Who's going to fly it? You or the *Hauptmann?*"

"I'll fly. He will ride in the rear lounge and read newspapers."

Kettering grunted, his belly rolling. "If so, all he'll see is Bruno Stachel, savior of little French schoolgirls."

Stachel blushed. "I've seen that stuff. Pretty awful, isn't it?"

"Yes it is."

Ziegel broke in: "Well, you can't help what the journalists do. After all—"

Stachel looked at him. "I don't have to talk to them."

Kettering said, "But you will."

"Sleep badly, Kettering? You're grumpy this morning."

"Any objections?"

Stachel, unaccountably, felt a surge of depression and regret. Two-dimensional Bruno Stachel . . .

"Why aren't we friends, Kettering? There was a time when I thought we might be."

Ziegel, who had been moodily contemplating a patch on the wing surface, looked up, new interest in his tired eyes. Kettering was caught off guard by the question.

"It requires two to be friends."

"There are two of us."

"Yes. But you're all take and no give."

"C'est la guerre. I'm going to get some coffee. Call me when Heidemann condescends to emerge from his sanctuary." He strolled off toward the mess shack. Later, after he'd gone, Ziegel shook his head slowly.

"Too bad."

"What's too bad?"

"Didn't you see?"

"See what? Goddamn it, stop talking gibberish."

"Stachel was trying to say something to us, I think."

"He's acting awfully contrite lately. I like him better when he's openly nasty."

"I think the poor bastard is lonely."

"Well, he works hard enough to make it that way. Frankly, I'm sick of talking about him."

Ziegel rolled the end of his thumb over the wing patch. When he spoke again, his voice was quiet. "So that's the trouble, eh?"

"What do you mean, for God's sake?"

"Loneliness. I've wondered about him. And he's lonely."

"Well, so is everybody else around this frigging hole," Kettering humphed. "What's so special about that?"

"It's a special kind of loneliness for him. I understand that kind of loneliness, the kind that comes when you find, for some reason you can't name, you're not a full-fledged member of the human race."

"What in the name of my uncle's testicles are you talking about, anyhow?"

"This puts his picture in an entirely different frame."

"Are you all right?"

"Yes, I'm all right."

They were silent for a time, watching the sun put golden streaks in the thinning mist. Ziegel said then: "Well, Stachel has one friend."

"Who could that be?"

"Me."

"Have you popped your bung?"

"We don't have the same problem. But we have the same load to carry."

"Load? What load?"

"Ourselves."

"Balls."

CHAPTER **25**

THE SUITE at the Hotel Bristol was the most lavish Stachel had ever seen. Of course, he could admit ruefully, he hadn't seen many in his life; among the few owned by his father, there was nothing that could come near this for sheer elegance and spaciousness. There was a foyer which could easily have passed for a deluxe double at the hotel in Schwalbe, and beyond it, through a splendid arch, he could see a great salon in which knots of men in uniform and women in high fashion chattered enthusiastically and clicked glasses and laughed against a background of insistent string music. There was that feeling of inadequacy again when he approached a haughty, negative-looking fellow with a red boutonniere who had taken station at the outer door and was checking the calling card tray. The man, sour-faced and dry, did not look up.

"I'm Bruno Stachel. I don't have an invitation, but I've been instructed by *Hauptmann* Otto Heidemann to meet him here. He says we are expected. . . ." Why, he wondered, did he have to sound so apologetic? Why did his face have to feel so hot? The carnation had turned toward him but almost at once had been nudged aside by a jolly-looking man in tweeds and knickers who had appeared magically. His grin was cordial and wide, and his voice was raised above the rumble coming from the room beyond.

"Ho, there! You are Bruno Stachel, eh? Welcome, welcome!" He pumped Stachel's hand.

Stachel, relieved, smiled back and couldn't resist giving the boutonniere a mild, triumphant glance. "Thanks. I wasn't sure I was expected. . . ."

"Expected!" The youngish fellow beamed. "Everybody's been waiting for you! Besides, no flier has to have a special invitation at Tony Fokker's place. Civilians, perhaps—they may be salesmen or revolutionaries. But fliers —never!" He took Stachel's arm and led him to the archway where he craned for the orchestra leader's eye above the crowd.

"What would you do if an English flier showed up, *Herr* Fokker?" Stachel asked, amused.

"Admit him, of course. All airmen are my friends. And it's Tony."

"Tony."

"As you can see, I haven't dressed. Just got in from Johannisthal myself. Where's Otto?"

"He'll be here soon. We arrived this afternoon, and he went directly to his home, of course. He asked me to meet him and *Frau* Heidemann here. He said you wouldn't mind."

"Delighted! I haven't seen Otto and Elfi in months. Months!" He raised an arm and whirled the forefinger. The violins and piano sounded a heavy, imperious chord and the crowd noises subsided. Everyone was looking at them, and again Stachel felt the heat rush behind his cheeks.

"Ladies and gentlemen! May I present the officer who has become the latest to join the ranks of Germany's most illustrious men of the air—*Leutnant* Bruno Stachel. . . ."

There was the music again and a crash of applause and *hochs*. Stachel wanted to run, as usual, but the host's hand was propelling him forward toward the advancing ranks of grays and blacks and reds and blues and the other more mystifying colors that constitute the gaudy armor of party denizens. There was a crescendo of geese-like gabble, shouted and empty salutations, introductions forgotten as soon as they were made; Stachel had the fleeting impression that all the faces were the same, as if

223

identical plaster casts had been inserted in a welter of costumes and topped with an insane variety of wigs.

He was passed from group to group (like a bucket in a fire brigade, he mused) and at each briefly held station the voices were pitched a key above those at the last, the comments were more vacuous, the wine-breath heavier, the perfume thicker, and his discomfort more intense. As changing as surf, the costumes surged up to break around him, smothering him in a foam of yammering faces. Somewhere, he noted anxiously, he had lost the host and he was alone in the noisy sea. His hand hurt from squeezing, his shoulders were sore from "stout chap!" pummeling, and his lips were stiff from the smile he had forced upon them. He shook his head in politely unbending refusal when tray after tray of drinks were swung before him; fighting the ancient battle, he was certain that he was the only sober person within miles, and the knowledge depressed and irritated him.

Then, unaccountably, he was free, and he made for the terrace, already forgotten, already just another of the reeds in the swamp. He was not unaware that the interest in him had diminished noticeably once the host had fallen away from his arm. This, too, depressed him somehow. (*All is ephemeral—fame and the famous as well. . . .*) The line came in on him from some small chink of the past, and he shrugged at one more irony confirmed.

A craggy man in evening dress and pince-nez was lecturing a fat colonel of cavalry who was deeply drunk and looked as if he'd crack the back of any horse, were he ever to mount one.

"I tell you, Kolbach," the tall one was saying, "paper shoes they're making now. Where will it all end? Burnt corn for coffee, sausage made of fish, no bread, no butter, no sugar, no fat—and now paper shoes. Where will it all end?"

The colonel belched, his paunch rolling. "The trouble with you, Hauser, is that you've been living off the fat of the land too long. If you'd broken out of your lace drawers long enough to leave that fruity diplomatic corps and get into the Army, perhaps you'd not feel the pinch so much these days."

"But I've a rupture. I told you that."

"How can you have a rupture when you haven't any balls?"

Stachel moved away, tense and a little sick. Two women came by, their hair in crazy arrangements and their dresses swishing. One was holding a cigarette in a long magenta holder and he realized that this was the first time he had ever seen a woman smoking in public. He had heard that some did, but such a brazen authentication of the rumor was shockingly embarrassing—like hearing a bishop break wind. The other was saying, "—and he wanted me to spend the month at Garmisch, put up in a horrid little *Gasthaus* like a fifty-*pfennig* whore." As they disappeared beyond the ferns, the one with the cigarette said, "I'd go with him anywhere, *Liebling*. And for nothing, too."

At a refreshment table beside the terrace doors, a pair of airmen flew their hands, and Stachel considered means to get into the conversation. He was struck by their advanced age; they were in their thirties if they were a day. The red-faced one laughed, his horselike teeth yellow in the light from the candles. He concluded his flight demonstration with a mocking shrug.

"And Tony says the triplane will remain a high spot in aviation history. Can you imagine?"

"Horse manure. He's always talking in superlatives."

"Jesus, the whole frigging country talks in superlatives. It's a German disease. . . ."

"Tony's no German. He's Dutch," the small one reminded gravely.

"The triplane's still a piece of junk."

"I hear his D-7's a barge, too. Alex said he took one up in Darmstadt one day. It damned near killed him. You ask anybody. The D-7 is a barge."

The pair gave no sign that they had noted Stachel's approach. To disguise the fact that he had indeed been heading their way, he went to the table and picked up a glass. As he studied the liquid, the red-faced one punched his arm and some of the wine ran over his fingers.

"What do you say, young fellow?"

"What do I say about what, Major?"

"You're a flier. At least you have a badge that says so. What do you think of the D-7? You know what a D-7 is?"

Stachel wished in silent chagrin that he'd not left the Blue Max with the hotel's jewelers. The ribbon catch had broken, and the house had assured him it would be repaired by morning. It was very apparent that these two had not interrupted their drinking long enough to be among the earlier welcomers of the latest officer to join the ranks of Germany's most illustrious men of the air. . . .

"I know what a D-7 is." He added: "Sir."

"What is it, my scrub-faced peacock?"

"It's a flying machine. Sir."

"Don't get snotty with me. What kind of flying machine?"

"It's a single-seater scout machine built by our host. It is variously fitted with the one-sixty and two-twenty Mercedes, or the one-eighty-five BMW; it's a biplane with wings of box-spar cantilever construction and a fuselage with welded steel tubing for longerons and spacers. It utilizes balanced ailerons, rudder, and elevators. Its upper span measures—"

"Who are you? One of Tony's men? Or maybe just a smart aleck?"

"Neither. Sir. I simply fly a D-7. I find it to be a very high-quality aircraft. Sir."

"I don't like your attitude."

"I don't like yours either. Sir."

The other gaped, and his partner giggled.

"You're trying my patience, *Leutnant*. Perhaps you'd like to accompany me to General Wurfl's office in the morning."

"General Wurfl? I'd be delighted. Sir," he said mildly.

"I think he'd like to hear how you address me in that sneering, snotty way of yours."

"From what I hear of General Wurfl, I'm certain he would. Sir. I hear he, too, makes short shrift of pompous drunkards who talk through their anuses. Sir."

"Why, you—"

Stachel felt a touch at his elbow. It was an attendant.

226

"Pardon, *Leutnant* Stachel. *Hauptmann* Heidemann is here and wonders if you can join him."

"Of course. Immediately."

He considered the pair, his eyes unblinking and indifferent. To the major he said: "May I offer a suggestion? Sir."

The man's face was now ruby with angry embarrassment.

"Well?" he gargled.

"Kiss my ass. Sir."

He turned his back on them and followed the attendant's red uniform through the crowd.

It was not *Frau* Heidemann's beauty that stunned Stachel. Actually, she was not what he would consider beautiful; she was interesting, to be sure, but certainly not the type he'd envision if someone were to say the two words, "beautiful woman." Her eyes, which her husband had described as blue, were not blue at all, but a cool green with dark blue flecks. Her hair was deep auburn; she wore it in a careful, almost severe style, perhaps as auxiliary to her gown, which he sensed, was subtly contrived to control a defiant voluptuousness. She was pale and erect, her smile quiet, and somehow remote.

His astonishment came, rather, from recognition: *Frau* Heidemann was the drunken nurse he had seen across the terrace while at dinner with the Von Klugermanns at Army those months ago.

Stachel clicked his heels and bowed, grateful for this means to cover his insane compulsion to laugh. *Jesus! Who said it was a small world?*

"Good evening, Bruno." Heidemann smiled. "I'm sorry we're late but we had many things to catch up." He was pink with prideful pleasure, and again it was all Stachel could do to keep a cap on the great guffaw that boiled in his chest when he weighed the *Jasta* leader's glowing superciliousness against his own secret knowledge. *Jesus to Jesus!*

"Good evening, sir."

"Elfi, may I present Bruno Stachel?" Heidemann waved with patronizing effusiveness.

"*Frau* Heidemann," Stachel acknowledged gravely.

"A pleasure, *Herr Leutnant*. Otto has mentioned you frequently in his letters." She gave him a clear green look.

At least, Stachel noted, she had the grace not to credit the newspapers.

"And he has often told me of you, *Gnädige Frau*. With all respect to your husband's way with words, he's done very poorly in his descriptions."

Heidemann laughed easily in his superior way. "How do you describe beauty *per se?*"

Frau Heidemann raised a tolerant brow at the saccharine flattery. As she examined the great room, she said evenly: "I dare say female beauty grows in direct proportion to male continence."

This time Stachel could not suppress the laugh. It came in a sharp burst, then accelerated when he saw Heidemann's face and its smile fading in confusion and embarrassment.

"You didn't tell me, sir, that *Frau* Heidemann was a wag."

She regarded Stachel curiously. "I'm not a wag, *Herr Leutnant*. Simply a realist."

"Some of the world's finest humor comes from the realists among us," he said.

"As do some of the most exquisite cruelties," she countered, her eyes studying the party again.

"True enough," Stachel chided, "but it takes a sentimentalist to recognize cruelty of any degree. One is hard put to be a realist and a sentimentalist at the same time; therefore, it's surprising to hear a realist acknowledge cruelty, let alone qualify it as being exquisite."

"Not," she said crisply, "if the realist is a sentimentalist reformed by a frequently bloodied nose."

Stachel studied her profile with puzzled interest. Heidemann had the air of a man left behind by a train. He ventured stiffly: "Would you like some refreshment, my dear?"

"No, I think not."

"Stachel?"

"No, thank you, sir." He could feel Heidemann appraising him.

"You're not drinking, old boy?"

Old boy? God, Stachel thought sardonically, there's no accounting for how the presence of a wife can alter a man's character. He tried to imagine Heidemann calling him into the office at the field and saying, "Well, old boy, how about a little balloon run, eh?" He couldn't.

"No. We may be flying tomorrow."

Heidemann's smile was faintly mocking. "Surely," he persisted, "you can join in one, at least. This is a party."

"Don't press the *Leutnant,* Otto."

Frau Heidemann's voice had not changed, but annoyance was there. Looking at her now, it seemed incredible to Stachel that this was the same woman who had been so superbly *besoffen* that distant evening. The other had been so plain. . . . This one was, well, different, that's all. In any event, he appreciated her stepping in and settling the drink business. This party was the first real test of his determination in that department and it was good to have an ally—even if it were a somewhat unusual woman with her own demonstrated drinking peculiarities.

"Of course not, my dear," Heidemann said blandly, "but I've never known Bruno to exercise such care simply because he expected to fly the next day. . . ."

She changed the subject. "I've looked and looked, and I don't recognize anyone here. Except for the Baroness von Klatow and that scandalous daughter of hers."

Heidemann put in, "Not always the best sort are found here. Tony is a very discriminating fellow in most respects, but when it comes to women he simply has no sense. He's anxious to show the front-line people a good time, and since he's heard they require feminine company to have a good time, he opens the door to anyone remotely resembling a female. But he could be more careful, really; after all, there are many first-rate ladies who'd be delighted to entertain our lads."

Stachel was tempted to point out the host's fundamental wisdom in not rounding up a corps of first-rate ladies to entertain the front-line lads (God—*lads!*), but held himself in.

"I believe," *Frau* Heidemann was saying, "our host has shown considerable wisdom in not assembling a group of

229

first-rate ladies to entertain the lads. If I were a front-line flier on leave, I doubt if I'd want to spend a precious evening with a first-rate lady—whatever that is."

"Elfi! Really. What makes you say such things?"

Heidemann, Stachel could see, was honestly shocked. The laugh was insistent in him again. The *Jastaführer* had his hands full with this dame, that was certain. She talked like . . . Who? . . .

She regarded her husband, not unkindly. "Don't you remember? I'm a realist."

"I don't know what to make of you," he said testily. "It's simply not proper. . . ."

"Just a little joke, dear. I meant nothing."

"What will Bruno think?"

Stachel covered his amusement by waving a hand disarmingly. "I think *Frau* Heidemann shows the most refreshing candor I've come across in ages. I only wish more people would say what they really think." Impulsively, he added: "Don't you, *Herr Hauptmann?*"

Heidemann was considering the question, his face dark, when the crowd parted to make way for a messenger outfitted in—of all things—a steel helmet, a dispatch case, gas-mask canister, and motorcyclist's puttees. He came clumping across the polished floor, his chin set in acknowledgment of his own importance. He saluted, clicking his heels in a climactic crash.

"Hauptmann Heidemann?"

"Yes. What is it?" The *Jastaführer*'s mood seemed to lighten with his awareness that many people were watching him.

"A message from *Kogenluft,* sir." The man flipped open his case and, with a parade ground flourish, presented an official envelope. Stachel wondered if *Frau* Heidemann had also been struck by the silliness of the tableau. He did not look at her.

Heidemann flicked the seal, withdrew the flimsy, and read briefly, brows knitted. He dismissed the messenger then, and although he retained his official posture, his expression had taken on a dim and frosty air of satisfaction.

"Laundry receipt, Otto?" *Frau* Heidemann asked dryly.

230

He gave her a narrow look.

"As a matter of fact, my dear, I've been asked to see General Wurfl immediately."

"Say hello for me."

"This is somewhat awkward, of course. I can't see you home. . . ."

"That's all right. *Leutnant* Stachel will call a cab for me." Was there relief in her voice? Stachel thought so. He realized Heidemann was looking at him questioningly.

"Why, naturally—" Stachel said quickly.

"No," Heidemann said authoritatively, appearing to make a decision, "there's no reason whatever to ruin your evening, my dear. Bruno will be happy to attend you here until I return, won't you, old boy?"

"Well, certainly. I'd be honored."

"No, Otto," she protested, "that would be a terrible imposition. *Herr* Stachel probably has other plans. . . ."

Stachel surrendered silently to the impossible development and reassured her, smiling. "I'd really be delighted."

Heidemann, anxious to be off, said: "I have an even better idea. Bruno will take you to Putzi's. He can order dinner for the three of us, and I'll join you as soon as I'm free."

"Putzi's?" Stachel asked.

"It's a first-rate little place on a side street whose name I can never remember. The cabby will know. Splendid food, atmosphere, all that. Well, until later, then."

"Otto, I—"

"At Putzi's. Later. *Wiederseh'n.*"

Watching him stride off it occurred to Stachel that the *Jastaführer* not once had asked his wife what she wanted to do.

CHAPTER 26

THE RESTAURANT was an island of Oberbayern placidness in the drumming of the city. Low oaken beams, candlelight, shelves lined with beer mugs of all sizes and colors, fresh-cut flowers arranged in careful disarray, and a couple who sang and played zithers made common cause. The resultant *Gemütlichkeit* gently mocked the glass and marble pomp that pressed in from the Berlin around.

Although their conversation had been intermittent and sparring, it had gone well enough, mainly because *Frau* Heidemann had had the shortages to talk about. Otto, she told Stachel with wry amusement, had been remembering Putzi's of several years before when he had recommended the food. The whole situation these days was becoming intolerable: it was virtually impossible for the average *Burger* to find real food, and bootlegging, even of staples such as potatoes and bread, was now a big business. No restaurant—even the very expensive Putzi's—could serve more than fish, turnips, and tired greens even at harvest. As for the *Hausfrau,* even the most conservative and law-abiding had long since been reduced to graft and barter, and to falsifying food cards.

Stachel welcomed her small-talk, because it was difficult for him to generate subjects on his own; the only thing he and this woman had in common was Otto Heidemann, and what was there to say about him? If he were to speak favorably of the *Jastaführer,* it would sound ingratiating; if passively, it might ring offensively. For a reason he couldn't quite label, he did not want to offend *Frau* Heidemann. So he quickly retreated into the role of polite listener, and it suited him.

But she was asking him a direct question now.

"Is my husband highly thought of? By his men, I mean."

He looked at her a long moment. The candlelight caught in her hair and the soft effect was pleasing. Her eyes were calm, and there was curiosity in them again.

"Yes. I'd say so."

"What do you think of him?"

His understanding of women was really quite limited, and he hesitated. Whatever she actually wanted to hear, he decided, was beyond him. So he plumped for—how had the *Graf* phrased it?—the blessed purgative of candidness.

"He's a first-rate airman, and I admire him for that. But he's also a stuffed shirt."

She smiled, a mere lifting of the corner of her lips. "That's Otto, all right. Does he still try to analyze people?"

"To the point of vexation."

She laughed then, her small teeth glistening in the rosy light. "And what are his pronouncements concerning you, *Leutnant* Stachel?"

"He says I'm a combination of contradictions."

"And are you?"

"Yes. He's right."

"He's always right."

Stachel considered the undertone of irony in her tone. He was anxious to avoid any family confidences from *Frau* Heidemann, that was certain, so he struggled for a way to change the subject. She did it for him.

"*Leutnant* Stachel, are you amused?"

"What do you mean?" he asked, startled.

"From the first I've sensed you've been secretly laughing at me."

"Well, no, I—" he stammered defensively.

"Is it," she persisted, "because you once saw me intoxicated? Somewhere, some place I don't remember?"

Jesus. This dame was a terror. He fought desperately to mask his surprise and confusion. "Well—"

"I thought so," she shrugged. "I guess it is funny at that. Otto such a proper fellow and all. Where was it? Here, in Berlin? Kreuznach? Köln? Or was it—?"

He broke in, annoyed suddenly. If she wanted sympathy, she was crazy if she thought she'd get it from him.

"It was at Army, last spring," he said crisply.

"Oh?"

"You were all rigged out in Red Cross gear. You were with a good-looking brunette."

She nodded. "That must have been Trina. She and I were visiting the field hospital there on an orientation tour."

"You were cockeyed," he pressed bluntly.

She smiled distantly, staring into the candle flame with

233

thoughtful eyes. "I usually was in those days. Was I especially offensive?"

"You didn't look like you look now, that's certain," he parried. "I barely recognized you tonight."

"So I was offensive, then."

"You brought up the subject, not I," he said irritably.

"I simply had to know, that's all. If I offended you— then or now—I'm sorry."

"Oh, you were all right then. Just blotto. Quietly and stiffly blotto."

"And now?"

"You're still all right. Perhaps a little odd, but all right."

She smiled that smile again and picked up her small evening purse. "You're bored. I'd like to go home now. Cab, please?"

"Now just a minute, *Frau* Heidemann," he blurted peevishly, "stay right where you are. You've got some explaining to do."

Her green eyes narrowed slightly. "You're being rude, *Leutnant* Stachel."

"The hell I am. I want to know more. You can't open up a whole great mystery and then simply walk away."

"I don't have to explain anything to anybody. Especially to you, my arrogant war hero."

"Now you're being rude, *Frau* Heidemann. I'm no more a hero than you are a sot. So that makes us even. So sit still and tell me about it."

Her eyes flashed anger, but he did not back down.

"I said tell me about it, goddamn it."

"Why?" she shot back hotly. "So you'll have something to gossip about when you get back to the barracks? So you can tell my husband's officers how funny it is that the *Jastaführer*'s wife is a reformed drunkard? So you can all snicker secretly at him while he goes through the agonies of leading you, worrying over you, hoping for you, protecting you—maybe even loving you a little?" Her eyes were defiant, and indignant tears were there.

"Oh, come now, *Frau* Heidemann," he snorted, "will you please calm down? For God's sake, you started this nonsense. Now finish it."

234

She tossed her head, and her voice was low and hard. "Listen to me, my overbearing peacock: you may be accustomed to barking at other people and getting your way, but you're wasting your time with me—it doesn't work. Once it may have, but not any more. I've stopped defending; I've stopped making excuses; I've stopped explaining. I've stopped doing these things even with people I care about, so I'm certainly not going to do them for an insolent, vainglorious parvenu I don't even know. I've brought up the subject because I wanted to stop your silly smirking. I'm very experienced at recognizing smirkers. I'm also very experienced at putting them in their places, and the easiest, cleanest way is to bring my former disgrace right out in the open, where it negates the smirkers' sole source of superiority. I can't help it if my little system annoys you."

"I wasn't smirking, goddamn it."

"You were, and you know you were. So, my dear *Leutnant* Stachel, it was really you who started all this —not I."

He sank back against the cushions, seething. They each resumed staring at the tablecloth while the pair of zithers strummed pensively. Stachel broke the impasse finally when he began to laugh.

"This is funny. It's been no more than three hours since we've met and we're snapping at each other as if we'd been married for years."

She looked at him. "Just don't provoke me, *Herr Leutnant*. I don't like to snap, but I don't hesitate to when I'm provoked."

"I'm sorry, *Frau* Heidemann," he said deprecatively. "I'm not much at getting along with people, particularly women. You'll have to make allowances. Meanwhile, you don't have to defend yourself or explain anything to me. It's none of my business, really."

"Now, then," she said, unmollified, "that's progress."

He laughed again, shaking his head. "How in pluperfect hell did a firecracker like you get tied up with a store dummy like Heidemann?"

"Otto is quite a fellow," she said without emphasis.

235

"No doubt. But I pictured his wife as somebody who'd be more his type."

"What's that—his type?"

"Well, sort of wishy-washy, I'd say. Somebody who'd fawn over him. I simply can't see you fawning over him, that's all."

"You really don't like my husband much, do you?"

He shrugged. "Oh, he's all right, I suppose. But he always *tells* people: he tells them what they are and what they should be; what they're doing and what they ought to be doing. I don't like to be told."

"You're an officer under his command. . . ."

"He can tell me what to do any time, any place, when it comes to military duty. But when he tells me the kind of person I am as compared to the kind I should be, he ceases to be a commander and becomes a meddler."

"But you're a German officer. As such, your commander has absolute jurisdiction over all departments of your life," she observed mildly.

"Not this German officer, he doesn't."

"Ah, a rebel, eh?"

"Call it what you want. My life's mine—and Heidemann and the Kaiser's whole Officers Corps can kiss my rosy cheek. I'll work for them, but I don't have to run for a napkin every time they belch."

She smiled stiffly. "Perhaps. But I still think you don't fully understand Otto."

"If you do, you're a genius."

"Otto is a man with very high ideals, a very rigid code of propriety. He's a perfectionist in a way; he wants the whole world—or at least his part of it—to be good, and, well, correct. He clings to his ideals with something approaching fanaticism, and he applies them to every phase of his own life. I envy him his ideals. They served as one of his main attractions when I first came to know him. They serve now as his single hold on me."

Stachel raised a brow. "What do you mean by that?"

"Well," she said in that deliberate way of hers, "as you can imagine, I haven't been the perfect wife. I say that easily because it's true. Therefore, I can say just as

236

easily that Otto has left a great deal to be desired as a husband."

"I'll bet."

She continued, ignoring his sarcasm. "Otto has been a rule-book husband: good, kind, an adequate provider. He's offered me everything but what I need most. Oh, I don't mean the silly, schoolgirl moonlight-and-flower-garden kind of love; I mean the deep down, look-you-right-in-the-eye kind. It's simply never been there. He treated me with a respectful and distant correctness from the very wedding. Do you have any idea what it can be like to be lonely and thirsting for a single, tiny word of love and be given instead whole paragraphs of arid courtesies? What it means never to be consulted as a dear friend, but always to be instructed—kindly and firmly—as a loyal but somewhat dim-witted employee?"

"I'm no woman, but it seems to me I'd raise a little hell about it."

She nodded. "I tried. But even then Otto reacted in proper form. Once he boxed my ears for what he thought was spirited behavior, as he calls it—he'd drowned some kittens, and I tried to smother the resentment with cooking wine, because in those days he kept the good beverages locked up for the few parties we could afford—and even then he was sort of academic, as if correcting a valuable hound who'd wetted a rug. I honestly would have been beside myself with joy if he'd have beaten me to death and shown some passion in the process. But he didn't, and it was then I realized that instead of a loving husband I had an idealistic, courteous employer."

Stachel said, "Tough. Why didn't you take a lover?"

She smiled vaguely. "I'm a thoroughly despicable person in many ways, *Herr Leutnant,* but I'm no conscious adultress. Loyalty is one of the few good traits I have left."

"Loyalty to what, in Christ's name?"

"Let me finish. I didn't—couldn't—take a lover. Simply let it rest with that. So I found a substitute."

"You began to work overtime on the old cooking wine, eh?"

She nodded again. "But not really in a bad way until after he'd been posted to the front, leaving me without even my kindly, tyrannical instructor. It grew worse rapidly. It still baffles me, the speed with which it all happened. I tried everything to stop; I tried even a tour of duty with the Red Cross—thinking things would be better with a change of scenery, with a rash of things to keep me moving and busy. But it wasn't any good. I soon found I couldn't run from myself; wherever I ran, I was still there. It was awful, and I did some awful things, I guess. There's a lot of it I don't remember. A lot I don't want to remember. Then, when things were absolutely the worst, a miracle occurred."

Stachel stiffened slightly. "Miracle? What do you mean —miracle?"

"My father sent a friend of his to see me."

"Who? A preacher?"

She laughed easily. "Hardly. It was one of the crustiest, bluntest old men I've ever known. A really quite unusual old fellow: the *Graf* von Klugermann. A prominent physician. Perhaps you've heard of him."

"I've heard of him."

"His nephew was in Otto's *Jasta*—"

"When did the *Graf* call on you?"

"I think it was about a month after that time you must have seen me. I'd left the Red Cross and was home in Munich. That was—yes, last May."

"You hadn't known him before, then?"

"No. My father had visited him at his summer place on the Ammersee several times, and he once did a series of articles on the *Graf*'s work. Father is the editor of a scientific journal, you see, and follows such things with considerable devotion. But although *Vati* had often discussed the *Graf* at home, I'd never actually met the old gentleman until he walked in on me that afternoon. Why do you ask?"

"I simply wondered." Stachel used a finger to worry a crumb along a crease in the tablecloth. "So he helped you, eh? How?"

Frau Heidemann studied him casually. "He told me many things in those first hours. But of them all, the thing I rushed to, clung to, embraced, was his assurance that I'd acted the way I had because I was suffering from a disease. He told me there was only one known medicine for my disease: not to take alcohol in any form. So long as I didn't, I'd not be compelled to do those awful things, but would instead have complete power of choice over good and bad—like any normal, sane person. Well, a disease was something I could understand, define, fight. I've been doing very well in my fight from that afternoon on." She added in a bemused tone, as if to herself: "What a marvelously simple medicine, really; simply don't take something. . . ."

"I've heard about the *Graf* and his disease tune. I understand the rest of his profession considers him a silly old fool."

She lifted a shoulder. "Perhaps. But for me he's been a miracle. Science, professions, philosophies, rationalizations—what do I care for them? Even if the *Graf*'s thesis is out-and-out humbuggery, he's saved my life."

"Still," he said, "you just drank too damned much, that's all. Will power would take care of that, wouldn't it?"

She gave him that cool green look again. "If I have to explain it at all, you would not understand. That's why I no longer explain things to anyone: those who need an explanation will never, never see; those who don't need an explanation already know. So why should I bother?"

Stachel thought about that for a time. Finally he said, "Well, the main thing is that you're feeling better now. But what's this business about Old Boy Heidemann's ideals? How do they figure in all this?"

Her eyes went moodily to the clacking cuckoo clock on the sideboard. "You're a rather peculiarly privileged person, *Leutnant* Stachel. I seem to be doing a considerable amount of explaining to you, despite my inclinations otherwise. I suppose it's because you're important to Otto, and therefore important to me. He thinks a good deal of you, you know. He's written of you many times, quite fondly, as a matter of fact. You seem to have been of great help to him out there, and you're probably one of the few people in the world he feels indebted to.

239

And more than that, you're one of the few he actually admires, I'd say."

"I don't know what I've done—any more than anybody else. And this isn't modesty; actually I've spent most of my time trying to save my own backside. . . ."

She spoke earnestly. "Whatever it is, there is something important he applies to you. Therefore, there's something I want you to understand about him, and something I want to ask of you."

"Well?"

"Please don't begrudge him his scrupulousness, his sense of the proper, his dedication to principles, honor, duty—all that. You don't have to like him; but for my sake let him have his stiffness and his penchant for meddling, because they're no more than symptoms of his very real idealism. I'm convinced of that."

"Why for your sake?"

"As I say, I've done many appalling things, I've suffered many losses. I guess the most important loss was my self-respect, and I'll be a very, very long time trying to get it back. It may never return entirely, but it's from the trying itself that I get some peace of mind, some sort of edge on living with myself. And Otto is critical to the success of this effort, you see. I've been unworthy of him; I've failed him in countless ways. He's clean, decent, honorable. He, well, personifies all the noble qualities that make up the professional officer's code, if that helps you understand. He's human, of course, and therefore isn't capable of achieving the perfection the code holds out; but I feel that he, too, finds his greatest reward in the trying. In other words, he's no real husband for me, but as a symbol of what's right he does what maybe no mere husband could do: he's a sort of goal to which I myself can aspire. If I can make him a good wife, if I can be worthy of his high principles, then maybe someday I'll have a dignity of my own. So don't laugh away his ideals, please. If he didn't have them, if they weren't there to inspire me, I'd simply die."

Stachel asked: "Does he know about all this trouble you've had?"

"No. There's no way he could, really."

240

"Well, take my advice and don't ever tell him."

She started to say something, but the same ridiculous fellow with the helmet and puttees appeared at the table, crashing his heels, saluting, and thrusting out his blue chin.

"Well, what is it?" Stachel demanded.

"A message from *Hauptmann* Heidemann, sir."

Stachel snatched away the envelope, flicked open the seal, and read quickly. He nodded testily at the messenger.

"Very well. Tell him you delivered the message."

When the man had left, Stachel looked quietly across the table at her. "Your husband," he said, "has been detained and will be unable to join us. He's instructed me to take you home."

"Oh, dear," she said absently, "I do hope he gets some dinner. . . ."

Stachel arose and gathered her wrap.

"*Frau* Heidemann," he said with a sigh, "You're quite a woman. Quite a woman."

"You've surprised me, too, *Herr Leutnant*. I expected a glaring man in armor, I believe. Those newspaper pictures make you look so surly and old, somehow. And you're so, well—decent-looking. . . ."

"I'm really quite precious."

CHAPTER 27

FOR OTTO HEIDEMANN there was a distinct sense of personal participation in the advent of a new era. The array of aircraft on the flight line at Johannisthal was something to catch the breath. Not that the machines were so different from those to which he had been accustomed; there was still the predominance of biplanes, still the familiar wood and fabric and metal, still the same snarl and blatting and sighing, and still the same elusive, pro-

241

vocative scent of lacquer and oil and petrol and leather that made aircraft things to ensnare men's souls. But a delicately curved fairing here, an absence of ugly guy wires there, an ingeniously contrived engine housing, a streamlining of a machine-gun mount, a sheltering wind-screen before a spacious cockpit—all these were indicators which of themselves were little but as an entirety spoke of revolution at hand. How far they'd come, he thought as he stood in the pale sun and autumn-promising wind, since those long-ago days when the machines had been little more than powered kites. He was proud of having been among the early ones, prouder even to be among the present ones. He loved these noisy, logic-defying things of the air with a deep love. Only Elfi had evoked a more telling measure of passion in him.

Elfi.

He thought of her now with a compelling poignancy. Strange how one could be so inarticulate, so inadequate, so fumbling when confronting the meaning of his life. For month after empty month he had envisioned that wonderful moment of confrontation. For day after day, night after night, he had lived the opening of the door, the pacing into the foyer with the unendurably sweet knowledge that she would be just beyond that inner wall, the tapping of her heels as she hurried to the meeting, the appraisal, the welcome. But when it had all become fact he had experienced a vague uneasiness, a haunting awareness of unfulfillment. True, the events had taken place much as he had anticipated, but when the final moment had arrived and the embrace was complete, he had been crude and stumbling and incapable of anything but a senseless prattling of formalities. How could he tell her how he loved her and had missed her and had wanted her and had yearned for her? How do you describe the sky to one born blind? Failing the words, you use mere words. And so there is the understanding that there has been no understanding, and the hours pass, given over not to the soul but to the inane.

She had been asleep when he'd returned from *Kogenluft* last night; she'd been asleep when he'd left this morning. At both times the desire to awaken her, to tell her, to show her, had been blunted by that somehow-empty afternoon of reunion. Elfi, he knew with an elusive dread, had changed. She was now more woman; but her growth, her new depth, disturbed him and made him inexplicably sad. Soon now (tomorrow?) she'd know how very much he loved her. Some sweet moment (tonight?) he'd be able to throw off the despicable cloth of the husband and stand before her in the unalloyed substance of the lover.

Now—after such a desperately long time—he would be with her, would have the chance to show, somehow, the things he never could say. Time was what he needed; time was what he had won. To achieve it had called for change in himself—difficult, costly change—but he knew he would have paid a hundred thousand times the price. The sense of victory now at hand was bitterly sweet.

He returned to the refreshment tent, and, balancing a porcelain mug of steaming coffee in one hand, took one of the camp chairs into the sun. He sat and sipped thoughtfully. He was still engrossed when Stachel came through a gate and approached him.

Stachel, he knew, had also changed.

He remembered the February ages ago when Stachel, a blushing, diffident schoolboy, had sat across the desk at Beauvin and had spoken so pridefully of his plans to write. So much had happened, and the youth had altered into a youth with an angry man's walk. He wondered if, behind the subtle physical metamorphosis, Stachel had developed the especial breadth and depth that would take him from his current notoriety to lasting greatness. If so, would he ever deign really to write, to share with others the fruits of the introspection he once cherished so glibly? Or would such greatness (if indeed it were to come) place him above and beyond any measure of sharing, as it had with so many of the Fatherland's military lions? Few symbols write, he mused; few statues can speak of the vast sweep of emotion and pain and spirit that underlies the history they suggest. Stachel, once so simple to divine, had, under the weight of the times, the press of coincidence, the clutch of the now-revealed flaw within him, become an enigma. The transition had been a portrait whose clearly depicted image had, by a running of

243

the colors, muddied, leaving an imprecise caricature. What, he wondered, had really happened to Stachel out there?

"Good morning, Bruno."

"*Herr Hauptmann,*" Stachel acknowledged, his eyes direct.

"I must say that you're looking well this fine day."

"Thanks. I got a good sleep for a change."

"So? Berlin agrees with you then, eh?"

"Perhaps. But I'm more inclined to credit the bona-fide bathtub and bed."

Heidemann smiled his thin, pale smile. "Awfully nice of you to attend *Frau* Heidemann last night. What do you think of her?"

Stachel continued to regard him evenly. The *Jasta-führer* seemed even more pleased with himself than usual, he decided.

"You're a very lucky man, *Herr Hauptmann.* She's an extraordinary woman."

"Yes. I knew you'd think so. You two are alike, remember." He raised a brow knowingly and his smile broadened.

"If I were like her I wouldn't have much to worry about. She certainly looks herself in the eye."

Two machines were engaged in mock combat overhead, and their insistent roar beat down. Stachel pulled up a chair and sat beside Heidemann, who was already absorbed in the contest.

Yes, *Frau* Heidemann was an unusual woman, all right. From the moment he'd left her at the door to her apartment he'd been preoccupied with her. He had never heard anyone talk with such utter acceptance of reality. Mankind, he mused, was veneered with deception. One person would think one thing but say another; his listener would react inwardly in one way and answer in still another. Consequently a simple, two-person relationship or encounter invariably became an unhappy compound of ploy and counter-ploy. *Frau* Heidemann had shown him what an exciting and somehow reassuring adventure it could be when such an encounter occurred in

244

the absence of deviousness and in the presence of humility. In any event, he sensed that something unusual had entered his life. He was conscious of having found, and at the very moment of finding, of having lost. It was as if he'd been on a train, and, during a brief slowing in the night, had seen into a lighted window beside the tracks. In that room had been something hauntingly familiar and immensely important and deeply desirable. He felt now as if the train were accelerating, leaving the meaningful window in the void behind; as if his mind were fighting to locate the room, so that he could flee the hateful thing that carried him and return, running.

One of the aircraft broke away from the *Kurvenkampf* and came down in a thinly whistling spiral. It corrected neatly and sideslipped toward a landing, its rotary blipping officiously.

"Awkward of me not to make dinner," Heidemann was saying. "But I was kept quite late."

"I only hope *Frau* Heidemann wasn't bored."

"She was asleep when I returned and, of course, I left before she'd awakened this morning, so I haven't asked her." Heidemann chuckled. "If she reports boredom, I'll have you court-martialed."

Stachel changed the subject, because he wanted to avoid being quizzed too closely about the evening. "How did you get along at *Kogenluft?*"

"I think you'll find my little absence worked to the benefit of us both," Heidemann said mysteriously, his smile persisting.

"How so?"

Heidemann shook the dregs from his coffee mug, then placed it on the grass beside his chair. "I have news," he said meaningfully.

"Well?"

"Effective the day after tomorrow, you will succeed me as *Jastaführer*."

Stachel's head came around quickly. "I'll what?"

"You will lead the *Jasta*."

"What about you?" he asked incredulously.

"I am being transferred to *Kogenluft*."

"To *Kogenluft?* Here? As what, for God's sake?"

"I'm to be special aide to General Wurfl, in charge of experimental propaganda."

"What in the name of Aristotle's ass is that?"

"The press. I'll try to devise more effective ways for the Flying Corps to conduct its affairs with the press."

"You mean like that silly pattycake Klingel? You're leaving your command when it's in trouble, just to become somebody like him?"

"Not like him, I hope. But in that general capacity."

Stachel sank back in his chair. "Dear Mother of God! We've just lost the war."

"Oh, come now. It isn't all that bad." Heidemann laughed dryly.

"Bad? Jesus! What are we coming to when *Kogenluft* takes first-class combat men out of the line to carry satchels for a bunch of peeping Toms? Bad? It's catastrophe, that's what it is. You know how bad off the *Jasta* is. It needs you now more than ever. . . ."

Heidemann held up a hand. "No. Wait a moment and think. What's more important than that the Air Service grow and become the really dominant branch of arms? You know as well as I that these machines we see here are changing all concepts of warfare. In less time than anyone really imagines, they will become the Fatherland's single most important military tool. But the trend has to be helped along. There has to be a conditioning of minds—not so much externally but within, within the military structure, from the General Staff down. That's why there has to be an organized propaganda program, carefully contrived to do the conditioning by glamorizing, dramatizing the significance of the air arm. . . ."

Stachel broke in: "There seem to be plenty of people trying to do that already. I know; I'm a direct beneficiary of the system."

"Nonsense. Oh, we have a helter-skelter propaganda bureau arrangement, and some brass hats are always maneuvering, but I mean organized, really organized. I have a scheme that will put some real teeth in the whole thing."

A vague uneasiness began to gather somewhere near Stachel's belly. "A scheme?"

"Yes," Heidemann said smugly. "A scheme. I have it all worked out and proved, and General Wurfl has authorized me to put it into formal play. Oh, we'll have to go a bit quietly and carefully at first, of course, because it won't work if too much fanfare accompanies it at the outset. But as we go along, it will become big—vital. Each *Jasta* will have an officer, someone like Kettering, for instance, who'll watch for things that can—if handled adroitly—reflect credit on the corps as a whole. He'll submit a report directly to me at *Kogenluft,* out of regular channels, and my office will see that it gets appropriate attention, either in the public press or in key staff summaries. This means we'll have a regular, organized program, a whole network of *Jasta*-size precincts reporting propaganda-worthy material on a consistent basis to my central bureau. With precise planting in fertile areas, these little seeds can grow into mighty appropriations for a growing aerial stature. . . ."

Stachel broke in, the uneasiness now a hard knot in him. "Just a minute. You say you have it all worked out and—proved?"

Heidemann's smile was maddening. "Indeed. Proved by a rather remarkable practical demonstration, as a matter of fact."

"You mean me?"

"You."

Stachel chewed his lower lip. "Everything that's happened to me has been—organized? Planted?"

"Precisely."

"By you?"

"By me."

"I see."

Heidemann laughed again. "Come now, Bruno, you needn't look so glum and shaken. After all, you've got what you've always wanted."

"What do you mean by that?"

"Why you've always been hungry for the hero's mantle, haven't you? You're quite transparent in many ways, you know. . . ."

"Transparent?"

"I wish I had a *pfennig* for every time I've seen you

247

staring wistfully at my Blue Max. You've wanted a Blue Max very badly. I saw to it that you got one, that's all. And, confidentially, I've been amazed at the incredible ease with which it could be done. Not the medal itself—they're cheap these days. But the fantastic gullibility with which the public and even our most sophisticated military people succumbed to my little exercise. Astonishing, really."

Stachel felt as if he were speaking through cotton. "The Blue Max has to be earned. You've got one. You know how it is. . . ."

Heidemann nodded agreeably. "Of course, of course. Those of us who wear it must actually achieve worthy things; no argument about that. But the difference, my boy, is that you're famous today—I am not. And why are you famous? Because I made you famous, that's why. Q.E.D."

Stachel studied the palms of his hands, brows knitted, face chilled. "So that's why you've been so inconsistent."

"Inconsistent?"

"Yes. From my first day at the *Jasta* I heard about Heidemann, the stickler for proprieties, the perfectionist. As a perfectionist, there are certain things you can do, certain things you can't do. But if any one thing stands out in a perfectionist it's his consistency. When it's come to me, though, your only consistency has been your inconsistency. Your—your constant looking the other way. . . ." His voice fell off.

Heidemann's eyes were slitted against the sun glare. The amusement stirred his lips. "Why worry about it? We've both got what we want."

"Both?"

"You have your Blue Max and your glory. I have my transfer to Berlin. All's right with the world."

"Transfer to Berlin? Is that what you wanted?"

"More than anything, my boy," Heidemann agreed easily.

"Why?"

"No matter. I simply wanted it."

"Why? *Why*, goddamn it?" Stachel had sat up, his shoulders hunched, his eyes narrow.

248

Heidemann turned his head away from the sun and smiled. "I'd say that's my business, *Leutnant* Stachel."

"You don't give a jug of bean breeze for your little propaganda scheme, do you? That isn't what you had in mind at all, is it?" His voice was husky.

Heidemann shrugged. "As I say: we both have what we want."

Stachel sank back in his chair, his face expressionless now. An engine started nearby, and a scud of dust from the propeller-wash drifted across the field. He watched the machine make a pigeonlike, strutting taxi run to a position by the starting flags. Finally he said: "Your wife's pretty important to you, isn't she?"

"She's all there is."

"You're a pretty sly little rascal, too."

"I like to think so."

The Adler offering was a biplane, conventional in appearance except for its cabane and interplane struts, which were of the single "I" configuration that Tony Fokker had used in the outer bay of his 1917 triplane. Stachel did not like those struts; they seemed flimsy and inadequate for the stresses he knew combat flying could generate. Nor did he approve of the smallish, spade-shaped vertical fin and rudder; he was no engineer, but it was apparent even to him that this component's area was insufficient to guarantee lateral stability. As he and Heidemann stood beside the idling machine and listened to the Aircraft Production Directorate's technical representative explain its various features, he became intuitively convinced that the Adler D-11 would prove to be a waste of time for everyone, from its designer to those who would fly it today.

His major problem at the moment was how to keep his mind on what the technical officer was saying. The depression that had fallen over him after Heidemann's disclosures had by now solidified and had become an empty, unfeeling sort of resignation. It was not so much the personal deflation that had weighed so, he decided; it was, rather, the awesome confirmation of the great role fraud and deceit actually played in setting the course of all things. There had been many small, niggling demonstrations of this in his experience, to be sure, but these he had merely accepted as stemming from the self-protective instinct developed by the human chameleon in his jungle. Disillusionment was no stranger to him; but to discover in the few casually amused words of a paragon that an entire bureaucracy could be established by calculated innuendo on the part of a paragon who was in fact no paragon was a cause for abject surrender to futility.

Dear God, he thought, *we're lost. We're all lost. Humanity is lost.*

"Do you have any questions?"

Stachel realized that the technical officer was looking at him.

"No, I guess not. It's just another airplane."

The officer turned his eyes to Heidemann.

"The *Jastaführer* will fly first?"

"No. *Leutnant* Stachel will go first," he said mildly.

"How about a parachute?" the man suggested. "I see neither of you is wearing the Heinecke harness."

Stachel said woodenly, "Only one man in our *Jasta* has used one of those things and he ended up skewered like a pickle on a toothpick. If anything goes wrong, I'll take my chances and stay with the aircraft."

"Herr Hauptmann?"

"I agree with *Leutnant* Stachel."

"Suit yourself, gentlemen. You both are expected at the Roland test station at thirteen-fifteen hours. Will you please time your trial of the Adler accordingly? Oh, yes— and please file your written comments on the Adler with me at the tent beside Hangar M. Thank you. Enjoy your flights."

They returned his salute and watched him stride away.

"Well, *Herr Jastaführer* Stachel." Heidemann smiled. "Bon voyage."

Stachel pulled his helmet strap tight and buckled it at the jaw. "Why do you bother?"

"Bother with what, Bruno?"

"With flying these kites today. The day after tomorrow your flying is done."

"That's the day after tomorrow. Today I'm still a *Jastaführer*."

"Propriety, eh?"

"I try to do my duty each day as it comes."

Stachel nodded at the mechanics and placed a boot in the stirrup. As he began his swing aboard, he paused. He dismounted and went to Heidemann, his expression thoughtful.

"What is it, old boy?"

"I want to ask you something. It's none of my business, of course, but I'd like to ask you a favor."

"Favor?"

"Yes. Please don't tell *Frau* Heidemann how you arranged your transfer to Berlin. Don't tell her, under any circumstances, how slick you've been in all this."

Heidemann's smile faded. "Well, as you say, it's none of your business, actually."

"Please don't, that's all."

"I can't promise anything of the sort."

"Why?"

Heidemann's eyes became indirect, his manner somehow defensive. "Really, I don't see why—"

"It's very important. More important than you realize. Can't you simply let the whole thing lie? She needn't know. She mustn't know. Just take my word for it. . . ."

"You're being presumptuous, Stachel," Heidemann said warningly.

"Oh, in Christ's good name," Stachel barked, his eyes hot, "will you just not say anything about it to her? Will you stop being such a frigging know-it-all and take my word for it?"

"You're acting awfully strange today, I must say," Heidemann snapped.

Stachel fought to restrain the fury that boiled up. He forced his voice to be calm. "I'm asking you as a friend."

Heidemann's face softened for an infinitesimal jot, then reassumed its stiffness. "I can't. It's the whole reason for all of it," he said coldly.

"Why? Just tell me why."

"I *can't* promise you such a thing. It's very personal, but since it seems so incredibly important to you, I'll tell you why. *Frau* Heidemann and I have not had it, well, easy together. Not as I would have it. She has frequently accused me of not caring for her. In a real way, that is. You know how women are. . . ." His gaze was averted and he seemed to speak laboriously. "I've never been able to show her how wrong she is. I can't seem to make the words or to do the things that she apparently believes to be necessary in a, oh, love affair, I suppose you'd call it. Well, I must tell her about how I achieved the transfer, that's all. She's been unhappy for so long because of my inability to unbend, my determination to follow the rules —the very things about me that annoy you and the other *Jasta* members so much—that this will serve as a clear demonstration of how much I do care for her. She'll see how I've moved mountains just to be—"

Stachel turned, white-faced, toward the airplane. As he clambered into the trembling cockpit, he shouted over his shoulder:

"You crazy, stupid son of a bitch!"

At the top of the long climb, he kicked the Adler over. Numbly he let the machine take its head, making no move to guide the plunge nor to ease off the accelerating power that set the wires to shrieking and the engine to pounding. It was with a physical illness that he watched the dun-colored earth rise to meet him; a liquid nausea flowed as the insignificant squares ballooned into hangars, as the rows of tiny crosses grew into aircraft, as the mottled patches became fields and trees and roads and houses and ponds and churches.

Churches, indeed.

How did it go?

When church yards yawn and hell itself breathes out. . . .
Built God a church, and laughed His words to scorn. . . .

Indeed.

He could almost hear an echo of the engine's roar as he pulled the Adler out of the dive, the sound booming up from the airfield's turf. The machine's shadow was a blurred thing that danced across the green, large and black and close. Then blue sky filled the space ahead and he sat back, breathing deeply and struggling to concentrate on the return to high places. Ever so slowly, as the wind sighed and the propeller churned its monotone, the paroxysm of frustration and disenchantment receded, to be replaced by an icy preoccupation.

For what seemed a long time he flew.

The Adler was monstrous. He noticed detachedly that it yawed considerably—that too-small vertical stabilizer falling short of its responsibility; it was sluggish in climbs, slow to head into maneuvers to the left; it was quick to stall and wanted urgently to spin.

He was in a spin now, and his eyes roamed about the beast, ignoring the nasty whirlpool of earth colors ahead.

Something moved.

It was nothing he'd actually seen. It had been more an impression, a suggestion of motion that was alien to the machine and its function. He adjusted the controls to counter the spin and resumed his inspection. The wild whipping slowed, but did not cease until he was a full fifty meters below the altitude he'd selected for complete recovery. He went into a wide, easy circle to the right and again examined the wings, the tail, those I-struts. Everything appeared to be normal. Tightening the turn and gradually increasing power, his eyes continued their search.

He saw it then.

One of the flying wires it was—the one that was turnbuckled to a spar at the top of the right interplane strut and ran to a longeron anchor just forward of the leading edge of the lower wing. It sagged, He made a steep turn to the left. The wire tautened. He made a shallow dive under power. The strut moved almost imperceptibly in its sockets, and there was a change in the sheen of the fabric aft of the upper wing's plywood leader, which meant its tension had eased sufficiently to cause a wrinkle in the linen.

The Adler, he knew, would kill at any moment.

Throttling back, he put the machine into a slow, curving glide, waiting patiently for the field to take its appropriate position atop and beyond the engine cowl. The wires sang dreamily and the propeller blades, catching the sun, flashed rhythmic sequences of light and shadow. He watched unblinkingly as the ground came up, fell off below the nose, and began its thumping and whispering under the kiss of the wheels.

He was in deep thought throughout the long taxi run to the starting line and parking area. By the time he had ruddered the machine between the flags and cut the switch, he'd still not made a decision.

CHAPTER **28**

THE ADLER representative, a man named Memminger, was exuberant—so much so he nearly bounced. He held out both arms to help Stachel climb down from the wing.

"Donnerwetter, Herr Stachel! You made our baby sing! Sing! *Ach,* what flying! You are merciless, yet adoring; like a lover you are, you young scalawag! Small wonder you have become so, so—fabulous! I have never seen such a demonstration! Ha, but our baby measured up to your fondling, did she not? She is built for such—caressing, eh? Ha-ha." He winked broadly.

Stachel pulled off his helmet and goggles and studied the little man. "Did you design this machine, *Herr* Memminger?"

"I cannot claim that honor, I regret to say. Heinrich Stolz is the one. A fine man. He could not attend today —*ach,* what a shame it is, too!" He burbled confidentially: *"Frau* Stolz was taken to the hospital yesterday and Heinrich felt constrained to be with her today. You know women. Ha-ha. But, oh, how Heinrich would have loved to see your flight just now!"

Stachel was impassive. "Yes. It's too bad. I would have liked to give him my comments personally."

"But you can tell me! Heinrich is my friend, and he will relish every word—even though it comes second-hand. . . ."

Stachel opened his mouth to speak, but broke off when

254

he saw Heidemann approaching. The *Hauptmann* was coolly formal.

"Ah, *Herr Hauptmann,*" Memminger chortled, "was not that a spectacular performance? You come to a lady who has felt the touch of a master seducer, I'm afraid. Ha-ha. It will be difficult even for someone as accomplished as you to stir her passion to greater heights. Ha-ha."

Heidemann considered him with disdain. "Aren't you off limits, *Herr* Memminger?"

"Eh?"

"I understand that civilian representatives of aircraft companies are forbidden to associate with military flight personnel during the trials."

The little man's face clouded. "*Ach, so.* I meant no trespass, of course. But I simply couldn't contain my enthusiasm over this marvelous—"

"You'd better leave. Now. Before the trial officer sees you and disqualifies your entry."

Memminger glanced nervously over his shoulder. "Yes, yes. I meant no harm, to be sure." He smiled again, suggestively. "There's to be a grand party tonight in our suite at the Bristol. I hope you can attend, for we've arranged some novel entertainment. Two Egyptian girls— directly descended from Cleopatra, they are—will exhibit the secret love techniques of—"

"Get out of here. At once!"

The tubby man retreated, sputtering.

Stachel said, "I had something I wanted to say to *Herr* Memminger about his airplane. Sir."

"Filthy little ogre. Egyptians, indeed. I simply can't *stand* improprieties. . . ." Heidemann's mouth twitched.

For Stachel, it was as if everything he'd seen, said, and done since landing had transpired within the field of a pair of binoculars that were being brought into focus— hazy and obscure at first, then shifting erratically, spasmodically, into brilliant and sharp perspective. The final precise adjustment came with that revealing tremble of Heidemann's lower lip, the restive travel of his eyes. Now, standing there in the sun, surrounded by the bustle and clamor of men and arms, it was as if he were seeing the smallish, irritable, and pinched face of hypocrisy itself.

The physical nausea he'd felt aloft came back in a silent rolling of juices somewhere far down, and it was with an audible, resigned sigh that he made his decision.

Heidemann looked at him, anger discoloring his face. "What's that?"

"Hiccups. I always get hiccups when I make a decision."

Heidemann's gloved forefinger jabbed Stachel's chest, three times. His voice was shrill. "A warning, Stachel: I don't want ever again to hear you address me in that contemptuous manner you used a while ago. You've not grown so big and so important that I can't still fix you. I don't *need* you any more. . . ."

Stachel jerked his head toward the Adler, whose engine was set to racketing again by its squad of mechanics.

"Do you want to hear how this puddle-jumper works? Sir."

"I don't want to hear anything more from you until your manners improve. Now get out of my way."

As he brushed past and mounted the stirrup, Stachel caught his arm. "May I say one thing? Sir?" he asked icily, a flatness in his eyes.

"Well, what is it?"

"This baby recovers beautifully from a spin. Try a good long one. It'll cheer you up."

If he had had any lingering doubt about the propriety (*Oh, God, God—that word!*) of his decision, it had gone with an orgasmic finality when Heidemann had made his summation.

"I don't *need* you any more," Heidemann had said.

So be it.

So be it, you bastard. . . .

It was a melancholic abstraction that settled over Stachel as he sank into the camp chair. Boots thrust outward, arms folded across his chest, he watched broodingly as the Adler waddled into the ground-maneuverability exercises that would precede Heidemann's test flight. Oblivious to the billowing dust, the barking and snarling of engines, the chirping of control officers' whistles, the distant thudding of a band, the clatter of the refreshment tent, and the surging of the crowd, he was held sullenly absorbed by the Adler and its awkward and uncertain jouncings across the taxi-and-turn courses. The sun spanking on the high gloss of its surfaces sent insolent stabs of light into his slitted eyes, and he loathed the thing with the impersonal malevolence of man for spider.

It was, in fact, the only emotion he could feel now—this idle, pensive hatred of an inanimate thing whose sole misdemeanor was that of inadequacy born of the inadequate minds of inadequate men. The sting of humiliation, the numbness of violated pride, the oppression of hypocrisy revealed, had died abruptly, leaving him in this dreary suspension. Even the awful fact of his now-total involvement as supreme arbiter of the bizarre and lugubrious affairs of the Heidemanns could not obtrude on his detachment. He sat for what seemed a long time like this, his gaze following the sluggish movements of the traitorous machine. Eventually, though, furtive thoughts gathered to snipe at the corners of his withdrawal.

She was, of course, worth ten of her husband. A hundred. A thousand. . . .

He clung to this, not so much as justification for the sentence he had pronounced on Otto Heidemann, but more as the rationale for what he recognized as his own unconditional surrender to the Great Fraud. That life was dirty, foul, and full of sordid deceit and irony and cruelty, he had long known; but for just as long, he had struggled, with steadily decreasing success, to resist the hardening conviction that his only survival was to commit himself to being dirtier, fouler, and more cruel than the worst.

How many times had he anguished over such a prospect? How many times had he fought to find the right? And how many times had he discovered that nothing could be taken for granted, nothing could be weighed right against wrong, nothing could be accepted as truth and holiness, because man persisted in mocking truth and the God he smugly alleged, and in muddying both of these noble concepts with his petty, animal chicaneries? Well, no more. He was tired. Now, for *Frau* Heidemann's sake, he had ceased his struggling and had joined—no, dedicated—himself to the jackals. The world could use a hundred million *Frau* Heidemanns;

instead it had a hundred million million Otto Heidemanns. So piss on the world; piss on all the Otto Heidemanns in it. Just this one last time, he'd do God's job for him and keep Otto Heidemann from destroying his own wife. But after this, God would have to handle His own affairs.

Refining and polishing this self-endorsement, Stachel was still watching the taxiing Adler when the brandy sloshed down his arm. At first he was mildly startled when the liquid stained the twill of his flight jacket, as if he had suddenly discovered an insect on a tablecloth. But when the dark area spread and the excess ran wetly across his hand, he jumped up in genuine outrage, spinning around and cursing. It was the major from the night before, the one with the horse teeth, and he was very drunk. He waved a brimming cup to punctuate his remarks to an embarrassed communications *Feldwebel,* and brandy splashed from it in sparkling, golden cascades.

"Why don't you watch what you're doing?" Stachel exploded, nearly inarticulate with rage.

The other turned, no evidence of apology on his face. His eyes, red-veined and swollen, roamed vacantly over Stachel's taut figure.

"Frigging lieutenants are getting snotty these days," he told the *Feldwebel* in elaborately confidential tones. Then, regarding Stachel again, he wheezed: "Who are you, you smart aleck?"

"Johann Sebastian Bach, you drunken bastard."

"I'm going to report you."

"Is that a guarantee? A solemn promise?"

"You're disrespectful of a superior officer. . . ."

"I'm disrespectful of a drunken swine who isn't superior to the lint in my navel."

The *Feldwebel* showed grateful relief when a motorcycle sputtered up to the dispatch tent down the line. He hurried off, without looking back. The major stood weaving, his puffy features contracted in a parody of injured pride. The stench of old alcohol was noticeable, even in the breeze. With exaggerated dignity he announced: "I am not drunk. I can assure you of that."

"I can poop diamond necklaces, too. Now get out of here before I call the *Feldpolizei*."

The man's expression turned to indignation. "Are you threatening me?"

"I'm telling you: get out of my sight. I've killed better men than you without thinking twice. You're lucky I'm thinking even once." Stachel felt himself trembling, and it surprised him somehow.

The major, his mouth slack and draining, belched. Then he stiffened, pulled his rumpled tunic to a semblance of straightness, and turned to wander off, his steps slow and deliberate. Over his shoulder he fired a resentful parting shot: "You'll hear more about this. I *hate* sanctimonious hypocrites like you. . . ."

Stachel stood in frozen ire, watching the man go.

It would have been impossible for him ever to point to the precise moment when the thought came. It was not a thought, as such, but a vague suggestion, a sensation that stirred and flexed deep in some dark, obscure corner of his soul—much as if a monstrous thing, buried in the primordial ooze, had turned in its infinite sleep. In the resulting tremor, he heard no voice, yet a voice he heard. There was no realization, yet a realization there was. No understanding, yet an understanding of stupendous, ineluctable clarity. The major, trudging away in his stiff-legged, gingerly retreat, was, in reality, Bruno Stachel. The major, in his sodden resentment, with his filthy, erratic, and anxious mind, his sullenly self-righteous and choleric denunciation of hypocrisy, was a mirror image of himself—reversed in every detail, but inescapably a representation of the reflected entity. Said the soundless, thunderous voice:

Who was a drunken swine?

Who was a liar, a cheat, a charlatan?

Who was a cruel, deceitful, arrogant, and covetous hypocrite?

Who had offered his surrender to the Great Fraud, when all along he was himself the Greatest Fraud?

"Dear God in Heaven! Bruno Stachel!"

Half accusation, half plea, the words rang out—a shrill, involuntary cry of indictment mixed with pitiable supplication. No matter that the crowd was staring, no matter that tears suddenly stung his eyes, no matter that he was running in choke-throated horror toward the dispatch tent. All that mattered was that he reach that idling cycle there, that he stop this insane, murderous thing he had been about to consummate. It mattered now more than anything in the world—the universe—that he get to Heidemann, that he stop Heidemann. He knew with a dreadful certainty that Heidemann's reprieve would be the first brick removed in Bruno Stachel's search for Bruno Stachel in the rubble of his spiritual bankruptcy.

He threw an agonized glance down the field as he ran, and saw through the film of alarm that the Adler sat in the downwind corner of the great meadow, waiting for another machine to land. Then he arrived beside the cycle and sidecar, panting and clutching the shoulder of the dispatch rider. His voice barely audible over the popping of the motor, he told the man: "Take me to that airplane out there. That one down there at the end of the field."

The driver looked at him in stupid surprise. The *Feldwebel* came out of the tent and asked importantly, "What's going on here?"

"I want this man to take me out to that airplane."

"Are you crazy? That's off-limits to all vehicles. That's a flying zone. I can't permit it."

"You'd better, you bastard, or I'll tie that brassard around your balls and drag you to Munich and back."

He vaulted into the sidecar, roaring at the confused driver: "Get going! Did you hear me? Get going!"

The chugging and barking dissolved into an angry snarl, and Stachel's head snapped back with the lunging start. The cycle sped across the turf, a million jarrings and rattlings tearing at it. As they careened into the open field, a trial officer's whistle sounded a far-off, furious series of warblings.

"Hurry."

"I hope you know what you're doing, sir." The driver's voice was muffled in the rushing air. The Adler's propeller had begun to churn as Heidemann made his turn

260

into the wind, and the driver added, "We'll never make it—he'll be gone before we get there. . . ."

"Can't you go any faster?"

"I'm wide open now."

"Keep going."

A whorl of dust kicked up to the rear of the Adler and Stachel could see its wheels begin to turn.

"Steer over into his path. He'll have to abort then."

"Sir?"

"Steer the goddamned cycle in front of him! And keep going!"

"Yes, sir!"

The Adler's roll quickened, and its tail skid lifted, dropped, then lifted again. The bellow of its engine came down the sun-soaked expanse and made itself known over the cycle's racketing.

"He'll hit us, *Herr Leutnant!*"

"Cut to the right a bit. His engine's hiding us. He can't see us over his engine."

"Jesus, sir, he's coming at us fast!"

"Cut to the right, I said! Right!"

"I want to get out of here. . . ."

"Keep going, you son of a bitch!"

"He'll kill us!"

"I'll kill you if you don't keep going!"

The airplane's propeller, a shining disc, slowed then, and the rumble fell off. A column of dust formed as the tail skid returned to the ground.

"He's seen us! He's stopping!"

"Now cut hard right."

"Yes, sir! Thank you, sir!"

Stachel clutched the cowling as the cycle heeled up and slithered into a skid. Dust stung his eyes and he cursed. The Adler made a loud, whistling sound as it clattered by.

"Now take me over there to him, soldier. Later, I'll see if I can get you a medal."

Heidemann raised his goggles and watched, face white with fury, as Stachel heaved himself onto the stirrup.

261

"Have you lost your *mind*, Stachel?"

"I'm not sure."

"What in the name of the good God Himself are you trying to do?"

"I want to keep you from flying this airplane."

"You nearly killed us all."

"I'm trying to keep you from breaking your ass in this pile of junk, that's all."

"It worked well for you."

"It's got a queer wing. It'll fold on you."

"Why didn't you say so before this?"

Stachel leaned close, his face hot. "Because, you stupid, self-satisfied son of a bitch, you wouldn't stop talking long enough to listen!"

Heidemann's eyes, marblelike in their rage, suddenly took on a glint of comprehension. In one instant there had been transcendent wrath; the next there was a mocking something that signaled discovery. He smiled that maddening smile for the thousandth (or was it the millionth?) time, and he shook his head.

"Stachel," he said scornfully, "it has never ceased to confound me how you manage to get so drunk so fast."

"Drunk?"

"You're drunk, Stachel. Good God—even over the exhaust I can smell you."

"I'm not drunk. . . ."

"With that fragrance? Oh, come now."

"I'm not drunk. . . ."

"Report to your quarters at once and remain there until my further orders."

"Why?"

"You're under arrest."

"What for?"

"For being drunk and disorderly on duty. And, I might say," he added disdainfully, "such charges are long, long overdue. . . ."

"Now *you've* lost your mind."

"Get off my airplane, you common, filthy sot!"

The engine's soft chuckling surged into a wind-lashing roar, and Stachel swung down.

He stood, staring through the dust for a long time.

What had she said?

It's the trying that counts?

He turned and walked slowly toward the cycle.

The Adler had risen a mere fifty meters when Otto Heidemann first sensed the movement to his right. He turned his head to search for the thing, but he never completed the motion. There was a thundering, and the sun was blotted out by the upper wing, which inexplicably hung above and to one side, billowing and snapping like a wind-torn sheet. A vicious twanging sounded as the flying wires tore loose, and there was a horrid shrieking. The horizon began an eccentric whirling, and his head slammed forward against the machine-gun butts. He forced himself erect again and cut the ignition switch with a slow, deliberate movement of his now-bloody glove. He thought of his goggles, and not wanting to endanger his eyes (he had always dreaded damage to his eyes, because what was more valuable?) he clawed them loose and threw them clear. It was a strangely wonderful experience to watch the ground change from a rocking green blur, to turf, to individual blades of grass. . . .

When it was quiet again, he could feel parts of his body shutting off, as if tiny hidden switches were being flicked. There was dirt in his mouth and nose, and through a small crack in the bloody paste over his eyes he could see a patch of sky and a wildflower nodding in the breeze. He had seen flowers like it. In a dreamy Taunus afternoon. The stem showed golden as the delicate, hairy tendrils caught the sun. The sun and Elfi. The sun equals Elfi. Elfi equals the sun.

As the switches disconnected, he was aware of a question unanswered, of something important unresolved.

What was it Stachel had said?

She needn't know. She mustn't know? It's more important than you realize?

Elfi?

Was something wrong with Elfi?

Dearest, sweetest, most wonderful Elfi?

He was still pondering when the final switch was thrown.

CHAPTER 29

IT WASN'T until late afternoon that the chief trial officer had permitted Stachel to return to his hotel. The questioning had been lengthy and close, but *Kogenluft,* Headquarters *Idflieg,* and the Aircraft Directorate seemed satisfied eventually that Otto Heidemann's death had been entirely accidental. There would have been little doubt of this if it hadn't been for the motorcycle incident. The spectacle of a dispatch rider's vehicle careening across the field to halt a rolling aircraft was a peculiar departure from the norm that had complicated what would seem to be a simple case of structural failure, and therefore it had been necessary to convene a preliminary hearing on the spot. Naturally, Stachel had been called upon at once to explain his extraordinary actions. This was fortunate, since at the outset a general air of shock still hovered over the proceedings, and the Officer-in-Charge had appeared unwilling to go hard on a well-known figure and Blue Max wearer who obviously was deeply anguished over the loss of his commanding officer. The subsequent account of the cycle driver to the effect that he had overheard *Leutnant* Stachel telling the *Hauptmann* that the Adler was a "queer one" had been helpful; indeed, the presiding officer had given Stachel a sympathetic glance at this confirmation of Heidemann's "strange behavior" and "argumentativeness" in face of the *Leutnant*'s "sincere efforts to convince the *Hauptmann* of the danger." Why, the driver had said (still working for his medal, Stachel decided), the *Jastaführer* had even accused the *Leutnant* of being drunk, and anyone could see that the *Leutnant* was as sober as a church door. Then a Directorate engineer by the name of Gittelmann had disclosed, with the injured air of a man nobody had listened to and should have, that three days earlier he had reported in detail on the Adler's unusual wing torsion under load. With this, the presiding officer had suspended the hearing indefinitely, and his dismissal of Stachel as a witness had been tantamount to official commiseration on the loss of a comrade under tragic circumstances.

Through it all, Stachel had been aware of a strange exhilaration.

He had told the inquiry precisely what had happened, and had been singularly moved by the rediscovery of the resounding impact that could be generated by bald truth. The *Hauptmann,* he'd said simply, had become annoyed at an official of the Adler firm, who had violated trial rules by attempting to interrogate and influence flight personnel. *Hauptmann* Heidemann, who had been a man of high principles and extreme sensitivity to matters of propriety, had become so upset he had begun his examination of the Adler machine without awaiting the preceding pilot's report. That pilot had resorted to exceptional means to intervene, but the *Hauptmann,* scenting spilled brandy, had chosen to level drunk and disorderly charges against the pilot in question. For Stachel, it had been peculiarly stimulating to watch the inquiry panel's sympathies shift subtly to his defense when he persisted in making no defense of his own.

But what had excited and impressed Stachel more than any of the day's grotesque events was the new thing that had come to himself.

For the actual fact of Heidemann's loss, he felt nothing; Heidemann's *act* of dying, however, was of enormous significance to him. Over and over he had told himself: *you tried, and yet he died anyhow, anyway, in any event, at any rate, nonetheless, and nevertheless, world without end amen.* His act of trying had been total, sincere, single-minded, and unequivocal, and still Heidemann had done the right thing—had conformed to the sense of propriety—by dying. And he felt that mysteriously related to this remarkable occurrence was the fact that Bruno Stachel had looked himself in the eye, had listed his transgressions and his weaknesses and his wrongs and his failures, and in the very listing—in the very act of admitting the enormity of his defeat—had come into a distinct awareness of having won. With some kind of surrender had come some kind of victory.

Somewhere, Stachel felt, Something had made things right.

It was heady, yet uncannily soothing.

He was still aglow with the thing when he locked the door to his hotel room and headed for dinner. Earlier, before bathing and dressing, he had stopped at a bookstore, and, after considerable innuendo, persuasion, and outright bullying, he had unearthed an especially salacious volume, profusely illustrated with coupling couples, which he knew would appeal to his new adjutant, Karl-Heinz Kettering, Pornographer First Class. Then he'd visited the hotel jeweler to pick up the Blue Max and, in the process, had arranged to have a cigarette case etched with a facsimile of a Fokker D-7 and the legend: "To Ziegel—here's the machine I owe you—Stachel." Together they came to an enormous sum, and as he entered the hotel lobby, he briefly considered canceling the whole silly business, since Kettering and Ziegel would certainly see the gifts as what he, himself, suspected they were—cheap solicitation of future good will. But to hell with it; he wanted to do it, and do it he would. . . .

The next thing he'd do, after a no-expense-barred meal, of course, would be to make a courtesy call on *Frau* Heidemann. By now, the authorities must have advised her of the accident, and by now she'd have brushed away the tear for herself in her new status, and possibly the tear for old time's sake.

That was something else to come out of this day.

In the moments he'd thought of *Frau* Elfi Heidemann, now the widow Heidemann—and they had been many—he had thought of her in a way he'd thought of no other woman, ever in his whole life. Since puberty, a female had been a convenience, an appliance to be considered in the terms of the ultimate function. Should a woman be sleek and trim, her functional quality would be correspondingly enhanced (it was always more pleasant to fly an airplane that had handsome lines). But he could not recall at any time having given Elfi Heidemann this

266

libidinous evaluation; from the first, he had been keenly aware of her femininity, but he had been so touched by her strangely compelling manner that the awareness had remained mere background, like the zither players and the cuckoo clock. Like her husband.

So Elfi Heidemann had worked a curious change in him. And he, he realized with solid gratification, had played a significant role in her life. She would never discover the true nature of this role, to be sure. For all time, she'd know only that the man whose principles she'd clung to had died, leaving the principles as his sole meaningful bequest. Then sooner or later, perhaps, she would find another man—one who could offer something eminently more satisfactory than a code to warm her nights; one who could, in turn, use her inherited ideals, her code, to enrich his own empty life.

Well, he thought with a secret smile, the least he could do would be to try. And it's the trying that counts. . . .

Someone seized his arm.

"Why, Bruno! My darling!"

Her face was impressively framed in a stunning fur, and the scent of soap was there.

"Why, my darling, I've never seen you so—incandescent! Imagine! What delightful chance!"

"Hello, Kaeti."

She swung him around and pulled him into the shadow of the vestibule. Her eyes were calculating.

"My sweet one. Oh, how I've missed you!"

"Careful, Countess. Someone here may know the *Graf.*"

"Where is that delicious smile that was on your dear face a moment ago?"

"What are you doing here?"

Her lips pouted. "You don't sound happy to see me at all. Imagine—you, here in Berlin. How wonderful! I've read every word there is about you, but I had no idea you'd be in Berlin until the Baroness von Klatow told me she'd seen you at *Herr* Fokker's yesterday. . . ."

"We still have a few military secrets."

"You sound angry. That's it. Angry."

"What are you doing here, Kaeti?"

"And disappointed."

He shook his head. "Not angry. Not disappointed. Surprised."

"Not angry?"

"Nothing can make me angry now. What are you doing here?"

"Delivering some of my husband's papers to Doctor Rademacher, Chief of the Medical Research Administration and one of the *Graf's* few professional champions."

"How is the *Graf?*"

"He died. Two weeks after you left *Sonnenstrahl*. He simply died. And I've traveled gloriously ever since."

Stachel's voice was soft. The depression tugged again. "I hadn't heard."

"It was in all the newspapers."

"I haven't been reading them lately. But it's too bad. He was quite a fellow, in his way."

"Perhaps. But such a bore. Now, my darling, where can we go for dinner? I have my car—"

"Thanks, but I have some important business."

"Nonsense! My limousine is practically at the foot of the steps. It's been waiting for us."

"You knew this was my hotel, then?"

"Of course, silly."

"Well, Countess, I've had a difficult day, and I—"

"Darling, don't be contrary." Her tone had sharpened a jot. "I do believe you're trying to avoid me."

"I simply have an important engagement, and I don't want to take you out of your way."

"'I have nothing I'd rather do than go out of my way for you."

God in loving heaven, he thought. *Wouldn't this day ever be free of complication and crisis?*

"Oh, all right."

In the car, Stachel took up the speaking tube and gave the driver the Heidemann address. The *Gräfin* laughed.

"That doesn't sound like a very businesslike address to me."

"It would if you knew the nature of the business."

"Aha. A lady? Are you still up to your business propositions with us girls?"

"That's enough of that."

She chuckled mockingly. "Oh, come now. I've agreed to meet your price, haven't I? It's not inconceivable that I've been your only—client, shall we say?"

"That's enough."

"Isn't it wonderful that we're together, darling? I can't bear to wait. I'm absolutely quivering all over—and I'm damp in all those secret little places. Do my eyes have that look? They must."

He did not look at her. "You're a tramp."

"Yes. But you don't seem to mind when the pit yawns. What is it the *Graf* used to say? 'An upright organ has no conscience'?" She laughed briefly.

"You make me want to throw up."

"Well, you'd better get used to it. You'll be seeing a lot of me from now on."

"In hell I will. Meanwhile, I have other plans."

Her voice was low, but suddenly waspish. "You'll be seeing a lot of me from now on. I've bought and paid for you."

He turned to regard her contemptuously. "You crazy bitch. I sent your money back as soon as it came. And the diary, too: that's on its way to *Sonnenstrahl* right now. You know damned well the deal's been off ever since it was made. I wasn't thinking straight that day. I was drunk. The deal's been off from the moment I sobered up."

She sat erect, and in the passing lights her eyes were glassy. "Oh, has it, now? I don't think so."

"Take it from me: it is off. Off. Off. *Off.*"

"Now you listen to me, *Herr Leutnant* Stachel, Hero First Class. You listen to *me*. You're going to see a lot of me because we're going to be married. Not right away, perhaps, but when I feel like it. . . ."

His mouth opened in incredulity. "Have you lost your mind entirely?"

"No. On the contrary. I've never been more excitingly in command of it."

"I wouldn't marry you if you farted hymns. Besides, I'm marrying someone else." (Strange how the fact formed so simply, how the words describing the fact came so readily. . . .)

"You'll marry me. Nobody else."

"Mad. Absolutely gibbering mad."

"No. You'll see."

"How—will you please tell me in simple, everyday German—just how do you expect to force me to marry you? And why?"

She smiled. "Ask me something difficult. You'll marry me because you're what I want. And because you have no choice."

"Don't tell me you're pregnant. You can't make that stick. I've been at the front too long."

"I'm not pregnant, silly. You know I've been—"

"Spayed?"

"Nastiness won't help."

"*Nastiness?* By my adorable, platinum-plated ass—look who's talking!"

"You'll marry me because you must."

"Look: I'll try to be sweetly reasonable. Why must I marry you?"

"Because you can't afford to be exposed."

"Exposed?"

"Yes. You see, I know you're a murderer."

He sat back against the cushions, staring. "Murderer?"

"Yes."

"Who was murdered?" Uneasiness crept in.

"Two Englishmen."

"You are really insane, aren't you?" he said, relieved somehow. "I've murdered many Englishmen. I can't count them all. I've got a medal to prove it."

"True. You're a real hero, a national figure. But you won't be very long if I speak my piece to the press. You will be a former hero."

"What in the name of my uncle's piles are you talking about?"

She took his hand and smiled. "Willi," she said mysteriously.

"Willi? What about Willi?"

"He was a great one for writing letters. Don't you remember?"

270

"So?"

"So he wrote me a letter. A very personal letter—delivered outside the censors, like all his others."

"What did he write about—a new mirror trick?"

She shrugged. "You may as well relax, darling; your smutty remarks don't affect me at all. I dote on smut. Actually, it was a letter about you."

"That's nice. And in it he reported my murder of two Englishmen?"

"In precise detail."

"Interesting. I guess I'll have to write an exposé of Willi von Klugermann and the assorted Allied types he did away with during his short and moody span in this vale of tears. I remember one he broiled in petrol at four thousand meters one afternoon. I wept for weeks."

"I dare say Willi never destroyed men who were helpless. Who had surrendered."

Stachel's sense of apprehension returned. His mind went back, racing, to the RE-8.

"Surrendered?"

"Surrendered."

"Oh, come now. There's a war on. We soldier types get paid to kill other soldier types."

"There's a difference, I understand. At least, Willi's singing prose makes a difference. 'Knights of the air, the last vestige of gallantry'; that sort of thing . . ."

"Just a moment, Countess. Let me get this straight. You say I must marry you—otherwise you'll reveal a letter from Willi that says I killed a couple of Englishmen who had surrendered?"

"Not killed—murdered. As Willi's letter begins: 'Today I saw murder. I could hardly believe my eyes, but it was premeditated murder.'"

Stachel threw back his head and laughed. She watched him, her face impassive.

"You," he managed finally, "—you are really to be pitied, lady. Honestly, if you weren't such an evil-minded, malicious little whore I could really pity you."

"Go on, dearest, laugh while you can."

"I'm laughing. Hard. For one thing, it's one man's word against another's. For another, no publication would

271

print such tripe. There are laws against such things, I believe. But if someone were mad enough to print it, I would sue him out of his cheese and you out of your bloomers."

"Perhaps. But won't the scandal be lovely?"

His eyes narrowed, and his sneer stiffened. "What do you mean?"

"I mean just that. Won't it be droll to have all this tossed about in the courts? The newspapers can always make fair game of court proceedings. I can see it clearly: 'Hero Sues Aunt of Dead Nobleman; Denies Murdering Prisoners as She Claims.' "

"But Willi's charges—your charges—aren't true."

"Prove it in court, my hero."

He stared at her, unblinking, for a long time. "I'd collect every penny you own."

"Worth it."

"You'd never get a publisher to go along with you in the first place, you little tart."

"I think so."

"Oh, horse manure. How?"

"Because I'm now a publisher. In addition to being a tart."

"You're what?"

"I've bought controlling interest in the newspapers formerly owned by Ludwig Niebergall, who is retiring due to poor health. My money has done some good, you see."

Stachel's uneasiness had burgeoned into full-blown alarm. "Hold on. You will publish Willi's letter in your newspapers. I will sue you for defamation or whatever they call it. I'll collect easily. That leaves me rich and you discredited. How will that make me marry you—before or after or at any time? Any way you look at it, you lose."

She chuckled again, and he could have throttled her. "It won't come to all that, darling. You'll marry me. Tomorrow, if I decide it's tomorrow."

"Why, why why why why?"

"Because you like being the hero. Willi told me how much it means to you. A good coat of tarnish on your medals would be more than you could stand, wouldn't

272

it? And there'd be tarnish, my dear. Scandal always destroys the image of those it touches."

"You're forgetting one thing, Countess. I'm a tough son of a bitch who likes money. Your money could wash away a lot of tarnish."

"Maybe. It's that 'maybe' I'm counting on."

He snorted in impatience and anger. "This is the goddamnedest rigmarole I've ever heard. Get this through your sex-crazed little head, sweetie: I'm not marrying you under any circumstances—tarnish or no tarnish."

"Yes you will."

"No. The cards you hold aren't strong enough."

She laughed outright then. "But, Bruno, my dear, I haven't played my trump."

He shook his head. "Now what?"

It had begun to rain, and lightning threw pale, flickering light across the roofs that made snag-tooth patterns against the sky beyond the streaming windows. She said simply: "There was a third murder."

"Whose now—the Kaiser's?"

"No."

"Whose?"

"Willi's."

He couldn't be sure if the thunder he heard was outside in the night or within his head. "Willi? Oh, my God. If it wouldn't be too much trouble, would you please explain that?"

"Do you know Gerhardt Rupp?"

"Rupp?"

"An *Unteroffizier* Gerhardt Rupp?"

There was a numbness. "Yes. I know him."

"I thought you would, since he served you so well with alcoholic beverages."

"He told you that?"

"Oh, yes. That—and many other things. I get very interesting mail, you see."

"Like what?"

"Like a letter that describes certain events that occurred on the day of my dear nephew's death."

"Go on."

"It seems *Herr* Rupp also cherishes money. He was

273

touring the French countryside that day, hoping to augment his meager funds by locating a supply of wine. It seems that one *Leutnant* Stachel was accustomed to paying handsome sums for such deliveries, despite a number of military regulations to the contrary."

He broke in, the sneer on his face again. "So where's the murder? Of course, I suppose you could say I was close to murdering myself with that cheap swill Rupp dug up—"

"I said it was Willi's murder."

"Oh, in Christ's good and lovely name—"

"*Unteroffizier* Rupp reports that he was in the yard of an abandoned factory that afternoon, negotiating with two Frenchmen. He names specific times, places, and names, incidentally. It was a very hazy day. But he describes—in rather colorless and stolid terms, I'm afraid —the accident in which Willi died. Only he says it was no accident. He says *Leutnant* Stachel deliberately forced the Von Klugermann aircraft into a crash. He says he and the Frenchmen were shocked by the appalling brutality of it all. . . ."

Stachel's voice cracked in its fury. "He's a stinking liar."

"He's a qualified military witness, familiar with aircraft and their operation."

"A dung-faced liar, a qualified witness? You amuse me. His word against mine? Really."

"His word. And that of two Frenchmen."

"Frenchmen are liars, too."

"It's three against one, nevertheless. And, what with Willi's little note about the Englishmen—"

"You're crazy! You'd never make it stick!"

"Maybe not. But in any event, darling, you can see how much—how very much—trouble I can make for you. You can avoid it all."

"By marrying you?"

"By marrying me."

He fell silent, and the rain sounds seemed to press in with fitful urgency. His head was turned away from the beast in the other corner. As the car turned off Unter den Linden, he stirred finally and asked, his voice thick: "Tell me something?"

"What is it, dear?"

"Two things. First, why did Rupp write you?"

"I rather imagine it was because he sensed a considerable reward somewhere."

"Yes. But why you? Why not the *Graf?*"

"*Unteroffizier* Rupp is one of us ruthless people, darling. Since Willi always entrusted *Herr* Rupp with our —private correspondence—so it would evade the censorship route, I dare say *Herr* Rupp was not above peeking now and then. As he put it in his initial letter to me, 'No doubt the Countess would be charitable with one who could lead her to the slayer of her *favorite* nephew.' Or words to that effect."

"The dirty bastard."

"Yes, isn't he? But you said you had two questions, my dearest. What's the other?"

"Why do you want me?"

"Because you're you."

"Oh, stop it. Why? Really?"

She laughed that laugh. "You said it once before. That day you made your own elegant proposition to me. You said I wanted to climb away from my humble origins, that I wanted to be the wife of someone important. Hugo is dead now. I therefore fancy being the wife of a great hero. It would give me a real lift, so to speak—I'm so tired of fat, ugly old husbands. I want a new model. A young one with a hard belly and tapered legs and bronzed face and that very special fame that seems to come to a German military lion. Or should I say 'cobra,' as Willi was so fond of saying?" She laughed again. "Won't I be splendid? 'There she goes, *Frau* Stachel, the lucky woman who shares the bed and board of the legendary Bruno Stachel.'"

"You won't, though. You know that."

"I won't what?"

"Share my bed. A cobra never sleeps with a jackal."

"I really don't care, darling. I can get all the hard and bronzed young men I want. You'll simply be window-dressing."

"For how long?"

"Until I tire of you."

"I see. And then you will exchange me for an even newer model?"

"Mm."

He thought a while. Then he said: "That isn't the real reason, is it?"

"What do you mean, darling?"

"You don't want me for window-dressing. You merely want to get even."

"So?"

"Yes. For my silly proposition that day at *Sonnenstrahl.*"

"Oh, my. There you go. You've discovered my secret."

"I was drunk that day, you know."

"*I* wasn't."

"But I didn't mean what I said. I—I do crazy things when I drink. I showed you I was sorry by returning your money and the diary—no strings attached. I was drunk, Kaeti."

"Are you pleading with me?"

"Yes. Yes, I guess I am. Don't force me to do this thing, please. Please."

She leaned toward him, her voice hissing. "You listen to me, you filthy swine. You hurt me badly. I admit I don't have the finest of characters. But I hurt when I'm hurt—just like anybody else. And nobody hurts me and gets away with it. You said you're a tough son of a bitch. Well, I'm tougher."

"I was drunk."

"What kind of an excuse is that?"

"I don't know."

"Well, darling, it isn't any excuse at all. You hurt me, and now I'm taking my revenge. So you may as well resign yourself to living at my whim."

The car pulled to the curb. He sat there, staring at the building with its large 122 set in brass against the streaming, rain-washed masonry. Slowly he reached for the speaking tube. To the driver he said: "I've changed my mind. Take me back to the hotel. . . ."

As the car started into its turn, he began to laugh. It

was difficult to determine whether it was a laughter or a sobbing; certainly he couldn't tell himself.

"What's so funny, dearest?"

"I was just thinking."

"Of what?"

"Of how you and I were meant for each other. God has arranged this union. Yes, indeed. He certainly has. . . ."

CHAPTER **30**

STACHEL PAUSED in the hotel lobby, not at all astonished that the world seemed so unmindful of the catastrophe into which he'd just plunged. The same haughty man in the same wing collar held cool command at the reservation desk, impervious to the sallies of the changeless horde that sought access to the refuge symbolized by his mahogany barricade. The same bellboys still hustled, hard-eyed and wise, on their mysterious and somehow furtive missions. The same orchestra moaned the same bland tunes, and everywhere was the same foul musk of wool that prevailed despite the management's stoutest defenses of cut flowers and incense.

"Help you, sir?" one of the mean-eyed boys wanted to know.

Stachel stared at him for a time. "I'm not sure anyone can help me, *Junge*."

"Sir?"

"Never mind."

"You're a guest here, *Herr Leutnant?*"

"Yes."

"Want a girl tonight? I can make arrangements."

He considered the narrow face, with its adolescent splotches and its ancient, knowing look. "How old are you, *Junge?*"

"Old enough."

277

"No. I mean really," he said softly. "How old?"

"Fourteen. Going on fifteen. So?"

Stachel shrugged. "Simply wondered. Want to know something?"

"What?" The boy's tone was guarded.

"I'm only five years older than you."

"Hurrah."

"Only five years older, and a murderer of at least three dozen men. Isn't that fine?"

"Have you popped your bung, *Herr Leutnant?*"

"I've murdered more people than years I've lived. Isn't that something?"

"Well, at any rate, you're old enough to service a cow. Do you want one or don't you? I'm busy."

Stachel laughed. "No. I don't want a woman. I'm betrothed, you see."

"Are you all right?"

"Why?" Stachel managed. "Can't a man be betrothed?"

"You're laughing awfully nutty. I think you are a nut. Excuse me."

He was still laughing as the pubescent pimp strode away; his eyes were still moist when he entered the bar and moved to the edge of a group of aviators gathered in a quiet huddle at the far end. A large *Oberleutnant* with a square face was holding forth in that asinine rhetoric cherished by barracks-room pundits.

"The war's nearly over, gentlemen," he was saying. "But for us—the elite—the war has just begun. Germany, God bless her, faces the severest trials in her history, trials that will make the sacrifices and losses of the past four years seem trivial indeed. All the proof we need of this are the reports of the thugs, the revolutionaries, already roving the streets this very moment. I'm no politican—I'm a German officer, like all of you. But I love my Fatherland, as do you, and, since all of my adult life has been spent at war, I shall continue to strive in the only way known to me for Germany's greater and ultimate glory."

His voice was low, and there was a catch of maudlin preciousness in the cadence of his phrases. The group was silent, all eyes on the gashlike mouth. Stachel gritted

278

his teeth against the returning laughter as the monologue soared.

"Do you feel defeated, gentlemen? Do you feel, honestly, deep within your hearts, that you have been beaten into craven submission? I doubt it. If you feel as I do, you are convinced that, had the home front been loyal to those of us who have fought the noble fight, our enemies would eventually have met our terms. If you feel as I do, you have within you an overwhelming sense of outrage over this perfidious betrayal of worthy men who championed a worthy cause. We here are no browbeaten shopkeepers, clerks, peasants; we are intelligent, illustrious, and moral individuals of especial cloth. It is therefore incumbent upon us to rid our beloved nation of the shameful ones who have brought on this national humiliation."

His eyes were glazed, and one hand toyed with the Blue Max at his throat. Stachel wanted to scream: *Pompous, fraudulent bastard.*

"There must be a leader. There will be a leader. We must apply extraordinary astuteness to find him, and, having found him, to give unstintingly of our energies, to dedicate our fortunes, our very souls in the holy, retributive crusade he will foster. Who will he be? Will he be you, Franz? You, Ludwig? You, Karl? Or you, Werner? One thing is certain: he will think like us, he will believe like us, he will—by any measure—be us."

There was a long silence.

The big one, his oratory still echoing, sighed dramatically. Voices sounded again, but in the afterglow of the soliloquy, they seemed oddly muted.

Would Germans, Stachel wondered in near hysteria, ever grow out of the fretful childhood that compelled them to fall, like emotional tenpins, before any ringing phrase uttered by any pretentious windbag of the moment?

Squareface came down the bar and signaled for his glass to be filled. Turning, he regarded Stachel speculatively. He held out his hand.

"Sorry I put a damper on the party. But I always was one to love the sound of my own voice."

Stachel took the hand and nodded, fighting for composure. "I thought you were first-class. I'm Bruno Stachel."

The square face showed recognition. "Yes, I know—the miracle of *Jasta* Heidemann."

"Well, hardly . . ."

"Too bad about Otto. He and I were great friends—classmates at Lichterfelde. I was very fond of him. He had a great knack for sizing up people. I'm Hermann Göring, late of *Jasta* 27, now commander—*pro tempore,* I'm afraid—of *Geschwader* Richthofen."

"I thought so. Otto mentioned you frequently." Then, stifling the same convulsion, Stachel said, "That was quite a speech. You make the German language ring."

"I feel very deeply about those things. Germany's future will be in the hands of men like you and me."

Stachel raised a finger to the barman. Giving Squareface his most sincere gaze, he said:

"I'll drink to that."